LIBERATING FIGHT

Book Five of The Extraordinaries

MELISSA MCSHANE

Copyright © 2021 by Melissa McShane

ISBN-13 978-1-949663-59-4

All rights reserved

No part of this book may be used or reproduced in any way whatsoever without written permission except in the case of brief quotations embodied in critical articles and reviews.

This book is a work of fiction. Names, characters, businesses, organizations, places, events, and incidents either are the product of the author's imagination or are used fictitiously. Any resemblance to actual persons living or dead, events, or locales is entirely coincidental.

Night Harbor Publishing

www.nightharborpublishing.com

Cover by Amalia Chitulescu https://www.amaliach.com

For Jacob,
whose insights into romance bring depth to everything I write

CONTENTS

Author's Note: Inca Measurements	vii
1. In which polite society encounters Amaya, and Amaya strikes back	1
2. In which Amaya receives a startling revelation	15
3. In which Amaya is bribed, threatened, and ultimately cajoled into service with the War Office	29
4. In which Amaya meets the most dangerous woman in England	45
5. In which the diplomatic party arrives in Madrid	55
6. In which Amaya meets a king, and is unimpressed	70
7. In which Amaya's relatives are not what she expected	83
8. In which someone again tries to command Amaya's loyalty	97
9. In which a legend comes to call	108
10. In which Amaya receives an unexpected proposal	119
11. In which a conversation ends rather dramatically	130
12. In which Edmund and Amaya experience a change of heart	139
13. In which Amaya uses her warrior's skills	152
14. In which battle is joined	166
15. In which Amaya and Edmund learn more of the glorious cause	177
16. In which Amaya's dance of death ends in an unexpected confrontation	190
17. In which Amaya learns a terrible truth	203
18. In which negotiations commence, and the power of a Coercer is discussed	217
19. In which different modes of travel bring them closer to their goal	230

20. In which Amaya does things not practiced among the Incas	242
21. In which an audience with the king does not go as expected	252
22. In which a more sinister revelation threatens to spark international panic	264
23. In which important information is ignored by those in power	274
24. In which retreat is discussed, and the nature of sanctuary explored	285
25. In which the power and limits of Extraordinary Scorchers are revealed	298
26. In which there is fire and blood	311
27. In which a new threat arises	324
28. In which cultures and customs are compared, and an agreement reached	333
29. In which Amaya is once more threatened, with predictable results	342
30. In which there is one final revelation	354
31. In which Amaya's happy ending is what she makes of it	366
The Talents	383
Historical Note	391
Acknowledgments	393
About the Author	395
Also by Melissa McShane	397

AUTHOR'S NOTE: INCA MEASUREMENTS

The Incas used well-defined units of measurement in their buildings, and Amaya still thinks in Incan terms. For readers who wish to compare, a *rikra* is equivalent to 1.62 meters, and a thousand *rikras* are slightly less than one mile.

(My thanks to Douglas McElwain for his informative article on Incan metronomy, found at http://www.electrummagazine.com/2015/03/inca-metronomy-an-intersection-of-cultural-elements/)

CHAPTER 1
IN WHICH POLITE SOCIETY ENCOUNTERS AMAYA, AND AMAYA STRIKES BACK

It was the smells Amaya found hardest to endure. The English had so many strange customs, so many rules about how one should dress and how one should eat, where one must sit at their absurdly high tables, who should receive a bow and who merely a nod, that she was overwhelmed in any social gathering, not just this evening's affair at Mrs. Eleanora Gates' home. So many people, few of them known to her. Amaya tried to conceal her discomfort so as not to offend her hostess, but she felt alien in this setting. The sounds of conversations in a language she still understood imperfectly battered at her; her hands in their uncomfortable gloves would have sweated had she not Shaped her body to suppress that physical reaction.

But the smells…oh, how the sweetness of fruit or flower mingled with the sharp bite of alcohol to hang cloyingly in the air, imperfectly covering the honest smell of warm bodies. The smells made her long for fresh, crisp mountain air, something she was unlikely to have ever again.

She might have deadened her olfactory senses, numbed her

nose, but as sick as the stench of civilization made her, she was reluctant to give up any advantage against her enemies. Her dear friend Bess had assured her she was in no danger here in England, but Bess was, despite her experiences amongst the people of Tawantinsuyu, hopelessly optimistic. Amaya knew that the most dangerous opponent was the one you did not see. And no warrior deserving of self-respect ever let down her guard.

"You must like that painting, to spend so much time admiring it," someone said from close beside her. Amaya let out a hiss of surprise and drew back her fist for a blow before realizing who had addressed her and lowering her hand.

Bess's brother, Edmund Hanley, regarded her with an amused expression. Though he was dressed as formally as every other man present, his relaxed, careless pose gave him an air of perfect confidence that comforted her, as if she need not face her enemies alone.

"It has been most of five minutes," he continued, this time in Spanish, "and I consider that long enough that you should direct your attention elsewhere. Unless I am mistaken, and you genuinely are interested as opposed to wishing to deflect the attention of admirers."

Amaya smiled ruefully. "It is easier than conversation," she said in the same language, "particularly with those who speak only English. Trying to understand their words makes me cross. And now you will say I should practice anyway, and endure my trials."

Edmund smiled more broadly. "You know me better than that. This evening is supposed to be enjoyable, and it can hardly be that if you are groping for words the whole time. I will simply have to amuse us both." He scanned the room, his eyes narrowed. "There, see Mrs. Broome? The lady in the unfortunate chartreuse gown? She is here alone because Mr. Broome has once more abandoned her company for the gaming houses. I would feel compassion for her were she not one of the most sharp-tongued women I have ever met."

Amaya covered her mouth to conceal a laugh. "You are terrible."

"Am I? I am simply being honest."

"Being honest does not have to mean being cruel, Edmund."

Edmund shrugged. "I agree, and to prove it, I will tell you of Mr. Dench, who recently made a large anonymous donation to the orphans' home. He is the man in the puce waistcoat. He looks like a miser, does he not, with his pinched face and straggling hair? And yet he is one of the most generous men in London."

Amaya regarded Mr. Dench, who did not look generous. "If it was anonymous, how do you know?"

"I have my sources," Edmund said. "And now that I have dispelled the look of gloom from your face, will you walk with me? You know there are many who wish to make your acquaintance. Ah, there is that scowl again."

"I dislike being on display, as if I am a captive jaguar rather than a woman." Amaya turned her attention back to the painting. She had, as Edmund had guessed, not seen it, had merely been staring in its direction. Now she realized it was a landscape of English trees and grasses and a slender river, and the sight made her unexpectedly homesick, not for England, but for Peru.

"I will not force you," Edmund said, suddenly serious. "But you must know how concerned your friends are for your happiness. You cannot be satisfied to lock yourself away from everyone, moping after what you cannot have."

Amaya glared at him. "You choose to lecture me?"

Edmund held up his hands in self-defense. "Merely expressing an opinion. Bess is concerned for you. She told me, before she left on her wedding trip to Italy, that she feared you felt lost here in England, unable to return home and unwilling to settle here. You know if you wish, we will return you to Peru."

His concerned expression dispelled her irritation. Edmund made a good show of being frivolous and light-hearted, but beneath his demeanor was a kind heart and a good mind. "I cannot return to the Incas," she said, using the European name for her people. "They are well hidden within the mountains, and even if I were able to find them, they believe me dead, and another is Uturunku in my place. I would have to kill that person to regain my position, and I am reluctant to do that."

"You might make a place for yourself among the Spanish."

"That part of my life is in the past. My people were killed, and I know no family to return to. And it is not as if I have any more place amongst them than I do here, a jaguar warrior in civilized society." Amaya shook her head slowly. "You are correct. If this is now my home, I should make an effort to find a place for myself within it."

Edmund sighed dramatically. "How glad I am you came to that decision, because I had no more arguments on my behalf. You know I am averse to telling people their business."

"I know you are not fond of being told your business by others," Amaya said with a smile, "and no doubt that influences your own actions."

"I believe in not doing unto others what you hope they will not do to you, and that is the closest I will ever come to being guided by scripture." Edmund extended his arm to her. "Come. Let me introduce some of these people to you. You may find their conversation interesting, after all."

Amaya accepted his arm without hesitation. It was one of the English customs she found most disconcerting, this hindering of a person's movement, and it was also the one that most surely drove home the point that this was not a warrior's society. But Edmund was a friend, and no danger to her, and he had also learned to take her left arm so her right would be free. Perhaps she could learn to fit in here, after all.

She spoke pleasantly, if stiltedly, to the men and women Edmund introduced to her. They, of course, knew who she was: Amaya who had been Imelda Salazar, formerly of the Incas, rescuer of an English Extraordinary Speaker, heiress to a fortune. That last was supposed to be a secret, but secrets, Amaya was learning, were impossible for the English to keep. She did not know who had revealed the existence of the Inca gold hoard England had retrieved thanks to her and Bess, but it was now common knowledge, though common knowledge had inflated the value of the hoard substantially.

Another quality of the English was a general reluctance to speak of certain matters directly, specifically money. No one ever asked her directly how much her share of the treasure was, nor what that meant in English pounds, but she knew from Edmund that speculation ran high. So the men and women she spoke with that night never mentioned it to her face, even as her enhanced hearing revealed those same men and women discussing the subject privately. It amused Amaya rather than irritating her. English manners aside, human beings were all equally preoccupied with questions of wealth. Though the Incas would never have dreamed of being allowed a share of the Sapa Inca's gold.

She permitted Edmund to lead her around the room, never stopping to converse with anyone for very long. Despite her discomfort, she had to admit it was a lovely room, if over-warm, with many paintings like the one she had stared at hanging on the walls and an empty fireplace surmounted by a creamy stone mantel. English art was so different. The Incas did not paint images of their surroundings as the English did—though the English did not sculpt images into everyday objects as the Incas did, something else Amaya missed.

"Miss Salazar, good evening," said a man who had been introduced to Amaya two nights ago and whose name she had forgotten. "I am pleased to see you again. How comes your reading?"

She remembered now that she had told him she was learning to read English, but this did not bring his name to mind. "It is well," she said. "Slow, but well."

"I of course have ulterior motives in asking, since I hope you will one day read my book," the man said with an arch smile. "Hanley, you agree with me, yes?"

"I am no reader, and I hesitate to make recommendations," Edmund said. "I am certain Miss Salazar can decide for herself someday."

Even Amaya's limited grasp of English caught Edmund's excessive formality of speech that suggested he disliked the man. "It is too soon," she agreed. "I regret."

"Not at all," the man said. He sounded disappointed, which annoyed Amaya—how dare he behave as if she were under some obligation to him? Then she felt ashamed for having such a cruel thought of someone she barely knew. She nodded and smiled and let Edmund draw her away again.

"Bess says his books are terrible," Edmund told her in Spanish once they were safely away. "He remains blissfully unaware of this."

"I feel pity for him, then."

"Don't waste your sympathy. He has no conversation that is not related to his writing, and is sometimes a dreadful bore." Edmund's head turned, and he released her. "That is Spofford—I should speak with him. Will you be all right if I leave you?"

"I am not made of glass, Edmund," Amaya said, half amused,

half annoyed again. "And you are correct that I should make friends. I will be perfectly well."

"Very well." Edmund touched his forehead as if in salute, which amused Amaya and dispelled her annoyance. He turned away to approach a short, rotund older man with grey-streaked black hair. Amaya wondered if he was someone with whom Edmund had business. She knew Edmund worked for the government as a translator, but that was all she knew—that, and how Edmund's parents spoke occasionally of his excellent prospects in that field.

She stood alone beneath the glittering chandelier that cast its light and warmth over the already warm room. No one seemed immediately inclined to speak with her, which relieved her mind even as it disappointed her. She felt slightly foolish, standing beneath the light as if she believed herself deserving of being set apart by its glow.

"Miss Salazar, I hope you are enjoying yourself." Mrs. Gates approached with her hand outstretched. She was one of Bess's Speaker friends, and Amaya clasped her hand briefly, smiling in a pleasant way. Being friendly to Bess's friends seemed important.

"May I introduce to you Mr. and Mrs. Ellery," Mrs. Gates said, indicating the couple beside her. "They have traveled extensively in Spain."

"*Buenas tardes*," Amaya said. Mr. Ellery chuckled, an uncomfortable sound. Mrs. Ellery looked confused.

"We don't speak Spanish," Mr. Ellery said. "Never could get the knack of foreign tongues."

"But Spain is lovely—do you, that is, have you much experience with your home country?" Mrs. Ellery added.

Amaya looked for Mrs. Gates to take up part of this awkward conversational burden, but the woman had moved on. "I was born in Peru and I do not know Spain," she said.

This apparently left the couple with nothing to say. More awkwardness descended upon their little group. "I know only my name," Amaya offered, then wished she had not said anything so potentially personal.

"Of course," Mr. Ellery said, then fell silent again.

"Lord Braithwaite," Mrs. Ellery exclaimed, "have you met Miss Salazar? Miss Salazar, this is Lord Braithwaite."

Lord Braithwaite was an attractive older man, possibly a Shaper by the regularity of his features and the broadness of his shoulders. "Charmed," he said, bowing over Amaya's hand. "You are an Extraordinary Shaper, are you not? I am also a Shaper, though I do not intend to trade upon any supposed connection our shared talent might give us. I've always said there is a great divide between Shapers and Extraordinary Shapers. It's the calling, don't you agree? The ability to Shape others, to Heal broken bones and other wounds—that suggests God intended you to use that talent to help others."

He spoke so rapidly she barely understood one word in five. Her enhanced hearing did not help; Lord Braithwaite's words tangled with more distant conversations until she felt even more confused. "I do not know. I think yes," she said, hoping she had not just agreed to something unpleasant.

"I disagree," Mr. Ellery said, but placidly, as if his disagreement was not personal. "Why should Extraordinary Shapers be held to higher expectations than other talents? If Miss Salazar, for example, chooses not to direct her talent in a medical way, should that not be her decision to make?"

"The War Office—" Lord Braithwaite began, but Amaya took advantage of their conversation to drop into the meditative state from which she Shaped her body. This, at least, was comforting and familiar, this sense of her physical form and how it moved and breathed and changed according to her will.

A Shaper's body, whether Extraordinary or no, differed from an ordinary human body in its elasticity, in its readiness to accept a new Shape. Amaya rarely had cause to Shape herself so rapidly it hurt; she was accustomed to taking her time, relishing the buzzing, tingling sensation that came with altering her body. Now, she instantly assessed her physical condition, a habit dating from her years as a jaguar warrior, and was satisfied at finding her body still as perfect as she could make it—better than perfect, as her senses were superior to the average human's, and her lungs and muscles would allow her to run for miles without stopping. No hidden defects, no incipient illnesses. Perfect.

She Shaped the delicate inner structures of her ears to be less receptive and came to herself to find both men looking at her expectantly. Dizzy from the heat and noise, she nodded agreement to something she had not heard. She needed air. "Excuse me," she said in English, then repeated herself when neither moved. The two men and the crowd surrounding her seemed ignorant of her distress. "Please to pass," she said.

Someone gripped her elbow. Without hesitating, she spun around and slammed her fist into her assailant's stomach, making him bend double and expel air in a great *ooph* of breath. With her other hand, she grabbed the man's hair and bent his head back to expose his throat. She pressed her claws against the jugular vein and shoved him backward, his feet scrabbling to keep him upright, until she had him up against the wall. A painting shifted and fell to the floor with a crash.

"Amaya!"

Her lips curled in a snarl. The man's eyes were white all around, and he held himself still, pressing hard into the wall as if hoping to escape her claws. She examined him closely. He wore formal English dress, those short pants that came only to the knee and the odd coat that was longer in back than in front, and was round of face and belly. He did not look dangerous, but she still was not entirely familiar with how English warriors looked.

"Miss Salazar," Edmund said from close behind her, "has this man assaulted you?"

The man swallowed, and Amaya's claws dimpled his flesh. "I didn't," he whispered, still motionless except for the convulsive leap of his throat as he swallowed again. "I beg your pardon, Miss Salazar, I meant only to attract your attention. I should not have touched you."

"Miss Salazar, if he has offered you offense, we will take him into custody," Edmund said. His words were heavily emphasized, the word *custody* a heavy stone pressing against her. She felt the man's pulse beating fast and hard beneath her hand, heard his heavy breathing, and realized her own body was poised to kill.

She slowly released the man's hair and lowered her claws. "You startle me," she said in English. "That not—it is bad manners to touch." The phrase *bad manners* was a familiar one; so many of her instincts that were appropriate among her people were bad manners in English society.

"It certainly is," Edmund said. He stepped forward to stand beside Amaya. "Lord Carstairs, apologize to the lady."

Lord Carstairs ran a quick hand through his disordered locks and bowed deeply. "Miss Salazar, I crave your forgiveness. I should never have done that. Please overlook my behavior, and know I hold you in the highest respect."

"Thank you," Amaya said. "I forgive." She could say nothing else if she desired to keep these people from fearing her.

"Miss Salazar, I came to inform you that your carriage is here, as you requested," Edmund continued. "If you would care to make your goodbyes to our hostess?"

She had not ordered the carriage, and she had never been so grateful for Edmund's perspicacity. "Thank you, I must go." She nodded to Lord Braithwaite and Mr. and Mrs. Ellery. They looked afraid, and the worried feeling centered on Edmund's words about taking her assailant into custody intensified.

Edmund handed her into the carriage without comment. Amaya settled her awkward skirts around herself and plucked at her gloves to remove them. The fingertips of both were shredded. She wadded them into a ball and closed her hand around it tightly. "He startled me," she said in Spanish. "Everything was so loud, and that is exactly the circumstance under which an attack is most likely."

"Will it do any good for me to point out you are not in Peru, and you are unlikely to be attacked in a London drawing room?" Edmund asked. He sounded, not angry, but resigned, and it made the worry deepen further.

"For ten years I have been a jaguar warrior," she said, "and those instincts kept me alive. They are not something to be easily overcome. And you yourself said he should not have touched me."

"His foolish mistake could have cost him his life." Edmund leaned forward to gaze at her directly, all frivolity vanished. When she protested, he added, "I don't mean that you might have killed him. You have better self-control than that. I mean that assaulting an Extraordinary is a serious crime, punishable in some cases by death. You owe it to society to be circumspect in your doings."

That explained the expressions of the others. Amaya clasped her hands in her lap and bowed her head to stare at them. Her skin was darker than most Europeans, darkened by choice when she was among the Incas, but no one ever commented on the difference. Her nails, however… She did not need claws here in England, and she might cut and Shape them to look like ordinary human fingernails. But the thought of doing so made her uncomfortable, as if in giving that small thing up, she lost another piece of herself.

"I would not be so vindictive," she said.

"Others might be vindictive on your behalf. If he had truly assaulted you, you would find many of those in attendance willing to testify to that fact." Edmund laid a hand atop her clasped ones. "I wish I knew how to help you."

She raised her head to look into his eyes. "Help me in what way?"

"You are not one to enjoy sitting idle. You are learning to read, and to ride, and you enjoy visiting museums and going for walks. And yet as busy as you are, you still seem restless, as if there is something you wish to do."

"I am grateful to your family, Edmund," Amaya protested.

"That is not what I mean. You have the air of someone whose destiny has yet to be revealed, if you will permit me a dramatic moment. I don't suppose you have given any more thought to Dr. Macrae's offer?"

Amaya frowned. "It is hardly an offer. It is more a thinly veiled threat. She seems to believe that, as a fellow Extraordinary Shaper, she has a right to dictate how I use my talent." So had Lord Braithwaite, she recalled. She could not help but wonder how prevalent this opinion was in English society.

"Medical training for all Extraordinary Shapers makes sense to me."

"It implies that my talent exists purely for the benefit of others. And yet—oh, I am saying this badly. I understand Dr. Macrae's perspective. Shaping others to be free of injury is a noble effort, and having all Extraordinary Shapers capable of doing so does make sense. But she would have me embark upon a years' long course of study, at the end of which my life would no longer be my own. I have no interest in becoming a physician."

"And yet you attended my sister-in-law's confinement and delivered her child." Edmund released her and sat back. "You clearly have the ability."

"That is different. I attended upon the Sapa Inca's wives when they gave birth, and Mary asked the favor of me. It is the *expectation*, Edmund, the assumption that because I am an Extraordinary Shaper, I owe it to humanity to Heal the injured. No one behaves as if Extraordinary Bounders should keep themselves ready to transport anyone who asks, or as if Extraordinary Scorchers must hie to the site of great conflagrations to extinguish fires regardless of the time of day or night."

"England has only one Extraordinary Scorcher, so that is unlikely."

Amaya waved that objection aside. "You understand my meaning."

"I do." The carriage came to a stop, but Edmund did not rise. "And I believe you will discover your calling, if you permit yourself time. You know you are welcome to stay with us as long as you like."

"I do, and I am grateful for your family's hospitality." She *was* grateful; she simply knew she could not go on like this forever, a hanger-on at the Hanley household, a poor relation with no home of her own. Well, she was not *poor*, obviously, but in every other respect she was a dependent.

"I am glad of your company," Edmund said. "With Bess gone, I have no one else behind whom to conceal my interest in antiquities. If you were to leave, I would be forced to go to the British Museum alone, and be mocked mercilessly as a bluestocking by my peers."

"I was under the impression only women were bluestockings," Amaya said with a smile.

Edmund stepped down from the carriage and extended his hand. "Then the male equivalent—an eccentric, perhaps, like my brother Vincent, so absorbed in his studies."

Amaya gave a moment's consideration to Edmund's younger brother, up at Oxford. He had enthusiastically welcomed her to that university, introduced many scholars to her, and was relentlessly engaged in academic pursuits. "I see nothing wrong with being interested in a life of the mind."

"I have a reputation to maintain, Amaya. It is that of a carefree man about town." Edmund held the townhouse door for her. "Suppose someone were to begin to take me seriously? So much for that carefully constructed reputation."

"Well, I like you whatever your reputation," Amaya said.

CHAPTER 2
IN WHICH AMAYA RECEIVES A STARTLING REVELATION

A maya woke late the next morning, emotionally weary from the previous evening's gathering. She lay in bed as she always did upon waking, marveling at the softness of the mattress. It had taken most of a week for her to feel comfortable sleeping on a thick mattress, and two weeks to learn to enjoy it. She had missed the firm support of a pallet at first, and struggled to climb out of bed for several days. Now she feared she would find a pallet uncomfortable, but as she was unlikely to return to the Incas, it hardly mattered.

She eyed the window; by the intensity of the light and the shadows it cast, it was an hour past dawn. Gone were the days when she would have risen with the sun. Sleeping late was one more alien habit to acquire, though Mary, wife of Edmund's older brother Charles, slept even later than she. Of course, Mary was still recovering from the birth of her child three weeks earlier, but Amaya was certain Mary enjoyed sleeping late regardless.

She rose and dressed in a white muslin gown patterned with

rosebuds. Mrs. Hanley had taken her to the warehouses to acquire clothing, back when Amaya and Bess were newly returned from Peru, but it was Bess who had directed the beautiful fabrics to be delivered to a woman who would make them up in the War Office style. "Women in the War Office may not be in a position to be waited upon," Bess had explained, "and our clothing is made to be donned unassisted." She had also introduced Amaya to something called *convenables* that went beneath one's clothing and shaped one's figure, but Amaya had declined the offer. She could Shape her own body to whatever mode English society demanded.

Now, fastening her gown, she once again was grateful to the absent Bess for knowing what would make Amaya comfortable. Amaya missed her friend terribly, but Bess was so happy with her husband, Lord Ravenscourt, she could not wish Bess here again. Soon enough, their wedding trip would be over, and then Amaya would go to live with Bess at her invitation.

The idea sent an unexpected twinge of annoyance through her. Dependent on the Hanleys, dependent on Bess... Should she instead look for a situation of her own? And yet, where would she go? The idea of being alone in a city full of people whose language she barely spoke unnerved her as no physical threat could.

She ate breakfast alone, then retired to the drawing room to read. It had been Edmund's suggestion that she practice her English by reading as well as by speaking, and that had been an excellent suggestion. She could take her time with her reading as she could not in conversation, and if a word stymied her, she could look for its meaning in the little book Edmund had procured for her, with its lists of English words and their Spanish equivalents.

The book she was currently reading had been recommended

by Mary, and Amaya was not certain she liked it. On the one hand, it provided an excellent portrayal of English society and culture, and the characters were lively and clever—clever enough that Amaya was certain she missed much of what was actually said. But she was not sure she believed a woman such as Elizabeth Bennet could exist, much as she wished otherwise. The character spoke with such easy confidence, even to men to whom she was not related, and seemed not to care that her existence was terribly precarious—Amaya needed to ask Edmund what an entailment was—and was nothing like most of the Englishwomen Amaya met. She wished Miss Bennet were real, because she felt certain they would be great friends.

She heard footsteps, and looked up to see Albert the footman enter the room. "Miss Salazar," he said in his ponderous voice, "you have a caller. May I tell her you are at home?"

Albert intimidated Amaya as no one else did, with his straight, unsmiling mouth and his fierce eyebrows. He always looked at her as if expecting her to do something uncouth. "Who is it?"

Albert extended a silver tray to her, upon which lay a rectangle of pasteboard. Amaya picked it up and squinted at the curly writing. "Mrs. Casper Neville," she pronounced slowly. "I do not know her."

"Very good, miss," Albert said. "Shall I show her up, or would you prefer not to be at home?"

Amaya examined the name again. "No, please to bring her here," she said. Curiosity had taken hold of her. She had had many callers, but they had always been men and women who had been introduced to her. A stranger. She might be anyone.

Albert left, and Amaya set her book aside and stood, straightening her skirts. She cast a quick glance around the room, ensuring it was tidy, though the servants were extremely thorough. It occurred to her that Mrs. Neville might be one of the many importunate fortune-seekers with a sad story to evoke Amaya's pity and open her purse-strings. Most of those interested in her fortune were male, and quick to offer marriage, but there were a few women who had laudable causes to which they wanted Amaya to donate. Well, if this were the case, Amaya would send Mrs. Neville on her way politely but firmly.

Footsteps sounded in the hall, and Albert reappeared, trailing a small, grey-haired woman with a careworn face. "Miss Salazar, Mrs. Neville," he said.

"Thank you, Albert, that is all," Amaya said.

Albert bowed and withdrew.

Amaya and Mrs. Neville gazed at each other. Mrs. Neville's clothes looked very fine, as far as Amaya's limited understanding of English fashion went; she wore a gown of striped muslin, pale green and white, and her bonnet was trimmed with a profusion of ribbons to match. She held a large silk reticule embroidered all over with an abstract pattern. By her clothing, she was wealthy, but her expression was not one of someone as free of care as Amaya felt a rich woman should be. Her lips were thin and pale, and wrinkles creased the corners of her eyes and dragged down her mouth. The blue of her eyes looked faded, as if they had seen much and been discouraged by most of it.

"Mrs. Neville," Amaya said. "I do not know of you. You are here why?" It was too direct for politeness, but Amaya's English was not up to the challenge of being polite.

"Miss Salazar." Mrs. Neville's voice cracked, and she visibly swallowed. "Miss Salazar, I am your grandmother."

The word at first made no sense. "You are..." Amaya began, thinking to ask the woman to explain herself. Then memory caught up with her. She took a step back and bumped into the round table whereon lay her books. "Grandmother," she whispered.

Mrs. Neville looked, if anything, more worried and nervous than before. One hand twisted in her muslin skirt, wrinkling the fabric terribly. She opened her mouth to speak, but no words emerged.

Amaya's hand closed hard on the table's edge. "I do not believe," she said. Her throat was unexpectedly dry, and the words came out as harshly as a rasp across stone. "I have no grandmother."

"I know it must be difficult to believe," Mrs. Neville said, "but I assure you I am certain you are my daughter Catherine's child."

This had to be the most unusual way anyone had yet tried to lay claim to her fortune. Amaya examined Mrs. Neville more carefully. She did not actually seem certain of anything, with the way her hand restlessly twisted her skirt around her fingers and the pinched look of her forehead. If she intended to make a claim on Amaya's ancestry, she had chosen a poor way to go about it. Despite herself, Amaya asked, "How can you prove it? My parents were Spanish, not English. This is a terrible lie—"

"Your father was Spanish, yes," Mrs. Neville broke in. "Don Ernesto de Salazar y Ortiz. He was of high-class Castilian nobility whose family fell upon hard times. He left Spain for London, where he was introduced to my daughter Catherine. They married, and he chose to pursue a life in the South American colonies. That is where you were born, Imelda Salazar."

Amaya's hand closed into a fist. "It is a good story," she said, "but someone tell you those names for you to say to me."

"Your name has been much in the news, yes, but not that of your father or your mother," Mrs. Neville said. Her brow was even more pinched than before. "And I do not believe anyone knows you were christened Imelda Magdalena Caterina Salazar."

It was like a blow to the stomach. "How?" Amaya whispered. "How do you know this?"

Mrs. Neville dipped her hand into her reticule. "Catherine wrote to me. Her—my husband would not permit me to receive her correspondence. These two letters were all I was able to hide from him, and one of them—" She withdrew a yellowing, much-folded paper covered with tiny writing— "gives the news of your birth and christening."

She extended the paper to Amaya, who took it reflexively. The date and salutation at the top were clear; the cramped handwriting beneath was impossible for her to interpret. She stared blindly at it, willing it to become comprehensible. The possibility that this was all a lie seemed less likely by the moment.

"I do not know any of this," she said, thrusting the letter back at Mrs. Neville. "You want things of me? Money? Why do you tell me this?"

"No, Miss Salazar, no!" Mrs. Neville's quiet voice rose an octave. "I did not come here—that is, I need nothing from you, but—"

She drew in a calming breath. "My husband is dead, Miss Salazar," she said, lifting her chin defiantly. "He cast Catherine off when she declared she would marry Don Ernesto. It was in part due to his stubbornness that they refused to make a life in England. Catherine was my only daughter, and—" She paused to blot her eyes with her gloved fingertips. "Forgive my selfishness, but you are all that is left of her. I wanted to know her child."

Words deserted Amaya, even words in her own language. Mrs. Neville continued to look at her with eyes brimming over with tears. She made no move to leave, or sit, and the challenge in her expression confused Amaya more even than the incomprehensible letter had. If Mrs. Neville was lying, this was the most elaborate scheme Amaya had ever heard of, more complex than even Amaya's well-honed sense of intrigue might have engendered. And Amaya felt deep within herself that Mrs. Neville was not lying.

She came to herself abruptly. "Sit," she said, and sank into the nearest chair without waiting to see if Mrs. Neville would comply. Her hands were shaking, and she clasped them in her lap to still them. She ought to call for refreshments; that was the proper thing to do for a guest. But she was still not certain she wanted to give Mrs. Neville a welcome that might indicate Amaya felt a connection to her.

"Your husband is dead?" she said. Turning the questions back on her unexpected guest might give her time to decide what she wanted from Mrs. Neville, if anything.

"These six years," Mrs. Neville said. "I have two sons still living. Both are married, both have children." A tentative smile touched her lips. "Your cousins. One is an Extraordinary Shaper like yourself."

The idea frightened Amaya, as if she were somehow no longer herself if she had relatives she had never heard of. "And my father's family?"

Mrs. Neville's smile disappeared. "I know almost nothing of them except the family name," she said, "and that Don Ernesto came from Toledo in Spain. I regret that I cannot tell you more."

Another unexpected flash of fear touched her heart, the fear that some other family member unknown to her might appear on the Hanleys' doorstep. She suppressed it and asked, "Do the sons—your sons, they know you come here?"

Mrs. Neville shook her head. "I decided, if you chose not to allow me entrance, it was better they not know of the connection. So you might choose what relation you wish to have with us."

"Thank you," Amaya said. "I do not know what to say."

"To be honest, I did not consider anything beyond convincing you I am not a liar or a fortune-hunter." Mrs. Neville settled her reticule on her lap. "May I ask, was she happy? Or is that too sensitive a subject? I know so little. Her letters simply stopped, you see, and then when you arrived in England, the newspapers said only that you were an orphan." The tears returned, spilling over the woman's thin cheeks.

"Do not cry," Amaya said, alarmed.

Mrs. Neville shook her head, wiping her eyes again. "I beg your pardon, I should not impose upon you. It is simply that believing one's child is dead is not the same as having it confirmed in such a brutal fashion. But—will you tell me what happened? I cannot bear my imaginings."

Sympathy for the woman displaced Amaya's disquiet. "Attackers. Raiders," she said. "It is a thing that happens sometimes to small communities far from where there is soldiers to protect. They attacked—" She swallowed as the memories threatened to choke her. Mrs. Neville did not need to know the details that burned in Amaya's memory, even thirteen years later. "All were killed. Mama, Papi, all in our home."

"But not you."

"No. I hide, and then I run. The Incas find me and give me a new home. I do not die."

Mrs. Neville nodded. "I regret so much that I did not—oh, it doesn't matter now. I feel such sorrow for your loss. How old were you? Nine?"

"Ten years." Mrs. Neville's unexpected sympathy made her blurt out, "There were more of us. More children. Ernesto and Rosita. They die too."

Mrs. Neville covered her mouth to hold in a gasp. "Oh, my dear," she said. "My dear child. To have witnessed such horrors."

Amaya's discomfort increased. "I am strong," she said. "I live and they do not. It is not to be sad for me that I live."

"Of course not. I apologize." Mrs. Neville's pinched expression reappeared. "Miss Salazar, I would very much like…that is, if you are willing…might you pay us a visit? I would like for you to know your family."

Amaya flinched. "I am—" She did not know the right words. How to explain that she did not feel the need of familial protection, that Mrs. Neville's offer made her feel as uncomfortably obligated as Dr. Macrae's demands on her talent did? "I have a place here," she said, and immediately wondered why she had not said "a home" instead.

Mrs. Neville's thin cheeks turned pink. "I did not mean to offend," she said. "It is simply that I know you are a stranger in this country, and hoped it might matter to you to have family here. No one will make demands upon you, I assure you. I only wished…" Her voice trailed off. Amaya, looking into her faded blue eyes, did not need to be a Discerner to perceive Mrs. Neville's longing.

"Am I like her? Like my mother?" she asked.

Mrs. Neville shook her head. "You look much like Don Ernesto, in the color of your hair and the shape of your nose and cheeks," she said. "But your eyes are grey like Catherine's."

Neither hair color nor eye color could be altered by Shaping. It was oddly reassuring to know there were parts of her that would always link her to the parents she only barely remembered. "Mama never spoke English," she said. "I am sad not to know of you. Of this birth. I may come."

Mrs. Neville smiled. "Thank you," she said, extending her hand to Amaya. It felt as frail as her smile. Then she rose, and

Amaya stood as well. "I will not keep you longer, but here is our direction." She removed another card from her reticule and handed it to Amaya. "Call on us whenever it is convenient. I rarely leave the house, so please do call."

"I will consider," Amaya said.

When Mrs. Neville was gone, Amaya returned to the drawing room and sat at the table, riffling the pages of her book. Elizabeth Bennet would have known what to say to Mrs. Neville. She would have asked the right questions. Amaya did not even know the extent of her newly-discovered relations. Cousins? She swiftly paged through her list of English words with their Spanish translations. *Primos*. Two uncles, and who knew how many cousins. She did not know whether to laugh or weep.

She stood and went in search of someone to talk to. She found Edmund in the small room that doubled as a library and a study for when Edmund's father was in residence. Its four walls were lined with bookcases that rose all the way to the ceiling, making the room dim even when both its lamps were lit. A desk occupied one corner, heavy and brooding and carved with images impossible to discern in the low light, and a short sofa took up the adjacent corner. It looked comfortable, but Amaya knew from experience it was actually lumpy and the velvet upholstery was worn thin in places.

Edmund was seated at the desk, pen in hand, papers spread out before him. "Good morning, Amaya," he said in Spanish without raising his head. He twitched one of the papers over another as if to conceal the second. "Did I hear the door just now?"

"You did. Oh, Edmund, I am so confused."

Now he looked up. "You sound distressed. Has something happened?"

Amaya sat on the lumpy sofa and immediately rose again. "I

have had a caller," she said, "someone who—Edmund, she claimed to be my grandmother, and I believe she was telling the truth." She began to pace restlessly in front of the desk, her hands clenched into fists.

Edmund set the pen down very precisely in front of him. "Such a claim is preposterous. She must be a fortune-hunter."

Amaya shook her head. "If you had met her, you would understand. It seems my mother was English, and her mother, Mrs. Neville—she says I have more family, her other children, and their children—Edmund, what am I to do?"

Edmund rose and came around the desk to clasp Amaya's hand and stop her pacing. "You need do nothing," he said in a quiet yet firm voice, "nothing you do not wish to do. Even if this Mrs. Neville is your grandmother, you owe her nothing. Do not feel you should pursue the connection if it makes you uncomfortable. It is not as if you need their name to give you consequence."

Amaya could not bear to meet his eyes. Instead she stared at his fashionably tied neckcloth, tracing its folds until her whole world was nothing but white cloth. "That is true," she said, "but I still feel like a stranger to myself. I was alone in the world, and now I have family, and it is as if I have been given a gift I am afraid to open."

Edmund's hand gripped her tighter, and now she looked into his eyes and saw nothing but compassion. "You are not alone, because you have friends. If you choose to make this family's acquaintance, we will support you. And if you choose not to, you are still Amaya, and you still have a home here."

Amaya nodded. The firmness of his hand reassured her, made her feel less alone, and without thinking she laid her other hand atop their clasped ones. Edmund's smile deepened for a moment, and then he released her. "A home," he repeated, "and many delightful occupations. Though it is a pity you do not read English well yet, or I might pass this task off to you."

"What task is that?"

Edmund returned to his seat at the desk and picked up the pen, tumbling it between his fingers. "Writing one of many letters to my associates, informing them that I will be leaving the country for several months. It is tedious because the message is the same for all, but I must still write it out for each." He laid the pen down and sighed. "How unfortunate we are not all Extraordinary Speakers. Bess tells me she is capable of Speaking a single message to several minds at once. If I could do that, my task would have been finished ten minutes ago."

"Do you mind, having no talent?" Amaya asked, feeling curious. She had been about to ask what took him out of the country, but his weary tone of voice when he spoke of his sister's talent disturbed her.

Edmund eyed her as if wondering what her secret intent in asking was. "I do not mind," he said. "Perhaps a hundred and fifty years ago, when talent was still new and the Stuarts gave preference to Extraordinaries, I might have said differently. But today there are still relatively few talented individuals, and England cannot afford to spurn those with intelligence and wisdom and wealth simply because they lack magical talent as well."

"And I suppose you are one of those intelligent, wise, wealthy people without whom England would surely collapse," Amaya teased.

Edmund smiled again. The wicked twinkle in his eye made him look even more charming than usual. "Naturally. Though I would quibble over 'wealthy.' I have sufficient for my needs and have shed most of the vices that would drain my resources. That makes me better off than half my peers."

A quiet knock on the door made them both look up. It was the footman Albert. "I beg your pardon, but there is a message for Miss Salazar," he said, proffering a silver serving tray. Upon it lay a sealed envelope.

Amaya resisted the urge to shut the door in Albert's face, denying this new mystery. Surely it could not be yet another unknown relative, imposing on her? She picked the envelope up and turned it over curiously as Albert shut the door behind him. "It does not say who sent it," she told Edmund.

"If you open it, you will be relieved of your ignorance," Edmund said with a straight face.

Amaya grimaced at him and used one of her sharp claws to break the seal. She likely should not have done so, but only Edmund was there, and he knew what she was capable of and was not horrified by it. She unfolded the paper and squinted at it in the low light.

"I cannot read it," she said. "Here. Tell me what it says."

"If it is a note requesting an assignation, I will be very embarrassed," Edmund said with a smile. He held the paper close to his eyes. "Ah. It is from the Ministry of the Treasury, requesting a meeting in two days' time. No doubt it is to do with the final disposition of your reward."

"I do not see why they need a meeting for that."

Edmund shrugged. "It is the government; they need no excuse to have a meeting, and I say that as a member of that government who has endured many such meetings. Your signature might be required, and I suppose they will need to know where you would like the funds deposited."

The idea made Amaya's head spin. "Will you go with me? I know so little of finance. I do not expect they will try to cheat me, but—"

"But better they not get the idea," Edmund agreed. "I would

be delighted to accompany you. Being in proximity to such wealth makes my skin tingle."

Amaya laughed. "You were satisfied with being well-off only minutes ago."

"Ah, well, when it comes to money, I am as much a hypocrite as anyone," Edmund said with a wry smile.

CHAPTER 3

IN WHICH AMAYA IS BRIBED, THREATENED, AND ULTIMATELY CAJOLED INTO SERVICE WITH THE WAR OFFICE

The Treasury building near St. James' Park had the reassuring solidity Amaya liked about English construction. Its builder had not only used the heavy rectangular stones so like those of her homeland, but had set stones in arches surmounting the many windows with their curved tops. Near the top of the Treasury, a triangular stone slab carved with intricate designs appeared supported by smooth columns, though Amaya was sure the builder would not trust to such fragile things to keep the slab from falling on passersby below.

She still marveled at the glass panes filling the windows. She had never seen glass before coming to London, and did not believe even her childhood home that had been destroyed by raiders had had such a luxury. What a convenience, to allow the sunlight in and keep the rain and wind out! And yet no one she knew ever behaved as if this were anything but a commonplace. Sometimes she could not understand how the English did not appreciate the things they had.

Edmund walked with her past the uniformed guard at the door, who did not acknowledge their presence. Amaya recognized a fellow warrior in how he covertly examined them as a potential threat. It reassured her that the English took their responsibilities seriously. She returned the favor by not smiling at him, a potential distraction.

The halls of the Treasury smelled of the sharp scent of the same cleanser the Hanleys' servants used, under which Amaya's keen nose smelled wood and lamp oil. Men dressed like Edmund in those odd coats that were longer in the back than the front passed through the halls in pairs or singly. They eyed Amaya with interest, no doubt because she was the only woman there, but did not accost her. She guessed, had Edmund not been with her, she would have been subjected to questions.

It was an English habit that annoyed her, this assumption that a woman needed a man to give her consequence. In Tawantinsuyu, men and women's roles were sharply defined, and women who were not jaguar warriors defended their prerogatives as fiercely as the men did. But here in England, where female Speaker and Bounders and the like had talents the equal of any man, and often did the work of men, women were still circumscribed as to how they could use those talents. Amaya did not understand why there were no women employed by the Treasury, nor why the English did not fully embrace the liberties they claimed to offer women.

Edmund, striding along beside her, did not seem aware of the looks Amaya received, but when they neared the door to which they had been directed, he said in Spanish, "They mean no harm, you know."

"I beg your pardon?" She should not be so quick to make assumptions about what Edmund did or did not notice.

"Many men of an earlier generation, which means most of

those employed by the Treasury, are not accustomed to the changes Napoleon's wars have promoted in our society. In their youth it would have been unthinkable for a woman to have business here. Many of them view the increasing freedoms of talented women with suspicion. They believe it is a woman's natural state to depend on a man for her livelihood."

Amaya made a dismissive sound that made Edmund laugh. "That is their class speaking," she said. "I know very well there are women all over London who must make their own living, and it is only your upper classes that can afford that sort of belief."

"True. And, as I suggested, it is mostly talented women who benefit from increasingly liberal modes of thought. You, as an Extraordinary Shaper, gain the most benefit of all. The fact that there are so many females with your talent has led to those women becoming doctors, which in turn has led to women without Extraordinary Shaper talent demanding entrance to our medical schools, on the grounds that female physicians are just as intelligent and skilled as men in medical matters, regardless of talent. Times are changing." He rapped on the plain wooden door. "I, for one, am fascinated by those changes."

The door opened. A balding man with a prominent forehead gestured to them to enter. "Miss Salazar," he said, "thank you for joining me. This is Mr. Hanley, yes? I am Sir Maxwell Price."

Sir Maxwell was not alone in the small room that smelled faintly of lilacs from the spray of flowers in a vase by the window. Two other men were seated in front of the desk that occupied most of the room, and rose when Amaya entered. One was short and round, with round, rosy cheeks that gave him the appearance of a cheerful apple. The other was not much taller than his companion, but very thin, with prominent bones and a slender neck that appeared in danger of snapping from the weight of his oversized head topped by thick grey hair. Neither smiled. The thin man indicated that Amaya should take his seat, and he and the round man retreated to stand near the window.

Sir Maxwell seated himself behind his desk. He did smile, a friendly expression that would have put Amaya at ease were she not painfully aware of the two strangers behind her. Her fingertips itched with the need to extend her claws in preparation to defend against them. She reminded herself they were likely not warriors, and no threat, but she had not survived this long by making assumptions.

"Miss Salazar, the assessment of the Inca treasure is complete," he said. "The total value comes to 432,000 English pounds, of which you will receive half of ten percent. I hope that is acceptable."

As Amaya had not demanded any share in the treasure, this struck her as an odd statement, but she put it down to English politeness. "I am thankful," she said. "But it is good the Sapa Inca does not know. It is danger, to take his gold."

"We are not afraid of savages," one of the strangers said. Amaya turned in her seat and observed it was the round man who had spoken. His hair was damp with perspiration along the hairline, though the room was comfortably warm rather than hot. Amaya suppressed the urge to show him why "savages" were to be feared.

"My people are not savage," she said, as politely as she could manage, "and you do not know that all gold is the Sapa Inca's to his people. They are not permitted to have it. But you are not Inca, and it is, how do you say it, spoils of war, yes?"

Sir Maxwell cleared his throat. "I would not put it precisely that way," he said, "but as I understand it, that treasure room is lost to the Incas, and someone might as well take advantage of it."

"The question is moot," Edmund said, "as we have retrieved it already, and there is no way to return it."

Sir Maxwell looked grateful for Edmund's interruption. "Naturally," he said. "So, Miss Salazar, if I could have you sign this document, accepting payment?"

Amaya read the document, or tried to; it was in language impenetrable to her imperfect grasp of English. She pushed it over to Edmund, who took his time reading it, to the point that Sir Maxwell said, "I hope you do not believe we would cheat an Extraordinary."

"Of course not. But you would not sign anything you did not know the full contents of, sir," Edmund said. Sir Maxwell had to concede the point.

Eventually, Edmund handed the paper back to Amaya with a nod. Amaya accepted a pen from Sir Maxwell and carefully wrote her name where he indicated. Sir Maxwell countersigned and put the paper away in his desk.

"There is one remaining matter," he said. "May I make known to you Mr. Fenton and Lord Baxter, both of the War Office. I beg your pardon, I should have introduced them when you entered."

Sir Maxwell's last words sounded too casual, and his eyes would not meet Amaya's. She realized it had been no accident; he had intended that Amaya not know their identities immediately. Why, she could not imagine, because she had no relationship with the War Office and certainly did not fear these men, either in their military roles or in their persons.

She turned to face them and said, "Is it that you wish to speak to me, gentlemen?"

Mr. Fenton's rosy cheeks rounded more fully as he smiled. It was an expression that did not suit him, despite how cheerful he looked; it was closer to baring the teeth. "Miss Salazar, you have English family, is that correct?"

Stunned, Amaya blurted out, "I do not know how you know this. It is not public."

"Then you admit to concealing this information?" Lord Baxter said. He did not bother smiling.

"Do not harass Miss Salazar," Edmund said sharply. He no longer looked like a gentleman of leisure; his coolly relaxed pose reminded Amaya of a jaguar waiting to pounce. "If you have something to say, out with it."

The men ignored him. "Miss Salazar, you are of English birth, and as an Extraordinary Shaper, you come under the direction of the War Office," Mr. Fenton said. "You owe the government four years' service. Failure to comply comes with it penalties, among them a heavy fine."

Amaya did not know all his words, but his meaning was clear. She was unsure whether they wanted her service, or her money for failing to give service, but it was obvious they intended to extract *something* from her. "I am not English," she began.

"I hope you would not be so dishonorable as to attempt to shirk your duty," Lord Baxter said. "We know the Neville family are your relations."

"You were raised in foreign lands, so we choose to believe you were unaware of this obligation," Mr. Fenton said. "But now that you are aware, we will require you to report to the War Office immediately to begin your service."

Amaya felt overwhelmed by all the rapid talk in English. She knew they were wrong, but she lacked the linguistic skills to challenge them. "You are wrong, and I believe you are trying to trick me," she said in Spanish, feeling desperate.

"That is enough," Edmund said, rising to confront the two men. "Your argument is void. Miss Salazar's father was Spanish, not English, and by both Spanish and English law this makes Miss Salazar a Spanish citizen. Attempting to confuse and deceive her is a despicable act."

Mr. Fenton's rosy cheeks paled. Lord Baxter glared at Edmund. "The law is not so definite as you suggest," he said. "We are willing to take Miss Salazar to court to claim our rights."

"You want my talent?" Amaya said. "You cannot make me use it."

"We can, and we will," Lord Baxter said. "Or we will see you punished."

Amaya stood, shoving her chair back. "You may try."

Lord Baxter stood his ground, but his skinny throat moved as he swallowed convulsively. "You would not dare attack me."

Amaya's lips curled ferociously. "I am an Extraordinary. It is you would be at fault."

"Please, Miss Salazar, Lord Baxter," Sir Maxwell said. His voice trembled, and he placed both hands on his desktop as if he needed their support. "We are civilized people. We can come to an agreement. Miss Salazar, I do not wish to be crass, but England has awarded you a fortune. Surely you feel some gratitude for that?"

Amaya turned on him, snarling, her claws extended. "You give a gift and then you demand I repay it? And you think my people are the savages?"

Sir Maxwell stilled dramatically. His eyes twitched like those of a mouse who had just seen the hawk's shadow.

"Miss Salazar, I beg of you, remain calm," Edmund said. In Spanish, he added, "If you turn your claws on these men, you will seem rash and ungoverned, and the English will fear you. Is that what you desire?"

Amaya turned her gaze on Edmund. "They wish to use me for their purposes."

"I know. They see your power and think only of how it might be turned to their need. Will you permit me to negotiate for you?"

"Negotiate? As if I were a parcel of land?"

Edmund grimaced. "No. You have talent, and you will choose how you use it. If you will permit me, I will see if I can turn this to your benefit rather than theirs."

Amaya hesitated, then nodded. "But I am not their property."

"I assure you, I will not permit them to treat you as such." Edmund turned to Lord Baxter. "May I ask, my lord, why the War Office is so determined? I was under the impression Napoleon was no longer a threat."

"Napoleon has vanished," Lord Baxter said. "His officers refuse to say where he has gone, and our Discerners believe those men do not know. Wellesley—I should say, the Duke of Wellington—brought the Army into France, and its advance no doubt made Napoleon fear for his control over his soldiers, hence his disappearance. But the War Office is not so foolish as to believe this means the end of the war. We will maintain our vigilance, and that includes continuing to require service of all our Extraordinaries."

"Regardless of your nationality, you owe England a debt, Miss Salazar," Mr. Fenton said. "One which you may repay with service, or with a fine to buy yourself free."

Amaya had never heard this suggested before. She opened her mouth to tell the men she did not care about her fortune and they were welcome to it, but Edmund overrode her. "It is unworthy of the War Office to make such a blatant grab for Miss Salazar's fortune. But I believe that is not what you are truly interested in, is it? Did Dr. Macrae speak with you?"

Now both men shifted uncomfortably. "Dr. Macrae is a

powerful advocate," Mr. Fenton said.

"She is powerfully determined to see Miss Salazar at Norwood College," Edmund corrected him. "And I believe Extraordinary Shapers with the War Office serve as battlefield doctors and surgeons, is that correct?"

Mr. Fenton nodded. Lord Baxter eyed Edmund as if wondering what trick Edmund intended to play.

"But Miss Salazar has little medical training, and that of a very specialized nature," Edmund continued. "If she were to enter the War Office, she would either be useless in the field, or she would have to gain medical training at Norwood, which would also remove her from direct service. In short, Miss Salazar's talent cannot be usefully employed with the War Office in a traditional role."

"And I suppose you have a nontraditional role in mind?" Lord Baxter sneered.

"Miss Salazar's medical experience is as a childbed attendant," Edmund said as if Lord Baxter had not spoken. "She has attended the deliveries of many women, including the Sapa Inca's wives and my own sister-in-law."

"I fail to see how that benefits the War Office," Mr. Fenton said.

"Perhaps you are unaware that Lord and Lady Enderleigh have been made ambassadors to the court of King Ferdinand of Spain." Edmund crossed his arms over his chest, once more the very picture of a gentleman at ease if one could not see his narrowed, intent eyes. "Lady Enderleigh is in a delicate condition and requires an Extraordinary Shaper to attend upon her, now and at the birth of her child. The Extraordinary Shaper attached to their ship must remain with the Royal Navy, leaving Lady Enderleigh without that resource to call on. And I am certain she would prefer a female physician."

"But Lord Enderleigh is an admiral with the Navy, not attached to the War Office. Such service as Miss Salazar would provide does not apply to the law." Lord Baxter took a step forward. He no longer sounded angry.

"I believe, if the War Office chooses, it might find a way around that difficulty. After all, Lady Enderleigh would have been attached to the War Office had she not voluntarily joined the Royal Navy." Edmund turned his attention on the silent Mr. Fenton. "Unless you wish to suggest that her ladyship is not deserving of some consideration, given her, ah, extraordinary service to the war effort?"

Mr. Fenton paled even more. "I would never criticize Lady Enderleigh. No, I believe you are correct. Miss Salazar may serve her term as attendant to her ladyship."

"You are mistaken," Edmund said. His words were polite, but there was steel behind them. "As I have said, Miss Salazar is not an English citizen. She owes you no service. Instead, she will turn her talent to assisting Lady Enderleigh as a token of her esteem for this country, which has shown her such hospitality and generosity."

All four men turned their attention on Amaya, who sank back into her chair. She did not know this Lady Enderleigh of whom they all spoke so respectfully, and she was not certain she wished to be her childbed attendant. On the other hand, she had come to trust Edmund over the months she had been his family's guest, and he would not have suggested this course of action had he not believed it would suit her. And she had fully understood his final words and appreciated their force.

"It is true I am fond of England," she said, "and I wish to help so long as I am not forced. This Lady Enderleigh, she is an Extraordinary?"

Mr. Fenton and Lord Baxter looked at each other, their faces very still as if holding back some strong emotion. "Lady Enderleigh is England's only Extraordinary Scorcher," Lord Baxter said. "The Countess is one of this country's strongest talents. I had not heard of the Earl's new assignment. Surely Admiral Lord Enderleigh is needed at sea?"

Edmund shrugged. "I am merely a translator attached to the ambassadorial party, and not privy to the government's decisions."

Amaya eyed him suspiciously. She was certain Edmund, in protesting that he was only a translator, was dissembling. He once more gave the impression of being nothing more than a harmless fop, but no fop could have argued so persuasively on her behalf. And yet she was certain if she challenged him on the discrepancy between his demeanor and his actions, he would look at her with an ingenuous expression and pretend not to understand her meaning. That he meant to seem foolish was clear, but she could not imagine why.

Sir Maxwell cleared his throat, drawing Amaya's attention back to the present. "We seem to have come to an accord," he said. "Miss Salazar, thank you for your service. England is indeed grateful."

"I am happy to be asked," Amaya said, emphasizing *asked* just enough for Sir Maxwell's complexion to redden. "Mr. Fenton, Lord Baxter." She refrained from thanking them; she still did not believe they meant well, and it was only Edmund's presence that kept her from snarling at them.

When they were safely outside the Treasury, and Edmund had hailed a hackney, Amaya said in Spanish, "I cannot believe they dared threaten me. I understood my talent would protect me."

"They hoped to take advantage of your ignorance," Edmund

said. He helped Amaya into the carriage and settled himself opposite her. "Feel free to thank me at any time."

"Thank you, Edmund," Amaya said sweetly. "I suppose you will not tell me where you learned to argue so persuasively? Your club, perhaps?"

It was a strong hint. Edmund simply raised both eyebrows and regarded her blandly. "I do not take your meaning," he said, smiling in the carefree way she now knew concealed a subtle mind. "I did only as anyone might."

Amaya considered pressing the issue more, but decided if Edmund had secrets, she owed it to him as a friend not to pry. After all, she herself had things she did not wish to share with the world. She dropped her falsely pleasant demeanor and said, "They were uncivil to make such a blatant grab for power."

"They were. And I regret that you were drawn into it. In truth, I almost wished I dared let you handle them your way. They should learn what it is to challenge a jaguar warrior. But, as I said, it would not be good for them to fear you. Fear is the sort of thing that leads men to act rashly."

"I fail to understand that, but I cannot recall ever being mastered by fear."

Edmund's eyebrows rose. He gripped the seat firmly as the hackney bumped over a particularly rough patch in the road. "No? Not even facing Uturunku?"

Amaya shrugged. "I knew I could defeat him. There is no sense in fearing an enemy weaker than yourself."

"I find that astonishing—not that you were stronger than Uturunku, but that you have never feared. What of the raiders who destroyed your home?"

A flash of memory struck her and vanished, leaving only the impression of hiding in a cupboard, her heart beating so hard she could hear it. She looked at the passing streets and the pedestrians enjoying the sunny day. "I suppose," she said in a low voice, "it is more accurate to say I have feared nothing since I became a jaguar warrior."

Edmund nodded, but said nothing. It was one of the things she liked most about him, that he knew when not to speak. For all he pretended to whimsical frivolity for no reason she could understand, he was the most sensible man she knew.

"Tell me of this Lady Enderleigh," she said. "You are so certain I will be acceptable to her as an attendant?"

The carriage jarred them again, leaving Amaya wondering what route they had taken that was so rough. Edmund leaned backward to keep his seat. "She is unusual," he said. "She and the Earl were not born to the nobility, but granted their titles for services rendered the Crown. I have met her only a few times, but she is unlike other Scorchers, who are erratic of temperament and tend to wildness. Are Inca Scorchers the same?"

"They can be. Wildness is discouraged, and those who show themselves to be incapable of or unwilling to control their talent are executed."

"I see. At any rate, Lady Enderleigh is poised, moderate in her speech, a very calm individual. One has the sense that she has mastered herself through great effort. She has a kind temperament and is deeply attached to her husband, who is devoted to her in turn." Edmund hesitated, then said, "When you meet the Earl, do not display distress at his appearance. He is severely scarred from burns."

"That is ironic, given that Lady Enderleigh is a Scorcher."

"Not ironic. She is the one who burned him."

Amaya gasped.

"I do not know the full story, only that he was burned fighting for her life. But it is a sensitive subject you should not allude to, even indirectly. His lordship takes great offense at any suggestion of criticism of his lady wife." Edmund's expression was as serious as she had ever seen.

"I would not be so impolite," Amaya said. "But you have not said why you believe she will accept your offer to make me her attendant."

A smile drove the serious expression away. "Because the two of you are very much alike," he said. "You are both dangerous in your own way, and simultaneously without malice toward any innocent person. I believe Lady Enderleigh will be curious about a woman such as you are, and as you are of the same rank, due to your talents, I hope you will become friends. I do not believe Lady Enderleigh has had much opportunity to gain friends during her years of naval service."

"You said she volunteered to join the Royal Navy."

"Her story is legendary. Perhaps she will share it with you."

The carriage bumped to a halt outside the Hanleys' home. Edmund gave Amaya his hand to help her down. She had almost become accustomed to this, given the narrowness of English skirts and how readily they tangled one's legs. "And you know of her because you are to translate for their party," she said. "Is that why you are leaving the country?"

"It is." Edmund followed Amaya into the house and up the stairs to the drawing room. "In truth, this is no ordinary assignment. What I will tell you now must be held in strictest confidence."

Amaya sat near the window and removed her bonnet, smoothing its ribbons. "You frighten me."

"Did we not establish you are not afraid of anything?" Edmund said with a smile. "I know you are circumspect, and besides, it is not as if your English is good enough to tell anyone the truth."

Amaya mock-snarled at him. "It is good enough for me to tell all the English *señoritas* that you are not to be trusted."

Edmund clutched his waistcoat over his heart as if she had stabbed him. "Perish the thought!"

Amaya laughed. "So, tell me this great secret."

"It is not precisely a secret so much as a diplomatic fiction. Everyone knows the Earl of Enderleigh is a naval man, and while he is intelligent and quick-thinking, he is no diplomat. That role will be played by Sir William Kynaston, who *is* a diplomat, and one with many years' experience. Lord and Lady Enderleigh are...it is not exaggerating to call them a veiled threat. The King of Spain and his government are a fractious lot, and their dubious military assistance in the late Peninsular campaigns has left England even less well-disposed toward them than before. But it is to our advantage to see peace in Spain, and to that end, we are sending this diplomatic party, with Sir William to negotiate treaties and Lord and Lady Enderleigh to remind Spain that England is the superior power."

"I wonder at Lord Enderleigh being willing to permit his wife to overshadow him."

Edmund laughed. "Lord Enderleigh is a highly-rated Extraordinary Mover, and from what I have observed, he is confident in his talent and not at all afraid of coming second to his wife. But that is why you must not speak of this to anyone. My assessment is from personal observation, not the overt statements of the government. As far as Spain is concerned, England is sending two of its most respected Extraordinaries as a mark of, well, their own respect."

"Even if everyone there will be aware of the truth," Amaya said archly. "Your assessment seems most subtle. Another thing you learned from your club?"

For a moment, Edmund's gaze sharpened, and he seemed about to speak. Then a lazy smile spread across his features, and he laughed. "You must give me credit for *some* intelligence," he drawled. "Even I must accumulate knowledge after spending enough time surrounded by those who swim in it. Perhaps I am the grit in an oyster that time will turn into a pearl."

"Perhaps," Amaya said, feeling obscurely disappointed. "Though I like the man you are now."

"High praise indeed." Edmund set his hat on a table near the door. "Shall I ring for tea? I am certain Mary and Charles will be here shortly."

"I feel the need for refreshment, after speaking with those men." Amaya rose and smoothed her skirts. "In truth, I am grateful for your assistance, Mr. Hanley."

"I am happy to be of service, Miss Salazar," Edmund said with a bow. "And, well, I am not certain how you will feel about this, but Spain is in a sense your homeland. Had you any ideas about locating your father's family?"

His words struck her like a fist to her stomach. "I had not considered," she said faintly. "Should I?"

"That is your decision." Edmund, having rung the bell, settled himself on the sofa with his legs outstretched, but his serious expression belied the ease with which he sat. "If you care for my opinion, I would wish to know."

Amaya sat opposite him, feeling as if her body were far away and she was manipulating it like a Mover might a puppet. "Mrs. Neville said my father was from Toledo. I do not know where that is."

"I will find you a map." Edmund leaned forward. "No fear, yes?"

She blinked, coming back to herself. "No fear." There was no reason to fear. It was her family, every bit as much as the Nevilles were. But the idea of meeting a cadre of relatives, English or Spanish, disturbed her calm for the rest of the day.

CHAPTER 4
IN WHICH AMAYA MEETS THE MOST DANGEROUS WOMAN IN ENGLAND

Amaya recognized the tall, brooding house whose curb the hackney drew up to; it was two houses to the right of the Gates residence, which Amaya had visited frequently because Bess and Eleanora Gates were close friends and fellow Speakers. This house had drawn her attention before because it was darker than the other houses on Grosvenor Square, and its windows had never been lit at any of the times Amaya had passed it. Despite its dour façade, Amaya was drawn to it—or perhaps it was because of its façade, which reminded her of the stony Inca city she had called home for thirteen years. Its dark stone, its relatively plain construction, gave her a twinge of homesickness.

"The Earl and Countess cannot have lived here long," she told Edmund.

"They have not. This is a temporary residence before the diplomatic party leaves for Spain." Edmund climbed down from the hackney and offered Amaya his hand. "You are not apprehensive, are you?"

"Should I be?"

"Of course not." Edmund lightly kicked the sole of his boot against the doorstep, though it did not appear dirty. "But some people are afraid of the Countess regardless."

Amaya felt a twinge of sympathy for this unknown woman. No one had ever been afraid of Amaya's talent, only of her martial prowess, and she felt it would be very hard to know others feared her for something she had not chosen. "I understand. It makes me grateful that so few of the Englishmen and women I meet know what it means that I am a jaguar warrior, because some of those who do fear me as well."

"Which is another reason I believe you and Lady Enderleigh will suit."

The door opened, and a footman showed them inside, accepting Edmund's hat with a placid expression. The hall was larger than the Hanleys', and brightly lit, which was such a contrast to its forbidding exterior Amaya gawked at the sparkling chandelier before gaining control of herself. The scent of roses filled the air, rising from an arrangement of pink and red blooms on a pedestal between two closed doors to Amaya's left. Roses were not a flower that grew in her lost home, and Amaya had become very fond of their robust, sweet scent. It increased her desire to know the Countess; this was one more thing they had in common, assuming Lady Enderleigh had chosen the flowers.

Ahead, stairs rose out of sight, their glossy wood gleaming with the pale reflection of the light high above. The floorboards, a lighter brown than the stairs, also reflected the lights like tiny dim stars. Amaya could see no way to raise or lower the chandelier, and wondered how it was lit. Then she remembered a Scorcher would have no difficulty with something so simple.

She followed the footman, who walked toward the stairs, but

turned left down a hallway before reaching them. Amaya admired the paintings hanging on the walls, which represented country houses of varying degrees of size and elegance. She liked English architecture for its regularity, though she was certain the Incas were more competent in how well they fitted irregular blocks with six or seven corners together. The English would never dream of such complexity; they turned their architectural efforts in other directions, such as glass windows and garden follies.

They passed an open doorway on the left side of the hall, through which Amaya saw a long table and many chairs lined up along both its sides. The table shone with polish and the light coming in from windows on the room's far side. Opposite this doorway stood a closed door the footman now opened. "Lady Enderleigh," he said, "Miss Salazar and Mr. Hanley."

Though the weather was clement, this room was very warm due to a fire burning high in the fireplace. Two windows illuminated the comfortable sofas facing each other near the fire, as did a pair of lamps on cabinets near the door. A bookcase between the windows stood handy for a reader who might choose to sit beside it. The fire burned hot enough that its smell filled the room—not the smell of smoke or resin, but the clean hot scent of the flame. Amaya had rarely smelled a fire so pure.

A woman seated on a sofa, her body angled toward the fireplace, rose awkwardly when they entered. "Mr. Hanley, welcome," she said. "And Miss Salazar. I am pleased to make your acquaintance."

Amaya examined this woman whom Mary Hanley had called, upon hearing what Amaya proposed, the most dangerous woman in England. Lady Enderleigh looked no different from anyone else. She wore her chestnut hair plainly arranged, with no curls or bands, and her gown was of fine blue wool with short puffed sleeves, over which she wore a shawl that did not quite match the gown. Sharp grey eyes examined Amaya every bit as closely as Amaya regarded her, though Lady Enderleigh's somewhat heavy eyebrows and strong chin gave her the unexpected look of a hawk stooping to prey.

"I apologize for the heat," Lady Enderleigh said. "I fear I am frequently cold these days. Dr. Hays says it is a usual change, and there is nothing to be done." She smiled. "It is at least something I am capable of managing for myself."

"That is fortunate," Amaya said. "The coldness, it is true many women with child feel it, or feel they are too warm, but it cannot be helped without hurting you."

The heavy eyebrows rose. "Oh? Dr. Hays did not say—that is, I believed it simply impossible." Lady Enderleigh touched her lips lightly. "I beg your pardon. Please, be seated."

Amaya sat opposite the Countess with Edmund at her side. Lady Enderleigh appeared to be in her seventh month and was moving as heavily as should be expected of a woman in her condition. She pulled the shawl closer around her shoulders as she sat. "So what is it you would do to make me feel less chilled?" Lady Enderleigh asked.

Amaya perched on the edge of her seat and clasped her hands in her lap. "There is a difference between the body and the air," she said. "You feel something is warm when it is hotter than you, and a thing feels cold when it is colder than you. It is in your head that you are cold now, though, not in your body. So it is that I can tell your head it is wrong. But that is danger. The head—it is that we know little of it, and small changes can make large problems."

"I can imagine it." Lady Enderleigh leaned back slightly and rested one hand on the sofa's arm. "Mr. Hanley tells me you are experienced at assisting women giving birth."

Amaya shot a quick glance at Edmund, wondering what else he had told Lady Enderleigh. "I have done it sometimes. With the Sapa Inca's wives, three, and with Mrs. Charles Hanley this past month. It is for women only to attend the Sapa Inca's wives, of course, and I am—was—the only Extraordinary Shaper among my people."

"He told me that, as well." Lady Enderleigh twitched the shawl closer. "Do you miss your people terribly? Your family?"

No one aside from the Hanleys had ever asked that question. Amaya's throat closed unexpectedly, and she swallowed before answering. "I have no family there. My parents and brother and sister were all killed, and I am alone among the Incas."

"I had heard that. But the Incas cared for you, made you one of them, so surely you left friends behind?" Lady Enderleigh's cheeks became a delicate pink. "I apologize, that was presumptuous of me. It is simply that I have made a home for myself at sea, amongst people who are not my blood relations, and I wondered if perhaps you felt the same. I know I miss my friends already, and I have not been torn from them as you were."

Amaya nodded. "They are all I know. Yupanqui and Quri, they are my...you do not have a word. We are together as warriors, live together, fight together. Inkasisa, she is the Sapa Inca's sister but she is also a Scorcher—she is a friend from when I live with the Incas. And Kichka..." She had not spoken of Kichka to the Hanleys, not even to Bess. She would not see him again, and it was better she forget what tenderness had passed between them. "He is also a friend," she finished.

"And you cannot return? I am afraid I know little of your situation, other than that your removal from Peru was rather abrupt and in a way that means the Incas are lost to you."

Amaya nodded. "But I have friends here," she said, feeling obscurely as if she should reassure the Countess. "And family. I learned my mother was English, and she has family here." At the moment, her uncertainty about accepting that family seemed irrelevant.

"How astonishing," Lady Enderleigh said. "And a possible family in Spain, Mr. Hanley tells me." A faint look of distaste tightened her features and vanished. "I hope for your sake they are wonderful people. I know from experience that blood relations are not enough to guarantee a pleasant intimacy."

"You do not like your family?" Amaya ventured.

"My father was not happy with my decision to join the Royal Navy," Lady Enderleigh said with a reflective smile, "and my mother follows where he leads. I fear even my success, my marriage, and my elevation in rank were not enough to appease him." She removed her hand from the armrest and touched her belly absently, suggesting to Amaya that she did not realize she had done so. "Perhaps if I produce talented offspring, he will change his mind. I, however, have not changed mine, and I have no interest in regaining his…oh, if I say 'affection' the word will curdle in my mouth. His regard, perhaps?"

Amaya glanced at Edmund again. The Countess was more forthcoming than Amaya was accustomed to. She liked the woman's forthright speech even as it puzzled her that Lady Enderleigh could be so unguarded with a woman she did not know.

Lady Enderleigh abruptly leaned forward. "I am making poor Mr. Hanley uncomfortable," she said, lowering those heavy brows until she looked very fierce. "I apologize for speaking so frankly, but if I am to trust my most intimate self to you, Miss Salazar, I would like there to be no false reserve between us."

"I am not uncomfortable, and you forget, my lady, that I am not unfamiliar with your history," Edmund said with a lopsided smile.

"Very true. Then I withdraw my apology." Lady Enderleigh turned her attention on Amaya, who did feel uncomfortable, but only because Lady Enderleigh's regard made her feel exposed, her nerves bared to the world. "Miss Salazar, let me be even more frank. I have been quite well these past several months, but my husband is concerned for my health as I draw near my confinement. He—and I admit to agreeing with him—would prefer not to rely on chance or a Spanish midwife to attend me. If something were to go wrong...well. You see why I have need of an Extraordinary Shaper." She smiled as wryly as Edmund had. "I am extremely valuable to my country, and they would prefer not to lose me."

"And valuable to yourself," Amaya said.

"Indeed." Lady Enderleigh's expression changed. For the space of half a breath, she looked very young and very uncertain. Then the moment passed, and she was herself again. "You are quiet," she said, "but I believe it is because you observe and study before you speak. I find that admirable. Will you join us? Be my companion? Because I would like to know you better."

"And because I do not fear you," Amaya said, making a guess.

Lady Enderleigh's eyelids drooped as she cast her gaze down, a moment's discomposure that disappeared as fast as her uncertainty. "Burns do not heal the way other injuries do," she said. "I imagine you know that."

Amaya shrugged. "Burns do not. But an Extraordinary Shaper, our bodies are not the same as yours. We do not burn the same."

"But that is not why you do not fear me," Lady Enderleigh said.

Amaya turned to Edmund, who was watching this interchange in expressionless silence. "You say we are both danger and we are both innocent of malice," she said. "Say why I am danger."

Edmund blinked at her impulsive request, but did not hesitate. "Miss Salazar is trained to fight," he said. "She had no experience with civilized society before coming to live in England. She has taken lives even as you have, my lady. And like you, she has never taken a life except in battle. You are both dangerous in theory, true, but you are neither of you to be feared."

Lady Enderleigh's hand, which had closed tightly on the armrest, relaxed. "Then you do understand," she said. "I hoped you would."

"We are the same that way," Amaya said. "And I tell—told Mr. Hanley I fear nothing, so I should not start by fearing you."

That made Lady Enderleigh laugh. "I think we will suit admirably," she said. She offered Amaya her hand, which was brown from the sun and small and well-shaped. "I am glad Mr. Hanley suggested this solution."

"Mr. Hanley is very intelligent. So he tells me," Amaya said.

Edmund chuckled. "Fortunately Lady Enderleigh knows I am of the most moderate temperament, and not at all proud, or you would convince her I am the most arrogant of men."

"You are not the man about town you would like others to believe, true," Lady Enderleigh said, surprising Amaya that Lady Enderleigh, too, had seen past Edmund's cultivated demeanor. "Tell me, Mr. Hanley, is it true Sir William wishes to use me as a bludgeon to keep our Spanish friends in check?"

Edmund did not flinch. He regarded Lady Enderleigh with unruffled calm, but one hand closed into a fist. "I am certain Sir William would never consider—"

"Mr. Hanley," Lady Enderleigh said, "do not try to deceive me. There is only one reason Lord Enderleigh and I would be removed from *Hyperion* when the entire fleet is out searching for

Napoleon. I would simply like to know what will be secretly expected of me."

Edmund pursed his lips and made his fist relax, spreading both hands on his knees in a gesture of apology. "Not a bludgeon," he said, "so much as a burning arrow, if you will pardon the comparison. I believe he would like King Ferdinand to consider carefully the consequences of defying England. Acting is unnecessary; you need only be present."

Lady Enderleigh made a sour face. "That is what Miles feared," she murmured, half to herself. "And yet we are sworn to do our duty."

Amaya felt a surge of compassion for the Countess. "It is not so bad," she said. "When you are feared, they do not make the little demands that pick and pick at you like birds with beaks." She tapped the cushion between herself and Edmund for emphasis.

"Very true," Lady Enderleigh said, regaining some of her cheer. "And it is surprising how quick people are to fulfil one's demands. I never need worry about finding a seat at some gathering."

"Then we will be feared together," Amaya said. "Now, may I examine you? I wish to see your body and if there is to be... complications, is the word."

"I should excuse myself," Edmund said, rising.

"No, wait here," Lady Enderleigh said. "I am accustomed to Dr. Hays' examinations, and they are not immodest, but they are boring to anyone not involved, or so my husband says." She rose, pushing herself off the sofa with both hands, and added, "I am grateful to you both."

Edmund bowed. "It was my pleasure to serve you—both of you," he added, including Amaya in his bow.

"Let us remove upstairs," Lady Enderleigh said, "and Mr. Hanley, feel free to ring for refreshment."

"Oh, Edmund will read a novel while he waits," Amaya teased.

Edmund groaned theatrically. "You will yet make me a bluestocking," he said with an answering smile.

CHAPTER 5
IN WHICH THE DIPLOMATIC PARTY ARRIVES IN MADRID

A maya sat in the well-appointed carriage, with its padded seats and open windows, and tried to relax. The road to Madrid was not as well-paved as similar country roads in England, and the ruts bounced the carriage's passengers mercilessly. Amaya had difficulty not clinging to her seat, trying to anticipate the next bounce.

Beside her, Elinor, Lady Enderleigh, sat with her eyes closed, though Amaya did not believe it possible for anyone to sleep given the rigors of the journey. She showed no signs of distress. In the nearly two weeks Amaya had known the Countess, she had become accustomed to the lady's placidity of temperament concealing a keen mind and robust sense of humor. This native good humor had made it natural that they should make free of one another's given names within only a few days of becoming acquainted. Amaya supposed Elinor was used to the movement of a ship, and this road might be no worse than a storm at sea.

On the seat across from them, Lord Enderleigh sat looking out the window, his one hand gripping the edge of the seat and his maimed right arm resting in his lap. Amaya did her best never to stare, but it was difficult not to wonder at the amount of damage he must have sustained for his hand to be removed, and consider the skills of the Extraordinary Shaper who had managed it so neatly. Almost it convinced her to accept medical training.

Sir William Kynaston, the other official representative of the King of England to the court of King Ferdinand, had sat with them in the morning, but he suffered from motion-sickness on these terrible roads. Although he never complained, his face had grown increasingly pale and green-tinged around the lips during the morning's travel, and after a stop for a midday meal, he had chosen to sit beside the driver.

He was a handsome man in his early fifties, lean and hawk-nosed with deep-set hazel eyes, and he might be a kind and generous man, but Amaya did not care for him. He spoke well, but Amaya suspected by how readily he smiled that he kept his true opinions well-hidden. Amaya distrusted anyone who could lie so readily for no discernable reason; such men and women reminded her of the Inca Seer Achik, whose deception and spite had nearly got Amaya and Bess killed. Sir William bore careful watching.

His wife, Lady Kynaston, rode seated beside Lord Enderleigh, having declared that the rear-facing seat did not disturb her. Where her husband was lean, she was round, with rosy cheeks made redder by the heat. She resembled one of Mary Hanley's porcelain figures, with flaxen hair and blue eyes, but she had a clever mind she concealed behind a sweet, diffident voice. Elinor had told Amaya, privately, that Sir William's success as a diplomat was due in large part to the presence of his wife behind the scenes. Amaya liked her to the same degree she misliked her husband.

She turned her attention to her own window. The warm, dust-filled air made Amaya wonder why she had ever disliked the dampness of the English climate. But the countryside was beautiful: a patchwork of yellow-greens and golds and rich, loamy browns that spread into the misty distance. At the edge of her enhanced vision, trees were visible, their low, spreading branches like grey-green clouds floating low above the ground. With the dust in the air, the trees made the sky seem to blend into the earth, gradually turning from yellowish-tan to pale blue to a vivid brightness that reminded Amaya of the skies above her mountain home, just before a storm.

A particularly bad jolt made Elinor open her eyes and Lord Enderleigh grip the seat edge more tightly. Amaya tensed her leg muscles to keep herself from sliding.

"I realize the war is to blame for the conditions of the road," Lord Enderleigh said with a smile, "but I'm resentful of it regardless."

"We are almost to Madrid, are we not?" Elinor said, leaning to look out the window. "I see a river ahead—I believe it is the one bordering the city. The Manzanares."

Lord Enderleigh rubbed his face with his right sleeve. "Say the word, and I will scout ahead."

Elinor laughed. "You dislike this cramped carriage, and the dust and heat, and you would like any excuse to Fly and leave the rest of us behind."

"You have seen through me, my dear." Lord Enderleigh had a long, interestingly bony face and fair hair bleached by a hotter sun than shone over England. Burn scars like a dozen bony, ropy fingers, livid against his tanned skin, sprawled across his right cheek and along that side of his face and crept into his scalp, making his hair above his ear patchy. The disfigurement never seemed to bother him, but Amaya would not draw attention to it in any way.

Now he turned his keen blue eyes on Amaya and said, "I would, of course, not leave you both to suffer while I escaped to the cool heights. Is there anything I might do for you, Miss Salazar?"

"No, thank you, my lord," Amaya said. "It is enough that this journey be almost over. I am not used to heat as this is."

"I imagine the mountains of Peru are much cooler." The Earl mopped his brow again. "The Caribbean is hotter still, but there is such a difference between being trapped in a carriage, eating dirt, and sailing through the waves and the sea breezes."

Amaya looked out the window again. Ahead, she saw the glinting ribbon of a river, and beyond it, the angular grey shapes of stone buildings. "Madrid is not as big as London," she observed. "Though it still seems large."

"It is a populous city, and one that has seen many centuries of growth and change," Lady Kynaston said. "Structures dating from the Moorish occupation still stand in the city, alongside European buildings. This co-mingling gives the city its unique character."

"I look forward to seeing the sights," Elinor said. "If we are allowed time for it."

Lord Enderleigh grimaced. "Say, more likely, if we demand time for it."

"I suppose I could use my notoriety to gain us greater freedom," Elinor said with a sigh, "but that would be cruel. And I dislike being feared."

"You might become like El Encendedor, terrorizing the countryside," Lord Enderleigh said with a twisted, bitter smile as if he were remembering something disturbing. "But you know I will not permit my wife to be a figure of dread."

"'Permit' is perhaps the wrong word, dearest," Elinor said. "Who is El Encendedor? I believed that to be the Spanish word for a Scorcher, but you make it sound like a title."

"He is half bandit, half bogeyman, and all legend," Lord Enderleigh said. "The stable hands at the last inn were full of tales about him. Apparently he is rather a thorn in the side of the government, being a rogue Extraordinary Scorcher at the head of a large guerrilla army. King Ferdinand cannot contain him, and the common people love him, as he fought against the *afrancesados* who would have had Spain remain dominated by the Bonapartes."

"It is that he is a folk hero," Amaya said. "Why is he feared by the government?"

"Because he does not always confine his activities to fighting the official enemies of Spain." Lord Enderleigh shifted his weight and rested his maimed arm along the windowsill. "Many lesser nobles have apparently been his victims. It is all to do with the Cortes, which drafted a democratic constitution that was ignored by King Ferdinand on his return from France. There are many who would see the nobility weakened, and the common man granted more freedoms. El Encendedor wishes that to happen immediately."

"How frightening," Elinor said, her brow furrowing. "Even if his motives are noble, I do not believe anyone is justified in hurting others in the pursuit of a cause."

"I agree," Lord Enderleigh said. "He may call himself a freedom fighter, but I daresay he is closer to being a brigand."

Amaya did not know what to believe. It would have been unthinkable for the Incas to rise up against the Sapa Inca, but he was a god to his people, and King Ferdinand was only a man. Suppose he did not have the best interests of his people at heart? Perhaps then it was the duty of those people to challenge him, as it seemed this Extraordinary Scorcher was doing. And yet she did not approve of vigilante justice, which so often became simply a justification for doing selfish, violent acts. Whoever El Encendedor was, he could not be entirely honorable.

"At any rate, I suspect if we are not assertive, we will find ourselves inundated with other people's requests," Lord Enderleigh said. "Though 'assertive' need not mean 'frightening.'"

Amaya silently agreed, though she was not the one whose time would be monopolized. She recalled Sir William, on the ship from London to Santander in Spain, talking a great deal about what would be expected of the diplomatic party, but he spoke in a florid, roundabout way she had difficulty following, and between that and her dislike of him, she had not paid attention. Now she wished she had at least asked Edmund to explain the situation.

All she did know was that the English diplomatic party was to be housed in the Palacio Real, that the Earl and Countess were to be presented to the Spanish king, and that Sir William intended to press the king and his government, the Cortes, to formalize their alliance with England. Amaya did not understand this last item. From what Edmund had said, Spain was in a subordinate position to England, so why would Sir William, or the English government, for that matter, wish to take the lead in promoting good relations between Spain and England? But it was nothing to her except a curiosity. She was here to care for Elinor and the child.

The idea of finding her Spanish family no longer compelled her as it had before the diplomatic party left England. Wherever they were, *whoever* they were, they could have no knowledge of her existence, and likely did not desire the connection. But late at night, when she lay wakeful in whatever narrow bed had been procured for her by Matthew Hestow, the man in charge of the details of their procession, she considered the possibility that she was wrong. Suppose her Spanish relatives were like Mrs. Neville, caring and interested in knowing her? *Suppose they are hateful and vile,* she told herself, and refused to think on the matter further, until the next night found her once more wakeful.

The carriage jolted abruptly once more, and then the rocking and bouncing diminished, and the sound of the wheels deepened. Amaya peered out and discovered the road was much smoother than before, though it still was not paved. Madrid was closer now, and she watched its grey stone edifices loom larger. The world was so much bigger than she had ever imagined when she was a jaguar warrior in Peru. That fact might have intimidated her were she not so curious about what made European cities, and people, different from her homeland.

She sat back and discovered Elinor was looking out the other window. "I see the palace," she said. "It is quite large. Our party will be swallowed up by it."

"How fortunate I brought my compass," Lord Enderleigh said with a straight face. "I hope I recall how to use it. We might end up wandering the halls, piteously calling for help in finding our way back to our rooms."

Elinor shot him an amused look. "I will arm myself with a spool of thread as Theseus did, and make a web of my wanderings."

Lord Enderleigh laughed. "How very practical of you."

A peculiar look, not quite pain and not quite pleasure, wrinkled Elinor's brow, and she splayed a hand across her belly. Lord Enderleigh's amusement vanished in an instant. "Are you well, Elinor?"

Elinor nodded, though the peculiar, inward-turned look

remained. "The child moved," she said. "It is still disconcerting, however often it happens."

Amaya was grateful Sir William had chosen to sit outside. He always looked embarrassed whenever anything drew attention to Elinor's condition. His reactions annoyed Amaya. She did not understand why the English were so reticent to discuss such a natural thing as childbirth, or why so many of them pretended a woman with child was not in that condition. She followed their customs, as she felt was polite, but the annoyance remained.

She laid a hand atop Elinor's where it rested on her stomach and let herself plummet deep into her awareness of Elinor's body. It felt like falling from a great height without striking the ground, the inner structures of her ears telling her that her body was moving even though she knew it was not so. She closed her eyes, unnecessarily, because her vision no longer perceived the outer world, but the shapes and structures of the human body.

Amaya was intimately familiar with how the human body looked on the inside, so she knew what she saw when she descended into this state bore no resemblance to reality. It felt, instead, as if she were asking questions of the body she Shaped and knew the answers on the same fundamental level she perceived the body from. Europeans had no name for the *sunqu*, the five parts of a human she had been taught by the Shapers of the Tawantinsuyu to call Heart, Sense, Need, Strength, and Release. She swiftly asked of each *sunqu*, *All is well?*

The responses welled up within her, feelings more than thoughts, as if her own body were linked to Elinor's. That could not actually be so, as that kind of linkage could be deadly if one body were ill or severely injured; it was merely a useful metaphor. Elinor was as healthy as ever, though Need was edging up on hunger and Release needed to urinate, a common enough occurrence in an expectant mother.

The unborn babe was a blank in Amaya's sense of Elinor's body, a separate individual Amaya could not directly touch and therefore could not Shape. Instead she dived deeper, becoming aware of the five nested *sunqu* centering on the womb. The babe moved then, sending ripples through the five. It had rolled rather than kicked, which concerned Amaya, as a too-mobile babe in the womb could roll itself into a dangerous position. But the child remained head-down, its life-giving cord coiled loosely around it, and seemed perfectly healthy.

She rose out of her meditative state and withdrew her hand. "The child is restless," she said. "It wishes to breathe free, I believe. But it is not ready, and it knows that, too."

"I admit to restlessness myself," Elinor confessed. "Only a few more weeks, and yet it feels like forever."

"Your time will come soon enough, my dear," Lady Kynaston said, patting Elinor's knee. "Every one of my five confinements passed in the space of a moment, or so it seemed. It is what comes after that is forever."

Shadows flashed over them, and Amaya once more looked out the window. They had entered the city without her knowing it, and tall buildings that looked much as London's did towered over the carriage, alternating with shorter buildings that lacked the ornamentation of their companions. Men and women passing in the street, most of them on foot, two or three on horseback, glanced at the English procession of carriages and then took a second, longer look, gaping.

Now the rattle of the wheels took on a hollow sound, as if striking stone, and the carriage took a broad left turn. Immediately ahead Amaya saw an enormous, pale grey structure whose many glass windows gleamed in the afternoon sun. It was her turn to gape in astonishment. She did not believe she had ever seen a larger building, even in London, though it was true she had seen very little of London in her time there. Even so, the Palacio Real was large enough to swallow up three of the Sapa Inca's palace.

The carriage came to a halt, and Lord Enderleigh stepped down and offered his hand first to his wife, then to Amaya. Once she had left the carriage, Sir William climbed down and offered Lady Kynaston his arm. The rest of the carriages in their train stopped smoothly nearby, and the diplomatic party began emerging from them. Amaya smoothed her skirts and took a few steps toward the palace, but came quickly to a halt when she realized how many people gathered around the entrance, standing in formal ranks like so many life-size dolls.

There were soldiers in the blue and red uniforms she had seen in Peru, lined up behind men in clothing that resembled English garb so closely she would not have guessed them to be Spanish. All of them had their attention fixed on a point somewhere between themselves and the carriages, not on any of the diplomatic party.

Amaya assessed the crowd, looking for potential threats. The soldiers were armed, but none held their weapons at the ready, and the gentlemen—for so she felt she should call them —did not appear to carry any weapons. Even so, talent did not show on the skin, and any of these people might possess talents they might turn on the English. Amaya flexed her fingers and let her claws extend a fraction of an inch beyond her fingertips. It was unnecessary, because Elinor's talent was far better suited to defending against a large body of warriors, but Amaya did not believe in letting down her guard in a strange place.

Sir William and Lady Kynaston strode toward a short, black-haired man who stood near the front of the Spanish cohort. Sir William bowed; the black-haired man bowed in return. In Spanish, Sir William said, "Lady Kynaston and I thank you for your welcome."

The black-haired man glanced past Sir William at the rest of the diplomatic party. His dark eyes narrowed for the briefest moment, and then his expression smoothed into affability. "It is we who are thankful that England shows us such respect," he said in the same language.

Sir William turned and bowed in Lord Enderleigh's direction as the earl and countess approached, arm in arm. "My lord, my lady, may I make known to you Don Martín de Ceballos y Beltrán, Count of Álava, *mayordomo de semana,* and representative of His Majesty King Ferdinand VII. My lord count, the Earl and Countess of Enderleigh."

"You are most welcome," Don Martín said in heavily accented English. "Permit me to introduce Don Pedro Borrero, who will have the charge of your household while you reside with us." He indicated a taller man whose light brown hair was longer than Amaya thought was strictly fashionable, but of course she had no idea what the Spanish thought appropriate. Deep lines made furrows from the sides of Don Pedro's nose to the corners of his mouth, and from the corners of his mouth toward his chin, giving his face a drooping, melancholy appearance. He bowed, but did not smile. Amaya wondered if he was capable of doing so.

"By 'our household' you mean, of course, our Spanish attendants," Lord Enderleigh said.

The count did not blink. "Of course. Not your own attendants, naturally."

"Naturally." Lord Enderleigh rested his hand atop Elinor's briefly. "We wish to rest after our journey. Please convey our regards to King Ferdinand, and express our desire to meet with him at his earliest convenience."

Don Martín stiffened slightly, a reaction Amaya supposed only someone watching him as closely as she was would notice. "I will express your wish to his Majesty," he said, managing to sound both polite and affronted. Amaya guessed the Earl's words were offensive in some way; perhaps he had implied that the King of Spain should bow to Lord Enderleigh's wishes. Amaya was cheered by this even as she felt slightly guilty that she should wish to see England triumphant over what was, essentially, her native land. But she had English friends, England had been kind to her, and yet she was no English citizen and likely should not choose sides.

The Earl nodded as regally as if he had been born to his estate, Elinor bobbed a curtsey, and the two turned to follow Don Pedro. Amaya walked behind them a few paces, watching the assembled Spaniards covertly. They did not stare openly at the Earl or Elinor until they were past—and then the gentlemen and a few of the soldiers turned their gazes on the Countess of Enderleigh's awkward form. So they well knew who had come to the Palacio Real, and who the real threat was. Amaya was annoyed again, this time on Elinor's behalf. Most of them looked as if they expected Elinor to burst into flame before them.

Beyond the wide front door, the palace opened up into a vast marble room, tall and majestic and well-lit by lanterns that burned high on its walls, out of reach of any but a Scorcher. The stairs leading up divided to rise again to a landing from which led three red-curtained openings, each large enough to admit three people walking side by side. Having left the soldiers behind, Amaya felt free to gawk again as Don Pedro led their party through many halls, cavernous and echoing with the sound of many footsteps. She had seen nothing like this in her life.

Almost every wall bore draperies or was covered with fine, brightly colored, intricately patterned fabrics; almost every ceiling was painted with scenes Amaya did not recognize, of men and women and creatures frozen in the act of dancing or making merry. Gold trimmed every conceivable surface, glinting warmly in the light of the lanterns. It was ornate enough to overwhelm her senses, and after a few minutes she had to look at Elinor's back as they walked, ignoring the beautiful but overwhelming scene.

They walked for some minutes before Don Pedro opened a door and said, his English not as accented as Don Martín's, "We are pleased to provide this apartment for our English friends. It was the home of Queen Maria Amalia, and we hope it will suit."

"Thank you," Lord Enderleigh said. "It is quite an honor."

Amaya eyed Don Pedro as she passed him. He continued to stand at the door as the diplomatic party entered, and did not seem to notice her regard. To her surprise, his attention was not on Elinor, but on Sir William. What it meant, she did not know, but Don Pedro's relaxed stance and inattention to the Extraordinary Scorcher suggested he did not fear Elinor. Amaya decided he bore closer watching. Either he was a fool, or he was very wise, and in the latter case he might be more trustworthy than Don Martín.

The "apartment" beyond turned out to be a series of halls lined with gold-rimmed doors, carpeted in plush, soft fabrics that gave slightly as Amaya trod them. A line of plainly-dressed men and women stood at attention along the wall, just inside the door. The woman at the head of the line, a plump lady with greying black hair and dark blue eyes, curtseyed deeply when Lord Enderleigh and Elinor approached. "I will to your comfort see," she said. "Ask for what you wish."

"Oh," Lord Enderleigh said. He sounded at a loss, not at all as confident as he had in speaking to Don Martín. "We—"

"Thank you," Elinor said smoothly. "Please show us to our rooms."

The woman turned and clapped her hands sharply, saying in Spanish, "Show respect to the lord and lady!"

Immediately the servants bowed or curtseyed, and spread out along the hall. Amaya followed Elinor again, this time watching the various servants as they disappeared within the doors lining the hall. She was so intent on them she did not at first hear Elinor say her name. "Oh—yes?" she said when Elinor spoke again.

"I asked if this room is suitable," Elinor said.

Amaya glanced inside the open door. The bedchamber was as ornate as the rest of the palace, the corners and edges of the ceiling gilded, the walls hung with red velvet draperies over patterned gold-and-red paper, the ceiling painted with some scene even her enhanced eyesight could not make out. It was not a room anyone could sleep in. But Amaya guessed it likely that every bedchamber in this place would look much the same, so she said, "It is very nice. Thank you."

Elinor shot her a look that said she did not believe Amaya was being completely honest, but said only, "Your maid will see to your things, if you would join me. I believe this lady wishes to show us our domain, and she will be more comfortable if she can speak her own language."

Amaya nodded. "I am Miss Salazar," she told the plump servant woman in Spanish. "My lady wishes to know your name."

The woman brightened at hearing her own language. "Mrs. Zambrano," she said. "But my lady need not lower herself to address me so. I am no one of importance."

"In England, it is how women of the household—the women who care for a household, I mean—are spoken to." Amaya relayed the information to Elinor, who nodded. "You will show us this place?" Amaya continued.

"It will be my pleasure," Mrs. Zambrano said.

Amaya paid more attention to Mrs. Zambrano than to the many overwhelming rooms she bustled them through. The housekeeper—though Amaya suspected that was a grander title than her Spanish masters would give her—seemed genuinely pleased to serve the English lord and lady, and Amaya felt confident she was no threat. She wished, though, that she understood more of the politenesses of civil society. Was it a subtle insult, for example, to assign Lord and Lady Enderleigh servants who could barely communicate in English?

Amaya inwardly chastised herself. It was not her responsibility to care about such things. That was on Sir William's head. Still, she could not help wondering, every time she saw an unfamiliar servant, whether or not he posed a threat.

CHAPTER 6
IN WHICH AMAYA MEETS A KING, AND IS UNIMPRESSED

Amaya's gown, chosen specifically as appropriate garb for meeting the King of Spain, was of heavy amber satin with a long train that felt as though it was weighted with stones. She preferred the necklace of faceted topaz gems that went with it; it reminded her of the golden *wallqa* she had worn, so briefly, as Uturunku, that even now resided deep within her jewelry case. European jewelry fascinated her in its difference from its Incan counterparts, particularly the gemstones cut to catch the light and sparkle. She ran a finger over the angular surface of the central topaz. Perhaps Edmund might take her into the city to see what kinds of jewelry the Spanish produced.

The lace *mantilla* over her head slipped, and she hitched it into place. It had not been part of her costume originally, but Mrs. Zambrano had hesitantly confided in Amaya that those veils were considered essential to ladies' dress when meeting the King, and Amaya had asked the housekeeper to procure them for the Earl's party. The *mantilla* was not uncomfortable, and it looked attractive, but it was one more thing to remember, however securely it was pinned.

She examined the rest of the diplomatic party as they walked through the halls of the Palacio Real. She, Elinor, Lady Kynaston, and Mrs. Paget, Lady Kynaston's secretary and a Discerner of no small talent, were the only women; the rest of Lord Enderleigh's train were men of ages ranging from the old Seer Lord Winder, whose hands shook violently but whose step was firm and confident, to Peter Grimly, seventeen years old and absurdly beautiful as only an English Shaper would be. Amaya did not know any of them well except Edmund, whose place was just ahead of her so she had a good view of his fashionable coat. None of the men had dressed any differently for this meeting, though all wore their finest coats and formal knee breeches.

Amaya had at first protested being included in the diplomatic party, arguing that she was there as Elinor's attendant, not as a diplomat, but Elinor had said, "An Extraordinary Shaper gives consequence to anyone," and Sir William had agreed, and that was that. Amaya had not liked the calculating expression Sir William wore, as if he were assessing his government's diplomatic strength and saw Amaya as a piece of that. But she did not like to disappoint Elinor, who she suspected wanted a companion of her own sex. And, she admitted privately, she had never seen a European king before, and was curious.

She looked past Elinor and Lord Enderleigh at a wide doorway set in a wall paneled in rich, dark wood. Very little of the room beyond was visible, but she had the impression of a great deal of red and gold. The men ahead of her slowed their pace, forcing her to slow as well and hope no one behind her would step on her awkward train. She smelled the unmistakable scent of dozens of warm bodies, not just the English but in the room beyond, and heard the rustling and murmuring of many people trying, not very hard, to be quiet.

Then their party came to a complete stop just outside the doorway. With her enhanced hearing, she clearly heard Don Martín tell Lord Enderleigh, "His Majesty will arrive shortly."

"Will he?" Lord Enderleigh said politely. His voice had that undercurrent Amaya was now familiar with, the musical lilt that said the Earl was not pleased but chose to conceal his displeasure. Whether the king intended discourtesy or not, Amaya did not know; she only wished Lord Enderleigh would continue on into the red and gold room so she could see it clearly.

At that moment, their little group surged into motion again, and Amaya followed Edmund into a room as rich and ornate as anything she had ever seen, the walls draped in red and hung with enormous mirrors reflecting the light from dozens of candles set in branches atop gilded tables. Directly opposite their entrance, a dais rose some three or four steps above the floor. Four golden lions, each with a paw balanced atop a ball, guarded the approach to the chair placed at the center of the dais. The gilded back of the chair reminded Amaya of the Sapa Inca's golden throne, though his had not been padded in red velvet.

Dozens of men dressed in red and black finery lined the walls as if they had chosen their clothing to match the room. They regarded the English delegation with vague curiosity, and then looked away, speaking amongst themselves in low voices of which Amaya could hear only that they spoke in Spanish.

Amaya gazed at the lions in awe. They were the first art she had seen among the Europeans that showed any similarities to her lost homeland. The temptation to sink down before one and touch its shining golden mane was tremendous. She found she had taken a few steps forward, putting herself next to Edmund. "How lovely," she said in Spanish.

"It is certainly a splendid sight," Edmund replied in a low voice. "It quite makes one feel in danger of being interred."

"In such golden richness?"

Edmund shrugged. "Velvet of any color makes me prone to funereal imaginings. I realize that sounds absurd."

Amaya was about to reply when the low, murmuring hum of the room sharpened, and all the Spanish nobles stood at attention. From a red-curtained door to the left issued a stream of well-dressed men, all of them in black coats trimmed with gold, fine black shoes, and white or red knee breeches. They crossed the room to the dais, compelling the noblemen lining the walls to bow deeply. Sir William bowed as well, and the rest of the English delegation followed suit.

Amaya curtseyed, but kept her head cocked just enough that she could maintain sight of the Spanish nobles. She could not tell which of them was the king until he sat on the chair and settled himself with his hands resting loosely on his knees. Then she felt disappointed. He did not look very kingly, with his round figure and large nose and fleshy face. She remembered the graceful power of the Sapa Inca and had to suppress a flash of homesickness. Such feelings were beneath her.

King Ferdinand said, in Spanish, "Rise, and welcome to my court."

Amaya straightened and heard Edmund repeat the king's words in English. Sir William stepped forward and said, also in Spanish, "We thank you for your welcome, your Majesty. Pray, permit me to introduce Lord Enderleigh and Lady Enderleigh, representatives of his Royal Majesty, George III of England, to your court."

Amaya let Edmund's continued translation wash over her and

paid close attention to King Ferdinand. He was not as old as she had imagined, no more than thirty, and by the way his gaze flicked in every direction Amaya guessed he was bored. Then his eyes came to rest on her, and his gaze sharpened. It was not a lascivious look, but one of keen interest, and it made Amaya feel uncomfortable.

"You are all very welcome," Ferdinand said, cutting across Sir William's words. "I would know the names of the diplomatic party."

Sir William's expression did not change. "Of course, your Majesty," he said, and began introducing each man. Ferdinand continued to watch Amaya; Amaya, unwilling to look away and possibly show weakness, kept her chin raised and her gaze confident.

When Sir William introduced her as "Miss Imelda Salazar, Extraordinary Shaper," Ferdinand said, "That is not an English name. Are you Spanish, Miss Salazar?"

Out of the corner of her eye, Amaya saw Edmund tense, though he continued with his translation as if nothing were unusual about the king addressing one of the Earl's attendants directly. "My father was Don Ernesto de Salazar y Ortiz," she said, "of Toledo. I was born in Peru."

"Salazar." Ferdinand's eyes narrowed. "I am unfamiliar with the family. But you are a Spanish citizen."

Amaya shifted uncomfortably. "My father was Spanish, my mother English. They were killed by Spanish raiders, and the natives of Peru, of Tawantinsuyu, cared for me."

Ferdinand did not seem to have heard her. "Why are you with these English?"

"I, well, England supported me when I fled Peru," Amaya stammered, "and I choose to attend on Lady Enderleigh. She is my friend."

The king's face darkened in a scowl. "You owe allegiance to your own country."

"Miss Salazar is—" Sir William began, glancing quickly between Ferdinand and Amaya.

"I serve Lady Enderleigh, not England," Amaya interrupted, "and I am free to make my own choices, your Majesty."

Ferdinand sat up straighter, and a flash of unease shot through Amaya that she had spoken so directly to him. She would never have dreamed address the Sapa Inca so irreverently, but this man had so little nobility about him it was easy to forget his rank. Ferdinand gestured, and one of his attendants joined him on the dais. He was younger and slimmer than the king, but otherwise resembled him closely. "Miss Salazar," the man said in Spanish, "you are an Extraordinary Shaper, and thus owe service to your country. Or do you reject your heritage?"

Amaya bit back her first hasty reply, which was to denounce any claim to Spanish heritage. This man annoyed her more than the king had. But she had enough remaining good sense to know her reaction for spite rather than her true desire. "I have many heritages," she said. "I am Spanish by birth. I am Incan by upbringing. And I am English by family. I hope you do not intend me to choose between them." She glared at the man, who stared back at her, unmoved.

The room fell silent. Amaya watched Ferdinand's face, and to her surprise noticed the subtle shifts and tics that said he was carrying on a conversation with someone in mental Speech, though he did not tilt his head back as an English Speaker might do. She had not realized the king was a Speaker, and wished Sir William or someone had mentioned it—although it was possible they had, and she had merely been in one of her inattentive moods. The man on the dais, too, looked to be Speaking to someone. It was far too coincidental that the two were carrying on separate conversations; they had to be communicating privately. Their rudeness increased Amaya's dislike of the men.

"Miss Salazar," Ferdinand said, drawing her attention back to him. "We are pleased to welcome you to our court. We extend you the respect due an Extraordinary Shaper. But we hope you will carefully consider your position here. An Extraordinary Shaper may go far in Spain."

Amaya curtseyed politely, unsure of what to say. She did not believe she could thank him for his magnanimity without snarling. And yet she also did not understand why he had not forced the issue. Extraordinaries in England were given great privileges, true, but Spain might be different—probably was different. She had expected the king to command her to serve him, as he clearly believed he had the right. Why he had retreated, she did not know.

Ferdinand removed a heavy gold ring from his finger and extended it to the man on the dais, who took it with a low bow. He came down the steps and held out the ring to Amaya. "A gesture of respect," he said. "And a reminder of the country to whom you owe allegiance by birth."

That had not been subtle at all. Amaya closed her hand over the ring, which was warm and smelled oily and sweaty, and curtseyed again, not to the man, but to the king. "I thank you for your generosity," she said. She wished she could return to her original position, but backing away was impossible thanks to her gown's train, and she did not wish to turn her back on the king.

Ferdinand leaned back in an almost relaxed position. "Spain is pleased to welcome England to her shores," he said. "You will attend upon us again, and we will discuss the future."

"We thank you, your Majesty," Sir William said before Edmund could finish translating. Amaya, from her new position near the front, saw Lord Enderleigh's hand close into a fist when Edmund reached "attend upon us."

"Yes, your Majesty, we appreciate your welcome," the Earl said, overriding Sir William. "It is a fine reminder of Spain's desire for good relations with England. Lady Enderleigh and I look forward to experiencing more of your famous Spanish hospitality."

Sir William flashed Lord Enderleigh a swift horrified glance, and translated Lord Enderleigh's words into Spanish. Ferdinand's rather florid face paled slightly. The man on the dais said in English, in a placating tone, "Of course, my lord, of course. In a few days, you will be presented to the Cortes, and we will discuss further."

Lord Enderleigh smiled at him. "We have not been introduced, sir," he said.

The man's smile hardened for the space of half a breath, then once more became friendly. "Don Carlos de Borbón, Count of Molina," he said.

That meant nothing to Amaya, but the Earl's hand relaxed. "Then I look forward to meeting with the Cortes," he said, "and thank you for your welcome, my lord."

He bowed. The Count of Molina bowed. Then everyone but the king was bowing politely, which seemed to be the signal for the English procession to leave. Amaya curtseyed again and gathered up her train to turn around. She still did not like turning her back on the king, but now it was because she felt certain he was to some extent an enemy. She did not believe he would attack her directly, but a king had no end of resources, and if he wanted her injured, or dead, there might be little she could do to defend herself.

Amaya held herself upright and walked at a measured pace next to Edmund. She could not react in any way that might look like fear. True, she did not think Ferdinand would strike immediately, not if he wanted the use of her talent. But if she continued to refuse him, she might be in danger.

"It should have occurred to us that the king would react that way," Edmund murmured in Spanish. "The Spanish attitude toward talent is very different from ours."

"I do not know what that attitude is," Amaya replied in the same low voice.

Edmund directed an amused look her way. "Amaya, you really must pay attention when Sir William speaks. You do at least know that Spanish Seers are venerated as holy, and are required to take holy orders, yes?"

Amaya scowled. "I know that, yes, Edmund, I am not entirely ignorant."

"Then you may also know that in Spain, talent is considered a gift of God, and those possessing it are of a higher order than the average man. They are known as 'the endowed.'"

Amaya had not known this, but she did not wish to admit to ignorance and have Edmund laugh at her again. He had used the word *dotados*, a word she had rarely heard before, and one she associated with religious faith. "Do the endowed have noble rank as well?"

Edmund nodded. "They are considered a class apart, lower than those born to the nobility but higher than the gentry. And unlike in England, it is irrelevant what talent they have or how strong or weak it is. Simply having talent is enough."

"That is not the implication I understood from the king. He sounded as if he intended me to serve directly." Amaya rolled the heavy gold ring between her palms. She would not for the world have put it on her finger.

"Extraordinaries are different. They *are* expected to use their talents to serve the country or the king. I am amazed King

Ferdinand did not order you to leave our party immediately to wait upon him. He must be more afraid of England than I believed." Edmund took Amaya's arm and drew her closer. "He is certainly afraid of something, did you notice?"

Amaya had not noticed this, but one of the many inconsistencies she had observed in Edmund's character was his uncanny ability to read people's faces and bodies, so at odds with his apparent lack of awareness of anything that did not directly involve him. "But England does not intend Spain harm."

"The king does not know that. And I am not certain it is England the king fears. He—" Edmund shook his head. "I should not speculate. And it is irrelevant. We are unlikely to have much contact with him, so it will not matter what he fears."

They neared the apartment door, and Edmund released his hold on Amaya. "Your gown is lovely," he said. "The color suits you."

The compliment warmed Amaya, as did the admiring light in Edmund's eyes. "Thank you. I am glad I do not have to wear only white as your young Englishwomen do. White does *not* suit me." Amaya had met any number of young, unmarried, non-Extraordinary women, and they were all without exception simpering, shy misses, which suggested to Amaya that they were either trained to behave that way, or that Amaya, as a stranger and an Extraordinary, inadvertently inspired in them such behavior. She could not believe their own natures were so universally insipid, and wished she might know them for who they truly were.

"I cannot picture it," Edmund said with a smile.

Elinor waited within the apartment, her hand on Lord Enderleigh's arm. "Amaya, we must talk," she said. She sounded so serious it startled Amaya. "Please, join us. And you as well, Mr. Hanley."

Puzzled, Amaya followed Elinor to the room the Countess had claimed as her private drawing room. Sir William and Lady Kynaston waited within, standing beside the tall, narrow window that overlooked the stone plaza in front of the palace. A fire sprang up in the fireplace as they entered, but Elinor paid it no attention. She lowered herself into a chair and arranged her skirts neatly but absently around her. Lord Enderleigh walked to the fireplace and stood looking down at the flames. Amaya had never seen him show any fear of fire, a fear that would in her opinion have been reasonable. But the Earl was not a fearful man, and he regarded the fire as if it were a curiosity he had never seen before.

"Do sit, Mr. Hanley. Amaya—" Elinor indicated the seat next to herself. The door swung shut unassisted, and Amaya heard the key turn in the lock. That frightened her more than Elinor's serious tone had.

"Is that necessary, Miles?" Elinor said, gesturing at the door.

"I have no idea how suspicious the king is, or whether he would stoop to setting servants as spies," Lord Enderleigh said, "and if Miss Salazar is in danger, I prefer to mitigate the risk."

"I? In danger?" Amaya said.

She looked from Lord Enderleigh to Sir William, who looked grave. He shrugged. "King Ferdinand was prepared to pluck you from our midst, and something changed his mind. I do not believe it was a sudden lack of interest in your talent. Nor do I believe he is so fearful of England's might as to assume our country would go to war, figuratively or literally, over you. No, the king has some other plan, and I would like to know what it is."

"But you are not safe here, Amaya," Elinor said. "Our diplomatic party is not strong enough to defend against an assault by

Spanish soldiers, and I cannot be everywhere at once. If the king found a way to kidnap you, there is little we could do."

Amaya laughed. "That is dramatic, yes? Kidnap is the thing of novels. He will not kidnap me."

"I am not certain of that," Sir William said. "An Extraordinary Shaper is a powerful talent, and one any country would be eager to control."

Amaya thought of Mr. Fenton and Lord Baxter, and had to admit he was correct. "Then what am I to do?"

"It might be best," Elinor said, "if you were to take a trip. To Toledo."

Amaya gaped. "You mean, to see if I have family."

"I do mean. It will take you out of the king's sight and provide you with a reunion." Elinor glanced at Edmund. "Mr. Hanley, would you be willing to accompany Amaya?"

"Of course," Edmund said. "I assume you mean us to depart secretly?"

"Of course," Elinor echoed with a smile. "You and Amaya will go south for a week, and take yourselves out of the king's sight."

"And Mrs. Paget will accompany you," Lady Kynaston said. "You are an Extraordinary, but you are also a young woman, and you should not travel alone with a man. Mrs. Paget is familiar with Spain and will provide you with companionship."

Amaya managed not to grimace. She did not like Mrs. Paget very much, as she was always conscious of her behavior being all wrong for an Englishwoman of gentle birth, and Mrs. Paget, while polite and respectful, sometimes had the wooden look of someone suppressing a mocking smile. But Amaya also agreed she could not travel in company with a man to whom she was not related without a companion. "It is a good plan, except that it takes me from you," she said to Elinor, "and suppose there are problems? And surely Lady Kynaston needs her secretary."

"I am perfectly well, and it is still many weeks before my confinement," Elinor said, clasping Amaya's hand gently.

"And you will only be gone a few days. No more than ten," Lady Kynaston added. "I assure you I am capable of handling my own correspondence for that length of time."

Amaya remembered the way King Ferdinand had looked at her, and the expression on the Count of Molina's face. Stay here, within the king's reach, or travel to where her Spanish family might welcome her warmly. "No more than ten," she repeated. "When can we leave?"

CHAPTER 7

IN WHICH AMAYA'S RELATIVES
ARE NOT WHAT SHE EXPECTED

※※※

A sudden afternoon summer shower brought them to Toledo, three days later. From the carriage, Amaya watched the rain fall, saw how it made the dry and dusty Spanish landscape green and vibrant, and could not help but compare it to Peru. In the forests south of the Incas' largest city, where she had lived her entire adult life, the rains fell heavily and regularly, and she and Yupanqui and Quri had frequently hunted there. But she had always been grateful to return to the drier uplands. This storm reminded her of one such hunt, when Kichka had joined them—

She closed her eyes briefly. Remembering Kichka hurt, a dull ache like overextended muscles, but in her chest. She thrust the memory aside and focused on Edmund, who sat on the seat opposite her. "You are certain of this Salazar family, that it is my father's?" she said, in English, though Mrs. Paget, who sat on her right, spoke Spanish nearly as well as Edmund.

"Certain enough," Edmund said. "There was only one Salazar

living near Toledo known to my informant, and he is of noble birth, if in reduced circumstances. He is a Scorcher, and therefore of the *dotados*, which rouses my curiosity. I did not receive a reply to my letter, but they know we intend a visit. We will introduce ourselves, and if he is not your relative, he will likely know who is."

Amaya nodded. "I hope he is the one. I do not like traveling all over this strange city, searching for another Salazar."

"It will not be so terrible," Mrs. Paget said. She sat stiffly, as if trying to prevent being jounced by the carriage through will alone. "Toledo is a beautiful city, and worth seeing even if you do not have relations there."

Amaya nodded. In the past three days, Mrs. Paget had proved to be a more amiable traveling companion than Amaya had expected, more friendly and less formal than she had been on the journey to Madrid. Amaya had learned she was a widow, and a childhood friend of Lady Kynaston, who had offered her the position as her secretary upon the death of Mrs. Paget's husband. While she still occasionally appeared to suppress her amusement at Amaya's mistakes, Amaya could now see the humor herself, and felt less mocked.

"I confess to a certain excitement over the prospect of meeting your Spanish relations," Edmund said, stretching his arms to make the joints pop.

"Excitement, how?" Amaya twined the strings of her reticule around her fingers, weaving a drunken spider's web and shaking it out, over and over. "I know nothing of them."

"My apologies, but it is the kind of excitement—or perhaps I mean anticipation—that arises from knowing there has been contention in the past. Naturally, I do not wish to see you unhappy, and I cannot help imagining a prodigal's welcome for you." Edmund tugged on his coat to make it lie flat again.

Amaya did not know the word "prodigal," and said, "You mean they will be angry?"

"They might, but I meant it is possible they will welcome you with great rejoicing, as you are all that is left of their lost son." Edmund eyed her restless fingers, but did not comment. She was grateful for that. She was not nervous, precisely, but her fingers seemed not to know that.

The rain, which had been pattering on the carriage roof like a fall of gravel, slowed and quieted until only a few random drops spattered the carriage. The sky remained grey and thickly clouded, as if it were undecided about its next action, so when the road curved, giving Amaya her first sight of Toledo, the city seemed ominous, a city under a curse. It rose upon its hill, rank upon rank of stone buildings all the way to the crest of the hill, where spires rose above tall, grey buildings that reminded Amaya of the stony edifices of London. Likely the grey color was a result of the storm, and in sunlight the city was brighter, but Amaya could not help feeling despondent. It seemed a sinister omen for the day.

The carriage clattered over a stone bridge crossing the river that meandered past Toledo, then followed the road as it carried them away from the city. "We do not stop?" Amaya asked.

"This Don Fernándo Salazar lives outside the city, on an estate," Edmund said. "Don Fernándo de Salazar y Ibáñez. Aside from his talent, that is the extent of what I know."

"An estate," Mrs. Paget said. "That sounds promising." Her thin features, barely lined though she was nearly fifty years of age, brightened.

Amaya turned her attention to the passing landscape. The rain had left it green and fresh-smelling, with low hills extending as far as her enhanced vision could see. Even the scruffy bushes that clung to the slopes with admirable tenacity were brighter than their usual grey-green. Low, spreading trees grew at intervals beside the road, and Amaya caught glimpses of white or pale blue birds nestled within their foliage, waiting out the storm. Beyond the hills, the land flattened out into fields of growing crops, and at the edge of her vision, she saw the spire of a church and a cluster of buildings marking a town. She had expected, from what she had seen of Madrid, that all the countryside around Toledo would be tame and cultivated, and this near-wildness comforted her, made her feel more at ease.

Presently, the carriage turned off the main road onto a deeply rutted path, almost as bad as the road leading to Madrid. But almost immediately, well before Amaya could become uncomfortable at all the bouncing, the carriage came to a stop, and Edmund alighted and gave Amaya his hand, then assisted Mrs. Paget down.

Amaya regarded the house at which they had arrived. She had expected something grand and tall, like the English estates she had visited, but this house was low to the ground, only one story tall with a long L-shaped wing extending from the main house. The walls were made of flat, long stones held together by thick, cream-colored mortar so that in some places the wall seemed more mortar than stones. Amaya, accustomed to the Inca way of fitting stones together so well they did not need mortar, was fascinated by the patchwork look of the walls—the ones that were visible. Much of the house was covered by spreading vines thick with narrow leaves as long as her longest finger. The many curved tiles of the roof, by contrast, were clear of encroaching greenery and reminded Amaya of the Thames on a stormy day, filled with small, choppy waves.

The vines did not cover the door or windows, the latter of which, to Amaya's surprise, were filled with glass panes. She had imagined, when she learned the Salazars were in reduced circumstances, that poverty would leave its mark. But this place, for all its rural appearance, looked quite luxurious. Amaya stopped her body from producing nervous sweat on her palms and turned to Edmund. "I..."

Edmund came forward, extending his arm. "There is nothing to worry about. At worst, they turn us away, and we explore Toledo. But I do not believe you need fear that."

Amaya drew in a deep breath and let it out slowly. She took Edmund's arm, and the three of them crossed the little yard to the three steps leading up to the door, which was of heavy oak studded with iron. It was cut in half, Amaya observed, top and bottom made to open independently so one might open part of the door and be polite without inviting a potentially unwanted guest inside.

Edmund rapped on the door. No one answered. "I sent word that our intended visit would be today," Edmund said in a low voice in English, as if he were imparting a secret. "I hope they did not decide to flee when they knew you were coming."

"You are not funny," Amaya whispered, not taking her eyes off the door. She felt superstitiously as if looking elsewhere would make the Salazar family disappear, leaving this house empty. It was a foolish, mad thought, but she could no longer toy with the strings of her reticule, and her nerves were looking for some other outlet for their anxieties. Mrs. Paget, on her other side, looked perfectly placid with her hands clasped loosely in front of her. Well, it was not her lost family they were about to encounter.

She heard footsteps, and shortly the upper half of the door swung inward, revealing a short woman, her black hair swept back tightly from her face into a knot at the back of her head.

Her face was lined, careworn as if she had seen, not a great tragedy, but a host of smaller horrors that had worn down on her over the years. She looked at Edmund first, then at Mrs. Paget, then fixed large, dark brown eyes on Amaya. "Yes?" she said. Her voice was inquiring, but the set of her lips and the direct certainty in her eyes told Amaya she knew who they were.

"Good morning," Edmund said, tipping his hat. "My name is Edmund Hanley, and this is Miss Salazar and Mrs. Paget. I wrote to Don Fernándo—he is expecting us, I hope?"

The woman regarded Amaya a moment longer. Then she extended her hand for Amaya to clasp. Amaya, surprised at the gesture, shook the woman's hand, but when she tried to withdraw, the woman held onto her. "Say your name," the woman said. "Your full name."

Amaya reflexively assessed the woman's health, noting that she was younger than she looked and that her bunions pained her. "Imelda Magdalena Caterina Salazar."

The woman nodded and released Amaya. "Please enter," she said. Her voice was soft, diffident, the voice of someone used to following orders. It did not at all match her directness in taking Amaya's hand. Amaya wanted to ask her name, but felt that might be bad manners.

They followed the woman through the door, down two shallow steps, and into a short, low-ceilinged hallway floored with warm red-brown wooden planks. This led to a wider space like the entrance hall of an English town house, but with the same low ceiling as the hallway, a large, ornately carved side table, and a wardrobe equally ornate.

"If you will wait here, I will tell Father you have arrived," the woman said, and before Amaya could react to that astounding statement, she was gone, vanished through one of the three doorways leading off this room.

"Father," Amaya said. "She is my aunt."

"So it seems. I expected to have a greater struggle to gain admittance," Edmund said. "After all, you might be a fortune-seeker or charlatan."

"I wonder," Mrs. Paget said, "if she has talent. That greeting is one I have made myself, taking someone's hand to determine through my Discernment if the speaker is lying."

Amaya examined the room more closely. The rug covering much of the floor, which was a boring beige color, was worn in a great swath across its center from generations of feet. The table's varnish had worn off in places, and black marks across its legs showed where someone had kicked at them as they sat there. She wished she dared open the wardrobe to see what was stored within. She was beginning to understand what "reduced circumstances" meant.

The woman returned. "Father will see you, she said, gesturing to them to join her at the doorway. Amaya followed promptly. Her earlier nervousness was gone, replaced by a great eagerness.

Beyond this doorway, the house opened up into a room with a high, peaked ceiling supported by black beams that made a stark contrast to the white plaster of the walls. Another rug, this one woven in an interesting floral pattern, filled the space imperfectly, as if it had been made for a larger room. Three sofas occupied much of the room, their arrangement centered on the fireplace, which despite the warm summer day burned high and bright with a fire that smelled deliciously of wood smoke and apples. A wide window, also paned in glass, let in wan sunlight to illuminate the room, which had no other light source.

An elderly man sat near the fire, bundled up against a chill Amaya did not feel. His thick white hair brushed his collar and covered the tips of his ears, and he gripped the head of an ebony walking stick in one hand. His brown eyes, so like the woman's, focused on Amaya. "You claim to be Ernesto's daughter," he said in a stern voice that sounded much younger than his apparent age.

"She is not lying," the woman said. "I know."

"Discernment cannot detect a lie the speaker believes to be true," the old man said. "Leave us, Graciela."

Graciela turned and left the room immediately, her head bowed as if the old man's words had laid a weight on her. Amaya felt an instant's pity for her. The old man had spoken with such peremptory dismissiveness Amaya felt the force of it as if he had directed it at her.

The old man tilted his head to look more closely at Amaya. He ignored Edmund and Mrs. Paget entirely. "So," he said, and tapped the stick against the rug, making a muffled rapping sound. "Prove you are who you say you are."

"I do not know what you would consider proof," Amaya said. She wished he had offered her a seat; she did not like towering over him, in a pose he might consider intimidating.

The old man snorted derisively. Beside him, the fire blazed higher as if he were an Extraordinary and capable of commanding it. "What are your parents' names?"

"Ernesto de Salazar y Ortiz, and Catherine Neville."

"And the year of your birth?"

"1791. In Peru."

"And your father's?"

Amaya shook her head. "I know very little of their pasts. They were Mama and Papi to me, that is all."

The old man's eyes fixed on her with a narrow ferocity that made her uncomfortable. "So you have nothing, no evidence, no identification, and you expect me to simply take your word for it that you are Ernesto's child?"

Amaya cast her mind back thirteen years and more. She was not entirely certain she wanted to claim a relationship with this man, but pride, and stubbornness, kept her rooted to the spot. "Papi had a scar on his left forearm," she said. "A wide, ridged red welt. It was on the inside of his arm. He liked to make up stories about how it happened—that he had fought brigands, that he had rescued Mama from a burning building, stories like that, but I think he never told his children the truth about it. How old it was, I do not know, but he had it my whole life."

The old man drew in a deep breath and let it out slowly. Then he got heavily to his feet with the aid of his stick. "It was an accident with a knife," he said. "Ernesto and his brother Joaquin were playing at pirates or some such nonsense, and Joaquin was careless. Both are dead now, and you…" He shook his head, slowly, as if he could not believe his own words. "I am Fernándo de Salazar y Ibáñez, and it seems you are my granddaughter."

Amaya could not think of anything to say. Fernándo gestured at the sofa across from his. "And who are your companions?" he asked, settling himself on his seat once more.

"Edmund Hanley, sir. Miss Salazar's friend and traveling companion." Edmund saluted Fernándo. "This is Mrs. Paget."

Fernándo grunted again and picked up a handbell on a nearby table. Graciela appeared almost as soon as he rang it. "Graciela, bring refreshments," Fernándo said. Graciela left without a word.

Amaya said, "She is your daughter?"

"Your aunt," Fernándo said. "She keeps house for me. We no longer can employ so many servants as when I was young. Graciela knows her duty."

Amaya still could not credit the daughter of the house

behaving like a servant. Perhaps Spanish households were different from English ones. She hoped Graciela would sit with them, because Amaya wanted to know her family better.

But when Graciela returned, it was to bring a tray laden with teapot and cups. She poured tea and handed the cups around, then left again and returned with another tray, this one bearing small, delicate cakes that might have been served in an English drawing room. She served each of the three without making any move to provide herself with refreshment.

"Send word to your brother and sister," Fernándo instructed her when she would have left. "Tell them to come immediately. Ernesto's child has returned."

Graciela nodded and once more vanished. So she truly was little more than a servant in her own home. Amaya felt another pang of sympathy for her aunt, and wondered how long she had been in this position.

"I do not know my other kin," she said. "You said, brother and sister?"

"I have three children yet living out of nine," Fernándo said. "My wife, God rest her soul, passed away some fifteen years ago. It seems Ernesto named you for her, as if that would make a difference. Ernesto was my eldest. Then Leocadio, who is a Seer and a priest, and Ynes, and Graciela."

"A Seer," Edmund said. "You must be proud."

Fernándo shrugged. "Who am I to deny God what He has demanded? If Ernesto—" He stopped, and his mouth closed in a thin, hard line. "Ernesto was a fool, and should never have left. But what is past is past."

Amaya and Edmund exchanged glances. Amaya took a sip of tea to keep from having to reply to this. She knew her father had left home under a cloud, but no more details than that. It sounded as if Fernándo still bore a grudge, but surely it could not be anything serious if he was willing to welcome her? She disliked not understanding a situation. She sipped again and resolved to observe without commenting until she knew better what she had got herself into.

Mrs. Paget, meanwhile, said, "Do any of your other children have talent?" She clearly had concluded, as Amaya had, that talk about Ernesto was a bad idea. Amaya wondered at her question, because she knew Graciela was a Discerner, but guessed Mrs. Paget wished to divert the conversation.

"Graciela is a Discerner, much good that may do her," Fernándo said. "It is not as if it makes her better able to keep house. My late wife was a Mover, but not one of great power or strength."

"My husband was also a Mover," Mrs. Paget said. "I am myself a Discerner."

Fernándo did not seem to feel this gave her a connection either to his late wife or to Graciela. "Have you talent, young man?"

"I have not, but I have never felt the lack," Edmund said cheerfully in a way that made him seem rather dim-witted. Amaya recognized at once it was a sham, though she could not guess why he wanted to deceive Fernándo. "My sister is an Extraordinary Speaker, and I believe she lives half her life in her reticulum."

Fernándo shrugged again and seemed to lose interest in Edmund. "An Extraordinary Shaper," he said, turning his attention on Amaya. "Did your mother have talent? Is that where your gift comes from? Certainly not Ernesto."

"I don't believe so," Amaya said. "She never displayed it if she had it, and her mother did not say—"

"Her mother? You know that family?"

Amaya, surprised at his sudden intensity, said, "We have met, yes. Mrs. Neville found me in London."

"A fortune-seeker, no doubt," Fernándo said. "Your mother was the same."

Amaya set her cup down with a sharp *chink* against the saucer. "I beg your pardon?" she said angrily.

Fernándo made a dismissive gesture. "Catherine Neville believed Ernesto would inherit. She attached herself to him in the hope of gaining this estate, which is not small."

"And how do you know this?"

"That is what her father told me. He wrote to me instructing me to order Ernesto to drop the connection. I told him Ernesto was disinherited and the English girl would be disappointed."

"And yet Catherine married Ernesto anyway," Edmund said, cutting off Amaya's incipient outburst. "Your theory is flawed, sir."

Fernándo ignored him. "But that is past," he said. "I forgave Ernesto his sins because it is my Christian duty. And I choose to welcome you as my granddaughter."

Amaya realized the points of her claws were digging into the flesh of her palms and relaxed her fists. She knew little of Christianity, but she did not believe a true Christian would be so quick to deliver insults and then claim he meant no harm. "My parents were happy together," she said, "and I do not believe either of them had such mercenary motives as you suggest. But I agree that all that is in the past, and I am glad you gave up your anger at my father."

Another shrug. Amaya was coming to dread the gesture, which simultaneously conveyed derision and lack of interest. Fernándo took a firmer grip on his stick and pushed himself off the sofa, causing the three guests to stand as well. "Let me show you the estate," he said.

It sounded like a change of subject, but Amaya's instincts told her Fernándo saw it as an extension of what they had been discussing. She wondered who his heir was. She knew Leocadio, as a priest, could not inherit a secular estate; the subject had come up on the journey to Madrid, as had the information that a priest in the Catholic faith was a priest forever. And yet she also knew that in most families, English or Spanish, the heir was the eldest son. Fernándo had no other sons, but he was old, and the estate must go somewhere at his death. She reminded herself to ask Edmund about it later. He had explained entailment; he likely knew what happened to inheritances under such conditions as this.

They passed through more low-ceilinged halls floored with the same short red-brown planks and out the back door. The vines grew thicker here, hanging low over the door so Amaya seemed to walk out through a living green curtain. She pushed a vine out of her face and followed Fernándo along a path paved with stones whose rounded tops felt smooth under her feet.

When they entered the garden, Amaya was glad she walked behind Fernándo, because in her surprise she failed to conceal her dismay. The garden would have been beautiful once, but now it was overgrown, with tall weeds encroaching on the former garden beds and a hedge that had not been trimmed in some time. Off to one side, nearly hidden by undergrowth, poked the curved top of a gazebo, its white paint flaking and peeling like dry skin. It was the most depressing thing Amaya had seen since arriving in Spain.

A man dressed all in black stood near the gazebo, his hands clasped before him as if in prayer. Amaya had never seen clothing like his before, the upper half tightly fitted, the lower half a long skirt like a woman's gown, with a long row of buttons down the front. He looked up and smiled at Amaya. He was missing a tooth on one side, but he did not attempt to hide the gap as Amaya had seen others do. His thinning black hair moved slightly in the light breeze.

"How good to see you in the flesh," he said. "I am Leocadio, your uncle. And you, child, you are our salvation."

CHAPTER 8

IN WHICH SOMEONE AGAIN TRIES TO COMMAND AMAYA'S LOYALTY

"Your—I beg your pardon?" Amaya said.

Leocadio's visage was serene, and he smiled as if her words gave him pleasure. "I have Seen it in Dream," he said. "Your return marks the beginning of a new chapter in this family's life. How good to see Ernesto returned to us, even in this small way. You resemble him greatly."

Fernándo made a noise somewhere between a grunt and a snort. Amaya wondered why he had not commented on the resemblance as he was pressing her for details that would prove her identity. He walked forward a few steps, leaning heavily on his stick. "What have you Seen, my son?"

Leocadio's attention flicked briefly to his father, and then his gaze returned to rest on Amaya. "Bright fire," he said, "burning away the shadows of the past. Links in a chain, forged and re-forged. You stand at the right hand of one who will bring change."

Amaya did not like how intently he looked at her, as if he

saw, not a woman, but a figure from Dream, highly symbolic and open to interpretation. "Do you know what your Dream means?"

"It is as I say. Change is coming," Leocadio said. "And you are at the heart of it. Father, where is Alejandro?"

Fernándo gave his son a terrible look. "You see this garden," he said, addressing Amaya as if Leocadio had not spoken. "It was Imelda's—my wife. It grows unchecked in her memory, and because I find beauty in wild places. Come, we will walk."

He walked in his halting, stick-assisted way past Leocadio and into a gap in the hedge that did not look intentional. Amaya supposed it might only be overgrown. She exchanged glances with Edmund, who shrugged, the barest movement of his shoulders, and then they and Mrs. Paget followed Fernándo into the hedge.

It felt like being swallowed by a great blue-green monster, with how closely the sides of the hedge pressed on Amaya. She and her companions were forced to walk single-file behind Fernándo, with Leocadio bringing up the rear, as the passage turned and then turned again. Overhead, the untrimmed tops of the hedges waved and bent in what were almost arches, giving Amaya the impression of walking through narrow corridors roofed with leafy branches.

She shortened her stride so as not to overrun the much slower Fernándo. His shoulders hunched slightly, and his white hair curled over his collar, too long for fashion. His overall appearance was that of a frail old man, yet his voice was strong and his opinions stronger. Amaya was coming to realize he ruled this household through iron will. Even Leocadio, possessed of a talent that gave him status and respect, bowed to his father. She felt even more pity for Graciela.

They emerged from the hedge maze on a broad field burned yellow by the summer sun. The farthest edge of the field gradually merged with uncultivated land, bristling with spiny gray-green bushes growing amidst the occasional clumps of green grass. More of the low, spreading trees dotted the landscape, offering shade. At the moment, with the sky still overcast, they were unnecessary, but Amaya admired them anyway.

Another house, this one with two stories, stood adjacent to the main house to define a yard of hard-packed earth, at the center of which lay a stone well that looked sturdier than either of the houses, as if the houses had grown up around it. A stable, weathered grey from what might have been a century of wind and storm, occupied the space opposite the second house, between the hedges and the field. A few horses ranged over the field, nipping at the dry grass or staring off into the distance looking noble. Amaya liked horses so long as she was not expected to ride them.

"Ah, here they come," Fernándo said. He was looking into the distance, beyond the field and the trees, to where a cluster of riders approached along a dusty road. There were five of them, Amaya observed, riding at a decent pace, with one bright bay out in front and the others, three chestnut and one black, gathered loosely behind.

As they approached, Amaya sharpened her gaze to examine them. To her surprise, the rider in front was a woman, dressed in shirt and trousers like the other four riders with her hair bound around her head beneath her hat. Amaya had not yet seen a European woman wearing men's garb. She knew female Extraordinary Movers wore divided skirts that were like very loose, wide-legged trousers for modesty's sake when they Flew, but this woman's clothing was clearly made for a man. She glanced at Fernándo, but he did not look angry or perturbed, and as he was the kind of man who would expect women to behave like women, his lack of reaction roused Amaya's curiosity.

The five riders came to a halt in front of the stable, and the woman dismounted. She strode toward Fernándo, removing leather gloves as she walked and slapping them against her palm. "So, this is she," she said, examining Amaya. Her expression was flat and hard and unwelcoming, making her lined face seem older than Amaya guessed she was.

"This is Ernesto's daughter," Fernándo said. "Miss Salazar, my daughter Doña Ynes de Salazar y Ortiz. Ynes, show respect. Miss Salazar is an Extraordinary Shaper."

Ynes' expression did not change. "How do you do, Miss Salazar," she said. "It is good to meet Ernesto's child." She gestured at the other riders behind her. "My sons Mateo, Marcos, Lucas, and Juan. Your cousins."

Three of the four men had dismounted and were approaching. The fourth, the rider on the black horse, kept his seat. He stared at Amaya with a frank, sensual appraisal that irritated her. He seemed the oldest of the brothers, the youngest of which was not yet adolescent. All three of the younger boys seemed more curious than hostile, which relieved some of Amaya's irritation with their elder brother.

"Mateo, leave that horse and greet your cousin," Fernándo snapped. Mateo's gaze hardened briefly, then he dismounted and walked slowly to Fernándo's side. Amaya had a sudden instinct that he was Fernándo's intended heir; he alone among the gathered Salazars stood as if he were not awed by Fernándo, and his stance was deferential, almost protective.

Ynes continued to slap her gloves across her palm in a slow, contemplative way. "I did not doubt Leocadio's Dream," she said, "but it is still disconcerting to see it come to pass so definitively." She turned her attention on Edmund. "And this is?"

"Edmund Hanley," Edmund said, bowing slightly. "Miss Salazar's traveling companion. She is my sister's dear friend, and I volunteered to escort her and her companion Mrs. Paget to Toledo."

Ynes' appraisal of Edmund reminded Amaya of the way Mateo had looked at her, and her aunt's casual, possessive air annoyed Amaya. "Mr. Hanley is my good friend as well," she told Ines, "and I appreciate his company."

"I am sure you do," Ynes said with a smile. She glanced over Mrs. Paget before returning her attention to Edmund.

"Inside," Fernándo said. "We will speak more. I wish to know of Miss Salazar's plans for her future."

Amaya was looking at Fernándo as he spoke, which put Mateo in her line of sight. She observed the way his lips tightened at this, and wondered at his reaction. It did not fit with the way he had looked at her as if he were considering what she might be like as a bed partner. She decided Mateo bore closer watching.

They did not return through the grasping hedge, but around the side of the house and through the front door. Fernándo returned to his seat near the fire, which flared as if in greeting, and rested his stick against the arm of the sofa. Ynes took a seat near him, her hands resting on her knees in a relaxed way that struck Amaya as masculine. Leocadio sat across from the fire, spreading the skirt of his odd garment across his knees and smiling pleasantly at Amaya. Amaya once more sat across from Fernándo, Mrs. Paget took a seat at the other end of the sofa, and Edmund, after a pause to observe that none of Ynes' sons intended to sit, sat between them.

"You are an Extraordinary Shaper. A doctor?" Fernándo said without preamble.

Amaya wished her youngest cousin—Juan, possibly, or Lucas?

—had not positioned himself behind her. His proximity made the back of her neck itch. "I do not wish to study medicine," she said.

"Nonsense. You have a duty," Fernándo said.

"I do not believe my talent is the property of anyone but myself," Amaya shot back.

"Then what will you do?" Ynes asked.

Amaya saw that Graciela had come to the door and stood just inside it, listening. "I have not decided," Amaya said. "Perhaps I will come to choose medicine, after all. For now, I intend to learn everything I can about European society. And I am companion to Lady Enderleigh, who is an English Extraordinary Scorcher. I feel I have purpose."

"A companion?" Ynes said, raising her thin eyebrows. "A subordinate? Surely an Extraordinary Shaper need not lower herself to such."

"Lady Enderleigh is with child, and it is custom among the Incas for an Extraordinary Shaper, if there is one, to attend upon a birth." Amaya disliked the way Ynes looked at her, as if sizing her up and finding her wanting. "And she is my friend."

"You seem to have many friends among the English." Now Ynes' eyebrows lowered and came together in the middle. Amaya amused herself wondering if Ynes and her eyebrows were separate entities.

"The English have been very kind," she said, choosing not to mention her fortune. She would not put it past Fernándo to try to claim it for his own, on the grounds that she was female and his descendent.

"Then you will stay in England," Mateo said abruptly.

"This is not your concern, Mateo," his mother said. "Miss Salazar, Spain will welcome you. This family welcomes you."

"I am grateful," Amaya said. "It is good for me to know my kin. I feel my father would have wanted me to meet you."

Fernándo eyed her with an expression she could not read. "Join us for supper," he said, "you and your companions."

Amaya suppressed a sigh. She could not understand why the other Salazars allowed this man to make demands. True, he was old, and among the Incas this would make him deserving of respect, but when one did nothing to earn that respect, one should not, in Amaya's opinion, behave with such peremptory disdain of others' desires.

Supper was a tense, strained meal. The food was unexpectedly good—Amaya hoped this was not also one of Graciela's duties—but conversation lagged, as everyone seemed conscious of the tension between Fernándo and Amaya. Mateo glared at her, all his earlier lascivious looks vanished. Leocadio might have eased matters, but he paid more attention to his plate than to Amaya.

Graciela did join them for the meal, which reassured Amaya, but all Amaya's attempts to draw her quiet aunt out fell flat. Mrs. Paget displayed the good manners endemic to her class; Edmund, seated beside Amaya, spoke as cheerfully and airily as if nothing were wrong, but even his affability did not change the mood. It was the most uncomfortable meal Amaya had ever had.

The women did not leave the table before the men as they did in England. Instead, Fernándo rose from his seat, disregarding the fact that a few of his relations had not finished their meals, and said, "You will join me in the drawing room. I have something to say."

Everyone promptly rose to follow him. Amaya and Edmund exchanged glances. "This is quite the household," Edmund said in English, his low voice not carrying beyond Amaya's ears.

"They fear him. I do not like," Amaya replied in the same language.

Again, they all took the seats they had occupied earlier. Fernándo said, "Miss Salazar, you have a duty to this family as well as to your country. Ernesto was my eldest son, and as his child, you are now my heir."

His words struck Amaya like a blow to the stomach. "I? But I am not—I am female; surely I cannot inherit."

"By law, a woman who is an Extraordinary can inherit in her own right," Fernándo said.

Amaya could not help herself; she glanced swiftly at Mateo, whose face was ruddy and scowling. So her guess was correct. "But I am not Spanish," she blurted out.

Fernándo sat up. "You mean to claim your mother's lineage? Reject the proud name of Salazar? Do not insult me so!"

Despite herself, the tiniest stirring of dismay rose deep within Amaya. She immediately quashed it. She was not afraid of Fernándo and would not allow him to cow her. "Spanish raiders killed my family, and would have killed me had I not hidden. I feel no connection to Spain. I am of Tawantinsuyu, Inca, and that is my heritage."

Fernándo's face was as red and furious as Mateo's. "Insolent, wicked girl," he shouted. "Disregarding your family's honor—you are just like Ernesto."

"Father, Miss Salazar has been through a great ordeal," Leocadio said. "Is it so strange that she does not feel an attachment to a place she has never known, or to family she has never seen?"

Fernándo sank back into his seat. "You will stay here," he told Amaya, "and you will learn what it is to be a Salazar. Do not think I will permit you to disrespect me."

Amaya rose, prompting Edmund and Mrs. Paget to follow. "I

must return to Lady Enderleigh. I apologize, but I cannot do as you request." It had been a demand, not a request, but Amaya felt it best not to increase the antagonism between herself and Fernándo.

"But you have only just arrived," Leocadio protested. "Surely you may remain a few days."

"That is not what Don Fernándo wishes," Amaya pointed out, her eyes still on Fernándo.

Leocadio leaned forward, his fingers interlaced. "Father," he said, "if you wish Miss Salazar to know our family better, to know her heritage, surely it would be better not to demand she give up all other loyalties? It speaks well of her that she desires to do her duty."

Amaya was certain Fernándo would explode with fury over this, but his expression grew contemplative. "True," he said. "Then—three days, Miss Salazar, I offer you and your companions hospitality for three days, and I hope you will honor us by remaining."

It amused Amaya that Fernándo had clearly forgotten Edmund and Mrs. Paget's names, it seemed so typical of him. She did not wish to stay at all, but her curiosity, and the fact that Fernándo was willing to make a total stranger his heir, overruled her. "Thank you, I appreciate your hospitality," she said. "I may not stay long, as I am needed in Madrid, but I do wish to know you all better."

Fernándo did not look as if this pleased him, but he nodded.

Ynes said, "Why is this Lady Enderleigh in Spain? If she is with child, surely she did not wish you to leave her."

"The Earl and Countess of Enderleigh are part of a diplomatic mission to the court of King Ferdinand," Edmund said, using the English version of the king's name rather than the

Spanish Fernándo. "She wished Miss Salazar to know her Spanish relations."

Edmund had spoken up rapidly enough that Amaya guessed he did not wish her to reveal that her companions were also members of the diplomatic party. She did not know why that mattered, but Edmund understood political matters better than she, and she was willing to be guided by him in that respect.

"How generous," Ynes said with a tiny smile. "Then it is true you should not remain here long. Is that not right, Father?"

Fernándo grunted. "You will remain, and in the morning I will explain your patrimony to you," he said, sounding as if the words tasted sour. Again Amaya caught a glimpse of Mateo's face, which was thunderously angry. She wished the old man were not so callous; he must surely know how Mateo's hopes had been dashed. It made her wonder what had passed between them, if Fernándo had made promises, or if Mateo had made assumptions. More knowledge might show her how to speak to her cousin.

Distantly, she heard the sound of many horses approaching, and turned her head instinctively to look for them, though the walls of the house prohibited such sight. "Do you expect visitors?" she asked.

Fernándo's eyes narrowed. "What do you mean?"

Amaya made a gesture near her ear. "I hear horses. They are coming this way."

"It must be Alejandro," Leocadio said. "Father, he will wish to meet Miss Salazar."

All rose, even Fernándo, who gripped his stick and stumped ahead of them to the front door. There, the carriage still waited, with the driver standing beside it. The skies had cleared, and the sun made everything golden with its tawny evening light. It was the time of day at which Amaya found Spain most beautiful.

Amaya turned to look back at the house and saw Graciela standing in the doorway. The woman did not look as downtrodden as she did when her father spoke to her; she held her head high, and gazed at Amaya as if willing her to hear her thoughts, though Amaya could not guess what she was thinking.

It was, in fact, many horses, enough that Amaya could not count them, as backlit by the setting sun as they were. They approached at a rapid pace, apparently not disturbed by the roughness of the road. Some of the men wore hats of an unfamiliar shape that slouched over their foreheads. All of them wore clothes that showed signs of having been worn and not washed for many days, the creases in their trousers ingrained with dirt, their coats dusty. Their horses, by contrast, were shiny and well cared for.

Their leader, or at least the rider in front, wore no hat, and his dark blond hair was made darker by sweat and road grime. He, unlike most of the others, was clean-shaven, and he was handsome, with a well-shaped face and a straight nose that did not appear to have been made that way through Shaping. He brought his horse to a halt some twenty feet from Fernándo and bowed from a sitting position. "Don Fernándo," he said. His voice was as handsome as the rest of him. "You have visitors."

"It is nothing," Fernándo said. For the first time, his voice sounded pleasant, almost ingratiating. "Please, join us."

The man slid down from his horse and walked toward them, his blue eyes fixed on Amaya. "I hope you will introduce us," he said with a smile. That smile, and the way he would not look anywhere else, told Amaya he already knew who she was.

"Of course," Fernándo said. "My granddaughter, Miss Imelda Salazar. Miss Salazar, this is Alejandro Valencia, El Encendedor."

CHAPTER 9
IN WHICH A LEGEND COMES TO CALL

✦

Amaya's breath caught. El Encendedor. He did not look at all as she had pictured him. Valencia bowed again, this time to Amaya. "What a pleasure to meet you," he said. "Father Leocadio's Sight is always dependable, but it is still a joy to see his Dream in the flesh, so to speak."

His eyes on her were warm and admiring, and they flustered Amaya. She curtseyed politely and said, "I did not know I was expected."

"Don Fernándo is much respected in these parts, and his family partakes of that respect." Valencia smiled at Amaya. "Though we did not realize you were so lovely."

Amaya, feeling more flustered than ever, did not know what to say to this. Edmund cleared his throat, a quiet but distinctive sound, and she clutched at his intervention gratefully. "Oh—Mr. Valencia, this is my friend and traveling companion, Mr. Hanley, and my other companion, Mrs. Paget."

"Your reputation precedes you," Edmund said. "All Spain talks of El Encendedor."

Valencia's smile faded slightly. "All to the good, I hope."

Edmund smiled, his expression showing no apparent awareness that Valencia's tone was cool and unwelcoming. "That depends on who does the talking."

Valencia looked Edmund up and down. "You are English, I believe."

"I am," Edmund said, bowing slightly. "I hope it is not my accent that betrays me. I have taken great care to learn your language as well as any native."

"No, but your dress..." Valencia again eyed Edmund. "You should take care instead, Mr. Hanley, that you are not mistaken for a French sympathizer. Such men are not treated well by the good citizens of Spain."

"I hope my allegiance is clear," Edmund said. His voice was pleasant, but his expression had turned neutral. Amaya had seen this expression before; it meant Edmund was suppressing a strong emotion.

"Naturally," Valencia said with a polite smile, and turned his attention to Fernándo. "Sir, I crave the privilege of a private word with you."

"Of course," Fernándo said. "Will you and your men stay the night? We would be honored to host you."

"If it will not be much trouble," Valencia replied.

"Not at all. Graciela! Prepare rooms for our guests. All our guests." Fernándo did not look to see if Graciela had heard him, or if she was even present. Amaya, however, saw Graciela turn to go back into the house, her expression as neutral as Edmund's. The sight made Amaya angry on Graciela's behalf, and angry with her aunt for allowing Fernándo to cow her.

The rest of Valencia's companions began dismounting and leading their horses around the side of the house, as casually as if it were a commonplace. Many of them stared at Amaya, some of them continuing to stare even after they had passed her. One, a young man with thick, curly black hair, kept his staring furtive, pretending not to be interested. His stride and his bearing were tense enough that Amaya realized the truth. How funny that young men were the same in every culture, keenly interested in women and just as keenly desirous of keeping that interest concealed.

Fernándo and Valencia had already retreated into the house. Amaya asked Leocadio, who stood near her, "Is Mr. Valencia a frequent visitor?"

"We support El Encendedor, of course," Leocadio said. "He defended this house against the French. Now he returns often, mostly to speak with my father." He gestured toward the door. "I must return for Vespers, and to prepare to Dream, but I will return tomorrow evening."

Ynes drew her gloves from her belt and put them on. "We shall return then as well. Come, my sons." She strode off in the direction Valencia's men had taken. Her sons followed, though one of them—Marcos, she thought—glanced back at her. Mateo walked with his shoulders hunched and his head bowed, like an angry bull. Amaya wondered for the first time if they had a father, and where he might be. If Ynes were as demanding and officious as Fernándo, perhaps her husband preferred to stay well away from her.

Alone, Amaya and Edmund looked at one another. "This is not at all what I imagined," Amaya said in English. "Señor Valencia, El Encendedor! Edmund, can you credit it?"

"I cannot," Edmund said grimly, all pleasantness vanished. "Almost I am persuaded to leave this place immediately."

"Why? He is not a danger, yes?"

Edmund glanced at the front door, whose top half was open, but no one was there. "El Encendedor does not have the most savory reputation. He has burned whole villages merely on the suspicion that they harbor enemies of Spain. You should not let his demeanor and his attractive face sway you."

"He is correct, Miss Salazar," Mrs. Paget said. "I have heard the most terrible things about him."

"He is a *guerrilla* fighter, and they must do terrible things to defend their country." Amaya found her earlier assumptions about El Encendedor's motives and honor less compelling now that she had seen him. She might not like Fernándo, but she did not believe him capable of giving respect to a villain.

Edmund's mouth tightened in a straight line briefly before he responded. "The Spanish *guerrillas* do not always limit themselves to fighting for their country. Far too many of them have made the war an excuse to loot and pillage their own people. Some have even destroyed churches and killed the innocents within."

"But we do not know this of Señor Valencia. And rumor may be false. I do not understand why you insist on him being a bad man."

Edmund sighed. "I suppose I simply do not like him imposing on your good nature. Very well. Let us ask your aunt where we are to sleep, and perhaps in the morning, Don Fernándo's temper may have cooled."

Amaya did not believe that was likely, but she was willing to borrow Edmund's optimism for once.

※

THE SPACIOUS ROOM GRACIELA SHOWED AMAYA TO FELT COZY thanks to the fire in the fireplace that took up an entire corner of the room. When Graciela had gone, Amaya climbed up into the deep window ledge to look out at the overgrown garden. The room would be brighter if someone would trim back the encroaching hedges, but to her surprise Amaya found she liked the feeling of being enclosed in a dark green curtain.

A knock at the door prompted her to jump down from her perch. She opened the door for a male servant, who had his hands full with Amaya's small trunk. "Thank you," she said. She had begun to wonder if Fernándo's household was limited to himself and Graciela, though of course that was impossible.

The servant, a man with brown hair that was silvery with age, nodded and smiled, but said nothing. He set her trunk down at the foot of the bed and bowed himself out. Amaya idly unfastened the trunk and looked inside, but found she did not wish to go to bed so early. The sun had not yet set, and if she were in Madrid, or in England with the Hanleys, she would be preparing for some diversion, a ball or a trip to the theatre. Here, she had no idea what would be expected of her.

She left her room for the hallway, which was long and plastered white with small framed portraits hanging in the spaces between the many doors. This was the side wing of the main house, and she believed it was exclusively for housing guests, so the presence of the portraits intrigued her. The Incas did not render human images in paint, and Amaya found the European tradition fascinating.

She stopped to examine one, which was set in an oval frame the length of her forearm. Surely this was a Salazar relation—but there was nothing to indicate the name of the painting's subject, who was a stern-looking man with black hair slicked down to his head and an enormous black moustache. Amaya gazed at him; he gazed back. That was another aspect of European art, that ability to paint faces that seemed to watch you wherever you stood.

A door farther down the hall opened, and Edmund emerged.

"More paintings," he said as he approached. "We must stop in Toledo before we return. The cathedral, and other of the public buildings, are home to rare works of art you will appreciate."

"I was wondering who this man was," Amaya said, gesturing. "I find myself increasingly interested in knowing my Salazar relations."

"Despite Don Fernándo's influence," Edmund said in English with a wry smile.

Amaya laughed. "He is not usual," she said in the same language. "I do not understand him. He is—it is perhaps that he is old, and likes to make people obey him. But he treats my *tía* Graciela as if she is servant and not daughter, and I do not understand that either."

"I have known far too many families in which the parents see their children as little better than drudges," Edmund said. He offered Amaya his arm. "Shall we walk in the garden? Perhaps it is less of a horror in the evening."

"I believe it will be more of one in shadow, but I am willing to see this experiment."

The guest wing attached to the main house near the dining room, which still smelled deliciously of supper. Amaya did not realize Edmund was taking them the long way around until she heard the murmur of two male voices, and saw they were near the drawing room in which they had conversed with Fernándo. She slowed her steps and found Edmund had done the same. "It is Don Fernándo and Mr. Valencia," she whispered in Spanish.

"Yes, I know," Edmund said. "I wish to eavesdrop."

Amaya frowned. "That is a terrible habit, Edmund. And I do not believe you can hear them at this distance."

"No, but you can." Edmund's expression was so serious she knew him to be suppressing amusement.

"You should be ashamed of yourself, making use of my talent

for your own purposes." But Amaya Shaped her inner ears to catch the faintest sound and bent her attention to the drawing room and its unseen occupants. The sound of the flickering fire made it difficult to make out words, so she closed her eyes to shut out distractions, and listened.

"...for a few days only." That was Valencia. "I am, as always, grateful for your hospitality."

"It is I who am grateful," Fernándo said. "Where will you go next?"

"Aranjuez, to start. There are towns in that area in need of my attention."

"Take care." Glass clinked against glass, and she heard the very faint sound of liquid sloshing.

"I will return in a week or more." Valencia's voice became quieter, and Amaya strained to hear him. "She will be here?"

A click, as of a glass being set on a table. "She believes not, but I will compel her obedience," Fernándo said. "And then she—"

"Are you in need?" A new voice, very close and very loud, interrupted Amaya's eavesdropping in a painful way. Amaya winced and swiftly altered her ears, which alteration hurt worse than the loud words had. Any Shaping done too quickly was painful, but continued exposure to that loud voice would be even more so.

She blinked back tears and realized it was Graciela who had spoken. The small woman regarded her curiously, but without the suspicion that would have suggested she knew what Amaya was doing. "Oh, Aunt Graciela," Amaya said. "We were—"

"I was admiring this room before taking a walk in the garden," Edmund said, smoothly inserting himself into their conversation. "Spanish architecture is an interest of mine."

Graciela's tired eyes narrowed. "The garden? It is nothing of interest."

"Oh, but it is so quiet and peaceful," Amaya said. "Or perhaps that is inappropriate, if it was your mother's and you wish it to remain undisturbed." She examined Graciela closely, but her aunt still did not seem suspicious of Amaya's motives.

"It is not inappropriate. Just ugly." Graciela's lips turned up at the corners in a faint, unexpected smile. "It is Father who wishes it to remain a memorial. Perhaps you will change his mind."

"I?"

Graciela shrugged. Unlike Fernándo, her shrug conveyed a nearly fatalistic sense of inevitability. "You are his heir, and his beloved Ernesto's child. I think there is very little he would not permit you." She gestured down the hall that ran past the drawing room. "I will take you to the garden door. We do not lock up at night, so do not fear being caught outdoors."

Amaya exchanged glances with Edmund. She wished Graciela had not come upon them, because she suspected the "she" Fernándo and Valencia spoke of was herself. But they could do nothing but follow Graciela to the side door that let out on the garden, and bid her goodnight once they were outside.

"I suppose that was to be expected," Edmund said in English when the door shut. "You did not learn anything exciting, such as Señor Valencia's plans to take over Toledo and burn the opposition to the ground?"

"No, it is not so exciting. That is only in novels, that someone listens in just in time for a secret about them." Amaya told Edmund what little she had heard, including her guess, and concluded, "But I do not guess it is me they speak of, because that is unlikely. I suppose it is that I wish this to be a novel."

"I do not know that it is so outlandish for them to speak of you," Edmund said. "Señor Valencia seemed intent on you in a way I do not like." His usual good humor had vanished, replaced by a serious expression that made Amaya feel not quite comfortable.

"Do you think he means me harm?" she asked. "He seemed more to look at me as if I am someone he wish to know better." She felt uncomfortable, again, admitting to that flustered feeling Valencia had caused, as if there were something shameful about being admired.

Edmund did not answer, but drew her along after him along the stone path into the garden. Amaya had been correct; the garden in twilight was not romantic or beautiful, but depressing, the weeds moving lightly in the night breeze, the hedge looming over the neglected beds like a monstrous creature with too many thin, grasping limbs. The gazebo was little more than a hulking, pale shape in the gloom, and although it benefited from the darkness in that its peeling paint was invisible, it was so enveloped by overgrowth it appeared caught in the clutches of some dire creature.

"Perhaps it is nothing," Edmund finally said, when the silence had stretched nearly to the breaking point. "And yet I am certain he knew who you were before Don Fernándo introduced you. That suggests his interest is more than simply that of a man who finds a woman attractive."

Amaya blushed. "Then you see it, too."

"I did." Edmund spoke with such finality it confused her.

"Do you disapprove?" she asked.

Edmund's eyes widened. "Disapprove? Of what?"

Amaya stopped and turned to face him. "Then you think it is wrong that a man see me as to want me."

One of Edmund's eyebrows climbed nearly to his hairline. "I did not realize," he drawled, "that you found Valencia so attractive as to desire his attentions."

Amaya's imperfect grasp of English could not interpret his whole meaning, but it was clear Edmund was angry and trying not to show it. "I do not wish," she began, stopped, then tried again. "You are not my brother, and you are not my father," she said, "so it is I do not understand why you should approve or not."

Edmund's lips compressed into a tight line as if he were holding words back like water battering a dam. "Señor Valencia is dangerous," he finally said, "and you and I both know you lack an understanding of European society to recognize his motives. I wish only for your happiness."

His eyes were fixed on her, his body tense, and Amaya suddenly found herself at a loss for how to respond. She did not understand European customs, it was true, and perhaps Edmund did understand Valencia's attentions better than she, but that did not explain this terrible tension between herself and Edmund, as if the conversation they were having was the wrong one.

Then the moment passed, and the intensity left Edmund's stance. When he spoke next, it was as casually as if they were discussing the terrible garden. "If you are correct, and he and Don Fernándo spoke of you, then Señor Valencia has a plan that includes you, and I dislike secrets that involve my friends. We will simply have to leave before he returns, and then you will be well out of it." He looked away toward the entrance to the hedge maze, then turned back to face her. "Forgive me," he said. "I should not make your decisions for you."

Amaya rarely saw Edmund as grave and serious as he was now. It made him seem a different person, and yet his face was so familiar, his eyes steady on her, that a shiver ran through her she could not explain. Her hand closed tightly on his sleeve. "I say you are right," she managed. "Señor Valencia is a romantic figure as El Encendedor, but he does things I cannot like, and I do not wish to be his tool, if that is what he intends."

Edmund looked down at where her hand rested on his arm. "Amaya," he began, then fell silent, his eyes searching her face for she knew not what. Then he smiled, dispelling the somber expression, and put his hand over hers. "I am yours to command, Miss Salazar," he said with a wry laugh. "We will remain here three days, and then, well, who knows what might happen in three days?"

Being free of that strange, serious moment relieved Amaya. "Very likely nothing," she said, "but I expect nothing and everything."

CHAPTER 10

IN WHICH AMAYA RECEIVES AN
UNEXPECTED PROPOSAL

Amaya woke to a servant entering her room with a tray filled to overflowing with a variety of meats and breads, far more than she could eat. She hoped Graciela was not responsible for the excessive nature of her breakfast.

After eating moderately and dressing, she set out to explore the house. Curiosity had supplanted her sense of European manners, and she investigated any number of well-appointed, moderately shabby rooms without feeling embarrassed at her nosiness. There was a part of her, also, that remembered what Fernándo had said about her inheriting the estate, and while she did not wish to be his heir, she could not help considering herself to have some right to investigate.

Every room she entered was empty of people, leading her to believe she was the only early riser. Though Graciela likely was awake too. This realization stirred in Amaya a desire to seek out her reticent aunt and learn more of why she behaved as she did.

She opened one more door, looked inside, and was startled to see someone within. It was so unexpected she exclaimed in

Spanish, "I beg your pardon, I should not interrupt," her heart beating faster as if she had come upon an enemy.

"It is no interruption," the man said, turning, and she realized it was Valencia. "Please, come in."

Amaya hesitated. Valencia's gaze upon her was direct and searching, not admiring as it had been the previous night, but every bit as intent. She told Heart to stop hammering at her—Valencia was no immediate threat—and entered the room. It was a library, or a study, perhaps. Bookcases lined all four walls of the small, windowless room, their wood stained dark and made darker with age. A lamp on a table in the center of the room illuminated it imperfectly; the room was so poorly lit reading would be uncomfortable, despite the two armchairs flanking the table that looked much newer than the rest of the furniture.

She was reminded of the study in the Hanleys' Wimpole Street house, which was as small and dim as this room. But unlike the Hanleys' study, the shelves here were not packed full of books. Large gaps in the rows showed where books had been removed, and some shelves were so bare the books lay flat on their faces rather than standing upright with the spines facing out. Amaya knew little of books aside from the novels she read, but she recognized that most of the remaining titles were old, their leather worn, the gilding on their spines faded into illegibility. It was not a library someone loved and cared for, and it saddened Amaya that it should have fallen into this state.

"I see you feel as I do that this library is sadly neglected," Valencia said with a smile. "I know Don Fernándo has been forced by circumstance to sell many of the more valuable volumes. But he is no reader, so perhaps to him it is not such a loss." He gestured at the chairs. "Please, sit. I wish to know more of Fernándo's granddaughter."

Amaya took a seat, and Valencia sat opposite her. The lamp

flared brighter, making a hissing sound, and Amaya looked at it reflexively. Valencia smiled. "Fire is a magnificent thing," he said. "So alive, and so bright. I take great joy in my talent—as I imagine you do in yours."

Amaya nodded. She wondered what she would do if Valencia turned his talent on her, whether she would be able to tear his throat out before she burned to death. Valencia was lean and moved like someone familiar with violence, almost as well as a jaguar warrior, but she was certain he was no match for her physically. That made sense for an Extraordinary Scorcher, who would naturally depend on his talent before his body. It would be a matter of speed, and of reflexes. She would need to act first.

Then she remembered that it was unlikely she would fight Valencia, and she should behave with civility. Civility, yes, and honor, but it never hurt to have a plan to defeat a powerful potential opponent.

Valencia raised a hand, and the lamp's flame flickered brighter for a moment before dwindling to cast his features into shadow. Another fire kindled along the length of his fingers, glowing pale yellow and shedding enough heat that Amaya could feel it from where she sat. "For me, it is as if the fire and I are one. I know its moods and its changeability. And when I touch fire, it is like nothing else in the world."

He paused, and in his pause Amaya heard an invitation to speak. "I am always conscious of my own body," she said, "and when I touch another, that person's self speaks to me. It is a beautiful thing to sense the human body working smoothly. So my experience is similar to yours."

"There is a connection between Extraordinaries that other talents lack—have you noticed?" Valencia leaned forward and closed his hand over the fire limning it, extinguishing it. "That purity of sensation, the deep knowledge of one's talent, is something common to all of us."

Amaya remembered how quickly she and Elinor had become friends. "I had not realized, but I believe you are right."

"Don Fernándo told me you do not consider yourself Spanish," Valencia said. His lips twisted in a wry smile. "He was very vocal about your betrayal, as he put it, of your heritage. Do you consider yourself English, then? I know Ernesto married an Englishwoman."

"Did you know my father?"

Valencia shook his head. "Only his reputation. Don Fernándo speaks of him often, always angrily, in the way men do when their hearts have been wounded and they wish others not to know this."

A brief sympathy for Fernándo touched Amaya's heart. "I am of Tawantinsuyu—Inca. They saved my life and accepted me among them for thirteen years."

Valencia leaned back again. "Don Fernándo also tells me you are not a doctor. Why is that?"

Guilt surged within her, unexpected thanks to Valencia's swift change of subject. Seeing Valencia ignite fire so casually made her feel as if in refusing to learn medicine, she truly was denying her destiny. "I—it is not the same among my people. We believe our talents, a Shaper's talents, I mean, are to be used in the service of the Sapa Inca. It is no different for an Extraordinary than for an ordinary Shaper."

"But you are not among the Incas any longer," Valencia said. "If you cannot serve your Sapa Inca, what purpose does your talent serve? That is a question you must ask yourself, because you no longer have the luxury of having it decided for you."

His words angered her even as they chilled her. No one had ever challenged her so directly. "Then you believe I am wrong."

"I am in no position to make that determination." Valencia ignited fire again and shaped it into a palm-sized sphere that he rolled from one hand to the next. "But I believe it is a mistake to make decisions solely out of a desire not to do what is expected of one. You chose to turn your talent to the service of the Sapa Inca because you believed in the traditions of the Incas, so why do you now reject the traditions of the people you live among?"

"You are impertinent, sir," Amaya said, resorting to coldness to conceal the uncertainty his words cast her into.

"I do not believe in mincing words," Valencia said. "And I do you the courtesy of speaking frankly because I believe you are the sort of woman who values action and honesty. I will not tell you you are wrong not to become a doctor. That is your own business. But I will express my opinion in the hope it might benefit you: whatever you choose, do so because it is what you wish to be, not because you intend to spite society."

"Why do you care?" Amaya exclaimed.

Valencia smiled again. "You interest me," he said. "You are a warrior, and that is rare among women indeed. I believe from what Don Fernándo said, and from what I observe, that you chafe at the restrictions of this culture and long for some way to use your talent as you were trained to do."

His frankness left Amaya speechless, caught between denying his assessment and the deep-down feeling that he had described her perfectly. "There is no way," she said. "The war with Napoleon is over, and I could not be a soldier even if I wished to. And Europeans do not fight as I do, in any case."

"That is only their lack of imagination," Valencia said. "Guerrillas fight from the shadows in any way necessary. You would be welcome among us."

"Welcome? I do not understand."

Valencia's blue eyes fixed on her again, intent and searching.

"I would be honored," he said, "if you would join my people. Fight for Spain."

"But I am not—"

"You are Spanish if you choose to be. And I believe you have a passion for justice that goes to waste while you pretend to be nothing but a society maiden." Valencia gripped her hand. His was warm and rough, the hand of a laborer. "Consider my offer. We ride out tomorrow morning. If you choose to travel with us, you will be welcome."

"That is sudden."

Valencia nodded. "You might consider longer—I will return from Aranjuez in just over a week. If you are still here…" He let go her hand and sat back again.

Amaya absently rubbed her hand where he had touched her. "I believed the French to have left Spain," she said. "Whom do you fight?"

"There are many who supported France and who continue to work against Spain. My people and I, we convince them this is a poor choice." Valencia's smile became wicked, his eyes lit with fierce pleasure.

His smile woke Amaya from the daze his invitation had sent her into. Those who supported France? He meant the *afrancesados*, who might or might not be evil, but who were certainly still Spaniards. "You fight to kill?" she asked.

"If needs must, then yes."

Amaya shook her head. "I cannot judge you, because I do not know your cause," she said. "But it seems to me that you are likely to harm innocents in your quest, and I cannot be a part of that."

Valencia's smile did not waver. "It is your choice," he said. "I will not give up on persuading you, because I believe I offer you an opportunity that will make you happy."

"I..." Amaya's words trailed off. She could not think of a good reply to that. She did not wish to insult El Encendedor, because she truly did not know enough about his work and his cause. "You will stay today?" she asked instead, then had to control a blush because her words had sounded more personal than she intended.

"I will," Valencia said, the admiring expression she remembered from the previous night returning to his face. "I would have regardless, but when a lovely lady asks so nicely, well..." He spread his hands in a gesture suggesting helplessness in the face of fate.

Amaya rose quickly. "Then we may speak again later," she said, cursing herself for once more sounding missish. She was not one of England's simpering maidens; she was a jaguar warrior, and one who did not allow an attractive face to sway her. "Please excuse me."

Valencia stood, more slowly, and bowed. "It was my pleasure, Miss Salazar."

Well away from the library and its unsettling occupant, Amaya slowed her steps and turned toward the garden door. She had no intention of doing as Valencia asked, and yet he had been correct in his assertion that she regretted not being able to use her talents as she had been taught by the Incas. She had no solution for this problem, short of returning to Peru and searching for her lost home.

Perhaps this was not such a strange idea. She might find a Seer willing to Dream the Incas' new location, might pay to be Bounded back to Peru. But the idea did not fill her with hope the way it might have two months ago. Now that she had encountered the wider world, she found she was not ready to leave it behind.

She slammed the garden door open with unnecessary force,

feeling angry with herself and wishing she might take out that anger on something. The rich green smell of the garden failed to calm her. She strode to the half-hidden gazebo and pushed vines aside until she could see its interior. There were two bench seats painted the same peeling, flaking white as the rest of the gazebo. One of the seats had collapsed and lay broken on the floor, which itself looked in danger of going the same way. Amaya decided not to risk it.

She stood in the doorway, holding fistfuls of greenery, and breathed in the damp scent. Somewhere nearby grew flowers that gave off a delicate smell, but they were not visible. Irritated, she tugged on the vines in her hands, then gave a sharp pull. With a crackling, tearing sound, the vines came free of the tangle, sending more of the damp green scent into the air. Amaya flung the vines aside and tore at more of them, using her claws on the recalcitrant ones, until the gazebo was clear of foliage and lay bare amid piles of shredded greenery.

Breathing heavily from anger rather than exertion, Amaya rubbed green stains from her fingers onto the grass, remembering in time that she did not wish to ruin her gown. The gazebo looked naked in the noon sunlight, its white frame the skeleton of some bizarre creature. Amaya kicked some of the vines aside and stepped back to examine her work. She felt a little better, less embarrassed about her conversation with Valencia and how it had ended.

"Well," Edmund said from behind her, making her jump. "I did not realize the vines had mortally offended you. Should I take shelter, or will you confine your violence to the trees and bushes?"

She turned around. "I cannot understand how you are able to sneak up on me."

"I am by nature a stealthy man," Edmund said, pretending to

great seriousness. "Are you well? Something seems to have disturbed you."

Amaya found she did not wish to share the details of her conversation with El Encendedor with Edmund. He already believed the worst of Valencia, and Amaya did not know what she thought of the man, except that he intrigued her. "Mr. Valencia wishes me to join his army," she said, "or whatever it is one calls a group of guerrillas."

Edmund's smile vanished, and his brow furrowed. "Why would he ask such a thing of a total stranger?"

"He knows I am a warrior—is that so strange, that he might ask me to fight with him?"

"And destroy innocents? Amaya, tell me you are not considering his proposal!"

Irritation surged within her once more, this time at Edmund. "I would not harm innocents, you know that. I told him I was not interested. And I cannot believe you imagined I would do anything else."

Edmund's lips tightened. "I did not believe it, but, Amaya, I know how you regret losing your place as Uturunku. It would not surprise me if you wished for an opportunity to be a warrior once more."

Amaya glared at him. "But not at that price. Mr. Valencia's cause is not mine."

"I—" Edmund lowered his head and muttered a curse under his breath Amaya was sure he did not intend her to hear. "You are correct," he said, looking at her once more. "I apologize for thinking so poorly of you."

His apology left her feeling drained, not only of her anger but of her emotional upheaval at how Valencia had looked at her. "No, I apologize, I was rude. And you are correct that I have regrets. I admit that were Valencia a general, leading an army against the French, I might have taken him up on his offer."

Edmund shook his head. "I am glad we are friends, to forgive one another our rudenesses. Will you join me for a meal? There are meats and cheeses and the like laid out in the dining room."

Amaya discovered she was hungry despite the breakfast she had eaten. "I have not seen Don Fernándo this morning. I wonder where he is? He wished to speak to me." She took Edmund's arm and strolled with him in the direction of the house.

"I heard he felt ill, and chose to rest," Edmund said. "Miss Graciela was forthcoming with this information. I cannot understand her. She seems completely worn down by life, and then she will look at me with a directness that makes me uncomfortable."

"I agree. I wish to know more of her, if I can find her at a time when she is not occupied. Where, by the way, is Mrs. Paget? I have not seen her all morning."

Edmund nudged a loose stone out of the path with the toe of his boot. "Mrs. Paget is not well, either, as Miss Graciela also informed me. I believe it is nothing more than a sour stomach, similar to what she suffered the night after we left Madrid."

He opened the door, and stopped. "I beg your pardon," he said to the young man who had been about to open the door himself.

Amaya immediately recognized him as the curly-haired youth who had pretended not to be interested in her the previous evening. His eyes, a peculiar greyish-blue, fixed on her briefly, then looked away; he studied the floor as if it were infinitely fascinating. "Please excuse us," she told him, "we are in your way."

The young man shrugged and pushed past them without a

word. Amaya half-turned to watch him go. "I believe he finds me attractive, and that makes him silent," she said.

Edmund chuckled. "That would be unexpected," he said, "as she is a woman."

Amaya gasped and turned around entirely, but the young man—young woman?—was already out of sight. "You must be mistaken."

"I am quite familiar with women, if I may say so without seeming indelicate." Edmund offered Amaya his arm again. "It is a good disguise, and she is built in such a way that bolsters that disguise, but I assure you she is female, whatever visage she shows to the world."

"Now I am intrigued," Amaya said. "Do you suppose Mr. Valencia knows?"

"I have no idea," Edmund said, "but we should not give her away, as that might prove dangerous to her if her comrades do not know her true sex."

"That had not occurred to me." Amaya let the door shut behind her. "Don Fernándo certainly has the most interesting acquaintances."

CHAPTER 11
IN WHICH A CONVERSATION ENDS RATHER DRAMATICALLY

Graciela appeared in the dining room when Amaya and Edmund had nearly finished their meal. "My father wishes to speak with you," she told Amaya in her diffident voice. "He asks that you join him in the drawing room."

Amaya laid down her knife. "Then he is well again?"

Graciela tilted her head to one side, considering. "He is very old," she said, "with all that suggests. He refuses to have an Extraordinary Shaper attend on him, though his heart sometimes does not beat regularly and his digestion is not what it once was. Some mornings are more difficult than others."

"I will join him—you do not mind, Edmund?"

Edmund pushed his seat back from the table. "Not at all. I will see how Mrs. Paget is feeling, and then I believe I will visit the stables and beg the indulgence of riding one of those magnificent horses. You should join me after your talk."

Amaya did not think they were all that magnificent, but she knew little of horseflesh. "I suppose," she said, making Edmund laugh at her lack of enthusiasm.

The fire in the drawing room burned hotter than before, and Fernándo sat, not on the sofa, but on an armchair drawn up close to the fireplace. Another, matching armchair faced his, and Fernándo gestured to Amaya to sit. "Has Graciela seen to your needs?" he asked. His voice sounded less forceful than it had the previous day, but his expression was as stern as ever. His hand gripping the head of the walking stick shook slightly.

"Aunt Graciela has been very accommodating," Amaya said. "But I do not understand why she acts as a servant instead of the lady of the house."

Fernándo scowled, deepening the lines beside his mouth and across his forehead. "Graciela knows her duty. Do you suggest I treat her poorly?"

This was exactly what Amaya wanted to suggest, but she did not feel comfortable accusing her grandfather of exploiting Graciela when she had only observed the household for a few hours. "I do not know what is acceptable behavior. I know only that were I a stranger to this place, I would assume Aunt Graciela was a servant and not a daughter of the house."

"It is none of your business," Fernándo said, raising his voice. "And we have other matters to discuss."

The emphasis he put on "other matters" filled Amaya with trepidation. "And those are?"

Fernándo shifted his weight, using his stick to push himself up enough to sit forward. "You are my heir, and should understand what that means. The Salazar family has possessed this land for centuries, through the rise and fall of kings. I will not see it lost to us."

"Then what would you have done had I not returned?" Amaya said.

"That is irrelevant, because you are here now." Fernándo's brows contracted and came together, furrowing his forehead more deeply. "We have much rich farmland, more than our neighbors. It supports this household well. You have seen our horses; they, too, are of the highest quality."

"And yet you sold the books," Amaya said.

Fernándo jerked back, the least controlled movement she had yet seen him make. "Who told you this?"

"Mr. Valencia."

"Ah. Yes." Mention of Valencia seemed to calm the old man. "You spoke with him this morning?"

"I did." Possibly the answer was too curt for politeness, but Amaya did not wish to discuss her conversation with El Encendedor with Fernándo.

"He is a great man. He wishes the best for Spain. You would do well to heed his words, as he has been a faithful friend these many years." Fernándo moistened his lips with his tongue and looked around the room. "Graciela!"

"If you are in need, I will fetch—"

"That is beneath you, to fetch and carry. Graciela!" The woman appeared in the doorway. "Bring water for both of us."

"I do not," Amaya began, then gave up. She was not likely to convince Fernándo to suddenly begin treating his daughter like a daughter.

"Alejandro Valencia is like a son to me," Fernándo continued. "And he understands the respect due a Salazar. You must learn this as well."

"But—what of Mateo?" Amaya blurted out.

"What of him?" Graciela returned with a tray, and Fernándo took a glass without acknowledging her.

"Was he not to be your heir?" Amaya had intended not to drink, as a gesture of defiance, but realized she was too thirsty for such gestures. The water was cool and sweet, and she drained half the glass in one gulp.

Fernándo waved her words away. "He knew the truth. If his hopes are dashed, that is his fault for building them high. And he is young and impetuous, not the sort of man one wishes for an heir. Ernesto—" He stopped abruptly and took another drink of water. "You are not like your father. You will care for this land."

His utter certainty that he was right, and that Amaya would obey his command, angered her. "You know little of me," she said, "and your assumptions are premature. I have obligations that will not wait, and I am not certain I wish to be your heir."

She expected this to throw him into a fury, but he only set his glass down with a faint *tick* of glass against the wood of the tray. "Alejandro told me as much," he said. "You cannot decide because you are yet ignorant of your destiny."

His casual certainty deepened her anger. "Mr. Valencia asked me to join his army. Suppose I agree?"

Fernándo delivered one of his typical shrugs. "Then you would learn to love Spain, and that will teach you to love this inheritance."

Amaya controlled an urge to leap to her feet and shout at him. Instead, she said, "I do not intend to join Mr. Valencia. I am not certain he is cautious in whom he attacks."

"It is of no importance," Fernándo said. He pushed himself slowly to his feet, wobbling slightly, and gestured toward the door. "Walk with me. I will show you your inheritance."

Amaya did not believe Fernándo capable of walking far, so she did not demur. It was not until they neared the stables that she understood Fernándo's intent. Inwardly, she sighed. She was certain Fernándo would not allow her to run beside him as he rode, but this did not make her like horses more than before.

Word had apparently gone before them, for two beautiful horses, one roan, the other the kind of white horse lovers call grey, stood saddled and ready in the yard behind the house.

Amaya mounted without assistance, wishing as she usually did that she might wear trousers rather than a gown, and turned the white horse to follow Fernándo out of the yard.

They followed the deeply rutted road that led to the house back to the main road, where Fernándo turned left, and rode in silence for several minutes. If Fernándo intended to sway her opinion, he had chosen some method other than conversation. Amaya surveyed the landscape. It was beautiful, she had to admit; fields green with summer's growth spread out as far as she could see, which was very far indeed.

Beyond the fields, the Tagus River flowed lazily past Toledo, which in the sunlight was as beautiful and golden as she had guessed it might be yesterday in the drizzle. Large spired buildings stood at the top of its low hill, and she amused herself by wondering what they might be—palaces, churches, or even remnants of the Moorish civilization she had been told once ruled Spain? She wished she had not promised Fernándo three days, because she was seized with a desire to explore those places.

Fernándo pulled his horse up short and waved a hand at the distant fields, dotted with tiny workers. "The land is what sustains us," he said. "I was not too proud to work the fields when I was a youth. It is your heritage."

Amaya doubted Fernándo had ever done the back-breaking labor of a field worker. More likely he had pulled a few weeds before leaving the rest to the servants. But she said only, "I have always wondered what it would be like to grow crops. In my home, the crops grow in terraces on the hills because there is little flat land such as this."

Fernándo scowled. "You persist in believing Peru is your home?"

"The Incas sheltered me and cared for me. They are my family."

Despite her care, Fernándo said angrily, "You do not know what family is. I—"

"You persist in saying that," Amaya said, finally goaded beyond politeness. "You treat your daughter like a slave, you are indifferent to the dashed hopes of your grandson, and you disowned my father for ignoring your wishes. It is you who does not know what family is."

Fernándo's jaw tightened. "We are Salazars. Our duty is to something greater than ourselves. The people depend on us not only to provide their livelihood, but to defend them against enemies. We fought off the French and we fought off guerrillas who believed themselves justified in taking what was not theirs." He brought his horse around so he could look Amaya in the eye. "You have a powerful talent you should turn to protecting others, if you refuse to take up an Extraordinary Shaper's traditional role. But this can only happen if you stop deluding yourself that none of this has anything to do with you."

Amaya, taken aback by his sudden intensity, said nothing. She still did not like Fernándo, but his speech showed her she had been wrong about at least one thing: Fernándo's devotion to his family name ran far deeper than personal aggrandizement.

Fernándo looked past her shoulder, and his eyes hardened. "And these companions," he said. "You should not need the English to give you protection."

Amaya turned to see Edmund approaching. She did not know enough to know how good a horse it was, but he sat it well, and it eased her heart to know she would no longer endure Fernándo's demands unaccompanied. "They are my friends," she said.

"Nevertheless," Fernándo said.

Edmund drew up even with them and saluted Fernándo. "Don Fernándo, I thank you for the privilege of taking out one of your horses," he said. "They are all excellent animals."

"You are quite welcome," Fernándo said stiffly. "I must return to the house now. I am in need of rest. But you must both continue your ride. The land for miles around is Salazar land; feel free to explore it." He looked meaningfully at Amaya as he spoke, then wheeled his horse around and trotted back toward the house.

When he was well out of earshot, Amaya said, "I believe you have rescued me." She spoke in English, just in case.

"Don Fernándo is no villain, unless I miss my guess." Edmund sat gazing after the old man's retreating figure. "But he has imposed on you, I believe."

"He wants me for his heir. I do not know what I am to do. Edmund, what will come to this place if I am not heir?"

Edmund nudged his horse into motion, and they followed Fernándo, slowly. "I do not know Spanish inheritance law, but I am aware the *dotados* owe much to the government. It is possible the Crown will take the lands and the money on the grounds that there is no other direct line heir. On the other hand, Doña Graciela is herself a *dotado,* and she might inherit in her father's place."

The idea cheered Amaya. "We must learn which is true, because I would wish my aunt to inherit. It is what is due her if she has been a servant for many years."

"Then you will not accept Don Fernándo's demand."

He sounded too neutral, as if he harbored an opinion he did not wish to share—an opinion she would not like. Amaya, feeling nettled at his unexpected reticence, said, "You do not believe I am to be heir?"

Edmund shrugged. "You are legally entitled, and I wondered

if you might not like the idea of regaining some of what was lost to you."

Amaya laughed. "I would feel...I do not know the word. I am a stranger who comes to the house and takes it over."

"A usurper."

"Is that the word? It is a strange one." Amaya sighed. "May we return now? Riding bores me, and as you will not permit me to run alongside, I have little pleasure in it."

"It is a skill you should master," Edmund chided her in a friendly way. "And you are not dressed for running."

Amaya sighed again, more deeply this time. "I do not know why my aunt Ynes wears men's clothing, but I feel I should ask, because perhaps it is a thing I can do here."

They turned the corner to the stables, where they found Mrs. Paget speaking to one of the stable hands. "Miss Salazar, Mr. Hanley, I regret not seeing you before you left," she said in Spanish. "I feel much recovered, and considered taking a ride—but of course I will not impose on you, if you are finished with yours."

"I would be happy to ride out with you," Edmund said. "Miss Salazar, however, has had her fill of riding for the day."

Amaya resisted the urge to make a face at him and slid down from her horse, not very gracefully. "If we were on foot," she began, then was distracted by the sight of approaching riders, moving very fast and throwing up clouds of dust. "Who is that?"

She had not addressed anyone in particular, but the stable hand walked past her, his hand raised to shield his eyes from the sun, and stared at the oncoming crowd of what Amaya could now see were ten or twelve riders. They dressed much as Valencia's people did, in plain clothes and slouching hats, and they were riding at a full gallop, as if desperate to reach their goal—or desperate to escape a pursuer.

Then the stable hand lowered his hand with an oath Amaya did not recognize, spun on his heel and ran for the stables at top speed. "Raiders!" he screamed. "'Ware raiders!"

Amaya immediately grabbed her horse's reins and urged it toward the dubious safety of the stables. Edmund rode past her, dismounting when he reached the stalls. "You must return to the house immediately," he told Amaya. "Take Mrs. Paget."

"And what do you intend to do? Edmund, you are unarmed—"

"I will see if I can rouse Mr. Valencia's men." Edmund turned to Mrs. Paget, who seemed not to have understood the cries, because she still stared at the raiders as if fascinated by them. "Mrs. Paget, we must get to safety!"

Mrs. Paget turned at that. The crack of a gunshot rang out, and the high-pitched whine of a rifle ball whizzed past. Amaya started for Mrs. Paget as more shots exploded. Men rushed from the servants' house, and the noise redoubled as they found sheltered spots and began shooting at the attackers. Some of them could find no better shelter than the sides of the buildings. Amaya had never felt more exposed than she did in the open yard.

She had almost reached Mrs. Paget, who had her arms over her head as if that would protect her, when another rifle ball grazed Amaya's shoulder, far too close to her head. Amaya let her body deal with the wound and ducked low to make herself a smaller target. "Mrs. Paget, get down!" she shouted.

Mrs. Paget nodded and began to crouch. Then she jerked, and a spray of red exploded from the back of her head. The crouch became an uncontrolled fall, and she hit the hard-packed earth without trying to stop herself. Drops of blood flew everywhere. Amaya, sliding to a halt on her knees beside the woman, saw Mrs. Paget's eyes staring back at her, glassy and dead.

CHAPTER 12
IN WHICH EDMUND AND AMAYA EXPERIENCE A CHANGE OF HEART

Amaya cried out and reached for Mrs. Paget's hand. Then Edmund's hands were around her waist and he dragged her away. "She is dead," he shouted over the noise of rifle fire, "beyond even an Extraordinary Shaper's power to restore. We must get inside, quickly."

Amaya freed herself from his grip, and the two of them ran for the entrance to the garden, ducking and weaving to make themselves less desirable targets. "What are we to do?" Amaya exclaimed in Spanish. "We cannot permit these men to kill others, or destroy this house."

"You have never used a gun, and I am a poor shot," Edmund replied. "We both of us are better at hand-to-hand fighting. Which in this case might be fatal."

Amaya peered around the edge of the maze. The riders milled about some distance from the yard, shouting and taking shots at anyone visible. From what she could see, most of their shots flew wide as their horses jigged and moved restlessly. As she watched, one of the defenders' shots found its mark, and a raider jerked backward before falling off his horse. The horse backed into another rider and jostled a second before finding its way free.

Then, as if in response to some unheard signal, the raiders wheeled their horses and rode away in a great clamor of shouting. A few of the defenders continued to shoot, but it was clear even to Amaya that the raiders were well out of range. One final crack of dull thunder, and the yard was silent.

Amaya and Edmund emerged from the shelter of the hedges and crossed the yard to where Mrs. Paget lay. Blood pooled beneath her head, which was shattered at the back. Edmund was right; she was clearly beyond the help of even the most skilled Extraordinary Shaper. Amaya crouched beside her, her mind numb. Mrs. Paget had not been a close friend, but Amaya had liked her, and she could not help thinking of Lady Kynaston, to whom Mrs. Paget had been dear.

"Three dead, including Mrs. Paget," Edmund said. Amaya looked up at him; he was surveying the yard, his expression grim. "Something is not right about this."

Amaya stood. "What do you mean?"

"I mean," Edmund said, "those men had no hope of doing real damage to this place, or even of killing many. Anyone who died was the victim of bad luck. This yard is not highly defensible, but it is secure enough. Well, you see it yourself. Only three dead, and I believe the defenders accounted for two."

Amaya chose not to comment on why Edmund understood the situation so well. She looked at where the fallen raiders lay. "Two," she agreed. "But then what was the purpose of the attack?"

"I cannot say. I have heard nothing to suggest that this kind of raid is common, or that Don Fernándo has enemies who are interested in harassing him." Edmund put a hand on Amaya's shoulder. "There is your uncle Leocadio," he said. "I wonder if he knows more."

Leocadio was hurrying toward them, his odd full skirts billowing as he ran. "You are—" he began, then noticed Mrs. Paget and recoiled. "God have mercy," he said, crossing himself. He crouched beside Mrs. Paget's body as they had, then stood as if he had realized there was nothing to be done for her. "What happened here?"

"The men said it was raiders," Amaya said. "Does that happen often?"

"Not often. Not since the guerrillas, two years ago." Leocadio mopped sweat from his forehead. "There are those who believe that my father, being old, is an easy target. I daresay those men, whoever they were, did not realize Alejandro's people were here." He shook his head. "I would laugh at their consternation had their violent behavior not cost so many their lives. Including your companion. I sorrow at your loss."

"Thank you," Edmund said. "But you say this is unusual?"

Leocadio blinked at him. "Unusual? I did not say that. Unlikely, perhaps. Spain suffers still from the depredations of war, and there are those who claim the guise of freedom fighters who rampage through the countryside, taking what they will and killing many who attempt to stand up to them. It is why Alejandro's work is so vital. He is a true hero."

"I would not call myself hero," Valencia said, coming up beside them. "It is simply what must be done. And when this brave lady lies dead before us, I feel my limitations most keenly." He, too, crossed himself and bowed his head briefly.

"It was a terrible accident, and you should not blame yourself," Amaya said. She saw servants approaching with armloads of tan or white cloth. "We must return to tell Lady Kynaston what happened."

"Permit these men to care for the body," Valencia said. "I believe Don Fernándo would like to speak with you."

"What could Don Fernándo have to say? He was not present," Edmund said, sharply.

Valencia smiled, one side of his mouth curving upward to make the expression wry. "I believe you will find Don Fernándo possessed of strong opinions on many topics. In this case, however, he wishes only to see that you are unharmed." He shot a glance at Edmund. "Both of you, naturally."

Edmund's neutral expression was the one Amaya recognized as how he looked when he was concealing a strong emotion. She wished they were alone so she might ask him what was wrong. She stepped back to allow the servants to wrap Mrs. Paget's body in sheets. "We will attend on him," she said with a nod.

Fernándo was not seated when they entered the drawing room. He paced before the fireplace, where tiny fires ignited, blazed high briefly, and merged to make larger flames that encompassed the logs laid there. "This is an outrage," he exclaimed. He brandished his stick as if he could beat the raiders into submission. "An outrage! That these fools, these cowards, think to attack me—despicable, craven men who think of nothing but their own foul needs!"

"Norales says he recognized two of them," Valencia said. "They work for Enrico Solano."

Fernándo spun to face him, faster than Amaya believed the old man could move. "Solano," he hissed, drawing out each syllable as if testing it. "Solano. That brute. Was he not defeated last year, and driven out of Castile?"

"I believed so," Valencia said. "I must beg your forgiveness for having failed."

Fernándo waved this away. "It is typical of such men. Chop off one head, and two more sprout in its place."

"It will not happen again," Valencia said. "I intend to ride out today in search of him." He looked at Amaya, then at Edmund. "Solano will be well-armed, and will have many fighters at his command. I would not reject your help if you chose to give it."

Amaya drew in a sharp breath. To fight? And yet her duty was not to Spain, it was to Elinor, and also to Mrs. Paget's memory.

"We must leave for Madrid today," Edmund said. "Mrs. Paget's body should be returned to her friends." He sounded polite, but distant, and once more Amaya wished she knew what was truly in his heart.

"Of course," Valencia said immediately. "Miss Salazar, will you return here?"

"I do not know." Amaya resolutely did not look at Edmund. "Eventually, yes."

"Eventually?" Fernándo exclaimed. "What is this 'eventually'? You have a duty to this family—"

"Don Fernándo, Miss Salazar has made promises she must keep," Valencia said. "She knows where her duty lies." He bowed to Fernándo. "I must see to my men, but they would appreciate your presence when we set off in an hour."

"Of course." Fernándo sounded less angry, but he did not look at Amaya again. Amaya took this to mean she was dismissed and hurriedly followed Valencia out of the room before Fernándo could renew his angry commands.

"Don Fernándo feels strongly about his family," Valencia said in a quiet voice when they reached the antechamber. "Do not judge him too harshly."

"He seems unfamiliar with the notion of his will being thwarted," Edmund said drily.

Valencia chuckled. "You will see us off?" he asked Amaya. "My men respect Extraordinaries and view them as good luck."

"I—yes," Amaya said. Once more Valencia's presence, his intent expression, flustered her.

"Good." Valencia nodded to both of them and left the antechamber.

Amaya let out a deep breath as if Valencia's overwhelming presence had struck her to the heart. "I will be glad to return to Madrid."

"I wonder," Edmund said. He was looking in the direction Valencia had gone. "He is…"

"Is what?"

Edmund shook his head slowly. "It is nothing. Or, rather, nothing that is a danger to either of us. He is simply too accommodating."

"Too accommodating?" Amaya laughed. "Because he is polite to Don Fernándo?"

"He is the kind of man who does as he pleases, and is polite when it suits him." Edmund no longer looked neutral; he scowled as if facing his worst enemy. "I fear what might happen were he to decide either of us were in his way."

"You said you did not believe him a danger to us."

"And I do not." Edmund sighed. "We leave soon, and it will no longer matter."

The idea of returning to Madrid both reassured and disquieted Amaya. "I must pack my things," she said. "We will leave when Mr. Valencia does."

It took very little time for Amaya to return her belongings to her small trunk. But when it was packed and fastened shut, she sat on the edge of the bed and reflected on the terrible events of the day. Poor Lady Kynaston, who would have no reason to believe Mrs. Paget in danger and would be devastated to learn the news. It would be a relief to return to Madrid, to leave behind Fernándo's demands and the oddness that was her father's family.

And yet the disquiet would not go away. The visit had not been bad, all things considered. True, Ynes was hostile and Mateo even more so, but Graciela had been kind, and Leocadio seemed an honorable man. Even Fernándo, despite his bullying nature, cared deeply about his heritage. It was not so awful a thing to be a Salazar. Had Amaya not made other commitments, she might have welcomed Fernándo's invitation.

And *that* was the source of her disquiet. Amaya's commitment to Elinor was a short-term one. Once the babe was born, and Elinor seen past danger, Amaya would once more be without purpose. Why, then, should she not consider returning to Toledo, to become a part of the Salazar family?

On the other hand, this was not her only family. Having made one connection, she found she wished to learn more of the Nevilles as well. That would be difficult if she were living in Spain. It seemed she would have to choose, if she wanted a connection to her family, which family to be connected to.

Amaya stood and collected her trunk before remembering a lady did not carry her own luggage. She set it down and looked out past the green veil that shrouded her window. The issue of which family to join was irrelevant at the moment because she had a duty that superseded it. She would return to Elinor and permit the question to lie dormant for a few weeks. Perhaps something might become obvious in that time.

She found Graciela at the front door when she went in search of Edmund. "Your carriage is in the yard," Graciela said in her flat, colorless voice.

Impulsively, Amaya said, "Why do you not stand up for yourself, Aunt Graciela? I understand if you wish to serve and run this household, but surely you need not let Don Fernándo treat you so poorly."

Graciela's hand rested on the lower half of the door, near the latch that connected the top and bottom. She flicked the latch with her thumb, idly, as if she did not know what it was for. "It is my duty," she said. "I promised Mama I would care for this place when she was gone. Father's behavior means nothing beside that."

"But—"

Graciela's other hand flew up between them, palm out to stop Amaya saying anything else. "It is my choice, child," she said. "And besides, where else would I go? The world is not kind to Discerners, even those who are not Extraordinaries."

"Did you never desire a home of your own?"

Amaya had meant it as an idle query, but Graciela reacted as if she had been slapped. "A daughter's life is in her father's hands," she said, her voice even quieter than before. "That is not my choice to make." She turned and hurried from the entrance.

Amaya stared after her. She felt uneasy at having pressed her aunt, though she did not believe she had been harsh about it. It was easy to imagine a thwarted romance, a suitor sent away—for Amaya was certain, though she knew little of Spanish customs, that a daughter would not remain in her parents' home once she was married. It would not surprise Amaya at all to learn Fernándo had kept Graciela a spinster so she would go on caring for him and his house. Amaya's irritation with Fernándo deepened. If she had charge of this family—but that was a possibility, was it not? She turned away from the door and walked through the house to the garden.

However overgrown the garden was, it was still cool in the heat of the day, and Amaya took her time passing through it. The yard, by contrast, radiated heat from its packed earth surface and from the white-plastered servants' house. There, the carriage waited, the horses already harnessed and the driver standing at their head. The baggage was already stowed, but Amaya did not see Edmund anywhere.

She did see Valencia, speaking to two of his men. Or, rather, one of his men and the curly-haired youth Edmund had said was female. Amaya examined the latter. Yes, if she knew what she was looking for, it was obvious the guerrilla was female; the curve of her hip and backside was too pronounced, and her cheeks were downy and had never felt the touch of a razor. But to the casual observer, she passed quite well for male.

Amaya heard someone come up beside her and said, "We should not leave before bidding Fernándo farewell."

Edmund said, "And the rest of your family. They are all present, I believe." He covertly pointed in the direction of the stables, where Ynes and her four sons were dismounting.

Amaya noticed Leocadio talking to Graciela near the servants' house. Graciela's expression was distant, the kind of look that says a person is not actually listening to what is being said. She wondered at Graciela's rudeness to a brother who had never been anything but respectful of her, but then Fernándo emerged from the garden and stumped toward her.

"You will return," he said without preamble. "Leocadio has Dreamed it."

Amaya shot a glance at Leocadio, whose attention was still all on Graciela. "Dream is not accurate over many days."

"Accurate enough." Fernándo harrumphed. "Humor this old man. Remember who you are. Please."

It was so unexpectedly humble Amaya was left with nothing to say. To cover her confusion, she watched Valencia, who had turned away from his comrades to accept the reins of a golden dun horse. He mounted smoothly, making the action look like part of a graceful dance.

"My friends!" he shouted, bringing all other conversations to a halt. "We ride today on a terrible errand. This very afternoon, we lost friends to a vicious, cowardly attack by men who think nothing of murdering a helpless woman simply because they can. This cannot be allowed to go unpunished."

A cheer rose from the watching crowd, all except Graciela, Fernándo, and Amaya and Edmund. Regardless, Amaya felt the power of Valencia's words. A comforting warmth centered on her breastbone filled her, and she could not help but remember times she had fought to keep herself and her companions alive, and how wonderfully right that had felt.

Valencia sat tall in the saddle, his head held high. "I know you wish for peace," he continued. "But peace is worthless if it is the result of giving in to evil. It is true, if we do as Solano demands, his men will no longer attack us. Is that what you wish?"

"*No!*" shouted the assembled crowd. Amaya saw Mateo and his brother shout as loud as anyone else. Across the yard, beyond where Valencia stood, the curly-haired woman stared at Amaya, her peculiar gray-blue eyes as fierce as the shouting.

"Then will you fight?" Valencia shouted over the voices.

"*Yes!*"

"You will fight for your homes? For your families?"

"*Yes!*"

"You will fight to make Spain great?"

"*Yes!*" The roar this time was overwhelming. Amaya's heart surged within her. The warmth suffused her body. She had felt this way so many times, surrounded by the other jaguar warriors, certain of who she was and what she was meant for. It had been many months since she had felt so powerfully connected to anything.

She found her objections to Valencia's request had faded. She watched her memory of them go with only a curious detachment, and then the warm passion flooded over her again, filling her with confidence in Valencia's words. She wondered where the new, unexpected feeling had come from, and then the wondering, too, vanished.

Valencia waited for the noise to subside. "Then you know what we must do," he said, his voice so quiet it made everyone else go silent to hear him. "We do not act out of pride or pleasure, but out of honor and love. I would give my own life for the sake of Spain, and I will be honored to fight beside such as you." He dismounted and gestured to Leocadio. "Father, we ask your blessing."

Leocadio walked forward and bowed his head. He prayed in some language Amaya had never heard before, though she could tell it was prayer by the way Valencia and everyone else in the courtyard bowed their heads. Leocadio finished by making the sign of the cross over Valencia, whose head remained bowed for a moment more before he stood straight again.

"We will fight," he declared, "and we will win. There is no other outcome. But remember, my friends—" He paused, and now his gaze fixed on Amaya. "Remember for what we fight. Remember for whom we lay down our lives. We are the protectors of Spain, every one of us. We seek not for glory, but for peace. And we are strong because we are one."

Cheering erupted throughout the yard, several dozen voices crying out in excitement and fervor. Amaya let out a cry of exultation she could not contain and heard Edmund beside her doing the same. She turned to him and saw his expression was as joyful and fierce as she knew her own to be. "Edmund," she began.

"I know," he said. "I cannot believe we did not see the justice of Mr. Valencia's cause before this."

"I will tell him," Amaya said.

She hurried across the courtyard to where Valencia stood beside the curly-haired woman. "We wish to fight," she told him.

Valencia's eyes widened. Then he laughed, a delighted sound that made the warmth in Amaya's chest burn brighter. "This is a rare joy indeed," he said. "You and your companion both are welcome to join us."

Amaya nodded. "I must have other clothes. I will not fight in a gown."

"Very reasonable." Valencia looked around. "I believe Doña Graciela can help you. We will wait."

"But I do not wish to delay you."

Valencia's smile grew warmer and more intimate. "For such a one as you," he said, "we will wait."

Amaya blushed and turned away, catching the eye of the curly-haired woman. She, too, was smiling, but her smile was not very pleasant. When she realized Amaya was looking at her, the smile disappeared. Amaya's warm feeling surged over her again. Comforted, she took hold of Edmund's hand and towed him to where Graciela stood statue-like near the servants' house. "We will fight," she told her aunt, feeling joy at the thought.

Graciela regarded her somberly. Amaya realized she was the only person in the courtyard not celebrating. Even Fernándo had shouted with the rest. "I will find clothes for both of you," she said, "if you will come with me."

"Aunt Graciela, is something wrong?"

Graciela gave Amaya another long, searching look. "Nothing

I can do anything about," she said. "I hope you do not regret your choice."

Amaya shook her head. "I have never felt so powerfully how right my actions are," she said. "Edmund, do you not feel the same?"

"Mr. Valencia's cause is the most just I have ever known," Edmund said. "I feel it in my bones."

"That is what I mean," Graciela said, and refused to elaborate further.

CHAPTER 13

IN WHICH AMAYA USES HER
WARRIOR'S SKILLS

Graciela found for Amaya trousers of a heavy, coarse weave, a fine linen shirt, and a coat that was slightly too large for her. As it left room for Amaya to enlarge her arm and shoulder muscles if necessary, she did not mind its size. The trousers came with straps that went over the shoulders to hold them up, but Amaya found her hips curved enough to make the straps unnecessary. Graciela also gave her a large cloth, bigger than a handkerchief and of soft red cotton, that she indicated was for Amaya to wear around her neck and pull over her face when the dust of the road became too much to bear. Amaya concluded it was simpler than altering her body to filter out dust.

She considered freeing her hair from the simple arrangement that was all she could manage on her own, but decided having her hair bound around her head was almost as convenient to a warrior as being clean-shaven. It left nothing for an enemy to grab hold of.

The riding boots were made for a man, and Amaya took a

moment to Shape her feet to better fit them. This left her slightly off-balance as she accustomed herself to her wider feet, but the moment passed, and she found her footing more stable than before.

Excitement, and the joy of newfound purpose, fizzed through her veins as she hurried to the stable yard. She had a moment's fear upon exiting the house that Valencia might have changed his mind, but he waited there with his dun horse, talking to the curly-haired woman. His eyes lit with appreciation when he saw her. "This clothing suits you," he said. "Far better than the other. Though I do not believe anyone would ever mistake you for other than a warrior, no matter what you wore."

His regard threw her once more into confusion, which she concealed. Regardless of her respect for Valencia, she did not wish to show weakness, even in such a small way as acknowledging his apparent attraction to her. "I thank you for the compliment," she said.

"And here is Mr. Hanley. Let us ride," Valencia said.

Amaya turned to see Edmund approaching, his walk no longer that of the careless fop, but powerful, his long stride suggesting contained strength. He was dressed much as she was, in trousers and a rough coat that strained somewhat across shoulders whose breadth Amaya had never noticed before. She had expected him to look odd, dressed like a laborer instead of a gentleman, but the rough garb suited him well. It was now not at all difficult to picture him as the skilled amateur pugilist he was.

Edmund nodded to Valencia as he neared their little group. "And where do we ride, sir?" he said.

"South and west," said Valencia, "as far as we can get this afternoon. I fear we will sleep rough tonight. My apologies to the lady."

Amaya laughed. "I have slept rough, as you say, for most of my adult life. You need not fear for me."

"It is your reputation I fear for." Valencia looked solemn. "Your aid is so welcome I cannot bring myself to reject it simply on the grounds that this is not what fine ladies do."

"I am no fine lady, Mr. Valencia, and this is what I wish to do." Amaya walked to where the horse she had ridden earlier that day stood, its saddle now a conventional one. Mounting was so much easier when one wore trousers.

"Drawing room manners are irrelevant in this situation, where we ride in the cause of justice," Edmund said. He, too, mounted, more gracefully than Amaya had, and added, "But I doubt anyone who might care about Miss Salazar's behavior will ever discover what we have done."

His words struck Amaya as odd. A tendril of doubt threaded its way into her heart. Edmund had always been more careful than she to guard her reputation, and for him to dismiss it as drawing room manners seemed strange. She said, "Perhaps I have been too hasty."

"Hasty? In what way?" Valencia asked. He brought his horse close beside her. "You know what must be done."

"Yes, but..." Her eye fell on the curly-haired woman, who was engaged in saddling a piebald gelding and did not seem to be paying attention to the conversation. Another rush of confidence swept over her, and she let out a long breath. "No, you are correct. I care nothing for the opinion of others, so long as I know my motivations to be pure."

Valencia smiled and put a hand briefly over hers where they held the reins. "That is good." He wheeled away and approached the curly-haired woman. "Ned, make haste. We lose daylight when we delay."

The woman, Ned, nodded curtly and swung herself into the saddle. Valencia shouted a command, and the rest of his men mounted and fell into a loose grouping around their leader. "Ride out!" Valencia exclaimed, and Amaya and Edmund hurried to bring up the rear of the procession.

"This is exhilarating," Amaya said. "I wonder what he will have us do."

"I find I care not, so long as I have a part in defeating this enemy," Edmund said.

Amaya lowered her voice. "Did you hear what he called that young woman?"

"Ned. That is not a Spanish name. I am increasingly curious about her."

"He must not know she is female." Amaya covered her mouth and nose with the neckcloth; the many horses riding before them kicked up a cloud of dust.

Edmund mimicked her gesture. "Or he knows, and does not wish to reveal her to the rest."

"That is possible." Amaya looked ahead to where Ned rode close beside Valencia. "I will try to speak to her. She is a mystery, and I dislike mysteries."

They rode south and west along the road, nearly facing the setting sun, until Amaya's posterior and legs ached from the unaccustomed exertion. Rather than alter her body to ease the pain, she decided to endure until they stopped for the night. Touching the horse to assess its condition revealed that it was not tired or in pain. It was a fine animal, she concluded, capable of running harder than she currently demanded, and some of her resistance to riding fled.

After almost two hours, they left the road to ride across the broad, dry plains that lay south of the Salazar lands. More trees grew here, sprawling and low enough that the party could not ride beneath them. The setting sun cast their shadows across the riders, however, and the evening was cool and comfortable after the heat of the day. Even the splotches of grey-green scrub that dotted the fields seemed less sere.

They came out of the fields into a series of low hills, brown and grey with bare earth and stones, and made their way west along their base. Amaya wished she had a slouching, wide-brimmed hat like most of Valencia's men had, to shield her eyes from the direct glare of the setting sun. Altering her eyes to provide protection was impractical, as it took far too long to Shape an inner membrane, and by the time she had done it, the sun would have set. So she shielded her eyes with her hand and did her best to look elsewhere.

Just as the sun's curve began to dip below the horizon, Valencia called a halt and gathered the riders around him. "My Seers believe Solano and his men to have taken shelter at his estate on the far side of these hills," he said. "We will discover the truth, and then we will attack. Until then, rest and eat. We must not lose strength just as we need it most."

The men dismounted and spread out, some caring for horses, others bringing out short loaves of bread and hunks of pale yellow cheese. Amaya brought her horse close to Valencia, who sat as if he were waiting for her. "How will you learn if Solano is there?"

"We will send scouts after the sun sets," Valencia said. "Then we will use the darkness to cover our assault."

"I understand," Amaya said. "I will go."

Valencia's brow furrowed. "That is not necessary."

"I assure you I am far more experienced at moving silently in darkness than any of your men, however skilled they may be.

LIBERATING FIGHT

And I am capable of seeing in very little light. You need only tell me what to look for, and I will find it."

Valencia regarded her with that steady, intent look for a long moment. "You should not go alone," he finally said.

"She will not," Edmund said. "I will accompany her."

Valencia turned his intent look on Edmund, and his lips twitched as if he were containing a smile. "You, sir?"

"Well should you laugh," Edmund said. "I know what I appear to be. But my role within the government is not only that of translator. I have been a spy these last five years, and I am accomplished at concealing myself in the course of discovering information others would rather keep hidden. I will not impede Miss Salazar on this task."

Surprise nearly made Amaya lose her seat. Edmund, a spy? It explained so much about the discrepancy in his character, his moments of seriousness, his unexpected talent for observation. But even she knew spying was serious, secret business. "Edmund, surely you should not tell us this," she said, feeling uncertain.

"Concealment is the nature of being a spy, that is true. But in this company, we must all trust one another." Edmund removed the cloth from around his neck and wiped his forehead, leaving a damp brownish smear from the dust. "And I wish to make my full skills available to Mr. Valencia and his cause."

"Very well," Valencia said. "We must verify that Solano himself is present. It will do us no good to kill his men if we cannot also destroy him. You must not enter the house, as even you, Miss Salazar, cannot be invisible. Instead, you will look for his horse. She is a piebald mare whose pattern is quite distinctive. Her head and throat are black, and her front legs and chest and shoulders are white, with one large black patch on her left side near her withers. She will be the only piebald horse in the stables. Find her, and bring word."

Amaya nodded. "We will go when the sun sets."

Edmund helped her care for her horse and remove its tack. In a low voice, he said, "I apologize for keeping that secret, but I am certain you see the need for it."

"I do, which is why I am so astonished that you should have revealed it at all. Surely your superiors will be angry with you, because how can you go on spying when your identity is known?" Amaya rubbed the horse down with a soft cloth as he showed her.

"I feel confident Mr. Valencia will not share it with anyone," Edmund said, and such was the confidence that rang through his voice Amaya's objections faded like the others. "Do you not feel it, that rightness and surety in this cause? It surges through me, and I know I can achieve anything."

Amaya nodded. "I have never felt so sure of anything. Returning to Madrid will feel dull by comparison."

Edmund turned away. "Perhaps we will not return to Madrid."

"Oh, but—I have a responsibility to Elinor." But even as she said this, a twinge of anxiety touched Amaya's heart at the idea of abandoning Valencia. There was so much good to be done, and Madrid must have many childbed attendants; it was not as if Elinor would be alone. "I believe she would understand," she said, and the anxiety lessened.

They ate standing up, hunks of bread that must have come from Graciela's kitchen and fist-sized lumps of cheese. It all tasted as wonderful as food does when one eats it out of doors, seasoned by Amaya's knowledge that soon she would do what she believed she had left behind forever. She watched the stars come out, prickling the dark blue sky. The moon would not rise for several hours. Conditions were ideal for concealment and swift, silent movement.

As she watched, she gradually Shaped her eyes to take in what little light there was. She could not see as perfectly as in daylight, but nearby shapes were clear. Then she Shaped Edmund's eyes as well. It was something she had done for her fellow jaguar warriors many times. For the first time, the memory was warm and pleasant, not a jagged pain in her chest. They were gone. She remained. And life went on.

When the last glow of light had faded from the western sky, Amaya and Edmund set out toward the hills. They kept to the low ground as best they could at first, making as straight a line as possible through the rises. Life in the mountains of Peru had taught Amaya the foolishness of silhouetting oneself against the sky at the top of a hill, and she led the way, gesturing occasionally to Edmund to follow her path exactly.

She slowly Shaped her muscles as they ran, building her arms and shoulders to more comfortably fill her oversized coat. Jaguar warriors depended more on speed than on muscular bulk to kill their prey, but she would not disdain any weapon in a fight where she did not know what to expect of her enemy. Guns, yes, but she intended to take the fight to them, and strength could not help but benefit her.

It took some time to pass through the hills, but eventually the slopes flattened out, and Amaya and Edmund slowed to observe the ground ahead. In the distance, perhaps five hundred *rikras* away—Amaya still could not accurately assess distances in European measure—warm lights flickered, like fallen stars. The lights were too distant to shed illumination on their surroundings, but Edmund said, "That must be the estate. It is larger than I imagined."

"Now is when we must be stealthiest," Amaya said. "There will be sentries posted."

Edmund nodded, his attention still on the distant lights. "We should pass to the left or right rather than approaching directly. That will permit us to see most of the estate without nearing it too closely."

"I agree. Stay close."

Amaya led the way again, hunched over to give any observers less of a profile to identify as human and therefore dangerous. Her heart beat steadily, the breath flowed in and out of her lungs just quickly enough, and she let the night breezes pass over her skin and listened to what news they might bring. Nothing. She might have been alone on the plains, because Edmund moved as silently as she did. A memory occurred to her of Edmund taking her by surprise, of how often he was able to approach her without her knowing, and she smiled. Now his skills made sense.

She heard footsteps—heavy boots, crushing the dry grass underfoot, not trying to be stealthy—and signaled to Edmund to halt. Crouching on the balls of her feet, she scanned the distance, looking for the sentry. There, to the right. He walked back and forth, covering the distance of perhaps two *rikras* before returning to his starting point. He carried a musket and wore a pistol at his hip. Amaya considered subduing him, but decided against it. If the sentries maintained contact with one another, one of the sentries finding his companion unconscious or dead would alert the estate to the presence of enemies. She gestured to Edmund, and they worked their way around the sentry to the left.

They saw no more watchers until the estate was visible as a poorly-lit building. Like the Salazar house, Solano's residence was low to the ground, only one story. Lights glowed in a few of the windows as well as from lanterns tied to posts some short distance from the house. They revealed stone construction similar to that of Fernándo's house, flat rocks embedded in thick white mortar, though without the vines that shrouded those walls. This gave the house a naked look as well as making it appear smaller, though Amaya's assessment of the proportions said the houses were almost the same size.

Edmund gripped Amaya's elbow to get her attention. He gestured to the left. Amaya nodded and headed in that direction. The night was so still and silent she could not believe no one had heard their breathing, though of course no one not a Shaper was capable of perceiving such faint sounds. Even the background shrill whine of a million insects such as Amaya had heard in her bedroom in Fernándo's house was absent. There was only Amaya and Edmund and—but there was another sentry, this one stationary and positioned beneath one of the lantern posts.

Now Amaya moved even more slowly. She was certain of her ability to silence the sentry, but the lantern cast a circle of light that would make her attack obvious were someone to look out of the house, or across the field, at the wrong time. She made a wide circuit around the house, staying well out of the light, until she and Edmund had left the sentry behind.

She paused, surveying her surroundings. They had reached the side of the house, which had no windows, and beyond that, a rail fence extended from the house into darkness. Edmund had already moved on and was gesturing to her to advance. When she joined him, she saw the rail fence connected to another fence to enclose a yard lit by only one lantern. The smell of horses drifted toward her on the breeze. Amaya squinted, and saw movement in the dark confines of a long shed open along one side.

Edmund made as if to advance again, and Amaya held up a hand, palm out, in a warding gesture. She sniffed the air. Horses, manure, and a fainter, sour smell of an unwashed human body. Yet she saw no one in the stable yard.

She pressed her lips nearly to Edmund's ear. "Someone is here," she whispered, "follow slowly," and crept, crouched nearly on her hands as well as her feet, toward the shed. The scent of unwashed male human grew stronger. Then she froze as a shadow detached from the depths of the shed and ambled across the stable yard. He was bulky, with a large stomach and sloping shoulders, and his thick beard obscured much of his face. He crossed to the rail fence and rested his elbows on it, leaning forward in a relaxed way.

Amaya and Edmund exchanged frustrated glances. The one light did not extend into the shed where the horses were. They would have to enter the stable yard to learn if Solano's horse was present. And as tempting as it was to remove this man permanently, without knowing whether his absence would be noted, they might simply be alerting Solano to the presence of an enemy.

Amaya scanned her surroundings once more, then gestured to Edmund and crept closer to the shed. The man continued oblivious to their presence, but assuming he would stay that way was foolishness. When they reached the shed, and were as far from the man as they could get without losing sight of him, Amaya once more whispered in Edmund's ear, "Watch him. I will look at the horses."

Edmund shook his head vigorously. "If you enter the stable, you may disturb them, and they will rouse the bandits," he whispered back. "Stay here. I have an idea." He vanished around the back of the shed before she could protest. Annoyed, she kept a close eye on the bandit, who seemed rooted to the spot. If only he would leave!

She heard Edmund moving, very faintly, and then all was once more still. The bandit stood upright and stretched. Then he turned and walked back toward the shed.

Slowly, so as not to make a motion that would draw attention to herself, Amaya pressed against the side of the shed and ducked her head to conceal the gleam of her eyes. The man moved without haste and without trying to be silent—of course for him there was no point, as he need not conceal himself from the horses. The noise of his feet on the packed earth obscured whatever noise Edmund was making, if any.

The bandit noisily cleared his throat and spat a great gob of saliva into the darkness. It landed barely a handspan beyond Amaya's foot. She held still. The bandit stopped, scratched himself in an intimate location, and then entered the shed. Amaya's heart beat too fast, and she slowed it, though not much because she wanted her body to be ready to act. Her claws slid out, ready to attack. If this man saw her or Edmund, she would kill him and risk his body being discovered.

Within the shed, a horse let out a sleepy murmur. "That's right, be easy, little one," the man said in a deep bass rumble. Amaya rolled her eyes. A horse lover. And one who might spend the entire night caring for their needs even though they were all asleep.

Someone touched her elbow. Discipline kept her from shrieking in surprise, but she did let out one startled breath she hoped no one noticed. Edmund tugged on her elbow and indicated with a jerk of his head that she should follow him.

They continued on the way they had been going, around the back of the shed and to the farthest point of the house. There, safely concealed by darkness, Edmund whispered, "The horse is there. I saw it clearly."

"How did you do that?"

"There are gaps in the walls, some of them large enough for one to put one's head through. Though I nearly gave myself away when that man returned and I was there, face exposed for anyone to see. It was fortunate he did not look beyond the horse he spoke to."

"Very well. I believe we should circle this place and see if we cannot get a sense of how many bandits there are. That knowledge will be useful."

They saw four more men standing sentry around the house, and heard the murmur of conversation punctuated by shouts for wine coming from beyond the open front door. Amaya made Edmund wait a full five minutes while she teased out individual voices, finally concluding there were at least fifteen men within the house. Then the two of them made their way back to the hills, where they ran.

Edmund was panting by the time they left the hills behind and saw the fires indicating Valencia's camp. They came to a stop by mutual unspoken agreement and watched the fires burn. "I envy you," Edmund said, putting a hand on Amaya's shoulder. "I believe you could run forever."

"Not forever," Amaya said with a smile. Her breathing was only slightly more rapid than usual, and her arms and legs felt warm and comfortably loose. She put her hand over Edmund's. At that moment, they were not just friends, but companions in battle, and the idea warmed her heart as well.

Edmund's face sobered. "Amaya," he said, "I do not..."

She waited for him to complete his sentence, but instead his hand gripped her shoulder more tightly. His nearness made her feel peculiar; it was not the discomfort she felt when Valencia looked at her, but something deeper and more satisfying, as if she were returning home after a long absence. She became aware of his hand beneath hers, how well-shaped and strong it was, and withdrew her hand, feeling shaken and uncertain as to why.

Edmund shook his head. "We must report to Mr. Valencia," he said, letting his hand fall to his side. "I find myself eager to return to Solano's estate. I do not love bloodshed, but he must not be permitted to attack any more innocents."

Amaya glanced over her shoulder as if she could see through the hills to the distant house and the men surrounding it. "He will learn the folly of attacking a Salazar," she said, and did not know if she meant Fernándo or herself.

CHAPTER 14
IN WHICH BATTLE IS JOINED

Valencia was crouched beside one of the fires when they approached. He rose and came toward them with his hands outstretched. "You return," he said. "With good news, I hope?"

"Good news," Amaya said. "Solano is there. We judge there to be at least twenty men in the house and surrounding it."

Valencia's eyes widened. "More than I asked. Thank you. Everyone, prepare to travel," he said, raising his voice so it carried to the far edges of the camp. "We will not ride, and a few of you will remain here to watch the horses and tend the fire."

As he spoke these words, three of the four large fires simply died out, extinguished as abruptly as if they had been mirages. Valencia had made no gesture, shown no sign that he had put out the fires. Amaya remembered watching Elinor manipulate fire and how she had behaved exactly the same, as if the fire were an extension of her and she thought no more of shaping it than another might think of lifting a hand to open a door. The memory of Elinor made her feel guilty for a moment, and then the guilty feeling left Amaya, and she remembered that Elinor would have many others on hand to assist her, and likely would not miss Amaya at all.

Valencia led the way into the hills, striding as confidently as a king with Amaya and Edmund close behind. Now that she did not have to worry about remaining unseen, or Shaping her body to withstand an extended run, Amaya was able to appreciate things she had barely noticed before: the soft dusty scent of the dry earth; the feel of the night breezes against her face; the richness of the blue-black sky arching overhead. It was a beautiful night, one it seemed a shame to ruin with bloodshed. And yet that was their intent.

When they came out of the hills, Valencia signaled a halt. "Half a mile to our destination," he said. "Wait to engage the enemy until my signal. We wish to conceal our presence as long as possible."

"What signal, sir?" Edmund asked.

Valencia smiled. "The signal only El Encendedor may give."

Now they ran, swiftly if not silently, though Amaya amused herself by stepping lightly so as to leave few tracks. The dark, hunched shape of the house loomed before them, as did another, shorter, narrower shape. Amaya saw the sentry before the others did and darted ahead, bearing the man to the ground and tearing out his throat before he could shout a warning.

Then the house erupted in flames.

Amaya rose, her fingers and claws bloody, and stared in astonishment. Elinor was reticent about the extent of her talent, and Amaya did not know how Valencia's talent compared to that of other Extraordinary Scorchers, whether distance and intensity mattered. All she knew was that the entire roof was on fire, the whole span of it, and beneath the crackling and roaring of the flame she heard men's screams of terror.

Soon, men flooded out of the house—into a rain of musket and pistol fire from Valencia's men. Some of the bandits fell back into the burning house, where the fire had spread from the roof to the wooden frame of the door; others who avoided the gunfire ran forward to engage with Valencia's men. Amaya saw Edmund drop his opponent with a well-timed fist to the jaw just before someone was upon her. She ducked, punched the man in the stomach, and raked her claws across his face, making him scream. He fell to his knees, and Amaya took his head in both hands and twisted, snapping his neck. She dropped his body and ran on, searching for another victim.

She could no longer hear anything over the noise of the fire and the screams of dying men. Such sounds told her nothing; now she depended on her eyes and the indefinable sense of her surroundings that rose from touch and scent combined. She stripped out of her coat to free her arms, snapped it into the face of someone who brought his gun to bear on her, and bore him to the ground. Wrenching the gun from his grip, she brought its butt down to smash his face. She sprang from his lifeless body and raced for the burning door, where men continued to emerge.

One man aimed a pistol at her. She dove, turned her dive into a roll, and a shot cracked the night over her head. Another shot followed that one immediately, and pain creased her back, but she ignored it. She ended her roll on her feet and took two steps to grab the shooter around the waist and knock the pistol from his hand.

The man gasped and flung his hands up. "Spare me!" he begged. "I will give you anything you require, everything I have—just spare my life!" He let his second pistol fall.

Amaya pressed her claws against the throbbing vein in his throat. "You beg for mercy after what you have done?" she said, breathing heavily. She hated it when an enemy disarmed himself in a plea for mercy. Killing an unarmed man went against all her instincts.

The man swallowed. His eyes were white and terrified, focused on her as if he might prevent her killing him by the power of his gaze. "We have done nothing," he said.

Amaya cut him off. "You raided the Salazar estate and killed my friend. That is hardly 'nothing.'"

Confusion touched his face. "You are mistaken," he said. "We have not attacked anyone. We live in peace with our neighbors. I swear this on my life."

Amaya snarled. "You lie. You are my enemy."

The man jerked as if he wanted to shake his head in denial, but feared her claws. "El Encendedor told me what would happen if I did not follow him. He is terrible in his wrath. Please, let me flee. Show mercy."

Someone approached them, someone who smelled of smoke. "Enrico Solano," Valencia said. "I warned you what would happen if you continued to attack the innocent."

Solano's gaze never left Amaya's face. "Please," he whispered. "Do not leave me to him. Kill me now."

Amaya released her grip on Solano's chest and stood. "He says he did not attack Don Fernándo," she said. "Why would he lie?"

Valencia took her elbow and drew her away from the man lying on the ground. "Does a villain need a reason to lie?"

"No, but he knows we know what he has done, and there is no point in lying about it." Amaya glanced over her shoulder at Solano, who lay rigid, his hands clenched and his face distorted as if in preparation for receiving a blow.

"His lies do not concern me," Valencia said. "Only freedom and justice."

Solano burst into flame, screaming.

Amaya gasped. The white heat of the fire battered at her, and Solano's screams cut to her heart. She took half a step toward the man and was restrained by Valencia's hand, still gripping her elbow. She turned to face Valencia. The man's handsome face was impassive, as if none of this had anything to do with him. Solano thrashed, rolled a short distance, and collapsed, still burning. The fire ignited the dry grass beneath him and died as abruptly as fire dropped into water does.

Valencia closed his eyes briefly. "And so it ends," he said.

Amaya found herself breathing far too rapidly, as if even she had reached her physical limit. "You burned him," she said.

"I destroyed an enemy of freedom," Valencia said, still in that distant, impassive way. He opened his eyes and looked at her. "As you have done. I watched you fight. You are extraordinary, and not just in your talent. I have never seen anyone more skilled at dealing death than you are. Thank you for joining my cause."

The sense of rightness that had carried Amaya all this way had faded into a faint memory. "But surely," she began, hesitated, then said, "Suppose you were wrong? Suppose Solano was telling the truth?"

Valencia laughed. "Truth, from that liar? Miss Salazar, you are new to Spain, and you do not know the depredations Enrico Solano has wreaked upon this country. And if he was not the one who attacked your grandfather's home? What of it? We have rid the world of a villain regardless."

"Then you do not believe his men killed Mrs. Paget."

"No, I believe it. But it is irrelevant." Valencia released Amaya and ran his hand through his hair, pushing it back from his sweaty forehead. "Take heart, Miss Salazar. You have done a good deed, you and your companion. He surprised me. I had not believed him anything but a fop and a useless hanger-on."

"Mr. Hanley is full of surprises," Amaya said. She looked around, searching the landscape that was hellishly lit by the burning house. She did not see Edmund anywhere, and her heart ached with worry and an inexplicable sorrow.

"We will return to the camp," Valencia said. Abruptly the fire —all the fires—extinguished, leaving Amaya blinking in the darkness as her eyes tried to adjust. "Tomorrow we ride east, to Aranjuez. I wish to show you my country, Miss Salazar, and show you what it is you have chosen to defend."

Amaya nodded. The powerful surety no longer flooded her veins; all that was left was a lingering sense that what they were doing was right. But the smell of charred flesh lingered in her nostrils for miles.

***

Edmund found her as their company emerged from the hills some distance from the lone fire left burning at their camp. "You are well?" he asked.

"Well enough. I always feel hollow after a fight in which I take lives. It is not a feeling I understand, since I never feel guilt over killing someone who would have killed me or mine. A good night's sleep will restore me."

"I have never seen an Extraordinary Scorcher in battle before. It was awe-inspiring, and terrifying." Edmund wiped soot from his face, leaving it streaky and dark. "I understand now why Lady Enderleigh is so feared."

"Elinor would never…" Amaya could not finish that sentence. Elinor had certainly done as Valencia had, killed in battle, and Amaya did not hate her for it, so why should she feel such doubt over Valencia's actions? "We succeeded," she said instead.

"That we did." Edmund stopped, forcing Amaya to stop as

well. The filth streaking his face could not conceal a look of concern. "You do not have doubts?"

Amaya shook her head. "It is as I said, that I feel strange after a fight. I feel in my heart we have done well tonight. And done good, which is more important."

Edmund gripped her shoulder briefly before releasing her. "And tomorrow we ride east, I understand. I feel eager to follow where Mr. Valencia leads."

"As do I," Amaya said, and a flash of uncertainty struck her. In half a breath, it disappeared, leaving her doubting what she had felt. But that instant prompted her to say, "Perhaps we should send word to Madrid of what has happened."

"That is unnecessary," Edmund said. "We will not be gone much longer than the ten days we agreed upon. Barely long enough for anyone to grow concerned. And whom would we send? We will finish the task, and return with glorious tales of adventure and battle." He grinned. "You did not believe this trip would be so exciting, did you?"

Amaya began walking again. "I did not expect anything of it. Perhaps my imagination is faulty."

"I doubt anyone could imagine what has happened to us," Edmund said.

※

THE FOLLOWING MORNING DAWNED CLEAR AND WARM AND windy, sweeping the scent of growing crops toward them. Amaya ate her small breakfast of porridge and bread with enjoyment. As she had predicted, a night's sleep whisked away her doubts, and she felt once more the confidence and surety that had propelled her all this way.

The curly-haired woman, Ned, neared the fire Amaya

crouched at alone, lugging a coffee pot big enough to serve an army. On impulse, Amaya called out, "Ned."

Ned jerked in surprise and stopped some ten armlengths away. Her wide, blue-grey eyes regarded Amaya with hostility Amaya could not explain. She ignored her discomfort in the face of that hostility and said, "May I have some?" She did not care for coffee, but it seemed the only way to have a word with the mysterious woman.

Ned stared at her in silence for a few moments. Just as Amaya was sure Ned would simply walk away, the woman came toward Amaya and indicated that Amaya should hold her cup ready. Amaya dumped the last of the water it held and extended the cup, and Ned filled it. The heat of the beverage warmed Amaya's hands.

As Ned finished and prepared to walk away, another impulse seized Amaya. "I know your secret," she said.

To her surprise, Ned recoiled as if Amaya had struck her. The pot slipped from one hand, lurching and sloshing and spilling coffee on the ground. Amaya had never seen anyone so terrified. It filled her with unexpected compassion despite the woman's hostility.

"No, please, do not be afraid. I would never tell," she assured her.

Ned's breathing was rapid, her pupils dilated. She said nothing. Amaya continued, "I do not know why you choose to pretend to be male, but I promise I will not give away your secret."

Ned's shoulders relaxed slightly, and her look of fear vanished, replaced by impassivity. She set the coffee pot on the ground carefully and said, "And I am to be grateful to you for this?"

"No." Amaya wished she understood why Ned seemed to

hate her. "It was a chance discovery—" she chose not to say it had actually been Edmund's discovery— "and one I do not believe I am entitled to share. But I wondered…"

Now Ned looked curious. "Wondered, what?"

"I wondered," Amaya said, "why you need the disguise. You have seen how Mr. Valencia treats me. He would not think less of you for being female."

"Alejandro knows all my secrets," Ned said. "But I am no Extraordinary Shaper. 'Tis easier that the others believe me male, so I need not fight a constant battle against my comrades who believe a woman is easy prey." She smiled, rather bitterly. "I suppose it is kind of you to be concerned about my self-worth."

"You intrigue me," Amaya said. "You are not Spanish, you are not male, so how did you come to be here?"

Ned picked up the coffee pot. "That is none of your concern," she said, but without the hostility that had marked her previous words. "We are not friends."

"No, we are not," Amaya said, feeling stung. "But I see no reason we should not be."

Ned's eyes narrowed. She seemed to be searching for more words. Then, in English, she said, "My name is Jennet," and hurried away before Amaya could respond.

Amaya watched her go, wondering at that interaction. It was true, they were not friends and did not need to be, but Amaya's curiosity, once roused, was hard to lay to rest. Jennet. She had never heard such a name before, though the faint accent in which Jennet had spoken English reminded her of Dr. Macrae. She determined at once that she would make Jennet like her. Then perhaps the woman would be forthcoming about her mystery.

She stood and went in search of Edmund, whom she found laughing and joking with several of Valencia's men. He saluted her with his coffee cup as she approached and left the group to join her. "What a glorious day," he said. "I swear I could ride for days and never tire. Did you sleep well?"

"I did." They were too close to the men for Amaya to share what she had learned about the mysterious curly-haired woman. "Walk with me?"

Edmund shrugged. "We will leave soon, and there is little time for a walk, but whatever my lady wishes," he said with a gallant bow that made Amaya smile.

"You are in rare fine spirits," she said when they were some distance from the others. "Edmund Hanley is not an early riser, and he rarely communicates in more than grunts before noon. Pray, what have you done with my friend?"

"I have never had such purpose before," Edmund said. "You feel it, do you not? That sense of rightness?"

"I do." Though she did not feel as elated as Edmund seemed to. "And I have made a discovery that will surprise you."

Edmund's jovial expression became pensive as she related her interaction with Jennet. "Astonishing," he said. "And you intend to dig to the bottom of her mystery."

"Would you not do the same? I feel she could be a friend."

"That may be, but if I were you, I would not be so sanguine about the prospects of my success. She looks at you as if she wishes to disembowel you."

"That is why it is such a challenge." Amaya stopped and put a hand on Edmund's sleeve. "She must be so lonely, never able to reveal her true self."

Edmund shook his head slowly, smiling. "I believe you see yourself in her, Amaya."

Amaya blinked. "Myself? How so?"

"So much of who you are must be concealed from polite society. Only a few of us see your true self." Edmund rested his hand atop hers. "If you feel compassion for this woman, it is because you know what it is to be hidden from the world."

Amaya looked away from his gaze to where their hands joined. She had rarely been so conscious of him, of how his hand was larger than hers and warmer, the palm slightly roughened in a way no gentleman's would be. "I hope that is not a criticism," she said, lightly so as to conceal the turmoil he had thrown her into.

"Of course not. Praise, and pride that someone such as you calls me 'friend.'" Edmund withdrew his hand, and a moment later Amaya let him go. "There, I see the signal for us to form up. Let us ride, and see what the day brings!"

They had walked quite a distance from the camp without Amaya noticing, and as she followed Edmund to where the horses waited, she could not help pondering his words. He was right, she concluded; she felt a kinship to Jennet, and the idea of befriending the prickly woman cheered her in a way unlike the warm glow of exhilaration that was her sense of Valencia's cause.

She mounted her horse and let it fall into line behind the others, with Edmund riding beside her. Ahead, Jennet rode next to Valencia as, Amaya suddenly realized, she always did. Amaya did not believe Jennet was Valencia's lover; they did not behave to one another in a loverly fashion. It was more as if Jennet were Valencia's lieutenant, quick to respond to his commands and first to ride where he ordered. More mysteries. Amaya flicked the reins, and her horse stepped out more smartly. She had all the time in the world to ferret those mysteries out.

CHAPTER 15

IN WHICH AMAYA AND EDMUND LEARN MORE OF THE GLORIOUS CAUSE

They arrived in Aranjuez at just after noon on the following day. Amaya had been content to ride at the rear, the dust notwithstanding, but as they set off, Valencia had sought her out, saying, "You will ride beside me, that you may see my country's beauty." So she rode at Valencia's left hand, Edmund on her left and Jennet on Valencia's right, and admired the countryside. Valencia was correct; Spain was beautiful with a stark, warm beauty that appealed to Amaya in a different way from England. The two could not have been more different, and yet Amaya liked them both. It would not be so terrible, she thought, to call Spain home.

They had followed the Tagus River, more or less, keeping a straight line where the river curved so that it flowed in and out of their sight. Amaya liked the sound it made as it washed along its banks, slower and quieter than the icy rivers that flowed from the mountain heights of Peru. She listened to its chatter and allowed the conversation Valencia and Edmund were having to flow past her unheeded.

"Do you not agree, Miss Salazar?"

She started. "I beg your pardon, Mr. Valencia, I was listening to the river," she said without thinking of how that must sound.

Valencia and Edmund laughed. "I cannot hear the river at all, from this distance," Edmund said. "It must be remarkable to be a Shaper, and tune one's ears to the most distant sounds."

Amaya glanced past Valencia to Jennet, whose rigid attention to the distant panorama told Amaya she was actually listening closely to this conversation. "I am certain every talent has aspects others might envy," she said.

"This is true," Valencia said. "I have great joy in my talent, and yet there is a part of me that wishes to be an Extraordinary Mover, to take to the skies whenever I wish."

"That would be my wish as well," Edmund said. "The power of flight is remarkable."

"I have never wished to have any talent but my own," Amaya said. Then, daringly, she said, "What is your opinion, Ned?"

Jennet flinched, casting a quick glance at Amaya, but said nothing. Valencia said, "You must excuse Ned; he is shy around strangers. You may yet make friends with him if you are willing to wait him out!" He laughed, and Jennet smiled mirthlessly before returning to her customary impassivity and dropping back a few steps so Amaya could no longer see her past Valencia. It was an intentional snub, but Amaya did not mind it. She was determined on befriending Jennet, however long it took.

"We were saying," Valencia said, "that it is unlikely Napoleon has given up his dream of conquest, just because the Duke of Wellington has swept across France. Say, rather, that he has gone into hiding to regroup and restore his forces. And that we must all be vigilant against his return."

"Which means, if the Spanish Army has stood down

LIBERATING FIGHT

according to King Ferdinand's wishes," Edmund said, "it is the guerrillas who must defend Spain against Napoleon's return."

Amaya eyed Edmund. His words no longer had the manic edge they had had before, but he was still more enthusiastic than she had ever heard him. "Do you suppose Napoleon will return to Spain?" she asked. "I believed him to be a Frenchman."

"He is Corsican, and therefore both French and not," Valencia said. "Spain has proved a tough nut for the Emperor to crack, but we have many more ports than France and a strong presence in Europe. When he has overrun France, he will assuredly come after Spain next. And we will be ready for him."

This did not strike Amaya as a conversation requiring her agreement, as it was clear Valencia and Edmund knew more of the matter than she did. So she said, "I am sure you will, but what of his Extraordinary Coercer talent? I understood such a talent to be nearly impossible to fight."

Valencia shrugged. "An Extraordinary Coercer is limited in his range and scope. Napoleon is powerful, true, but he can only Coerce so many people at a time."

Jennet had gradually come forward until Amaya could see her once more. Her continued attention to the distant hills suggested she was still listening closely. Amaya wished she might change places with Valencia, to converse with Jennet more directly. But that would likely make the woman shut down entirely.

"I do not know exactly what a Coercer's talent is," she said. "We had none amongst the Incas. There is not even a word in Quechua to express the idea."

"A Coercer's talent is to shape the emotions, and to some extent the thoughts, of others," Valencia said. "A Coercer can make someone feel anger, fear, desire, even love—any emotion imaginable, a Coercer can generate within one."

"That does not seem very powerful a talent. Surely it is obvious that such feeling is not real?"

"Not from what those who have been under a Coercer's thrall and been released say," Edmund said. "There is an element of Coercion that convinces the victim that their feelings are natural. And once Coerced, the unnatural emotion persists until the Coercion is removed or some other emotion takes its place."

"That is horrid, and I find it difficult to credit," Amaya said with a grimace.

"It is unlikely you will ever suffer such a fate, Miss Salazar," Valencia said. "And it is said there are those strong-minded enough to fight Coercion. It would not surprise me to discover you are one."

Amaya made herself meet his gaze without blushing. "I thank you for the compliment, sir."

"It is only the truth." Valencia's regard was warm, his smile a peculiarly knowing one, and a shiver ran through Amaya that she could not account for.

"Still, I wonder where Napoleon might have gone to ground," Edmund said. He seemed unconscious of what had passed between Amaya and Valencia. "There are very few places he might conceal himself without being given away."

"I have heard it rumored that he is in Paris, hiding in plain sight." Valencia looked away from Amaya, relieving her mind. "He has many followers whom he has not Coerced, and their loyalty is said to be unshakable."

"It is more likely he has retreated to some distant stronghold," Edmund said. "A country estate, or an island fortress."

"In either case, he cannot depend on Coercion without giving away his location. He must be plotting a grand return." Valencia brought his horse to a halt. "There, that is Aranjuez. I see the watermill—there, across the river, do you see?"

LIBERATING FIGHT

Amaya looked where he pointed and saw a wood and stone contraption perched beside a weir across the Tagus River. "What is a watermill?"

"It grinds wheat into flour. The force of the water propels it so it can work as tirelessly as a man cannot." Valencia flicked the reins, and they set out walking again. "It is beautiful because one may see it from the palace, and the kings of Spain have always insisted on being surrounded by beautiful things." Sarcasm tinged his words. "They ignore that which is unpleasant or ugly, which leads them to ignore the plight of their people. How I wish to rid the world of such thinking!"

"Surely you do not believe ordinary folk ugly, simply because their lives are not so refined as the nobility?" Amaya said.

"Certainly not. I mean that the nobility believe anything not fitting their aesthetic preferences is ugly. And poor folk do not have the luxury of fine clothing, or homes whose roofs do not leak in the rain." Valencia's jaw was set tight with anger. "The Cortes claimed they would prevent the king from abusing his power, but it was all a lie. Now we cannot depend on the government; we must strike for ourselves."

"The Cortes is the governing body that ruled while King Ferdinand was a captive in France?" Edmund said, relieving Amaya of the need to ask for clarification.

"Yes. The Cortes wrote a constitution that should have limited the king's power and awarded benefits to those who were not noble." Valencia let out a short bark of mirthless laughter. "Of course, the men of the Cortes are themselves noble, so why should it be a surprise that they wrote a document that favored themselves? Nobles, educated men, the endowed, the wealthy gentry, they all had a hand in writing themselves preferences. And again the common man gets nothing."

Amaya could not think of a response to this. Before meeting

King Ferdinand, she would have said it was right and reasonable for the king of a people to receive their adulation. The Sapa Inca was a god; should not his people worship him, and give everything they had into his possession? But Europeans did not believe their kings were gods, and having met Ferdinand, Amaya could understand why his subjects might be unwilling to let him exercise unnatural dominion over them. He had nothing of the Sapa Inca's power and presence.

"It is true such behavior is unjust," Edmund said. "In England, the law is intended to apply equally to all men. Whether that happens in practice is another matter. But the intent is there."

"Spain will not stand for this injustice any longer," Valencia said. "You will see, in Aranjuez, that I speak the truth."

Aranjuez was a green blotch on the landscape, masses of trees surrounding many buildings, with the Tagus a bright streak beside it. Valencia led his company into the city, whose streets looked as old as Madrid's and whose buildings resembled those of London. The sight made Amaya curious about whose decision it had been to build all these European cities alike. Surely someone, somewhere wished to impress upon a city its national character?

She had to admit the design was a sensible one. The walls of the houses and shops were straight, and they filled all the available space in an orderly fashion. They rose high above the streets, taking advantage of the vertical space to double the area people might use. Windows paned with glass dotted the façades of the finer houses, shining in the noon sunlight. It could not have been designed more perfectly to make Amaya feel once more a stranger. Edmund seemed unmoved by the splendor. Well, to him it was likely a commonplace.

The building Valencia ultimately brought them to was big enough to look to Amaya like a mansion, with its gabled roof and Spanish tiles combining to give it the appearance of a Spanish villa that had fought a war with an English manor. The stable yard could hold twice as many horsemen as rode with Valencia, and teemed with riders and stable hands making enough noise for an army.

Valencia dismounted and handed his reins to a young man whose awed expression said he knew who had come to the inn that day. "Is Rodrigo in?" Valencia asked.

The young man nodded. "Yes, sir, please go in, I am certain he will wish to speak to you."

Valencia gestured to Amaya and Edmund. "Join me. I would like you to meet my friend. He, too, is a champion of justice."

The inn's front door opened on a dark, narrow space Amaya had not expected, given the size of the building. She blinked rather than Shaping her eyes to see in the dimness, and made out two doors and a staircase before Valencia opened the left-hand door, saying over his shoulder, "Juan, fetch Mr. Cisneros, and I will sit with our guests in the private dining room."

The room beyond, a large, low-ceilinged room, was as brightly lit as the little entrance chamber was not, its many glass windows looking out on the stable yard. A dining table ringed with chairs, all made of some dark wood Amaya did not recognize, occupied the center of the room, with armchairs pulled up to smaller, round tables beneath the windows. The room smelled of dinner, of roast pork and chicken and new potatoes that might have come direct from Peru, they smelled so familiar.

Valencia pulled a chair away from the dining table and gestured to Amaya. "Please, be seated, Miss Salazar."

Amaya sat, amused at his good manners even though she was not garbed like a lady. Edmund and Valencia sat on either side of her, while Jennet took one of the armchairs. Amaya's amusement dwindled. She supposed, as Jennet was passing as male, Valencia could not give her the same courtesies he gave Amaya, but he ignored Jennet completely. Amaya could not understand their relationship. Not lovers, not friends; were Jennet not human, Amaya would have said Valencia saw her as a pet, or a support like a walking stick, something one depended upon but did not give the same respect one did another person.

The door swung open again. "Alejandro, my friend!" exclaimed the very large man who came through it. Valencia stood, smiling broadly, and the two men embraced with the heartiness of old friends who had not seen one another for years.

"Rodrigo, thank you for your welcome," Valencia said. "May I introduce my companions, Miss Salazar and Mr. Hanley. Miss Salazar is an Extraordinary Shaper, and she and Mr. Hanley are newly come to our cause."

"Salazar," Rodrigo said. "Not Don Fernándo?"

"I am his granddaughter, sir," Amaya said. She rose from her seat and extended her hand politely.

Rodrigo did not take it. His gaze surveyed her closely, as if her talent were visible on her skin and he wished to analyze it closely. "Extraordinary," he said. "What a blessing." Finally, he took her hand and bowed over it, somewhat clumsily as if he had little practice in doing so. His skin was damp and warm, and out of habit she surveyed his five *sunqu* and observed that Need was taxed nearly to breaking and Heart worked more rapidly than it should. She judged this was due to his physique and not because he was afraid of her, and released his hand with a polite smile.

"We will eat, and you will tell me of your great exploits,"

Rodrigo said, clapping Valencia heartily on the back. "Ned, join us, you need not sit in a corner."

Jennet rose and took a seat at the table as far from Rodrigo as she could manage. Amaya saw the way she looked at the man and judged this was on purpose. She smiled at Jennet, whose expression became briefly confused before settling back into displeasure.

"Rodrigo has long been a friend of the true Spain," Valencia said. "He was among those who captured the traitorous minister Godoy and forced him to resign his post, which led to the ouster of King Charles."

Rodrigo ducked his head and smiled, pleased and embarrassed at this praise. "I would that we had rid ourselves of Ferdinand as well," he said, "but even a revolution must have humble beginnings."

"We make progress. Enrico Solano will no longer plague Spain," Valencia said. "Though I regret that his men took three more lives before being destroyed."

Rodrigo's mouth drew down in a scowl. "Let us be grateful there will be no more. And of Don Balthasar?"

"Balthasar Rubio has gone to ground on his estate, and I judge we would lose many lives in a frontal assault. Even with the use of my talent." Valencia gestured at Amaya. "However, we may have an alternative solution."

Rodrigo turned his attention on Amaya. "And that is?"

"Miss Salazar has proven adept at stealthy reconnaissance." Valencia smiled at Amaya, once more that warm, admiring look that flustered her. "I believe she might be capable of infiltrating the estate and eliminating Don Balthasar."

Amaya's discomfort rose. "Mr. Valencia," she said, "I would appreciate it if you did not treat me as your weapon. Wishing to do good is one thing; killing someone not known to me on your direction is something else entirely."

Valencia's smile vanished. "I beg your pardon, Miss Salazar. I forget you do not know the extent of what you are fighting for. Please accept my apology."

A scraping noise from the end of the table caused Amaya to glance at Jennet. The woman had her fierce attention on Amaya, but at Amaya's look, Jennet lowered her head. Amaya looked back at Valencia. Once more the feeling of rightness in his cause surged through her. "I accept your apology," she said. "Now, who is this Don Balthasar, and why is he your enemy?"

"I have no enemies but the enemies of Spain," Valencia said, "and Don Balthasar is the worst of them. He is an Extraordinary Discerner, Count of Aranjuez and the king's deputy in this district."

"I believed all Extraordinary Discerners to be madmen, driven insane by their talent," Edmund said.

"There are some few who overcome the burden of feeling every emotion of every person they encounter. Don Balthasar is one such." Valencia had answered Edmund, but his attention was fully on Amaya. "He is canny and cruel and uses his talent to oppress the people. He knows when someone near him has even the slightest revolutionary feeling and does away with that person instantly. Even those whose desires are simply those of any man for freedom from oppression."

"That is terrible," Amaya breathed. "I know a Discerner can tell truth from lies, but I did not realize they could Discern one's deepest thoughts."

"Not thoughts," Edmund said, "but the emotions surrounding such thoughts. Don Balthasar must be skilled to identify someone's intent from how they feel. Unless he simply punishes at whim and uses his talent as justification."

"He has done both," Rodrigo said. "And his talent prohibits us from getting anyone close enough to him to kill him. Alejandro, what plan have you in mind?"

Valencia regarded Amaya again. "His estate is too large, and his people too numerous, for me to simply burn it to the ground. And there are many innocents who work for him, mostly under duress, who would suffer if I did. But Rodrigo is correct that Don Balthasar is aware of the intentions of those around him, and has defended against several assassins in the past."

"And yet you wish me to attempt it," Amaya said.

Valencia smiled. It was not the warm smile he had so often bestowed upon her; it was the look of a predator, one Amaya was familiar with because she had worn it so often herself. "No assassin is as deadly a fighter as you are, Miss Salazar. It will not matter if Don Balthasar knows you are there, because I am certain you are capable of killing anyone who stands between you and him."

Amaya did not like the predatory look on his face. "I," she began, then fell silent. The others said nothing, waiting for her to finish. "I am no assassin," she said. It was a word she knew from the novels Bess had pressed upon her, the ones filled with dread horror and violence. Amaya marveled that gentle Bess found such pleasure in them. "To take the life of a man I do not know—"

"Amaya," Edmund said, leaning forward, "you need not fear. If this Don Balthasar is half the villain Mr. Valencia says he is, you would be doing Spain a service. Think of all the men and women he has terrorized."

"Yes, and of those whose property he has claimed after driving their rightful heirs off the land," Rodrigo said. "I assure you, he is a dreadful villain."

"Your reticence does you credit," Valencia said. "You have a powerful thirst for justice, and justice dictates that one must never take life lightly." He pushed back his chair and rose. "Permit me to show you something that might convince you."

Amaya followed Valencia back into the stable yard, where he stopped a spotty lad crossing the hard-packed earth. "Where is Maria Consuela?"

The boy swallowed and pointed rather than answering verbally. Valencia nodded his thanks and walked around the corner. There, a side door hung open, from which emanated more of the delicious smells. Near the door stood an old stone well, its construction as sturdy as anything Amaya had ever seen. A young woman, barely more than a girl by either Incan or European standards, worked the windlass. As Valencia and Amaya approached, the dripping bucket hove into sight, and the girl hauled it onto the stone lip of the well.

"Maria Consuela, permit me to help," Valencia said. The girl started, took a step back from the well, and ducked her head as if frightened. Valencia lifted the bucket and set it on the ground beside her.

"Miss Salazar, this is Maria Consuela Gonzales," Valencia said. "Her father was a tenant on Don Balthasar's estate. Maria Consuela, show Miss Salazar your throat."

The girl hesitated. Then she lifted her chin far back, revealing a slim neck. Amaya gasped. A dark red slash of a scar at least a handspan in length curved around Maria Consuela's throat.

"Mr. Gonzales denied Don Balthasar what the lord deemed his rights," Valencia said in a low voice. "Don Balthasar's men attacked and slaughtered almost everyone in Mr. Gonzales's house. Maria Consuela was left for dead; it is a miracle she survived. But that miracle cost her her voice." Valencia put his hand on Amaya's shoulder and turned her to face him. "Do you see what it is I ask of you?"

Amaya could not stop staring at the girl's scarred throat. "I do," she said. "Tell me where to go, and I swear I will end that man's life."

CHAPTER 16

IN WHICH AMAYA'S DANCE OF DEATH ENDS IN AN UNEXPECTED CONFRONTATION

It was easy to find Don Balthasar's country estate, just as Valencia had said; there was only one road, and it led directly north from Aranjuez with no branching side roads. Valencia, Rodrigo, and Edmund accompanied Amaya as far as the outskirts of Aranjuez, from which she would begin her journey. Amaya declined the offer of an escort to the estate itself from Edmund, who did not look entirely happy that she was embarking on this quest alone, but understood the need.

He drew her aside as she was preparing to set out and said, "You will take care, yes?"

"Of course. Edmund, you do not believe I would take this step if I thought I could not succeed, do you?"

Edmund's face was still with concern. He shook his head. "No, but so much of this is unknown. Being informed about the estate's geography, and studying a map, are no substitute for seeing a thing in person."

"Which is why I shall survey the estate in detail before

attempting entry." Amaya gripped his hand tightly. "You know why I must do this."

"I do." Edmund put his other hand over their joined ones. "Amaya, I…"

She waited for him to finish, but he merely shook his head again and said, "There are things I wish to tell you, but they will wait for your return. Fare well, Amaya."

She nodded and released him. Saluting Valencia, she said, "I will return to the inn when the deed is finished. Do not go sleepless on my account."

"I doubt any of us could sleep knowing the errand you pursue," Valencia said with a smile. "Go with God, Miss Salazar."

Amaya cast a final look at Jennet, standing beside Valencia. Jennet's eyes were cast down, fixed on her boot tracing a loop in the dirt with its toe, and her fists were clenched tight at her sides. That Jennet might not meet her eyes, Amaya did not find surprising, but the young woman was the picture of uncertainty, and Amaya had never seen Jennet look uncertain in all the time she had known her. It was a mystery whose depths she could not afford to plumb, so she merely nodded and took off running along the northward road.

As she ran, she gradually Shaped her leg muscles to carry her swiftly and tirelessly along the road. Her lungs and heart were already tuned to the same rhythm, so after half a dozen *rikras*, she was running as fleetly as she ever had across the mountains of Peru.

It was a joy to run without fear of what European society would say, without the need to rein herself in to accommodate someone of lesser ability. At these times, she felt most connected to her five *sunqu* as they surged and thrummed within her, as if they were living creatures bound to her will. Being a Shaper felt like nothing else in the world.

With her pupils dilated to catch the faint light of the moonless sky, and her eyes Shaped to make better sense of what that light revealed, the landscape she ran through was pale with grasses burned yellow by the summer sun, with darker blotches where the spreading trees grew at random. She had admired the irregularity of the scene as they rode toward Aranjuez; now she examined the trees with an eye to concealing herself when she neared the estate. The trees did not grow closely enough together to provide true cover, but she was accustomed to making her way through the craggy, treeless heights of her mountain home, and this would be as good for hiding as fog by comparison.

Valencia had said the estate was five miles north of Aranjuez. Miles meant nothing to Amaya, and she did not know how to convert them to *rikras*, so she remained watchful for signs that she was approaching the estate. She noted that the trees were growing thicker and closer together after she had run for some six hundred heartbeats, and had just slowed to consider what this might mean when the road came out of the trees into a vast, empty space.

And there it was, a house well lit by lanterns, its tiled, gently peaked roofs a slightly darker contrast to the white walls turned yellow by flame. To the right stood a much smaller building with the same gently peaked roof. The road continued to the house through a wide, treeless plain that Amaya guessed had been deliberately cleared, to give those at the house unimpeded sight of any approaching attackers. It gave the estate the appearance of being encroached upon on all sides by a forest, though in truth, the trees did not grow very thickly in their ring around the house. More trees grew near the building, only a few, nothing that would interfere with line of sight.

Two men bearing long guns strolled back and forth in front

of the house, guarding the long, pillared portico. The front door, visible in the portico's shadow thanks to two lanterns flanking its doorposts, looked massive and ominous, like the guardian to a villain's fortress high in the mountains. Amaya shook away this fancy, product of more of Bess's books, and crouched low so as not to be seen by the sentries. She saw no one other than the two men, but it was likely they had compatriots on the far side.

Keeping close to the tree line, she circled the estate, making note of anything that might prove useful. Don Balthasar was a sneaky man, she concluded, suspicious and clever. He had thought of almost everything: lanterns lit every part of the estate's walls; the trees near the house, which would provide shade during the day, were close enough to the building that anyone hiding there would have to take great care not to be seen; and there were, in fact, two more sentries guarding the rear of the house. It was actually a courtyard formed by two ells extending back from the main house, paved with light-colored stones and centering on a fountain that flowed sluggishly, barely visible from Amaya's perspective. The men patrolled outside it rather than entering the courtyard.

When she had circled the entire estate, Amaya crouched in the shelter of a low, spreading tree and considered what she knew. Europeans had a tendency to put more effort into guarding the front door of a house than the back, even if the back were an easier entry. Amaya's first instinct was to approach the rear of the house for this reason. But her assessment of Don Balthasar's personality suggested that he was not a typical European.

She watched the men at the front of the house, counting their steps. One moved faster than the other, making their circuits irregular. This meant there were times when both men were out of sight of one another around the corners of the house. And she had seen that the man at the back right corner never ventured around to the side of the house, but satisfied himself with a quick glance in that direction. She would make her move there.

She crept around to the best vantage: a place where the ring of trees came closest to the house, across from a clump of trees next to the estate that was slightly thicker than most. She waited. The man at the rear of the house reached the end of his circuit, paused to look along the house's side, and turned back. Two heartbeats later, the man at the front reached the corner and took a few steps along the side facing Amaya. He paused for what felt like an eternity, then turned and walked away. Amaya rose and sprinted for the trees beside the house.

She did not run as fast as she was capable, feeling the need to remain silent, but it took only ten heartbeats for her to cross the distance, faster than any horse, faster than a jaguar after its prey. Breathing heavily, she crouched within the shelter of the trees and waited again.

Presently, she heard the man at the rear make his usual stop and turn around again. This time, it took more than four heartbeats for the man at the front to appear. He walked toward Amaya's hiding place. Just as he turned his back on her, Amaya leapt.

She bore him to the ground with her arm across his mouth and her other hand wrapped around his throat. A silent command to his Sense *sunqu* sent a pulse through all his nerves, paralyzing him and silencing him. The man stiffened into perfect rigidity. Amaya lifted him over one shoulder and swiftly hid him beneath the tree where she had waited, then ran for the corner of the house and peered around it. The other sentry had not yet turned back to complete his circuit. By her count, he would notice his partner was gone well before the man at the rear came back to glance this way.

The sentry turned and walked toward her. She could tell the moment he became suspicious because his steps slowed and he looked off toward the distant ring of trees, searching. Amaya held her breath. Now was when she would learn how truly devious Don Balthasar was. If *she* gave these men orders, those orders would be to raise the alarm if anything unusual happened. She hoped this sentry was cautious enough to come looking for his partner before making a stir.

"Francisco?" the sentry said in a loud whisper. "Francisco, what have you found?"

Good. He had jumped to conclusions that would get him killed. Amaya waited until he was close to the corner, then jumped. He dropped as easily as the first, and Amaya took a moment to make sure of him before returning to the corner and waiting for the man at the rear to make his usual stop.

This time, he paused longer than before. Amaya cast a swift glance over the tree where her paralyzed victim lay, suddenly certain that despite all her care, this other sentry could see his fallen companion. Then the man came along the side of the house toward the front.

Amaya's claws slid out involuntarily, though she hardly needed them. She watched him approach, step by step. Her fears aside, she had concealed the paralyzed man well enough, but only from someone approaching from the front of the house. This fool was going to ruin all her plans.

The man paused. He looked around, peering past the trees toward the open plain. Then he turned and headed back the way he had come.

Amaya did not release her bated breath until he was well out of sight. Then she carried the body of the second guard to where the paralyzed man lay, did a more thorough job of concealing both, and stopped the heart of the first man so that there was no chance of either recovering to give her away. She felt no qualms about doing so; these men were servants of a vile betrayer, and would have killed her themselves had they had the opportunity.

Then she ran lightly to the front door and listened for signs that there were more men waiting inside. Her enhanced hearing perceived nothing. She felt horribly exposed against the nearly black wood of the door, with both lanterns shining brightly upon her, and had to remind herself that she had eliminated the nearest threats and could afford to be slow and cautious.

After a few more heartbeats in which she satisfied herself that no one lurked beyond the door to attack her, she eased down on the latch—and found the door locked. Not barred, which would have been a nearly insurmountable challenge, but securely locked. Amaya allowed herself a moment's smug pleasure. Yes, Don Balthasar was a worthy opponent, though likely he would find that no comfort when her claws tore out his throat.

She drew in a deep breath and released it slowly so it spiraled out of her like a warm wind. Bracing herself, she drew on Strength, and bit back a moan of pain as her muscles expanded and grew denser. The muscles of her arms and shoulders strained the fabric of her shirt as they grew. Another command to Strength enhanced the muscles of her chest, an important balance to her upper body, and one she had neglected only once before learning wisdom.

The pain in her torso and arms throbbed for what felt like several hundred beats and was really only ten. It had not fully subsided when Amaya once more took hold of the latch, but she was disinclined to wait. She gripped the latch, hoped it was as sturdy as it appeared, and with a single hard shove and an *oof* of breath, she broke the door free of the lock to swing silently and gently away from her.

Amaya flattened herself against the doorpost so as not to offer herself as a silhouetted target. But the hall beyond was empty, and lit by a single lantern on a stand beside stairs leading up. Square stone tiles the color of Valencia's dun horse covered the floor; a man in boots might have trouble moving silently across them. Amaya had gone barefoot for this task, the soles of her feet thickened and roughened to protect them, and she slipped noiselessly around the door and sniffed.

Many doors led off this hall, which was large enough to be a room in itself. The faint smell of several kinds of meat reached her nose from one of them, and she ignored that door and focused on the others. The stairs lay to the right and made two turns before disappearing into the upper floor. Two more doors lay beyond the stairs on the right, both of them standing open. One led to a dining room far more ornate than the Hanleys'; it, too, smelled of dinner, though even more faintly. The second opened on a narrow hall that ended at a drawing room, angular and filled with overstuffed, over-embroidered furniture.

Amaya suppressed the urge to run up the stairs to find Don Balthasar's bedchamber. There were more men here somewhere, and she would be more successful in her goal if she did not leave them behind her to take her by surprise.

A dim glow radiated from the third doorway, a hall on the left. Amaya listened closely and heard the low murmur of voices and some rustling of cloth and tapping of boot soles as if someone were pacing. Silently, she crept down the hall, counting voices. Three. Men, by the deepness of their voices and the heaviness of their tread.

The glow brightened as she approached the end of the hall, but not by very much. She discovered a closed door with a gleam of light limning it, brightest where it imperfectly met the floor. Or, not entirely closed; another crack of light ran from floor to near the ceiling, and whoever paced inside the room occasionally dimmed the light by passing between it and the door.

Amaya listened. Two of the men within spoke in calm, unhurried tones about some event due to happen in a few days, something at which Don Balthasar would be expected to preside. The third man contributed little more than grunts to the conversation, but they were enough for Amaya to place him some distance from the door. The pacing man had the highest-pitched voice, and his conversational partner seemed to Amaya to be his superior, based on his tone of command. Amaya closed her eyes to give herself a better sense of where each of the three stood or sat.

She heard the pacing steps grow louder just as she realized the man was coming toward the door. Instantly she assessed the situation. She was too far from the entry hall to reach it before the man opened the door. It was time to attack.

She slammed into the door with all her strength and weight. It struck the pacing man, who let out a cry of pain and staggered backward. Amaya was on him, bearing him down and slashing at his throat, before the other two men could do more than rise from their seats. Blood fountained, and Amaya was up again, kicking the door shut with one foot and launching herself at another man with the other. He, too, fell over backward, and Amaya pressed him into the ground with one knee, took his head between her hands, and snapped his neck.

The third man shouted, "We are under attack! Guards!" He was bigger than the other two, nearly as heavily muscled as Amaya currently was, and his darkly tanned skin was ashen with fear.

Amaya snarled and turned on him, her bloody hands reaching

for him. The man stumbled backward and managed to evade her claws, shouting all the while and fumbling for a pistol holstered at his side. Amaya wished in passing she knew how many guards there were to begin with, and then she had her hand around his throat and commanded his Heart to stop entirely, the entire *sunqu*. A peculiar look crossed the man's face, and he grabbed at his chest before toppling, wheezing as if it were Need's grasp of his lungs she had stopped instead.

Amaya calmed her breathing and wiped her hands on the dead man's shirt. She heard running footsteps nearby. Likely it had always been going to come to this. She concealed herself behind the door and waited.

The footsteps grew louder. A handful of men poured into the room, slowing rapidly and falling over each other as they saw the carnage. Amaya waited for all four to enter, then slammed the door shut and leaped to the attack.

She only resorted to her claws once; the rest fell to her Shaping their *sunqu*. When all four were dead, Amaya once more waited for her Need and Heart to subside and stared at the bodies. Dr. Macrae would not be so swift to urge Amaya to take up medicine if she knew what Extraordinary Shapers were capable of—though how could she not know, being an Extraordinary Shaper herself? Possibly doctoring was how Dr. Macrae soothed her conscience, for Amaya could not imagine the stately, composed woman capable of taking lives in such a fashion without being overpowered by guilt. True, there was some balancing of the scales if one could Heal others as well as Shape their deaths, but Amaya felt no need to justify herself to anyone.

She once more wiped her hands and listened at the door, just in case. Distant shouts and screams told her the man's warning had penetrated to the entire house, but no more men approached this room. She wrenched the door open past a body blocking it and ran for the stairs.

The entry hall was chaos. Men and women dressed for sleep thronged the hall, shouting at one another. Soldiers shoved them aside as they ran outside. No one noticed Amaya, standing at the edge of the commotion. She pushed past the servants and darted up the stairs.

She heard the men waiting above—well, there was no more need to be stealthy. She ran lightly around the turns of the stair and came bursting out, diving at the nearest man before he could bring his pistol to bear on her. One touch, and his heart burst within his chest. She rose, snarling, and the remaining men opened fire.

She was fast, but not fast enough to dodge every pistol ball. One struck her shoulder, cracking the scapula and sending pain shooting down her left arm that she ignored. Another hit her in the stomach, and a third grazed her right temple. As she bore down on her next victim, her body Shaped her injuries without more than a passing intent from her, the bone realigning and fusing together, the stomach Healing fast enough to eject the deformed ball at speed from the entry wound, the skin of her temple re-growing at a rate that made her head ache for a couple of heartbeats before fading. The pain of the rapid Shaping filled her, but the clear sharpness of battle lust made it distant, something easily ignored.

As she Healed herself, she killed; a swipe to the throat here, a touch of the hand there. Men dropped like stones into a clear pool, their blood, when there was blood, soaking the planks of the floor. She reached the end of the hall, swiped blood out of her eyes, and regarded her fallen victims dispassionately. If there were more men, let them come. She had nearly reached her goal.

Light came from beneath only one of the doors along this

upper hall. She pushed the door open and flattened herself to one side, in case whoever was within was armed. Instead, she heard a man's voice saying, "Let's not waste any more time, shall we? Do come in."

Amaya slid around the door and shut it behind her, locking it with the key she found waiting in the lock. She had never seen a more comfortable room. Furnishings in English houses always seemed designed to remind one of one's status as guest rather than to invite one to stay and visit. The bed and chairs in this room were made of honey-colored wood that smelled of distant forests rather than lacquer; they were low and spreading and altogether inviting. The carpet, too, asked a visitor to settle in for any amount of time he chose, its reds and browns reminding Amaya of the weaving of her lost home.

The man who sat in the chair nearest the window was enormous, easily the fattest man Amaya had ever seen. His weight suited him; his features were large and well-formed rather than coarse, and when he rose from his chair he seemed almost to float, as if his weight did not bear down on him.

He stood beside the chair and said, "You won't sit, I know. But since you intend to kill me, I ask the courtesy of you telling me which of my many enemies sent you."

Amaya hesitated. She well knew a villain did not have to appear villainous, no matter what Bess's novels said, but this man's demeanor did not strike her as that of someone who could order a village razed. He seemed, rather, like someone who would insist on doing the razing himself.

Don Balthasar smiled. "So, I am not what you believed," he said. "Will it help to tell you I likely am guilty of whatever you were told? Or—no, that seems to have confused you further." He gestured. "Sit, or not, but I truly do wish to know who sent you."

Amaya swallowed. Her throat was inexplicably dry. "It was

Alejandro Valencia, and you deserve death for what you have done."

Don Balthasar's smile fell away. "Valencia," he said. "I might have guessed. Only he has the power to inspire such loyalty." He shook his head. "Even if it is Coerced."

CHAPTER 17
IN WHICH AMAYA LEARNS A TERRIBLE TRUTH

"Coerced?" Amaya's mouth fell open. It was not at all what she had expected. "What lie is this?"

Don Balthasar's hand closed over the chair back. She would have suspected him afraid if his demeanor were not so confident, as if he were not facing death. "Do not feel ashamed," he said. "Coercion is impossible to fight."

"I have not been Coerced." Amaya took two steps toward Don Balthasar. "You intend to make me doubt—that is impossible. I know what you have done to the innocents of Spain."

"This is a hard time, and we must do hard things. As I am certain you know." Don Balthasar shrugged. "Believe me, or not. But I am a Discerner, and we are immune to Coercion. I know when a Coercer uses his talent. And I know Valencia uses his pet Extraordinary Coercer, whoever that is, to reinforce his charismatic speeches. You are not the first to fall under his sway."

"You cannot prove that," Amaya said in a low voice. Her instincts were screaming at her to kill this man, to end his lies. And yet, was it not peculiar that she and Edmund had changed their minds so thoroughly about helping Valencia? Had she not felt a powerful desire to fight for him, like no emotion she had felt before? She wet her lips, which were dry, and said, "No one has Coerced me to kill you. That is all my own choice."

"I realize I cannot dissuade you," Don Balthasar said. Now he sounded weary, as if he had ridden all day without rest, and he gestured with his free hand in a dismissive fashion. "But you are remarkable. No assassin has got this far before. I should not admire you, since you intend my death, but I find it sickeningly wrong that one such as you should be so foully influenced. Better you kill me cleanly than because you have been manipulated to it."

Amaya's breathing came too rapidly, and her heart pounded as if her body was preparing to flee. "Impossible," she said. "I am not—I would have known—"

"No, you would not." Don Balthasar sounded pitying. "No one ever does. It is why Coercers are evil, taking one's will and one's very heart."

His pity enraged Amaya. Anger surged within her, and she leaped at him, claws and teeth bared. Don Balthasar made no move to step away. She shoved him against the wall, pressing her claws against his throat and punching him hard in the chest to knock the wind out of him. While he gasped, she said, "I am no man's tool."

"Prove it," Don Balthasar wheezed. "Kill me in fury. It will break the Coercion."

Amaya released him and stepped back a pace. "What?"

Don Balthasar bent double, gasping for breath. "Coercion cannot stand in the face of some other strong emotion. A different Coercion, perhaps, but also real hatred or fear or even love. The body cannot sustain both at once."

He looked up at Amaya, and smiled, a bitter expression. "You are angry with me for challenging you, angry at what I have done. Let me tell you more. I have presided over the slaughter of a village whose elders would not give up a revolutionary hiding among them. I have watched my soldiers rape women and cut their bodies open while their husbands watched helplessly. I have ordered the death of someone who did nothing but deny me my rights as his lord. I—"

With a scream, Amaya launched herself at Don Balthasar, claws raised. She raked him across the face, stopping his words and making him cry out in pain. Rage filled her, a good clean rage that made her veins pulse and her body tremble with fury. With another swipe of her claws, she tore through his jugular vein and rejoiced in the blood that spurted from it.

She released her victim, who sagged to his knees, clutching vainly at his throat. Blood welled from between his fingers. He closed his eyes—and smiled. "Be free," he whispered, and fell face first on the beautiful red and brown carpet.

Amaya stood over him, breathing heavily. Her whole body still trembled with anger. How *dare* he? She stepped over the body and looked out the window. Soldiers raced here and there like frightened ants, drunk on sap and utterly leaderless. She felt as clear-headed as she always did in a fight, where everything around her seemed to slow and she moved through the world like water running downhill.

Behind her, she heard more booted feet coming up the stairs and down the hall. She glanced out the window again. Only a few soldiers remained outside. It would be her best exit.

She unlatched the window and climbed out, clung to the sill for a few heartbeats, then jumped. It was not a far distance, and she had jumped from much farther without injury, her leg bones dense and strong. A soldier came to a halt only a few arm spans away and raised his musket in shaking hands. Quicker than thought, she wrenched it away from him and swung it at his head. He collapsed from the impact, and Amaya threw the gun atop his recumbent body and ran.

Shots rang out, but only one struck her, low in the back near her kidney. She Shaped herself whole, barely noticing the pain. In a dozen heartbeats she reached the trees' shelter, and the shooting stopped.

She had come out some distance from the road, but rather than waste time following the trees to where the road entered them, she struck out across country, running as easily and as fleetly as the jaguar. Dry, dead grass tickled the sides of her feet, though her soles were too thick and roughened to feel more than the sharpest of stones. She ran until she judged she was halfway back to Aranjuez, and well out of range of any pursuit. Then she stopped and permitted her body to return to its resting state, Need and Heart subsiding so she no longer heard them pulsing in her ears.

Now that her rage had subsided, she could ponder Don Balthasar's words. He had been lying, certainly, but to what end? Not to save his life; he had seemed determined to force her to kill him, which made no sense. And she had succeeded at Valencia's task. She had rid Spain of a villain—

Amaya's breath caught. She had killed a man on Valencia's word. Had killed many men that night for the sake of Valencia's cause. Which was not her cause.

She clutched her head in bloody hands and keened as memory struck. That speech in Fernándo's stable yard. Her sudden change of heart. How true and passionate she had felt about Valencia's words. Nothing about that had been right. And yet it had all seemed so *reasonable*. Don Balthasar was right; she had been Coerced. And now that she knew the truth, she could not believe how easily she had fallen under the Coercer's sway.

She fell to her knees and vomited what little was in her, for the first time since manifesting her Shaper talent not in control of her body. What a violation, not of her body, but of her mind and heart. She vomited until she was wrung out and gasping for air. Then she knelt a while longer, staring blindly at the puddle of bile soaking into the bare earth of the road.

Don Balthasar had not known the identity of Valencia's Extraordinary Coercer. Amaya had a bitter suspicion that she did. Someone Valencia kept close to him, someone no one would suspect of being capable of such horror, someone so innocuous no one ever noticed her. Amaya could not believe she had ever felt sorry for Jennet. She would kill the young woman and take pleasure in her death.

Except, if she threatened Jennet, the Extraordinary Coercer would simply turn her talent on Amaya again, this time making her even more willing a victim. Jennet would have to if she wished to save her own life. Amaya would have to find a way to eliminate Jennet without exposing herself to more Coercion.

And Edmund. Edmund was still under Jennet's thrall. Amaya wanted to weep, but she felt too weary for tears. She must free him from the Coercion before killing Jennet. Don Balthasar had shown her the way, if she could only enrage Edmund, or terrify him, or—she could not conceive of other emotions she might reasonably induce in her dear friend.

She remembered Edmund's excitement about fighting beside Valencia and her heart burned with anger. That Jennet had dared turn Edmund's courage and strength to that foul cause! It was possible, whatever Don Balthasar had said, that Jennet was responsible for controlling Valencia too, that she had turned him to her own cause, but Amaya could not quite believe it. For one, Jennet was not Spanish, so why would she care about Spanish independence? No, Valencia had somehow convinced Jennet to act for him, to turn her talent to his cause.

Amaya was certain, now, that Valencia was not the innocent crusader for justice he portrayed himself. Some of the guilt for Jennet's Coercion lay at his door, because Jennet did whatever he told her to. A part of Amaya whispered, *Suppose she is as much a victim as you were,* and she ruthlessly quashed the idea. Jennet's talent was evil, and she had chosen to use it at the behest of a villain. That made her complicit, and guilty.

Amaya rose and continued toward Aranjuez, slowly now, barely able to put one foot in front of the other. She would have to pretend to still be an ardent supporter of Valencia's cause. She was not certain, after what had happened that night, that she had the fortitude to do so. But it was either that or be returned to the condition of a mindless slave. So she had no choice.

The city was dark when she returned, well after midnight. The inn at which Valencia's men stayed looked ominous in the darkness, though a lantern burned beside the door and two more wanly lit the stable yard. Amaya paused at the well to draw a bucket of water to wash her hands. The blood staining them sickened her now. She reminded herself that, Valencia's manipulation or no, those men had done terrible deeds and were deserving of death. The reminder felt empty.

She could do nothing about the blood on her clothes. Perhaps someone at the inn knew where she might find others. She hated the idea of being dependent on any of Valencia's people, now that she knew he had manipulated her and likely lied to her, but she could not go on wearing the reminder of the night's bloody work.

She donned the boots she had left beside the inn's back door and entered. The door led to the kitchen, which was unlit. The scent of roasted chicken overlaid older smells, of bread and ham and sausage, none of which roused her appetite. She made her way through the darkened room and followed unlit halls until she came out in the small, high-ceilinged entry. A line of light shone beneath the door to the private dining room. Amaya took a deep breath, released it, and pushed the door open.

A fire crackled in the fireplace, sending up the bitter smell of smoke and char. Valencia sat beside it, staring into its depths. Edmund, across the room, reclined in an armchair beneath one window with his legs outstretched. Both men sat up when she entered. Their identical looks of anticipation made Amaya wish she could vomit again. Her gaze lingered on Edmund, and anger supplanted the sick feeling. She would free him, or die trying.

She almost did not see Jennet, who was curled up asleep in a chair as far from Edmund as possible, but then her shadowy figure moved and sat up, blinking. Amaya looked away, certain if she did not, she would launch herself at Jennet and be Coerced once more.

Valencia rose. "Well?"

Amaya nodded once. "It is done. Don Balthasar will trouble Spain no more."

A slow smile spread across Valencia's face. Edmund let out a low cry of exultation that pierced Amaya's heart to the center. "Well done, Amaya," he said. "You should be proud of what you have accomplished this night."

"Indeed," Valencia said. He walked toward Amaya and fingered her collar, whose tip was stiff with blood. "New clothing for you in the morning, I believe. We must make haste to turn Don Balthasar's death to our advantage. I will speak to Rodrigo, and we will gather those capable of taking the city."

Uncertainty touched Amaya's heart. "Taking the city?"

"The Count of Aranjuez is dead, and no one remains who can quickly take his place." Valencia turned to Jennet, who was watching the conversation as curiously as if it were in a language she did not speak. "Summon Rodrigo, Ned, and ask him to join me at the stables. We will yet make of this city the center from which a new order will spread."

Amaya hoped she appeared as eager as Edmund did. She covertly watched Jennet. Don Balthasar had not said whether a Coercer, Extraordinary or not, could tell if her Coercion had failed. If so, Amaya was doomed no matter what she did. But Jennet only cast one quick glance her way before quietly leaving the room.

"You have earned your rest," Valencia was saying, and she turned her attention back to him. "Are you in need of anything else? Food? Not Healing, surely." He laughed as if it were a great joke. Nothing about his words amused her. "Anything you require, we will provide. You have done Spain a great service tonight, Miss Salazar."

"I must sleep," Amaya said. Now that she had completed her task, weariness would not be far behind, the result of repeatedly Shaping her body and making demands of her *sunqu*. She had only once pushed herself to the point of collapse, and that had incapacitated her for days. She would not make that mistake again.

"Of course," Valencia said. He took her hand and pressed it to his lips. "We will speak again in the morning. Rest well, Miss Salazar."

When the door swung shut before him, Edmund said, "I wish I could have joined you. I feel an overpowering desire to fight for this cause."

His words struck Amaya to the heart. "You would not have survived it," she said, casting about for something else to say. "I was shot many times and had to jump from a second-story window to make my escape."

Edmund let out a low whistle. "I had not fully appreciated your talent until now. Shot? Amaya, suppose there had been enough men to overwhelm you?"

"But there were not, and you should not be afraid for me." Instantly she wondered if fear for her was enough to break Jennet's Coercion. She surveyed his face, but found only concern there. Clearly, he was not afraid enough. She felt lost, desperate for a solution and ready to snatch at any straw of hope. The need to hurt or frighten or anger Edmund warred with her desire to protect him, because he was her dear friend—and yet because he was her dear friend, she could not permit him to go on a captive. She did not believe she could make him fear her. Anger, though…

"Though I suppose I should not expect anything else from you," she said, letting sarcasm and disdain sharpen her voice. "You who insist on accompanying me everywhere, as if I were a child."

Edmund blinked, his eyes going wide. "What—Amaya, I don't understand."

"Of course not," Amaya said, more angrily. "You see only what it suits you to see. Did my awkwardness in society satisfy you? Permit you to feel strong and capable in shepherding me around? I suppose you sought ways to keep me tied to you, keep me docile like an English miss so you might puff up your consequence."

"Amaya, what are you talking of? This is nonsense!" Edmund raised his hand as if to grip her shoulder.

Amaya took a step back before he could touch her. "Nonsense? I think not. You use me to make yourself more important, you follow me everywhere—even to my own family's home—pretending it is to protect my reputation, when you know I am an Extraordinary and the keeper of my own honor. I cannot understand why I permitted it for so long, but it ends tonight!"

Edmund lowered his hand. His eyes narrowed. "Is that what you feel?" he said in a low, angry voice. "That my friendship has been a sham? I wonder that you have endured my presence at all, if it is so objectionable to you."

He turned and made for the door. Desperation lent Amaya greater speed even than Shaping, and she beat him there. He was not angry enough. She could not permit him to leave. "Of course it is objectionable," she said, ignoring the clamoring of her heart that said she was doing something he might never forgive her for. "You are a fool and a fop, capable of only the most superficial emotions. I cannot tell you how often I have laughed at you in private, you are so ridiculous. You are not even worthy of my hatred, only of my disdain."

Edmund's lips curled in a snarl. "I might have expected as much from a savage who knows nothing of true feeling."

"Better a savage than a self-indulgent ninny. How much did it gripe you to have to trail after me to all those museums, pretending an interest you could not feel?" Despair threatened to overwhelm her. This ruse would not work, and Edmund would hate her as well as remaining in Jennet's thrall. "You ridiculous, prating fool! I do not understand how Bess tolerates your company, you are such a burden on her."

"You believe—" Fury distorted Edmund's features. In the next moment, he punched Amaya in the face.

She had not been expecting the blow, and it rocked her back on her heels. Startled, she dropped to a crouch, and the second blow passed harmlessly over her head. She rose from her crouch in an explosive leap and took Edmund around the waist, bearing him to the ground and pinning his arms to his side. He was strong, but at the moment, she was stronger.

He struggled against her grip briefly, then wrenched himself free with a twist of both wrists she was unfamiliar with. He grabbed her by the upper arms and sat up, driving his forehead at the bridge of her nose. She twisted to one side, and his head struck her cheekbone, sending a shooting pain through the side of her face.

She broke his grip with a shrug and leaped backward, still keeping herself between him and the door. "Edmund, stop," she gasped. "Stop. You must feel different."

Edmund growled and rushed her. She did not dare step out of his way, so she let him shove her into the wall beside the door. She took his face in her hands and said, "This is real, this anger. What she did to you is not. Please, Edmund, tell me you can feel the difference."

He blinked at her again, and his grip slackened slightly. "I—difference? What do you mean?"

Her eyes ached along with her heart. "We were Coerced, Edmund, into believing Mr. Valencia's cause was just and right. It was all a lie."

Edmund released her and stepped back. "I don't understand," he said. "I..." His eyes were wide, the whites showing all around the dark irises. "But his cause—no, Amaya, it is impossible—" His jaw tensed as if he were suppressing his revulsion, and Amaya's heart ached for him.

"Remember," she begged. "You must see now how false the feeling was. I felt it too, Edmund. But it was all a lie. All Coercion."

Edmund rubbed his face with one hand. "I can feel it now. It was too perfect." He turned away and staggered to lean against the dining table. "It is all so terribly obvious, and yet I remember how right it felt. How did you know?"

Amaya rubbed her sore cheek, choosing to hold onto that

pain rather than Shape it away. "Don Balthasar knew," she said. "He convinced me. He infuriated me, saying that another emotion may supplant a Coerced one. Anger, or fear…"

Edmund bowed his head. "And you made me angry."

His words were so bleak tears came to Amaya's eyes. "Oh, Edmund," she said, despair once more surging over her. "Please, forgive me. I meant none of that, nothing at all—you are my dear friend, and I admire you, and—you must forgive me, you must, because I cannot bear your hatred!"

She buried her face in her hands and wept, unable to remember the last time she had done it. She had forgotten how it felt to cry, how her eyes were hot and wet at the same time, how her body shook, how her chest and throat ached. It was painful, and embarrassing, and she would not have stopped it even if that were possible.

To her utter surprise, arms encircled her, and Edmund drew her close to his chest and held her. "I know of no one else who would make such a sacrifice to save me," he whispered. "Thank you."

The ache in Amaya's chest faded. She unfolded her arms from where they were pressed between their bodies and returned his embrace, reveling in the simple joy of human closeness. He was warm and strong and he smelled of sweat and horses, not unexpected given how much riding they had done in the past few days, and the smell reassured her because it was simple and homely and uncomplicated.

Then she became aware of his hands, how they touched her so gently, of his breath sighing across her forehead, and a different kind of warmth spread throughout her body. She turned her face to rest on his shoulder and sighed with pleasure. A flash of memory struck her, of lying quietly with Kichka on her pallet, how peaceful she had felt just as she felt now. Kichka could not be more different from Edmund; he was somber and serious and almost never laughed. And yet the feeling was the same.

Edmund shifted his position, but did not release her. "Forgive me for striking you," he said. "I cannot believe I lost control so greatly that I could attack you. I am ashamed. Hitting a woman—"

"I am a warrior as well as a woman. Though yours was a foolish attack, and almost certainly arose from your Coerced state. Had I truly meant those things, I might have killed you."

"True. Still, I beg you to forgive me."

Amaya nodded, her face rubbing against his shirt. "We forgive each other, and will say no more about it, because what matters is what we will do next."

"You said 'she' did this," Edmund said. "You must mean Jennet. She is the Extraordinary Coercer responsible."

Mention of Jennet sent cold fury rushing through Amaya's veins, dispelling the peacefulness she felt. She stepped away from Edmund, wiped her eyes, and nodded. "There is no other possibility. She was present every time I felt that rush of emotion. And Mr. Valencia keeps her close beside him. I believe she is his tool."

"You do not suggest she is not to blame?"

She felt a moment's uncertainty that she refused to entertain. "It is her talent. She is to blame. But I believe Mr. Valencia has an equal portion of blame, since it is impossible she is doing it without his knowledge. Don Balthasar said Jennet makes Mr. Valencia's rhetoric potent and irresistible."

"Indeed," Edmund said with a grimace. "Then what are we to do?"

"We must leave tonight," Amaya said. "We will return to

Madrid, I suppose, and warn the king or his ministers of what Mr. Valencia proposes."

"We certainly cannot stay here. Suppose Jennet knows we are no longer Coerced?"

"I had wondered that myself. I do not know if it is possible, but it is not a risk we should take. If she Coerces us again—"

Edmund shook his head. "Surely now that we know of the possibility, it will not happen again. How can she convince us of a feeling when we know it is not true?"

"Again, I do not know what more a Coercer is capable of. I have no desire to find out." Amaya turned. "We should hurry, before—"

The door swung open. Jennet entered. She stopped when she saw Amaya and Edmund, and swiftly scanned the room, no doubt looking for Valencia. The three stared at each other. Amaya felt as if she had unexpectedly come across a predator who might or might not be hungry.

Jennet's gaze passed from Amaya to Edmund and back again. Her eyes narrowed. Then terror like Amaya had never felt before swept over her, making Heart and Need and Release contract painfully. She gasped, and heard Edmund cry out, an anguished sound as if his soul were being ripped from his body.

Jennet bolted for the door.

CHAPTER 18

IN WHICH NEGOTIATIONS COMMENCE, AND THE POWER OF A COERCER IS DISCUSSED

Horrors filled the shadows, unseen figures Amaya knew in her heart were there, ready to tear her flesh from her bones. She cringed away from the door, crying out and gasping for breath. Edmund staggered away from her, and she saw him curl up on the floor beside one of the armchairs before she closed her eyes and flung her arms over her head. Something was attacking—

She made herself raise her head and scan the room for threats. Nothing. There was nothing there but the shadows and Edmund, keening out his fear like a child. Amaya turned toward the door, which had swung shut. Fear still battered at her, but she ignored it. Memories of hiding in a cupboard surfaced and were swept away. She was no child, helpless against adults who would kill her. She was a jaguar warrior, and fear meant nothing to her.

She slammed the door open in time to see the outer door shut. Swiftly she crossed the little room and flung that door open as well. Jennet was halfway across the stable yard, running as fleetly as a non-Shaper could. Amaya snarled and raced after her, painfully shaping the muscles of her legs to give her a burst of speed nothing could outrun.

Jennet looked over her shoulder once. Her eyes widened. Then, to Amaya's surprise, she slowed and turned around to face her oncoming death. "Don't," she said in English. "He'll die of fright if you kill me, because I will not release him."

Amaya did not slow. She grabbed Jennet and dragged her to the low wall of the stable yard, forcing her up against it with her claws poised to tear Jennet's throat out. Fear still battered at her, but distantly, something easy to ignore. Jennet regarded her unblinkingly, seeming unafraid, though Amaya could feel the woman's heart pounding. "Release him," Amaya said in English.

"No."

Amaya's claws drew tiny pinpricks of blood. "You will do it."

"He is the only thing that stands between me and death. I will not. You will let me go, and he will go free. If I die, he will remain locked in his fears until he, too, dies."

Amaya examined her face. Jennet seemed utterly certain of her words. Amaya wished she had some way to know if the Coercer was lying to her. But Edmund's life was at stake. She withdrew her claws, but kept Jennet pressed against the wall. "I should kill you for what you did to us. What you have no doubt done to so many."

"I will not justify myself to you," Jennet said. "I did what I had to for my survival. You of all people should understand that."

"I? I do not ever—have not ever Coerced someone into a belief that they feel what they do not feel. It is foul." Amaya pushed a little harder, and Jennet gave out a low grunt of pain.

"You have killed in defense of yourself and others. I have

never killed anyone. How does that make you my superior in character?"

"It—" Amaya shook her head. "I will not speak with you. Why do you not Coerce me now? Convince me to love you and let you go?"

Jennet said nothing. They stared at each other in silence for a time until Amaya became uncomfortable being the focus of Jennet's strange light-colored eyes. Finally, Jennet said, "I choose otherwise. I do not obey every one of Alejandro's commands."

"You obeyed him when he told you to make us follow him. I cannot imagine what else you might do to us."

"Can you not?" Jennet shrugged with some difficulty. "Alejandro wanted me to make you desire him so you would go to his bed willingly. I refused."

It was like a blow to the chest, stunning Amaya. "I? But why? Why refuse?"

"I may be damned, but there are evils I will not partake of." Jennet's eyes on Amaya were unflinching. "And you are a fool, but you do not deserve that fate. Why did you care about keeping my secret? The other one? Why care about me at all?"

Amaya had almost forgotten there had been a time when she pitied Jennet. "Because I am curious. About who you are and why you pretend not to be female. About why you are in Spain with a revolutionary leader. I wanted to be your friend."

Jennet laughed, a dry, bitter sound. "I have no friends unless I make them my friends, and that is unsatisfying. I am always aware they only like me because I have enthralled them."

Amaya's lips curled back in a snarl again. "You and I are not friends."

"No. That is impossible."

"And yet we speak friendly. As friends."

"Because you are a fool. I know you will kill me as soon as I release your love."

Amaya's grip slackened. "Edmund is not my love."

Unexpectedly, Jennet smiled. "Then your friend," she said, but Amaya could tell she was suppressing some other comment.

She chose not to pursue it. "I swear I will not kill you if you free him." It was a stupid, terrible promise, but she could see no alternative.

"You must let me go to him," Jennet said. "I cannot Coerce someone I cannot see."

Amaya hesitated for a moment. Then she changed her grip on Jennet to hold her by the right arm in a way that would dislocate the woman's shoulder if she tried to escape. She marched Jennet back to the inn, saying, "If he has injured himself—"

"That fear will not kill him immediately," Jennet said.

The way she emphasized "that" prompted Amaya to say, "Then there is a fear that will?"

Jennet glanced at Amaya. "There is," she said, and her following silence was that of someone who would say nothing more no matter what Amaya did.

Edmund still crouched by the armchair, but he was on his hands and knees, breathing heavily. As they entered, he crawled two paces, raised his head, and said in a faint voice, "Amaya...run..."

Amaya sucked in a horrified breath. Edmund in a rage had been terrible to see. Edmund in the grip of terror broke her heart. That someone so strong could be reduced to that condition! She had to look away, feeling as if she had intruded upon him in his most vulnerable state.

She heard him draw in a deep breath, felt Jennet's arm in hers stiffen briefly, and then there was the sound of someone getting to his feet. She looked back to see Edmund rising, pushing himself up with the chair's assistance. His shirt beneath his arms and across his chest was dark with sweat, his hair disordered, but his eyes were clear, and the dread within Amaya gave way as her own distant fear subsided.

Edmund closed his eyes and tilted his head back, calming his breathing. Jennet tugged at Amaya's arm, trying to free herself, but Amaya did not let go. "You promised," Jennet said in a low voice, still in English.

Jennet's words brought Edmund out of his reverie. He opened his eyes, and a furious expression swept across his face. "Kill her," he said, his voice low and flat.

"I promised I would not," Amaya said.

"That was a stupid promise. We cannot permit her to live." Edmund strode toward them, one hand clenched into a fist.

Amaya held up a hand palm-first in a warding position. "Edmund. I swore."

"But I did not," Edmund said.

Jennet took a step forward, which was all the farther Amaya's grip would permit. "I could make you believe you adore me," she said. "I could convince you I am your dearest friend. I have not done either of those things."

"And you believe that should make me trust you? Make me forget what you *have* done?" Edmund stopped within striking distance, his fist still clenched.

"No. I cannot be forgiven. I know this." Jennet regarded him unflinchingly. "But if you leave now, no one will know it until morning, when you will be beyond Alejandro's reach."

"He cannot harm us as you have."

Jennet tilted her head like a curious bird, as if Edmund had said something incomprehensible. "You think not? You do not realize the extent to which Alejandro has acted to ensure you follow him. It was not Enrico Solano's men who killed that woman, your friend. Alejandro ordered her murder. He meant you—" She jabbed a finger at Edmund— "to die as well, but in his words, you are luckier than a cat."

Amaya let go of Jennet's arm. "That cannot be true. Why would he do that, when all he needed was your Coercion?"

"Because she was a Discerner, and immune to Coercion," Jennet said. "She would have known it when I enthralled you, and might have acted to prevent you following Alejandro." She shrugged. "What is one small death in the name of freedom? It is how he thinks. Now, you must leave."

Amaya shook her head. "He will blame you for our flight."

Jennet turned her gaze on Amaya, her lips quirked in a smile as bitter as her laugh. "Why should you care?"

Amaya did not have a ready answer for that. She opened her mouth, closed it again, and finally said, "I should not. But I do. Tell me why you do not make me Señor Valencia's lover."

"I know what it is like to be taken against one's will," Jennet said, "and I swore I would never do that to another woman." Her smile deepened. "There are no laws for one such as I, so I must make my own. I will not kill with my talent. I will not Coerce feelings of love. And, it seems, I will not turn my talent on someone who has shown me mercy, however unwillingly."

"That does not excuse you from all the other evils you have done," Edmund said.

"I have not asked for forgiveness or absolution," Jennet said. "You cannot give them to me in any case. But if you are looking for reasons for my mercy toward you, perhaps I feel it redresses the wrongs I have done you in some small way to help you escape."

Amaya stepped away from Jennet, knowing this left the woman free to escape, or at least gave her the illusion of freedom. Amaya could still outrun her. "Señor Valencia will be angry. Or is he not already angry that you do not make me love him?"

Jennet's smile became amused, and her eyes lit as if in appreciation of a good joke. "Alejandro is clever, but he is not as intelligent as he believes, and he never doubts what I tell him my talent is capable of, or not. This is the first time he has asked me to enthrall a woman, and I convinced him the act of love is unsatisfying when one partner is only there because she has been Coerced. That is a lie, but a believable one. He was not happy, but he is very attractive to women, and I am certain he believes his wooing of you progresses nicely."

Amaya felt ill. She recalled the many fond looks Valencia had turned on her, and imagined herself in his arms. No, it was impossible. Gratitude to Jennet welled up in her heart, replaced by anger that she should feel grateful that Jennet had not turned her foul Coercion upon her. "But he will know you are the one who makes us free," she said. "We do not leave except you do not Coerce us more."

"He does not know we encountered each other this evening. I will suggest that your emotions were overwhelmed in your attack on Don Balthasar, and that you found a way to free Mr. Hanley. Alejandro knows what will break Coercion, and he will believe my words because he cannot imagine I would ever lie to him." Jennet pulled out a chair and sat at the table, resting one elbow on it. "You waste time talking. Go, now, before someone else comes and you are forced to kill to secure your escape."

Amaya turned toward her. "Come with us," she said.

Jennet's eyes widened. "I? No, why would I do that?"

"Yes, Amaya, why would we wish to have her along?" Edmund said angrily.

Amaya ignored him. "You do not need to be his slave. Come with us and be free."

"Amaya—" Edmund repeated.

"Edmund, it is wrong that Jennet make people follow Señor Valencia. She can act for herself." Amaya returned her attention to Jennet. "I do not believe you are so certain as you sound. If Señor Valencia learns the truth, either he will kill you or you will have to Coerce him so you can flee. I do not believe you desire to make others fear or love you or whatever else it is you do. If you come with us, you can do other things. Better things."

Jennet's eyes and mouth were both round with astonishment. Then she laughed. "You are so very odd," she said. "Do you suppose your offer a noble act? Saving the sinner from Hell? I am already damned for what I have done, Miss Salazar. Leave me to my damnation."

"But—"

"She is right, Amaya, we must leave immediately if we wish to escape pursuit," Edmund said. He took hold of Amaya's arm and tried to steer her out the door.

Amaya stood firm. "You are not damned," she said. "I am no Christian, but I know you must choose evil to be evil. And you have chosen merely...I do not know the word, but it means the need of the moment."

"Expediency," Edmund said automatically. He swore and added, "Amaya, *now*."

Jennet rose. The amusement had left her face, and she looked as somber as she had in the stable yard. "Almost you convince me to have hope," she said. "Go, and I hope we never meet again, because if Alejandro orders it, I do not know if I could refuse to Coerce you into obedience."

Edmund tugged on Amaya's arm once more, and this time she let him pull her through the doorway. The last Amaya saw of Jennet was the woman resuming her seat at the table, her face thoughtful and her hand closed loosely along the top of the chair.

She and Edmund hurried through the darkened inn, out of the kitchen into the small yard with the well. "How are we to go?" she asked, reverting to Spanish.

"We will take our horses," Edmund said, hurrying around the corner of the house. "They are Don Fernándo's animals, and therefore you have more of a right to them than Mr. Valencia does. Though in truth, I do not mind stealing from him after what he did to us."

Amaya followed Edmund closely. "Then you blame him and not Jennet."

Edmund scowled. "I blame them both. Do not try to change my mind. Coercion is evil, and we have both been betrayed by that woman."

They slowed their steps as they approached the stable, where lights still burned. A man detached himself from the shadow of the stalls and said, "Who is it?"

"Mr. Hanley and Miss Salazar, on an errand from Mr. Valencia," Edmund said in a slightly bored way. It was exactly the tone of voice Amaya would expect from someone who had been roused from his bed to ride somewhere in the middle of the night. "We need our horses. Mr. Valencia asked us to ride to speak to Jorge Cantos."

Amaya did not know the name, but the stable hand did. Clearly Edmund paid better attention to Valencia's speeches than she had. The stable hand waved them onward without another word.

In the stalls, they swiftly saddled and bridled their horses. Amaya's every sense was alert for signs that they had been betrayed. She felt stretched wonderfully taut, her pulse quickened to give her a greater readiness to fight or run. The sensation tingled through her bones and her veins and her muscles. She wished they had time for her to pass that sensation on to Edmund, but haste was now their friend.

Having led the horses into the yard and mounted, they trotted off down the dark streets of Aranjuez. Amaya continued to listen for shouts, or running footsteps, but heard nothing but the sound of their horses' hooves and Edmund's breathing. Her own light breathing made almost no sound.

"Don't keep looking back," Edmund told her the third time she turned around. "Ride as if you have purpose and no fear of being followed. Continually looking behind you makes you seem as if you have something to hide."

Amaya nodded and resolutely kept herself facing forward. "I wish we could run."

"That, too, would draw attention. We must move at a rapid but unhurried pace."

"I am glad you are a spy. I am certain Edmund Hanley the man about town would not have this rarefied information."

Edmund didn't laugh as she had intended. "I will be grateful for my knowledge once we are free of the city. My shoulder blades itch as if a blade were poised there."

The knowledge that Edmund was as apprehensive as she quelled her amusement.

Now they rode in silence, never stopping, until they reached the outskirts of the city. "We will ride faster now?" Amaya asked.

Edmund shook his head. "We must wait for moonrise, and even then we dare not ride full-out. But in truth, I believe we have escaped as perfectly as possible."

"We must return to Madrid, and tell them what we know," Amaya said. "I do not know the way from Aranjuez."

"I have seen the maps of this area, and we are close enough to Madrid that the road makes the journey swift. But we will need a place to rest, and clothing for you. You look like the denizen of an abattoir."

The blood spattering Amaya's clothes now sickened her. "I will feel better once I have changed my clothes."

Edmund brought his horse to a halt. "Amaya," he said, "do not blame yourself."

"For what?"

"For having killed for the sake of a cause you did not actually believe in. We were both victims. I took lives as well. There is no way to reverse that." Edmund put a hand over Amaya's where she held her reins. "We can only attempt to make up for those deeds by revealing Mr. Valencia's plan to those who can stop him."

Again, the touch of his hand warmed her. "I understand," she said. "But—"

"But, what?"

Amaya sighed. "Mr. Valencia did evil in having Jennet Coerce us to join his cause. But I am not certain his cause is wrong. Don Balthasar admitted to having done horrid things, and I cannot regret his death even though I might not have killed him except for Coercion. And I have met King Ferdinand, and he does not strike me as a noble ruler who has a care for his people. What if we are wrong about who the villain is?"

Edmund withdrew his hand. "You did not listen closely to Mr. Valencia's plans. He may have noble ambitions, but his methods are as violent as any lord's. Many hundreds, perhaps thousands of men, women, and even children will die because of his revolution. I cannot permit that to happen. And Spain is not my country, and I am disinclined to decide how it should be ruled. Amaya, there are no good solutions in this fight."

"No, I suppose not." A smile tugged at Amaya's lips. "It is

good you are not a frivolous man about town, after all, for such a man would not understand Mr. Valencia's plan."

Again, Edmund did not respond. His lips pressed tightly together, and he cast his gaze down the dark road unspooling like a black ribbon away from Aranjuez. "Better for me if I were," he murmured. "I revealed my true employment, and I have betrayed my government in so doing. If I did not hate Jennet for anything else, it would be for that."

Amaya did not like the way he sounded, full of anger and, beneath the anger, self-loathing. "Edmund, you are not to blame," she said.

"Am I not?" Edmund said, his voice harsh. "No amount of Coercion should have lowered my reserve to that extent. And now Mr. Valencia has a weapon he may use against me, or worse, against England." He let out a short, hard laugh that hurt Amaya's heart. "I suppose I should count it a blessing that I did not spill for him every intelligence secret I know."

"Oh, pray, Edmund, do not talk so!" Amaya edged her horse close to Edmund and gripped his wrist. "If I am not to blame for killing under Coercion, why should you blame yourself for your indiscretion under the same condition?"

Edmund opened his mouth to speak, and Amaya overrode him. "Jennet took advantage of your natural desires to see justice done, and you wanted only for Mr. Valencia to know what your true capabilities are. You told him nothing else, correct? No secret plans, no details about England's intentions toward the Spanish government? Then I do not see the harm in one or two people knowing the truth, especially since they are in no position to do anything with that knowledge."

A faint smile touched Edmund's lips. "I cannot believe my situation is as simple as that," he said, "but I take your meaning. And I cannot wind back the clock and prevent myself revealing my identity. I will simply have to confess to my superiors what I have done, and pray they will be understanding. Beyond that, there is nothing more I can do."

Amaya still felt Edmund chose to take on more guilt than he deserved, but he was smiling again, and perhaps that was the best she could hope for. He still looked downcast, and Amaya wished she knew how to comfort him. Instead, she said, "You were here as a spy? What were you meant to do? Unless you feel you should not tell me."

Edmund let out a low, bitter *hah*. "Likely I should not, but since I trust you with my life, I suppose I cannot be damned a second time for speaking my secrets, and only to you. My assignment—my secret assignment—is to evaluate the strength of the Spanish government and determine what form English assistance should take, if any." He sighed. "I feel it an extension of that duty to prevent Spain's government from being overthrown, as England's interests are not best served by a Spain in internal turmoil. That is my goal. I cannot afford philosophizing."

"I understand. And I truthfully do not wish Mr. Valencia to succeed, because I would rather my claws in his throat for what he did to us. But—oh, I am so muddled. I thought, after all this, that I am Spanish, but now..." Amaya flicked her reins. "The moon will rise soon. Let us ride as fast as we may."

Edmund nodded.

As the moon rose, they sought out the road to Madrid, riding as fast as they dared under the waning moon's blue-tinged light. Amaya no longer looked behind them. She was certain Valencia would not know how to follow them. But she felt pursued nonetheless—not the pursuit of men, but of terrible memories. She recalled how it had felt to tear Don Balthasar's throat out and shuddered. For the first time in her life, she felt ashamed.

CHAPTER 19

IN WHICH DIFFERENT MODES OF
TRAVEL BRING THEM CLOSER TO
THEIR GOAL

Exhaustion caught up to Amaya well before the sun rose, the bone-deep weariness that was the result of too-frequent Shaping. Her inability to keep her eyes open and her head from nodding caught Edmund's attention, and he said, "Do you need rest?"

"I must sleep." Her whole body ached with tiredness. "I did not realize, but I have drawn on my body's reserves too deeply. But we cannot stop. We must—"

"We must stop for a few hours of sleep," Edmund said, catching hold of Amaya's shoulder as she swayed in the saddle. "It will slow us more if you fall asleep while riding and tumble off your horse."

Amaya's eyes slid shut again, and she forced them open. Edmund was blurry in her vision. "A few hours only, and I will be recovered," she agreed.

They stopped in a village large enough to have an inn for travelers, if a small one. Amaya waited in the tiny space not big enough to deserve the name of courtyard while Edmund attempted to rouse the innkeeper, leaning heavily against the stolid horse and trying desperately not to fall asleep. Her *sunqu* all felt sluggish, barely awake themselves. The horse did not seem to mind her leaning on it. Perhaps she should feel guilty at stealing Fernándo's excellent horses, but emotion was too distant to be more than a shadow on her conscience.

Then Edmund was beside her, putting a hand on her elbow. "The stair is on the outside, fortunately for us, because I would have difficulty explaining your bloodstained condition. Can you walk?"

She nodded, and let go of the supportive horse. She hoped it would not be stolen, because it was an excellent horse that deserved better than to be ridden by a desperate man. Of course, she and Edmund were desperate, so she did not know what that said about her.

She focused on putting one foot in front of the other, one at a time, watching her booted feet stir the dust in little puffs barely visible in the darkness. She could not remember the last time she had seen rain. No, it had been on the road to Fernándo's estate, and Mrs. Paget had been alive. Once more emotion stirred her heart, distantly, and then she realized her eyes were closed and wrenched them open with an effort.

The stairs were nearly insurmountable, and it took her one or two tries to remember how to mount them. But at the top, Edmund opened a door to a beautifully warm space she did not attempt to Shape her eyes to see clearly. Then there was another door, and a bed with a scratchy blanket, and she curled up on it and fell unconscious.

She woke as if to the sound of a bell some time later, clearheaded and alert. Edmund lay on the floor nearby, sleeping as soundly as she had. Even in sleep, he was silent. She could not believe she had never associated his ability to sneak up on her with that of a warrior. She had been as fooled by his casual, carefree demeanor as anyone.

Swiftly, she assessed her condition. Her exhaustion was gone, and her *sunqu* responded as readily as ever. That was the trouble with too much Shaping; one's reaction to it was always hours delayed from the exertion that caused exhaustion, and it was too easy to overextend oneself without knowing. She had been fortunate this time, because in her Coerced state she had not given any consideration to how much of her reserves she was expending on Valencia's deadly errand.

She rolled off the bed and crouched beside Edmund, carefully shaking his shoulder. Edmund came alert as abruptly as she had, grabbing her wrist, and as swiftly released her. "Are you recovered?" he asked.

"I am. We should continue on."

Edmund sat up and rotated one shoulder. "We must eat, and you must acquire new clothes."

"But we are in a hurry."

"We are not so much in a hurry that we can neglect basic needs. If we exhaust or starve ourselves, we will fail in this mission. Stay here. I will return with food and clothing."

"I can come with you."

Edmund shook his head, smiling ruefully. "You do not fully appreciate your appearance. I shudder to think of the carnage you must have left behind you."

When he was gone, Amaya examined her clothes more closely. Spatters of blood stained her chest and shoulders, and her trousers, which had been grimy with road-dust to begin with, had gory brown splotches across the thighs that could not be mistaken for anything but dried blood. Tears in the shirt revealed where the pistol balls had struck her. She sat on the bed and tried not to remember, but the images of men dying at her hands would not leave her thoughts.

Ordinarily, she felt neither guilt nor shame at killing. When it had been Spanish soldiers in Peru, she had killed in defense of her people. She tried to tell herself that Don Balthasar and his men were evil, and she had rid the world of villains who would hurt innocents, but the fact of Jennet's Coercion—that Amaya had effectively killed without choosing her victims—filled her with horror.

She lay back on the bed and stared at the ceiling, which was low and dark with age. Webs gathered in the corners, too old to host spiders, and the one window shed dirty yellow light across the floor. The scratchy wool blanket had once been dark blue, but had faded to a softer color that was the only attractive thing about the small room. The smells of dust and old wood, bitter and resinous, combined with the fainter smell of unwashed body from the blanket to make Amaya feel slightly ill. She sat up and stilled her stomach, making Need remind her that she was hungry—another aftereffect of excessive Shaping. Or it could simply mean that it was past breakfast time.

A short while later, a rap at the door preceded Edmund into the room. He carried a bundle of fabric under one arm, a bucket in one hand, and a covered basket in the other. "I believe these will fit you," he said, offering her the bundle, "and there is fresh bread and fruit. I will see to the horses, and as soon as you are ready, we can leave." He set the bucket on the floor; water sloshed up its sides. "I guessed you might wish to wash. Do not dawdle, though. We must make good time today if we are to arrive in Madrid tomorrow morning."

Amaya paused in the act of reaching for the bucket. "We cannot arrive tonight?"

"We are still some distance from the city, and we slept longer than I anticipated. I doubt the horses will make it that far. If possible, we will see about exchanging mounts this evening, and ride through the night. But it is more likely we will have to rest, and arrive in Madrid in the morning."

"Then go, and I will hurry," Amaya said.

When he was gone, she stripped out of her gory clothes and sponged herself off, wincing again at how the blood made the water pink. Then she dressed, marveling as she did so how well Edmund had chosen for her. The shirt and trousers were only a little too large, the coat a little too snug, and she pulled on her own boots and wriggled her toes in satisfaction.

Gathering up her armload of ruined clothes, bucket, and basket, she hurried down the stairs, dashing the water across the parched side yard. It was larger than the front and was surrounded by a low fence twined with bright green vines that looked more alive than anything else near the inn. Edmund was just bringing the saddled horses out of the shed that apparently passed as a stable. The horses did not seem put out at the quality of their lodgings.

Edmund flicked aside the napkin covering the basket and helped himself to a yellow-green pear and half a loaf of crusty, delicious-smelling bread. "Eat quickly, for I find eating while riding to be hard on the digestion."

Amaya thrust her ruined, bloodstained clothing deep into a saddlebag and bit into her own pear, wiping away the juice that spilled over her chin. "This bread smells unexpectedly good."

"Because the inn is unexpectedly bad?" Edmund said with a smile. "I admit I did not expect such quality from this kitchen." He finished his pear and tossed the tiny core of seeds aside. "You are certain you are well enough for travel?"

"I am quite well, Edmund, do not trouble yourself over me."

Edmund's gaze did not waver. "I have never seen you in such a condition. I did not realize Shaping could be so exhausting."

"It can be, but I am careful," Amaya said. "And it takes very little sleep to restore me. I promise I will not collapse like that again."

Edmund looked as if he wanted to say more, but he merely shrugged and emptied the rest of the contents of the basket into his saddlebags. "We will eat again on the way. For now, we ride."

Amaya dropped her own core at her feet and mounted. "We ride," she agreed.

It did not take long for Amaya to regret her agreement. Until leaving Fernándo's estate, she had never ridden all day, certainly had not ridden astride for any length of time, and the sedate pace Valencia had set had convinced her riding was not such a feat of endurance. Now only five or six hundred *rikras* of hard riding showed her how wrong she had been. First she Shaped her thighs, then her posterior, then her lower back, and yet no matter what Shape she gave herself, she still felt sore.

Finally, when Edmund slowed, she said, "I cannot endure this any longer. I will run instead."

"Amaya, we cannot slow our pace," Edmund objected. "We are already traveling more slowly than a full-out gallop so as not to exhaust the horses."

"Why do you believe I will slow us?" Amaya scowled. She removed her boots and stuffed them into her other saddlebag, the one containing her clothes. "I can run faster and longer than a horse. Try me, and you will see."

Edmund rolled his eyes and took Amaya's reins. "I suppose we will travel faster if I can change mounts occasionally," he said. "But if you cannot keep up—"

"It is you who will have to keep up with me," Amaya said, and darted away.

Running was so much better than riding. Amaya re-Shaped her legs to make herself as fleet-footed as a jaguar and ran smoothly along the road until Edmund caught up. Then she ran just fast enough to keep ahead of him and the horses, not wishing to eat dust all the way to Madrid.

The road unrolled straight as a furrow through sere yellow fields untilled or tended, dotted with low, spreading trees placed at random. Some grew close enough to the road for Amaya to observe as she ran. They seemed in her haste to blossom from the ground in the distance, rising to their full height like flowers blooming as she approached, and then their shadows flicked over her and they were gone as if snatched out of the ground. She enjoyed the illusion, as few trees grew in her mountainous home, and those that did had fatter, darker green leaves than the small dusty green-grey ones of Spanish trees.

They stopped once for a few minutes to eat and to rest and water the horses, and then moved on. Edmund said nothing about Amaya's speed or endurance, which told Amaya he had acknowledged the truth of her assertions. She liked that he did not make much of her skills or deprecate his own concerns, which meant he was sensible and not inclined to give condescending praise.

The sun rose high in the parched blue sky and then began to sink in the west. Amaya ran fast enough that the breeze generated by her passing cooled her, and she felt comfortable enough to run for days. It was an illusion; she did tire, just not as quickly as a non-Shaper or even a horse. But with her muscles warm from exertion and her thick-soled feet thumping the ground, she fell into a haze in which she ran mindlessly, not contemplating anything in particular, just a body in motion whose heart and lungs moved as smoothly as she did.

They ran through a handful of villages without stopping,

resting between settlements on occasion for the horses' sake. Amaya wondered in passing whether anyone noticed her, and what they thought of the woman who raced with the horses. Surely there must be other Shapers in Spain whose abilities were known, for it did not take an Extraordinary to Shape one's body for speed and endurance. And yet she could not recall seeing any other Shapers who did so. In England, the Shapers she knew, the ones not Extraordinaries, made their bodies beautiful rather than functional. That was civilization, she supposed, the way England defined it: a society not on the edge of survival could afford to spend its resources on nonessentials.

Having considered this, she found herself unable to return to her mindless state. She recalled what Valencia had said to her in Fernándo's library, that she had adapted to Incan society but refused to do the same for European. Her first instinct was to reject anything Valencia had said, on the grounds that he had either wished to convince her to join his cause or to convince her to come to his bed. But his words struck something deep within her, something she could not easily cast aside.

She was Incan. She was convinced of this. And yet she could never return to that home. So what was the point of clutching at her traditions rather than choosing to embrace something new?

Considering this sent a shiver of discomfort through her. There was nothing so wrong with English customs, certainly no more than there had been with Inca customs—for she could admit that the Incas were not perfect. It was only that there were *so many* English customs that chafed at her. Their multitudinous rules of polite behavior. The way gently-born women were hemmed in on all sides that went far beyond the division of sexes the Incas believed in. And, not least, the expectation that she should use her Extraordinary talent according to society's rules and not her own will.

And yet she could not help suspecting that her disinclination to embrace an English identity, or a Spanish one, arose from fear. That was unacceptable. A jaguar warrior never let fear master her. She should have the courage to consider what her life would be like as an Englishwoman, or a Spaniard, and make a choice.

For the first time in her life, her courage failed her.

"Amaya," Edmund called out, his voice nearly drowned by the thrumming of horses' hooves. "Amaya, we should stop for the night."

She cast a glance westward. "It is not yet dark. We can continue to run."

"Despite our care, the horses will not last much longer," Edmund said, "and we are nearing another village. I have no idea what other settlements lie along this road. We should not risk riding past full dark and not finding another place to stop."

Amaya nodded and slowed her pace. She disliked the necessity, but could see the sense of Edmund's words.

Far ahead, a cluster of houses abutted the road, stretching out along both sides of it, and a cart drawn by a donkey ambled along between a number of pedestrians that could almost be called a crowd. This was closer to being a town than the places they had passed earlier. Despite herself, she could not help imagining a hot meal and a comfortable bed. Perhaps she was closer to English society than she believed.

To either side of the road now grew rows of short, fat bushes heavy with green leaves. They grew in such an orderly fashion Amaya knew they were crops, cultivated deliberately. She wondered what food they produced, and whether any of it would appear on her plate that evening. It was something she might ask the innkeeper.

As they neared the town, Amaya observed many trees growing between the buildings, their leaves a lusher green than those of the plains. Their evening shadows cast the many stone buildings with their cream and tan façades into a comfortable shade, and an evening breeze brought the scents of cool green leaves and onion and garlic and spicy meat to Amaya's nose. Rather than relax her, the smells increased her sense of urgency. It would be good to settle into this beautiful place for the evening, but who knew what Valencia might be doing in Aranjuez right now?

Edmund came to a stop before a two-story stone house from which more of the delicious smells emanated. "Here is as good an inn as any," he said. "But you might put your boots back on."

The way he said it, the amused and resigned tone of his voice, made Amaya wish to laugh. "I should wash first," she said.

"Let us see about stabling the horses." Edmund dismounted and led the shivering, sweating horses around the side of the house. Amaya had not seen any sign that this was an inn rather than a particularly large house, but she trusted Edmund's instincts.

While he negotiated with a stable hand, she drew water for herself and washed her feet, drying them on her trouser legs. It made for a streaky and none-too-clean job, but now the road dust would not fill her boots. She put the boots on and wriggled her toes again. It was a sensation she enjoyed—a peculiarly European sensation, as boots were not a thing the Incas had.

The house turned out to be, not an inn precisely, but a tavern with rooms to let. The tavern owner gawked at Amaya the whole time Edmund was speaking to him, asking about rooms. She could not tell if he gawked because of her masculine dress or her road-grimed condition, but she glared back at him, daring him to make an issue of it, and in the end he said nothing but, "There's two rooms at the top of the back stair you can have. Payment in advance."

The expression on Edmund's face told Amaya they were running low on funds, but the journey was almost over. When they had gone outside again and around the back, Edmund told her, "I asked about buying or borrowing new mounts. It seems there are none to be had. We must let the horses rest, and begin our journey again in the morning."

"In the early morning," Amaya said.

Edmund grimaced. "As early as we can manage. I have never so much wished for Bess's talent as I do now. I might have Spoken to Madrid last night, and this journey could be for pleasure."

"I do not know that I could take pleasure in it even if our message went before us. What do you suppose is happening in Aranjuez?" Amaya pushed open the back door of the inn, revealing a short, dark hallway that smelled not only of garlic and onions but of heated olive oil and the yeasty scent of bread. A staircase on the right, narrow and as dark as the hall, extended upwards out of sight.

Edmund, laden with their saddlebags, indicated that she should precede him up the stairs. "With luck, nothing much. Mr. Valencia must gather his support, and I do not imagine Don Balthasar had the only soldiers in the city at his estate. So taking Aranjuez will not be as simple as whistling for it. If we are fortunate, our message will arrive in time for an Army detachment to march on the city, and Mr. Valencia will be caught off-guard and surrender."

"But he must know what we intend. And he is still an Extraordinary Scorcher."

"I know. I choose to be optimistic rather than to fall into despair."

The staircase came out on a hallway much more brightly lit than the one below, thanks to a series of windows in the right-hand wall. They were small, no more than head-size, but they were clean and they faced west, letting in the warm orange light of the setting sun. Four doors spaced very closely together faced the windows. "This is more than I expected from this place," Edmund said. "The first two rooms, he said."

Amaya opened the first door and looked inside. The room was comfortably small, though the whitewashed walls made it feel bigger, and held nothing but a bed beneath another window as small as the ones outside. A brightly colored blanket that seemed to have been pieced together from many small scraps of fabric covered the bed. "Yes, unexpected," she said.

Edmund handed her her saddlebags. "We should eat, and then sleep, and perhaps we can start before dawn."

Amaya did not feel sleepy, but she was an experienced warrior and knew it made sense to catch sleep where and when one could. She stowed the bags beneath the iron frame of the bed and followed Edmund downstairs.

CHAPTER 20

IN WHICH AMAYA DOES THINGS NOT PRACTICED AMONG THE INCAS

They ate a delicious meal, rice and chicken and crumbled sausage in a thick sauce, that was of the same unexpectedly good quality as the rest of the tavern. Amaya had not yet gained a taste for the alcoholic beverages served with English suppers and at English social gatherings, but the ale the tavern owner produced was delicious. It tingled the tongue like the *chicha* she had drunk in Tawantinsuyu.

Neither Amaya nor Edmund spoke as they ate, and Amaya was reminded once more of the urgency of their journey, though she did not feel urgent at all at the moment. She felt slightly guilty at enjoying the wonderful food and the thought of a night's rest in a European bed. No Inca warrior...

She closed her eyes, prompting Edmund to say, "Is anything the matter?"

"No," she said. And then, because she trusted Edmund with her life, she added, "I have simply realized I am no longer an Inca warrior. But I do not know what that makes me."

Edmund's lips quirked in a sympathetic smile. "It makes you Amaya," he said, "and you are whatever you choose to be."

Amaya shook her head. "I do not believe I will ever be an English lady like Bess. I cannot imagine returning to Don Fernándo, since he supports Mr. Valencia. And the longer I spend in England as an Extraordinary Shaper, the more wrong I feel in rejecting medical training—and yet I truly do not believe I am suited to that destiny. Everywhere I turn, I see doors shutting."

Edmund opened his mouth to speak, then closed it again. His face was for once expressionless, and it unnerved Amaya, though she could not explain why.

"What is it?" she asked.

Edmund's lips tightened briefly. "I know little of talent, and what it means to those who have it," he said, "but Bess has always said she cannot dream of not using hers. That it is so integral a part of her, that it gives her such joy, means it is not something idly laid aside. You must feel much the same. I was about to say, suppose you find a purpose that is not Shaping, but I realize that is impossible."

Amaya blinked, surprised at his words. "I—it is not impossible, merely unlikely, because it is as you say—I use my talent as easily and as instinctively as breathing. To set it aside simply because I see no use for it in proper English society fills me with horror."

"I fear I have no answers for you," Edmund replied. "But perhaps you should speak with Lady Enderleigh. She, too, has a talent not easily exercised within society, and she may have given the question some consideration."

"That is an excellent idea, Edmund."

Edmund smiled, dispelling his earlier somberness. "I have a great many excellent ideas. It is one of my best qualities." He pushed back his chair. "If you are finished, we should repair to our rooms."

Amaya stood as well. Across the room, the tavern owner turned away from setting tankards in front of a couple of men, and his gaze met hers. His mouth fell open slightly, giving him the appearance of a drowsing cow. Amaya nodded without smiling, and he reddened and looked away.

When she and Edmund were in the narrow back hall, Edmund said, with some amusement, "You should not taunt that man."

Amaya, who had not realized Edmund had seen that interaction, said, "How, taunt him? I have never even spoken to him!"

"It is hardly his fault he finds you attractive and knows no other way of expressing his feelings."

It was Amaya's turn to gape. "But I..." she managed, then said, "You are mistaken."

They reached the top of the stairs, and Edmund stopped outside Amaya's door. "I have great experience when it comes to the ways in which women and men interact, and I have seen that look on men's faces more times than I can count. Do you find it so strange that a man might feel an attraction to you?"

Amaya remembered Kichka, and felt a pang of regret that the memory was a faded, dull one. She could barely picture his face. "Yes, I do," she said. "I do not Shape my face and body to the kind of beauty Europeans expect. And I do not have the pretty manners of an Englishwoman. I am strong, and capable, and I have learned this is not something European men wish for in a woman. They prefer to be the strong and capable ones."

The amusement fell away from Edmund's face, leaving him once again somber and unfamiliar. "Not all European men," he said. "And there are those who find the artifice of Shaped beauty inferior to what Nature gifts a woman with."

"Like the tavern owner." Amaya could not help staring at Edmund, at the line of his jaw, covered with dark stubble, and the smooth curves of his lips. He did not have the strong nose or dark skin of the Sapa Inca, who was Amaya's standard for male beauty, and yet the way the last light of the sun cast his cheekbones and brows into shadow made her breath catch.

Edmund nodded once. "Like the tavern owner. Yes."

Amaya's heartbeat thudded in her ears. "But he is not the only one."

"No," Edmund said. "He is not."

They both fell silent, their gazes intent upon each other. Amaya's whole body trembled with the need to act, to do something, even if it was to open the door of her room and escape within. Why she might need to escape from Edmund, she did not know, because in truth what she wanted was to reach out to him, to discover the meaning of what passed between them now. She had never felt this powerful anticipation, not even with Kichka, her every *sunqu* poised on the brink of an unimaginable future.

Edmund closed his eyes briefly. When he opened them, his face was even tenser than before, his jaw tight, his lips compressed. "Sleep well," he said.

Though she could not have said what she had expected, she knew it was not that. She took half a step backward in her surprise. "Edmund—"

"We must rise early," he said. He put his hand on the door latch. "Good night."

"No," Amaya said. She put her hand over his where it rested on the door. "That is not what you desire."

Edmund turned his head away to look out the window and let out a deep sigh that seemed to come from the depths of his soul. "What I desire is irrelevant," he said. "I will not compromise your reputation—"

She understood at that moment what shadow had touched his heart, and impatience seized her, impatience that something so ridiculous as the opinions of others might destroy this fragile understanding they had found. She stepped closer, slid her hand around the back of his neck, and pulled him to her for a kiss.

He had not been as reluctant as he seemed, for his lips anticipated hers, curving to return her kiss with a sweet passion that swept over Amaya. She knew little of kissing, as it was not something the Incas did, and what she knew came from having observed Bess embracing her husband when she believed no one was looking. Those observations had made Amaya curious, as kissing was clearly enjoyable to both parties. She understood now that "enjoyable" was a pale, limp word for the lightning-sharp sensation that shot through her at the touch of his lips. Her hand closed reflexively on the nape of his neck, and she kissed him again, tentatively matching the movement of his lips with hers.

Edmund drew her closer, his hand resting on her hip, his other hand cradling her face. The gentle touch of his hand sent another thrill through her. She put her other arm around him, wanting him as close as possible, enjoying the sensation of her body pressed against his and the scratchiness of his unshaven cheek against her smooth one. She imagined someone coming up the stairs and finding them like this, and discovered she was incapable of caring what anyone else thought.

Edmund's hand slipped from her face to her shoulder, and he drew back, prompting a noise of protest from Amaya. "We should not," he began.

"If you apologize, I will never speak to you again," Amaya said.

That made him smile. "Then I will not, for that is the worst threat I can imagine. But I should not take advantage of you."

"That is worse than an apology. As if I am incapable of deciding for myself the intimacies I allow!" Amaya scowled. "If I choose to kiss you, that is my own affair."

Edmund's eyes widened. "I...do you know, I had never considered the matter in such a light. It is tradition, I suppose, that Englishwomen of gentle birth do not have those desires, or at any rate do not act upon them outside marriage. And by the way you turn that scowl upon me, I wish I had not said that."

The amusement in his expression made him no longer seem a stranger, and Amaya smiled as well. "It is as well for you I am no Englishwoman, because you seemed to enjoy it."

"I did, I assure you. But we are alone in a place where there is no one but ourselves to control our desires, and I choose not to permit kissing to lead to anything else."

Her irritation, which had begun to wane, flared up again. "And again you speak as if you are the one who may make that decision for me," she said hotly. "Is it because English society wishes to protect its women from themselves?"

His amusement faded, replaced by the direct, searching look that never failed to unsettle her with its intensity. "It is because I have a history of indulging in temporary pleasures of the body," he said, "and I will not make the woman I love nothing more than one of those pleasures."

Amaya's breath caught. Her heart, beating strong and fast, seemed ready for her to flee, and yet she felt rooted to the floor, unable to move or turn away. Words rushed into her mouth, preventing her from speaking any of them.

Edmund took both her hands in his. "I did not believe I was capable of love," he said, "at least, nothing that lasted beyond a night, and whether that was the fault of the women I met or, more likely, my own fault, I neither knew nor cared. But you are like no woman I have ever known, fierce and loyal and terrible in battle, and the longer I know you, the more convinced I am that you are the only woman I could spend my life with."

He let out a heavy breath. "And now I feel a fool for opening my heart to you in such a place and time. I should not impose on you when I have no idea of your feelings for me, but I—" He let out a short laugh. "That damned tavern owner. I saw the way he looked at you, and I could think of nothing except making him disappear."

Amaya's hand flew up to cover a smile. She could not bear it if he believed her amusement was at his expense; it was just that the idea of her turning to the tavern owner, who was a good twenty years her senior with greasy hair and a blue-veined, bulbous nose, in desire was utterly ridiculous. But Edmund laughed too, relieving her mind that he also saw the ridiculousness in the situation.

"We need never speak of this again, if the subject is repellent to you," he continued, releasing her hands. "I hope you will always consider me a friend, because I am that."

Amaya regarded Edmund closely, saw how the tiny lines at the corners of his eyes belied the casual indifference he showed, and could not understand how anyone might be capable of pretending his whole heart was not caught up in her answer. Her own heart ached at the possibility that they might only be friends, that what had passed between them meant nothing. Kissing had been wonderful; she knew she desired Edmund as a woman desires a man, and that the idea of welcoming him into her bed made her giddy with anticipation; but she found she understood his reluctance to make what they felt for each other nothing more than a physical interlude.

"I do not believe," she said slowly, feeling her way to an

understanding she had never before contemplated, "that I could be happy if you were nothing but a friend. I have never loved a man before, not in the way you mean it, but I have seen love—I have seen Bess, and Elinor, and the way they look at their husbands—and I want that. I had never considered that I might find that love with you, and yet it is not a strange or unpleasant notion. And when I consider everything I have experienced since leaving Peru, I realize that you have been by my side almost since the beginning."

Edmund smiled, but the tiny lines did not disappear. "Dare I press you to tell me what you mean by all that?"

She smiled back, and touched the corner of his eye, pressing gently to smooth the wrinkles. "I mean that if I do not love you now, I am certain I will love you soon. I hope that is not too strange an answer."

"Not at all," Edmund said. "No, not at all." He put his arms around her and kissed her again. This time, his kisses were slow, and intense, and as Amaya returned his kisses, she could not help thinking that for a man intent on not taking her to his bed, he certainly kissed as if that intimacy were just a heartbeat away.

She rested her palm flat against his chest and pushed, very lightly, and Edmund kissed her a final time and drew back. Amaya brushed his hair back from his forehead and said, "Have you changed your mind, then, about physical intimacy?"

Edmund laughed. "I have not, but as you were so insistent on being permitted to have desires, I felt it only fair to indulge you."

That made Amaya laugh as well. "Then I should retreat to my bed before I convince you otherwise."

"You will not, because these rooms are small and the walls are thin, and I do not believe you deserve to experience that intimacy for the first time in such a setting."

Amaya arched her eyebrows. "I said I did not know love, not that I had never lain with a man before, Edmund."

Edmund's own eyebrows shot up. "You have—I did not realize—"

"The people of Tawantinsuyu do not care so much about female virginity as Europeans do." A flash of fear shot through her, that perhaps Edmund had expected her to be virginal and would think less of her for what had passed between her and Kichka. But another look at his face told her he was not upset; in fact, she almost imagined a look of relief. That could not be possible, but it did not matter.

"Perhaps you can explain it to me," she continued. "I do not understand why it is acceptable for you to have been with many women, but not for me to lie with many men. It is not as if I will become a mother against my choice. So why—"

Edmund's face had turned bright red. "It is not a subject for polite conversation," he said, "and in truth I don't know the answer. Possibly there is no answer you will find acceptable."

Amaya sighed. So many of her questions had the same non-answer. "Then I will bid you goodnight, for we must still rise early."

"Good night, Amaya."

She closed the door of her tiny room and removed her clothes for sleep, though she was sure, after kissing Edmund and realizing what she felt for him, sleep would elude her. She lay beneath the blanket and permitted herself a few minutes' memory of his lips on hers. What a remarkable discovery, kissing.

After her brief indulgence, she closed her eyes and sank deep into her awareness of her *sunqu*, stilling each with soothing impulses. Her moments with Edmund had temporarily driven away her disquiet over what Valencia might be doing in Aranjuez, and whether their message might not be too late for the people of that city. Or were the citizens of Aranjuez in favor of Valencia's revolution? She did not know how many people Jennet could affect, but even without her Coercion, Valencia's words were compelling.

She soothed Sense again, calming her disordered nerves, and eventually slept.

CHAPTER 21
IN WHICH AN AUDIENCE WITH THE KING DOES NOT GO AS EXPECTED

They prepared to leave before dawn, eating what was left of their supplies from the first inn. The tavern owner did not make an appearance, which relieved Amaya's mind. Now that she knew his demeanor was a result of his attraction to her, she was uncomfortable at the idea of being in his presence, despite knowing he would do nothing more embarrassing than stare.

Edmund did nothing to allude to the previous night, not even in passing or through a glance. It surprised Amaya to discover that gave her a twinge of unhappiness. She covertly watched him as he saddled his horse. He looked no different than he ever did, and yet she found herself drawn to the motion of his hands on the buckles, how well-shaped and masculine his fingers were. His brow was furrowed slightly in concentration, his lips pursed, and she remembered how it had felt to kiss him and shivered with the memory.

He glanced her way. "Surely you are not cold?"

Amaya shook her head, suddenly afraid to trust her voice.

This was foolishness. She should not permit her new romantic feelings to affect her behavior to someone who was, after all else, her friend.

Edmund smiled then, a wry expression that made his mouth curve up on one side. "I feel it, too," he said in a lower voice. "I have carried my feelings for you secretly for so long it is strange to know I need no longer hide them."

That warmed her to her core. "How long?"

Edmund made a great show of pondering this. "Oh, since I went with you to the Treasury and you threatened to eviscerate those War Office functionaries."

"That cannot be true," Amaya said, laughing.

"I swear it on my life. When you called Sir Maxwell a savage—he is known to be the most upright and punctilious of men, and I could hardly stop myself from laughing at his reaction. And then I realized what it would mean to me if I were ever to lose your company." He took her hand and squeezed it gently. "You are dear to me, just as you are, and I anticipate much joy in seeing who you will become."

The intent, searching look was back, and this time it made Amaya's heart beat faster with happiness. "You are dear to me as well," she said. "You should kiss me now."

Edmund smiled, and kissed her lightly on the lips. "We must rejoin polite society now," he said when she protested, "and were we to engage in such displays of affection publicly, it would expose us both to censure. You must take my word for it that such would be the case, and that we would suffer for it, as I know more of that world than you. I promise nothing would please me more than to be able to kiss you whenever the mood strikes."

Amaya scowled, but she recalled that Elinor and Bess both

were circumspect in how they showed their husbands affection, and she had to admit Edmund was right.

Edmund was also right, she realized an hour later, about the need for her to ride rather than run. Riding was extremely uncomfortable, and she had already proved she could outpace the horses, but they would return to Madrid disheveled and road-grimed despite the slower pace imposed by the not fully rested horses. Their appearance would cause enough of a stir without her being even filthier than the journey on horseback would cause. So she rode, and cursed silently, using English words Edmund likely did not know she had learned from him.

They had made better time than she realized, because the stones of Madrid's many buildings appeared on the horizon a mere hour after the sun did. Upon seeing them, Amaya's discomfort vanished with the anticipation of delivering their message. She did not know to whom they must speak, or who would know best how to relay their message to the king, and hoped Edmund had a plan. The delay of the previous day's journey chafed at her, tainting even the memory of her time with Edmund. Surely Valencia, even with Jennet's Coercion, could not have taken Aranjuez so soon, but her impatient heart could not believe it.

They rode through the streets more rapidly than was likely safe, passing open-air markets thronged with people and dodging pedestrians who seemed certain they and not the horses had the right of way. Amaya, focusing on the need not to run anyone over, did not realize they had reached the Palacio Real until her horse's hooves clattered on the great stone plaza in front of the enormous palace.

Edmund came to a halt and dismounted before they could progress further. He glanced around and beckoned to a grimy urchin who regarded their horses with open-mouthed awe, tossing the lad a coin. "Watch them, and I will give you another on our return," he said, thrusting his reins into the child's hand. "Come, Amaya."

Amaya dismounted and grabbed hold of the saddle to steady herself. She opened her mouth to ask if they should take the saddlebags, but Edmund strode across the plaza without looking back. It was not as if they were carrying anything they cared about. She handed her reins to the lad and hurried after Edmund.

Edmund had already reached the front door and was confronting the guards as she ran to join him. "We must see the Count of Álava at once," he said in Spanish. "It is a matter of national importance."

The guards did not acknowledge him. They continued to stare straight ahead. But Amaya saw one moisten his lips with his tongue, a nervous gesture she hoped meant he was listening.

"I know there are other guards within," Edmund said. "Simply have them send word to Don Martín. We are members of the English diplomatic party and he will verify our identities."

Now the guards glanced nervously at Amaya, then at each other, the merest twitch of the eyes without turning their heads. The same guard touched his lips with his tongue, but still said nothing.

Amaya's impatience surged. She dropped the reins and stepped forward, extending a hand to touch the first guard's throat. A command to his Sense sent a pulse through his nerves, making him collapse, paralyzed. Before the second guard could do more than gape, she did the same to him.

Edmund looked as astonished as the guard had. "You killed him," he said, his voice faint. "You touched him, and—"

"He is paralyzed only," Amaya said. "It will pass soon, and he will not suffer further." She stepped over the guards' bodies and opened the door.

Edmund followed her. "I did not realize you were capable of that," he said. "A single touch? It is astonishing."

She glanced over her shoulder, hurrying her pace. "Any Extraordinary Shaper can do it. I am not exceptional. I am surprised you did not know it."

Edmund shook his head, but said no more.

They ran up the marble steps, passing more guards whose slow reactions irritated Amaya. Their responsibility was to prevent intruders from attacking the king or his officers, and yet all they could do was stare as Amaya and Edmund, two people as villainous-looking as any enemy might be, rushed past them toward their king. If they had been jaguar warriors, their lives would have been forfeit.

Once past the marble stairs and through one of the red-curtained doorways, Amaya was utterly lost. All the halls with their fabric hangings and gilded moldings looked the same; the decorative urns and statuary did nothing to show her where in the palace she was. Edmund, however, ran as if he had a direction in mind. When a familiar wide opening appeared in the distance, Amaya's relief eased her worries that they might simply run through the corridors of the Palacio Real, wishing they had Elinor's proposed spool of thread.

The throne room was as full of men in formal dress as ever. They all turned at Edmund and Amaya's abrupt entrance. Edmund, breathing rather heavily, said, "I wish to speak to the Count of Álava. It is most urgent that I see him immediately."

"Who permitted you entrance?" demanded an elderly man whose white hair reminded Amaya of Fernándo. He was taller than her grandfather, though, and his face was a mass of wrinkles like an unmade bed. "You will leave immediately."

"I am Mr. Edmund Hanley, a member of the Earl of Enderleigh's diplomatic party, and I bear urgent news for the king,"

Edmund said, not wavering. "I am not entitled to speak to the king directly, but a royal steward may convey my message. I repeat, I must speak with Don Martín immediately."

The elderly man looked as if he wanted to protest, but another man, this one younger and slimmer, stepped forward, holding up a hand. "You may give me the message, and I will pass it along," he said.

"Forgive me, but this news must not be made public until the king has heard it." Edmund had regained his breath and now looked as composed as if he were dressed as finely as the many hangers-on. "Please send for Don Martín immediately."

The man regarded Edmund closely for a long moment in which Amaya assessed the room and concluded she could not incapacitate everyone before the guards would be upon her. Finally, the man said, "You will wait here," and left through one of the side doors.

Edmund and Amaya looked at each other, then at the waiting men. None of them seemed inclined to go back to the conversations they had been having; all of them stared at Edmund and Amaya as if they were rare species of birds that had somehow fluttered their way into the palace and were now flaunting their plumage and demanding acknowledgement. Amaya said, in English, "Why the Count of Álava?"

"Because he is the diplomatic liaison, and will recognize us," Edmund replied. "A *mayordomo de semana* is one of the king's personal attendants and accompanies him everywhere, particularly to important functions and at meals. They guard their privilege closely. King Ferdinand showed respect to Lord Enderleigh by assigning Don Martín to his household while he is in Madrid. He is the only person I know here who can gain immediate access to the king. And if he will not see us…" Edmund's voice trailed off.

"Then we must tell Lord Enderleigh, because he will be able to speak to the king," Amaya said.

"You are correct, though I fear I see in that course of action nothing but delay." Edmund took a few steps away from Amaya, causing the hangers-on to tense. Edmund paused, then returned to Amaya's side. "We should not have delayed on the road."

"You told me we could not have traveled faster."

"Not without killing the horses." Edmund blew out his breath in an impatient sound. "Even so."

"I understand."

Amaya heard footsteps approaching, softened by the thick carpet, and turned to see the man returning, followed by Don Martín. The Count of Álava's short black hair was unexpectedly in disarray, as if he had been running, but neither he nor their impromptu messenger bore any other signs of haste. Don Martín strode forward. "What is so important that I must leave my king's side?" he said. His superficial politeness covered what to Amaya looked like profound irritation.

"Let us be private, and I will tell all," Edmund said.

Don Martín glanced at Amaya, then looked at her more closely. "You are Miss Salazar," he said. "I beg your pardon, I did not recognize you immediately."

"I understand, my lord," Amaya said. "But we truly must speak privately. I assure you it is a matter of great importance."

Don Martín turned his attention on Edmund. Finally, he said, "Walk with me."

They left the throne room and walked through halls Amaya was certain she had never seen before. She listened with only half her attention to Edmund quickly telling Don Martín of their experiences and what Valencia intended to do in Aranjuez. The rest of her was preoccupied with watching for anyone who might try to listen in. She understood the value of concealing important facts that might cause panic in the wrong listeners, and surely this qualified.

Don Martín said nothing, did not even make noises of surprise, but when Edmund finished, he said, "El Encendedor has long been a thorn in my king's side. Has he plans to march on Madrid next?"

"I regret that I do not know," Edmund said. "My understanding is that he intends to pacify Aranjuez and use it as his capital, from which he will extend his armies. Though what armies he might have, I also do not know. But..."

"You have some speculation?" Don Martín pressed.

"Mr. Valencia's Coercer is quite powerful, as we know from experience," Edmund continued. "It would not surprise me to learn she had suborned the remaining regiments in Aranjuez."

Don Martín cursed under his breath, too softly for anyone but Amaya to hear. "We must tell King Ferdinand," he said, but he did not sound certain.

Edmund heard his uncertainty as well. "Is there nothing the king can do?"

Don Martín hesitated. "He can order the troops to march on Aranjuez," he said, sounding less certain than before. "A quick, clean strike may rid us of El Encendedor for good. Finally we know where he is, and he is unlikely to leave that city immediately."

"Then you mean the king may not order such an attack," Amaya said.

Don Martín shot her a quelling glance. "I do not criticize my king," he said, and would say no more.

Amaya's apprehension rose. She understood little of kings and European armies, but she knew there were many men in command of the fighters, and the king was only one of them and, she guessed from what Don Martín did not say, the least well-informed about strategy. Were she Uturunku over the Spanish warriors, she would command them to secretly spy out the enemy forces and bring her word so she might plan an attack. But she was not Uturunku, and she had no say over what the Spanish warriors did. She hoped they had leaders who might convince the king of what was best.

Presently, they arrived in a dining room as ornate as every other room in the palace. Amaya, to her surprise, found herself longing for the relative simplicity of an English house, or of Fernándo's estate. Walls draped in blue velvet hushed conversation to a soft murmur, unintelligible even to Amaya's ears. The smell of food, of half a dozen kinds of meat, filled the room. The effect was as overwhelming as the ornate furnishings and décor, and Amaya's stomach gave her a moment's queasiness before Need soothed it.

The king sat at one end of the long table. His companions flanked him on both sides, standing rather than sitting and not partaking of the sumptuous meal. Amaya recognized the Count of Molina, who had spoken to her upon her meeting King Ferdinand. He was the first to look up at their entrance. His eyes narrowed briefly, and then he looked away before Amaya could guess at how he felt.

The king, eating with great gusto, did not put down his knife and fork immediately. Amaya stood beside Edmund and watched him eat, feeling an unaccountable uneasiness. Obviously King Ferdinand could have no idea what news they brought, but their presence here, interrupting his meal, must surely stir his curiosity.

Finally, the king looked up. "I assume you have good reason for intruding upon our presence," he said.

"Your majesty," Don Martín said, "Mr. Hanley and Miss

Salazar bring news of El Encendedor. He has killed the Count of Aranjuez and taken over that city."

A murmur rose up from the other royal attendants. King Ferdinand did not show surprise. "Has he," he said, with no more emotion than if he were commenting on his meal. "And you know of this how?"

Edmund stepped forward and bowed. "Your majesty, Miss Salazar and I traveled with El Encendedor, Alejandro Valencia, and observed his actions. Our understanding is that he intends Aranjuez to be the starting point for his revolution."

"You traveled with him?" The king patted his lips with a white linen napkin and set it down delicately on his plate. His tone of voice suggested that their having traveled with Valencia was at the very least a weakness in character and at worst a crime.

"We did, but not by choice," Edmund said, not flinching. "Mr. Valencia's much-vaunted rhetoric is enhanced by the talent of an Extraordinary Coercer whose obedience he commands. People follow him because they have no choice. Miss Salazar and I fell under the Coercer's sway, and it was only good fortune that freed us."

"I see." The king rose, prompting every other man to step back respectfully. "What an extraordinary story."

Amaya did not like the way he referred to their experience as "story." "It is the truth," she protested. "And we have ridden hard to bring you the news. If you act now—"

"I do not permit my actions to be dictated by women," King Ferdinand said. "Tell me, what precisely did you do while you were...Coerced?"

Amaya felt like a small animal who senses the approach of the hawk. "I fought for Mr. Valencia," she admitted, "but it was not by choice."

"So you say." King Ferdinand approached them, but halted some distance away, well out of Amaya's reach. "How am I to know you are not still Coerced, and here to do El Encendedor's bidding? To kill me and my brother and open a way for my enemy to take the throne?"

Amaya's mouth fell open. Edmund said, "I beg your pardon for my bluntness, your majesty, but that supposition goes against all reason. Were we truly here as Mr. Valencia's agents, we would not have bothered approaching you formally."

"And I take *that* as a threat against my person," the king said. "Take them into custody, pending trial for treason."

Amaya snarled and extended her claws. "You would not dare."

"Amaya, no!" Edmund exclaimed. He put a hand on her shoulder. "You cannot."

The king's royal stewards had not moved. King Ferdinand said, "I command you to seize these two."

Don Martín cleared his throat. "If you are innocent, you have nothing to fear," he said, his voice calm and certain. "Please cooperate, and you will be unharmed."

"It is you who should fear us," Amaya said, still poised to attack.

"Amaya." Edmund's grip tightened. "If you kill these men, there will be no saving us. Don Martín is correct; we must go quietly."

All Amaya's *sunqu* were roused to attack. She soothed them, calmed Heart and Sense and Need, and retracted her claws.

"You will send word to the Earl and Countess of Enderleigh," Edmund said. "They will insist we be released, even if it is to their custody instead of yours."

"That remains to be seen," the king said. "Take them away and confine them. We will learn if their words are true."

The royal stewards looked at one another as if willing someone else to fulfil the king's command. Finally, four men stepped forward. They looked extremely disinclined to lay hands on Amaya. She raised both her hands in a pacifying gesture and said, "You need not touch me. I will go with you and will not fight."

Don Martín bowed to her as he had not to the king. "Thank you for your cooperation," he said, and Amaya could tell he meant it. At least one person understood what she might have done.

CHAPTER 22

IN WHICH A MORE SINISTER REVELATION THREATENS TO SPARK INTERNATIONAL PANIC

The room in which they were confined was in another unfamiliar wing of the Palacio Real, one as gaudy with gilding and velvet as the rest. It was not a single room, but a suite of five chambers, most of which were empty of furnishings. The walls were all covered with fine silk, patterned in gold and white, and Amaya's steps on the bare wooden floors, which were scuffed and free from wax, echoed off the fabric. Gold drapes tied back with thick golden ropes the size of Amaya's wrist absorbed some of the echoes, but for the most part, the rooms felt as hollow as mountain caves, if warmer.

Amaya explored the five rooms, though she was not certain what she hoped to find: an exit, a weapon, even an unburned log with which to attack anyone who approached with evil intent. The fireplaces were all bare and swept clean of ash; there were no blades decorating the walls nor even empty urns capable of battering an enemy; and the windows, while offering a grand view of the gardens behind the Palacio Real, were not made to open.

She returned to where Edmund sat in the first room. It alone was furnished, but only with a low-backed sofa, an armchair, and a narrow table beneath one of the windows. The upholstery of the sofa and armchair did not match, and the table, painted white with the ubiquitous gilding, was not a partner to either. Amaya suspected the furniture was simply stored here, but then why not fill all the rooms with castoffs? She did not understand the Spanish at all.

Edmund eyed her as she paced restlessly before the door. "You should sit," he said, "and conserve that energy for the point at which we might have to fight our way out of this place."

Amaya made an impatient gesture with one hand. "I can break down the door at any time, Edmund. And I must pace or go mad. I cannot believe King Ferdinand is so stupid."

"Not stupid, but paranoid and, if I dare say it, rather self-absorbed. He seems to see the situation only in terms of what it might mean to himself and his rule, not to the country." Edmund rested his elbows on his knees and buried his face in his hands. "I doubt we will be here long. And we have delivered our news, so it matters little if we are."

"You are far too patient." Amaya resumed her pacing, flexing her hands open and shut. It did not relieve her *sunqu*, which wanted to be free of this unpleasant room.

"I am simply very good at disguising my impatience." Edmund's voice was muffled by his hands. "I assure you I am no happier about this situation than you are."

"I know you are correct, and it does not matter if we are free," Amaya said. "But do you not wish to have *some* part in fighting Mr. Valencia? I feel, not guilty, but culpable, if that makes sense, and I wish my claws in his throat."

"It makes sense." Edmund raised his head. "But you need not attack him with claws. Not if you can paralyze with a touch."

"That is true," Amaya said, taken aback. His tone bewildered her; he sounded distant and impassive in the way that suggested he was actually in the grip of a strong emotion. "But you knew this. Why do you speak as if my abilities are a surprise?"

"Amaya, I assure you, I had no idea you were capable of such..." Edmund's voice trailed off. "How is it done?"

"I cannot explain the way in which I command a body, my own or another's." Amaya came to a stop before him. "I touch, and I know every *sunqu*—you have no word for it in either Spanish or English—every part of the body. And it does what I tell it. If I say to the legs, grow strong, they grow strong. If I say to the nerves, be still, there is paralysis. It is who I am."

Edmund's lips thinned in a tense line. "Then you might tell a heart to burst," he said, "or you might crush veins. Amaya, you can kill with a touch."

His suppressed emotion frightened her. It was not the terror Jennet had Coerced in her, but a more subtle, insidious fear as if she were losing something precious. "You must have known this," she insisted. "All Extraordinary Shapers are capable of it. And it is not as if I have ever killed innocents in that manner. I have taken lives, yes, but in the cause of protecting those who cannot defend themselves. Edmund, do not look at me that way!"

Edmund's head turned away so he was looking out the window at the gardens. She did not believe he saw them. "No English Extraordinary Shaper can use his talent in that way."

"That is not true, Edmund. I am certain that it is inherent to the talent. They must have a reason for not revealing it, but it is not that they lack the ability." Amaya followed his gaze and saw a pair of blue birds banded with black swooping and diving in perfect harmony. They swept past, separated, and were gone.

"Of course they would keep it a secret. No one would

welcome the touch of someone who could take a life as easily as breathing." Edmund let out a deep breath, as if demonstrating how easy the act was. "Not even if that touch meant life instead."

Amaya felt frozen in place. She wished she dared go to him, make him look at her as he had before, not with that dreadful, empty, almost fearful look. "Edmund," she said, her voice almost a whisper, "you should not fear me. I would never hurt you."

He rose from the sofa and walked to the window, rested his head on the frame, and let out another breath. "I know," he said. "It is simply impossible to comprehend. All those Extraordinary Shapers concealing such a terrible secret."

"Is it so terrible?"

Finally, he turned to look at her. "There would be no stopping someone who chose to use that talent for evil," he said. "And I shudder to imagine the rioting and massacres that might occur were ordinary people to learn about that aspect of an Extraordinary Shaper's talent. It would be the Frenzy all over again."

"I do not know what that is."

Edmund's thumbnail scraped the window sill restlessly, peeling up thin curls of paint. "When talent first arose, it was in the wake of plagues that killed thousands, perhaps tens of thousands. People were terrified because no one knew where the plagues came from or how the illness was transmitted. When those who had been taken for dead woke, that terror transformed itself into what in Europe was called the Frenzy. People feared the dead were rising, and since those who woke had talent, that frightened people even more. In some places, the newly talented were torn apart by mobs of people they had once called friends. It took fast action by courageous community leaders to prevent the Frenzy from spreading."

Amaya nodded slowly. "And you believe it could happen again."

"Ordinary people do not fear the talented because the talented do not, for the most part, abuse their talent and the status that comes with it." Edmund's thumbnail dug deeper. "No one fears Scorchers as a whole, for example, rather reserving their animosity for those who use their talent to commit criminal acts. Were it to turn out that Scorchers are capable of, for example, igniting fire miles away from where they can see, instead of being limited to no farther than their range of vision, people would not be so generous of spirit."

"But *someone* must know," Amaya insisted. "I assure you this is not a part of my talent I was unaware of until I was instructed. It is an obvious extension of Shaping."

"I daresay you are correct," Edmund said. "In fact, I wonder now if that is not what Sir Maxwell and the War Office functionaries feared you might do, and not your claws and physical strength—ow!" He raised his thumb to his lips.

"What is the matter?"

"Merely a splinter driven beneath the nail. It is nothing."

Amaya hesitated. Then she came toward him, her hand extended. "May I?"

Edmund lowered his hand. They stared at each other, and Amaya was reminded of that narrow hall in the inn, where they had faced one another on the verge of another extraordinary moment. If he would not permit her to Shape his injury, it would be the end for them. Her heart ached at the thought that she might never touch Edmund again.

Then Edmund held out his hand. "Please," he said, his face once more empty of emotion. Amaya took his hand gently and plucked the splinter out, then Shaped the tiny blood vessel to seal itself, made skin grow over the spot.

"It does not take a doctor for such a small wound," she said.

Edmund removed his hand from hers and wiped a trace of blood on his already filthy trousers. "Thank you."

Her throat seemed to have closed up, rendering her incapable of speech. She merely nodded.

Edmund closed his eyes and tilted his head back, releasing another deep breath. "Forgive me, my love," he said, reaching once more for her hand. "I do not know why it should unsettle me to learn you have other ways of killing, if I am not disturbed by knowing that you have killed at all. Forgive my foolish reaction."

Amaya took his hand and was drawn into his warm, solid embrace. The strange, insidious fear faded and died. Of course Edmund would not hate her for having a deadly talent. "Scorchers can kill with their talent," she murmured into his shoulder.

"I know, and I cannot explain why that is different from what you can do." Edmund gripped her shoulders and held her so he could look into her eyes. "I suppose because there is an element of subterfuge involved. Any Extraordinary Shaper could be an assassin, an undetectable assassin. Imagine forming a blood clot in someone's veins that does not kill until hours or days later. No one would ever suspect foul play."

"Or every Extraordinary Shaper would be suspected of crimes they had no reason to commit," Amaya pointed out.

"Which is no doubt why they have kept the ability a secret." Edmund no longer looked impassive; he looked as if he were pondering some great puzzle. "And yet—Amaya, it is impossible that no Extraordinary Shaper in England has ever killed this way. How many murders have gone unpunished, or even undetected, because of this secret?"

"That is impossible to say, and I do not know that it

matters," Amaya said. When Edmund began to protest, she added, "I mean that the lives of the innocents, the Extraordinary Shapers who are not murderers, must surely outweigh bringing those few to justice. If you are correct that knowing this could spark a panic—"

"It goes against my instincts to see justice robbed like that," Edmund said, "but you are probably right." He put his arms around her again and pulled her close. "Is it easier? For you, I mean."

"Easier to kill with a touch than another way?" Amaya considered the question. "I have never used it as my primary weapon. It is not as honorable as a warrior's claws or blade. I paralyzed Uturunku before killing him to show that I have more abilities than an ordinary Shaper to turn toward protecting my people. But I took his life with my claws."

Edmund let out a low chuckle. "You realize most Englishmen would indeed find you terrifying. I am remarkable in how I do not feel intimidated by the powerful woman I love more every hour I am in her presence."

That filled Amaya's heart with joy. "You are remarkable because you are strong enough not to fear being underestimated because you appear weak and foolish. It is what draws me to you, that you are strong in ways different from mine."

"If I believed my foolish ways made you think less of me, I would change them in a heartbeat," Edmund said. He touched her face gently, tracing the line of her eyebrow and then the curve of her cheek. "Because I can bear anything but that."

The sound of the door opening made them separate, fast enough that Amaya felt bereft. She considered extending her claws, imagining the many possibilities of who might come through the door: soldiers, Don Martín, the king.

But it was Elinor.

LIBERATING FIGHT

She turned and spoke quietly to someone out of Amaya's line of sight; Amaya heard the words, "Turn the key if you feel you must, but you might remember that the door is made of wood." Elinor sounded perfectly composed, but Amaya could imagine the face of whatever servant or even *mayordomo de semana* might have accompanied her there.

Elinor entered the room and shut the door behind her. Amaya did not hear the click of the lock. "I hope you can explain what has happened," Elinor said. "No one tried to stop me coming here, but neither would they permit me to release you. Lord Enderleigh has gone to speak to King Ferdinand, and I am here to speak to you."

Amaya was not sure where to begin. Edmund had no such difficulty. "We encountered El Encendedor," he said, "who has an Extraordinary Coercer in his train. She Coerced us into believing his cause was just. When we managed to escape, we came directly here with news that Señor Valencia—El Encendedor—has captured the city of Aranjuez and intends to make it the center of his revolution."

Elinor's eyes widened. "How unexpected," she said, her calm voice at odds with her expression. "How did you escape? I believed a Coercer's talent to be unbreakable."

"Another strong emotion can be in its place," Amaya said. "And she—the Coercer is not so loyal to Señor Valencia as she or he believe. She helped us escape."

"Also unexpected." Elinor took a seat on the sofa. "Forgive me, but standing for very long makes my ankles ache. Did you see El Encendedor use his talent? What is its extent?"

"I do not know what an Extraordinary Scorcher is capable of," Edmund said. "He was able to ignite the entire roof of an estate, several hundred square feet, and extinguish it as readily. And he controls fire with ease."

Elinor's expression was thoughtful, her eyes unfocused as if seeing something not in the room. "He might be more powerful than that," she said. "But that alone is powerful enough. If he attacks Madrid, I will not be able to challenge him directly."

"Why is that?" Edmund's gaze sharpened, and he took a few steps toward Elinor.

"Because the child can be burned," Amaya said.

"That, and I dare not permit myself to be overcome by fire a second time." Elinor's gaze focused on Amaya, and she smiled a thin, self-mocking smile. "My husband only has so many hands to sacrifice."

Amaya wished dearly she could press Elinor for more details about this extraordinary statement, but now was not the time. "Why can we not leave? We are not traitors."

Now Elinor's expression was sour. "King Ferdinand sees an opportunity to make his English 'guests' supplicants. His pride is engaged, and with such a man as him, that pride prevents him seeing clearly. As the two of you are the only ones who know even a little of El Encendedor's plan, you should be consulting with his generals so they might determine a course of action. But that would not suit the king's pride."

"They cannot keep me if I choose not," Amaya said.

"And none of them are willing to challenge me. But we must yet maintain a diplomatic appearance." Elinor looked even more bitter. "I regret that you must be confined a while longer. I hope you will not grow bored with one another's company."

Amaya could not help glancing at Edmund. His eyes were alight with amusement and affection, and she blushed before she could stop herself.

Elinor regarded them both. "I see," she said, and now she sounded amused as well. "Then I shall leave you, but I promise I will return as soon as Lord Enderleigh judges we have pandered to King Ferdinand's self-love sufficiently." She smiled, gripped Amaya's hand, and said, "You must tell me what passed between you and your Salazar relations—but later."

When the door had closed behind her, Amaya tried and failed to hold back laughter. "She knows," she said in Spanish.

"I wish everyone to know, because I am just selfish enough not to wish to see you courted by tall, handsome Spanish grandees," Edmund said with a wink.

"I have yet to see a Spanish grandee I prefer to you." Amaya sat on the sofa and patted the cushion beside her in invitation.

Edmund sat beside her and once more took her in his arms. "High praise indeed, Miss Salazar," he said, and bent his head to kiss her.

CHAPTER 23

IN WHICH IMPORTANT INFORMATION IS IGNORED BY THOSE IN POWER

By the time the door opened again, the sun was low in the afternoon sky, casting the suite of rooms into shadow. Amaya, standing by the window looking out over the gardens, turned to see a pair of soldiers enter, followed by Don Martín. Don Martín looked as placid as ever; the soldiers cast nervous glances at Amaya.

"You will come with us," Don Martín said. He made a little gesture toward the door as if he feared they had not understood him.

"We are free to go?" Edmund said.

"The king wishes to speak with you," Don Martín said. He still looked unconcerned. Amaya regarded him closely, but saw nothing to indicate he saw this request as extraordinary.

Edmund glanced at Amaya, then left the room with her immediately behind him. Don Martín took up the lead, and the soldiers fell in behind. Amaya's neck prickled with her awareness of how close they were. Unlike most of the soldiers she had seen guarding the palace, these men were armed with pistols as well as the long poles with blades attached to their tips. This difference worried Amaya, as she could see no reason for it. True, she had not seen every soldier attached to the palace, so these might merely be a different kind of guard, but combined with the request that they speak with the king, the pistols unnerved her.

She paid close attention to the path they took, in case she might need to make a rapid escape. She had never seen anything manmade as large as the Palacio Real. The residents of her city in the mountains of Peru might disappear into it without a trace. Occasionally windows revealed glimpses of the gardens, and once she saw an enormous glimmering pool, its sides regular as no natural pool would be. She never saw any people.

Eventually, Don Martín opened a door and bowed to indicate Edmund and Amaya should enter. The room beyond was as ornate and gilded as all the others, though the walls were covered in a rich patterned purple fabric and the ceiling, rimmed and decorated with gold leaves, did not have a picture painted at its center. Curtains matching the wall fabric shrouded two other doors, while a third set of curtains was drawn back to reveal a window that overlooked the garden. Though the afternoon light illuminated the room, the darkness of the walls and drapes absorbed it, dimming the chamber, though an enormous chandelier, unlit, hung from the center of the ceiling.

Soldiers stood at attention in pairs at every door, including the one they entered by, and flanked King Ferdinand, who stood at the window, looking out. He did not turn when they entered. More men, these dressed like the courtiers Amaya had seen in the throne room, stood near the walls at random. Their soft conversations ceased when Amaya and Edmund entered. With a quiet *click*, the door closed behind them.

Amaya turned reflexively and saw only an unfamiliar pair of

soldiers flanking the door. Don Martín and the soldiers had not entered with them. Amaya's disquiet intensified.

She took a step toward the king, and the soldiers all shifted at once, bringing their long weapons into a threatening position. She stopped. The soldiers did not relax. Amaya assessed the room. Getting inside the reach of those weapons would be difficult, but the soldiers could not defend themselves once she was close enough. She might kill one soldier and take his weapon—it was unfamiliar, true, but—

"Your majesty," Edmund said, "have we offended you in some way?" He sounded polite, not at all as if the soldiers were poised to attack.

The king said nothing. Amaya continued planning her attack. The soldier on the left behind her; he would be an excellent target, as he clearly believed he had an advantage over her.

Finally, without turning, the king said, "Do you take me for a fool?"

"If we have given you the impression that we do not respect you, I assure you this is not the case," Edmund said, still as polite as ever.

The king made a dismissive gesture. "You claimed that El Encendedor seized Aranjuez, that he killed its count and intended to make the city the center of his revolution?"

"That is what he told us, yes." Edmund's politeness now sounded slightly confused.

The king turned to fix his gaze on Edmund. His voice had sounded calm, but his expression was furious, startling Amaya. "Then how do you explain the army on our doorstep?" he said. His hand, closed into a fist, trembled with suppressed rage.

"I—your majesty, what do you mean?" Edmund now sounded completely bewildered. Amaya did not dare look away from the king. She feared, irrationally, that if she did he might erupt into violence, and she did not wish to be responsible for killing a king.

The king pointed out the window, his hand still shaking. "El Encendedor is marching on Madrid. His fires go before him. Your story is nothing but a lie, concocted to lull the Army into a false sense of security and prevent them reacting in time to defend this city."

"No," Edmund said, taking a step forward.

The soldiers moved, two of them stepping in front of King Ferdinand, the others blocking the exits. And Amaya was seized by an unseen force, held in place though she had not tried to move. It did not feel like her paralysis, in which nerves forbade the body to move; it felt like being restrained by an outside force, an invisible hand gripping her arms and pinning them to her sides. She tried to move her legs and discovered them similarly bound. Only her head could move, and as she turned it from side to side, hoping it might help her free the rest of her body, she saw the courtiers standing as still as if they, too, were bound.

She cast about for the source of the restraints and heard Edmund say, "You need not turn your Movers on us. I assure you we mean you no harm. We told the truth as we knew it."

Movers. Amaya looked again at the courtiers and realized they were not frozen; they were deeply intent on her and Edmund. She had seen Movers among her people, though none of them had been Extraordinaries, and they always required intense concentration when maintaining a hold on something, or someone, that wished to escape.

Amaya strained again against the invisible grip. She found she could twist from side to side, exactly as if her arms and legs were bound but she was not tied to anything. The grip tightened, and she cried out involuntarily. "Amaya, do not fight!"

Edmund exclaimed. She ignored him, twisting until she overbalanced—and another invisible hand prevented her from falling. Breathing heavily, she let herself hang supported by nothing but air.

"You expect me to believe you are not my enemy?" King Ferdinand said. "When you English came in power and status to remind me of my country's inferiority to yours? Did you believe I would not know what it means that two such powerful talents head your embassy?"

Edmund said nothing. Amaya twisted her head to look up at him. He wore the impassive look Amaya knew so well, the one that said he was prepared to attack. How, she had no idea, as they were both held fast.

The king walked toward them, his pace measured. Amaya strained against her invisible bonds again, then let herself go limp, as if she had given up or fainted. "I should have you killed," King Ferdinand said, "but I am certain your Lord Enderleigh will cry diplomatic immunity. But I cannot permit you to go free, not while you are the victims of a Coercion that might see me dead."

"We are not Coerced," Edmund said, somewhat breathily as if a hand compressed his lungs.

"Precisely what someone in the thrall of a Coercer would say." King Ferdinand stopped in front of Amaya. With her head hanging low, she could see nothing more of him than his brown, pointed shoes and his stockinged legs that disappeared into those odd trousers that came only to the knee. Then she felt his hand on her chin, lifting her head. "I will show—"

Skin to skin contact was enough. Amaya sent a command to his Sense, shooting paralysis through his every nerve. King Ferdinand collapsed.

She heard gasps and cries of dismay, and the grip holding her vanished, dropping her. She landed lightly and she stepped backward, inside the reach of the nearest soldier's pole weapon. She slammed her elbow into his face, and when he cried out in pain, she wrenched his weapon from his hand and used it to disarm his companion. She whipped the blunt end around to slam into the second soldier's head, sending him to the ground.

Edmund grabbed the fallen pole weapon and rested its blade against the fallen king's throat. "Do not use your Moving on us again," he said. "You know you cannot hold us entirely, and it will take very little movement for me to strike."

The courtiers raised their hands to show they were unarmed, a pointless gesture, Amaya thought, as they did not need touch to Move anything. The soldiers across the room held their weapons at the ready, though Amaya saw one of them tremble with fear. She snarled at him, and he took an involuntary step back and was glared at by his companion.

"Is he dead?" Edmund murmured for Amaya's ears alone. She shook her head. "Then I suppose you have not completely lost your mind." In a louder voice, he said, "We have not killed your king even though I am certain you realize we could have. England means Spain no harm, and we do not wish El Encendedor to destroy your government. I suggest, if you have not already, that you mobilize the Army's forces to meet Mr. Valencia before he enters the city."

Two of the soldiers took a step forward. Edmund brought the sharp blade closer to the king, and they froze as if paralyzed themselves. "We should leave," Edmund murmured.

Amaya dropped her polearm atop the first soldier and opened the door, backing through it without taking her eyes off the soldiers. Once she was through, Edmund reversed his grip on the pole weapon and flung it like a spear at the soldiers, then hurriedly backed out the door and slammed it shut.

Without a word to each other, they ran back the way they

had come, speeding through the corridors until they reached the grand entrance. The soldiers stationed there looked at them curiously, but made no move to stop them. Edmund had begun to slow, and when he stumbled, Amaya grabbed his hand and hauled him along. "Where can we go?" she said.

"Back...to the ambassador's...quarters..." Edmund panted. "Amaya, this pace...I cannot maintain..."

Amaya focused on his Need *sunqu*, and with a thought, she made his lungs open up, taking in more air and using it more efficiently. Edmund gasped, his eyes wide. "Run," she told him.

They ran faster now, dodging servants and palace functionaries until they reached the door of the ambassadorial apartment and dove through as if their pursuers were dogs on their heels. Edmund leaned against the door, breathing more easily. "I feel dizzy," he said.

"It will pass. Your lungs are not made to maintain that Shape, and they will gradually return to normal." Amaya leaned against the wall and waited for her own *sunqu* to subside, for Heart and Need and Strength to realize the danger was past.

"Thank God you did not kill the king," Edmund said. "I do not believe we could come back from that."

"He was gravely misinformed, and afraid, not evil," Amaya said, "and I do not believe he should suffer for that. Do you suppose he will do as you instructed, and send the Army?"

"I hope he has already done so." Edmund stood upright and ran his hands through his hair, disordering it further. "Now we must decide what we are to do."

"What, decide? We will fight."

"This is not our fight, Amaya." Edmund walked away down the hall. Amaya hurried to catch up to him.

"It *is* our fight, Edmund," she said. "We helped Mr. Valencia take Aranjuez. Even if we were wrong about what he decided to do—"

"Yes, and that concerns me. He was very clear that he intended to subdue that city. His decision to march on Madrid instead can only be a result of our escape."

Amaya grabbed Edmund's hand and made him stop. "How is that?"

Edmund's jaw was tight with anger. "If he knew we were free of Coercion, he must have guessed we would return to warn the king. That means he would lose the element of surprise he would otherwise have in capturing Aranjuez and Coercing its troops. And given that, there would be no point in his waiting to capture Madrid—would be actively detrimental to his plan, as our warning would permit the Army to amass in such numbers as even Jennet is unlikely to be able to sway."

Amaya nodded. "I understand. I wish Jennet had come with us."

Edmund scowled more deeply. "I wish you had killed her."

"I told you, I swore not to in exchange for your life."

That startled him. "You did not say that."

"Did I not?" She could not remember. "At any rate, I do not believe she is as evil as one might think. I believe she wants to be free of Mr. Valencia but does not know how."

"You are hopelessly optimistic," Edmund said. "And it doesn't matter now. We must tell Lord Enderleigh what has happened, in case the king decides to mount an assault upon our position here."

Amaya let him pull her along after him. She did not believe it was unnatural to wish Jennet to free herself, but she could not have explained why. They had nothing in common save a terrifying talent, and even that was a slim connection, given that it seemed no Europeans knew how deadly an Extraordinary Shaper could be. But Amaya could not help remembering how Jennet had looked when she offered the Coercer the chance to leave with them, how for the briefest moment, Jennet had seemed hopeful, like a prisoner who sees the light of day for the first time in years.

Edmund threw open the door to Elinor's drawing room with greater force than it required. Amaya could sympathize with the urgency that propelled him. Within, Elinor sat in her accustomed place near the fire, with Lord Enderleigh seated across from her. Sir William stood by the window and turned at the noise of the door slamming open. Under their collective stare, Amaya was conscious of her disheveled state, of her hair hanging in a horse's tail down her back, and for the first time since entering English society felt embarrassed.

Edmund seemed to feel no such thing. "My lord, my lady, forgive our intrusion," he said.

Elinor rose from her seat, saying, "Not at all. You must permit me to call Señora Zambrano—I cannot imagine anyone bothered to bring you food."

"We have no time," Amaya said. "Señor Valencia—El Encendedor—he marches on Madrid, and the king believes we bring him here."

Lord Enderleigh stood as well. "Explain," he said.

Amaya was grateful the earl was not a man to waste time on irrelevancies such as "who" or "what." "The king—" she began, then could not imagine what to say first.

"You know the king believed we were Coerced and under orders to kill him," Edmund said. "It seems El Encendedor, rather than consolidating his power in Aranjuez, chose to bring his forces north to Madrid. The king believes we lied about El Encendedor's plans so the man might come upon the city secretly."

"How close is El Encendedor to the city?" Lord Enderleigh asked.

"We did not see," Edmund replied. "But by the king's reaction, he has already reached the outskirts of Madrid."

"I can learn," Amaya said. "I will go to the roof."

"No need," Lord Enderleigh said. "I will see what I can discover. The rest of you—" He looked at Elinor, and a flash of understanding passed between them. "You should make plans to evacuate."

"Miles!" Elinor protested. "And leave these people helpless against a monster who thinks nothing of burning men alive? I may be their last line of defense!"

"You cannot fight El Encendedor directly," Lord Enderleigh said, "and I will not risk my wife and child for what is essentially a Spanish affair."

Sir William, who had had his head thrown back in the attitude of a Speaker, lowered his chin and walked forward to join Elinor by the fire. "I have spoken with my liaison in England, and he is quite clear that we should not endanger ourselves. If El Encendedor is on his way here, even your talent, my lady, will not be enough to dissuade both him and his forces. And the majority of our diplomatic party are not fighters, save perhaps Sir John. They will be a liability."

"My lord, Sir William, it is true we might leave," Edmund said, "particularly since King Ferdinand believes we—Miss Salazar and I—are his enemy. In fact, we should remove from the palace to some safe location, as it is possible the king will send soldiers after us here and we are not capable of defending against such force. But it is in England's best interests to have Spain indebted to us, something we might accomplish by fighting on their side. And, if I may be blunt—the world will know what happens here, and their fear of Extraordinary Scorchers will grow out of control if they believe one is capable of taking down a government."

Now Amaya looked at Elinor, who reddened, though Amaya judged her angry rather than embarrassed. "I do not fear you," she told her friend, "as you do not fear me. But if you wish to leave, I will help."

"There must be *something* we can do," Elinor insisted.

"With both El Encendedor and King Ferdinand against us?" Lord Enderleigh said. "This is no naval battle, Elinor. Neither of us know how to fight on land, or how to defend a party of noncombatants. It is best that we leave." He put his hand on her shoulder. "Please, do not permit your thirst for justice to override your good sense."

Elinor scowled at him. "You will not take me against my will, Miles."

"Of course not. Which is why I ask you, again, to go willingly."

Elinor rested her hand atop his. "You are too sensible," she said. "Very well. But if it comes to a fight—if we cannot flee in time—"

"Then we will stand together, as always," Lord Enderleigh said with a wry smile.

Elinor sighed and patted his hand. "You should spy out the land, and see what route we should take. I will prepare the others for evacuation."

"And I will help too," Amaya said. "It is that the king may send his soldiers, and we will have to fight them to get free."

"Let us hope that is not the case," Elinor said.

CHAPTER 24

IN WHICH RETREAT IS DISCUSSED, AND THE NATURE OF SANCTUARY EXPLORED

The sun had nearly set by the time Lord Enderleigh returned. The ambassadorial apartment was in a flurry of packing and racing to and fro, deciding what must come and what could be left behind. Amaya stayed near Elinor, who was as calm as ever in directing the servants and answering questions from her position in the drawing room. "I would leave everything," Elinor confided, "as there is nothing here that cannot be replaced. But people are usually calmer if they know their possessions are secure."

Amaya touched Uturunku's *wallqa* that she wore beneath her shirt. It was the only one of her jewels she treasured, and she had chosen to leave her jewelry box in favor of a swift flight. The shirt's fabric slid along the *wallqa's* flat, hammered surface, reassuring her that she had not left everything behind in Peru.

A door slammed in the distance, and soon Lord Enderleigh appeared in the doorway. Elinor gasped. The earl's clothes were charred, and he smelled of burned cloth and hair. "I am well, do not fear," he said, clasping Elinor's hand. Behind him, the sitting room door closed, and Amaya heard the key turn in the lock.

Elinor heard it too. "El Encendedor caught you," she said, her eyes wide.

"Only once, and I was at a great enough distance that his fire could do no damage," Lord Enderleigh said. "But—" He hesitated, and Amaya saw his grip on Elinor's hand tighten. "I believe his range is greater than yours, my darling."

"Range is only one aspect of a Scorcher's talent," Elinor said. "But you seem concerned with more than that."

The sitting room door latch rattled, and then someone knocked on the door. Lord Enderleigh ignored it. "It is growing dark, and that he saw me in the gloom concerns me. We must hope to slip away unnoticed."

"I am not afraid," Elinor said.

"You never are. Permit me the indulgence of fearing for you." The earl let go Elinor's hand. "We must leave now. The fighting has reached the southeastern end of Madrid, and if we are to escape the city, we cannot delay."

The knocking on the door redoubled. The earl glanced over his shoulder, and the key turned in the lock. Edmund opened the door. "We are nearly ready, my lady."

"We must go now," Elinor said. "Tell everyone to take what they can and leave the rest."

Edmund nodded and disappeared around the corner.

Despite Elinor's command, it took some ten minutes for everyone in the ambassador's party to gather. Amaya waited with Elinor by the outer door, chafing at the delay. Elinor's calm grated on her, for once; she wished her friend would shout or demand obedience or anything that would get all these people pointed in the right direction.

Someone hammered on the door, startling Amaya. Elinor

jerked in surprise. The pounding resumed, and someone said in Spanish, "Open and release the traitors to us, by order of King Ferdinand of Spain!"

"They are here for me and Edmund," Amaya whispered, though it was unlikely the soldiers could hear anything over the noise they were making.

Elinor muttered something under her breath that sounded like profanity. "Tell them this is sovereign territory of England," she said, "and do not permit them entrance." She hurried away, moving awkwardly but swiftly.

Amaya repeated Elinor's words in Spanish. The pounding ceased for a few moments. Then the same voice said, "If England protects traitors, they are an enemy to Spain. Give up the traitors and prove your friendship."

Amaya was not certain this was reasonable, but it hardly mattered, given that she was no traitor. "You will not provoke war between our countries, will you?" she said. "Consider carefully what you intend."

Silence. Amaya paced restlessly before the door. Perhaps the soldiers would see sense where their master had not. On the other hand, they were sworn to obey the king, and might not believe themselves responsible for preventing a war if it meant disobeying orders.

The pounding began again, several hard thumps, and then the speaker said, "The traitors work against England as well as Spain if they support El Encendedor, who wishes only death and destruction. Hand them over, or we will be forced to break down this door."

"You will not. You desire peace with England, and this is not the way to achieve that." Amaya was running out of words to fend them off. She extended her claws and sent commands to Strength and Heart, preparing for a fight.

"Stand aside, Miss Salazar," said Lord Enderleigh from behind her. Amaya turned to see two chairs and the sofa from the drawing room swaying toward her, untouched by human hands. The earl walked behind them with no indication that he felt any strain at Moving the heavy furniture.

Amaya stepped to one side as the pounding began again. The chairs and sofa settled against the door firmly, stilling the vibrations that ran through the door. "We must go," Lord Enderleigh said, indicating that Amaya should follow him. "It will take them some time to break through, and by then we will be well away."

"But there is no other exit from this place," Amaya protested.

"There is now," the earl said.

He led her to a bedroom at the far end of the apartment. Amaya did not know whom it had belonged to, but it was larger than her own and had two tall windows instead of one. It was also full of people, nearly the entire ambassadorial party. A strong wind whistled through the open windows—no, that was wrong, the windows were not made to open. The glass was entirely missing from both windows, whose frames gleamed with shattered fragments from where something had smashed them open.

Lord Enderleigh pushed through the crowd to stand where he could see outside. "Two at a time," he said, "and you need only remain still, this is perfectly safe."

Two men climbed up into the casements, taking care not to touch the jagged glass still clinging to the openings. As Amaya watched, they lifted off the sills and floated smoothly downward and out of sight. Amazed, Amaya took a few steps forward, but halted when someone put a hand on her arm. "We will go last," Elinor told her, "in the event those soldiers are more dedicated and stronger than I believe."

"I do not know a Mover can do such," Elinor said.

"Sir John is almost as highly rated a Mover as Lord Enderleigh, and between the two of them, we should be able to escape cleanly." Elinor spoke absently, as if her mind were elsewhere. Amaya smelled fire, a sharp, hot, smokeless scent, and realized Elinor's hand was limned with flames that burned with gemlike colors, lapis and opal and ruby and gold. She took in an astonished breath. Elinor looked at her, then down at her burning hand. She smiled, and the fire vanished. "I had believed myself in control of that reaction. Forgive me."

"It does not hurt me," Amaya said.

She heard footsteps, and Edmund entered the room. "We have left nothing important behind," he said, "and the soldiers at the door continue battering at it impotently. I don't believe anyone knows what we intend."

"There are so many carriages," Elinor said, for the first time sounding worried. "I know Miles said the Army and the guards have been pulled away to the fight, but surely someone must see."

"Let us be hopeful that they will not," Edmund said.

The room was nearly empty, and Amaya watched young Peter Grimly climb into the window and be Moved gracefully down. Then it was her turn. Suppressing a twinge of nervousness, she stepped up, feeling grateful for her trousers. Lord Enderleigh gave her a reassuring smile. "Do not struggle," he said.

A feeling as of gentle pressure, like a giant, invisible hand, rose up around her. It reminded her of being held by the king's Movers, but flexible, as if she could resist if she chose. She moved one arm, felt the pressure increase slightly, and reminded herself not to struggle.

The rooms were on the first floor, well above the ground, but it took almost no time for Amaya to reach the paved plaza. She stumbled as her feet touched the ground, felt the invisible hand steady her, and turned to watch Edmund and Elinor descend. Edmund took a few awkward steps as she had, but Elinor alit with grace, as if she had done this a thousand times. Likely that was true.

It was full dark, but lanterns lit the palace's façade, giving Amaya a clear view of the plaza and the streets beyond. Gunfire, and shouting, dispelled the illusion of a placid, warm summer night. The noise was loudest to the southeast, and Amaya looked that way and saw beyond the buildings lining the streets the glow of a dozen fires. Her heart longed to race through the streets until she found Valencia, but she calmed her impatience. Elinor would need defending, and it was irresponsible of Amaya to go running off into the darkness.

Finally, it was Sir John's turn to be Moved, and Lord Enderleigh stepped out of the window behind him and Flew, not down to join them, but up to hover near the roof. Amaya shielded her eyes against the setting sun to watch him. He appeared to be scanning the distance.

"Come, Amaya," Elinor said. "Miles will follow."

Amaya climbed into the nearest carriage, where Sir William and Lady Kynaston already sat. Edmund and Elinor followed, making the carriage very crowded. "There were not enough carriages available," Sir William said, rather apologetically. "I fear it will be a tight ride."

"So long as everyone is safe, I daresay we can endure," Elinor said. "Lord Winder Dreamed while we prepared for evacuation, and his Sight suggested this was the best course of action."

"It chafes me—" Edmund fell silent, his lips pressed tightly together.

Elinor glanced his way. "I as well," she said. "But—"

The carriage jerked into motion, throwing Elinor into Amaya. Elinor put a hand on the window to steady herself. "But it is the only reasonable course of action," she continued. "It is not as if we can seek out El Encendedor and attack him directly. There are too many of us to protect."

A light thump sounded from the carriage roof as of something large alighting on it. "I will ride outside in case we must fight our way through," Lord Enderleigh called out. "But it seems much of the fighting is happening at a distance, to the southeast, and we travel west."

The noise of the carriage wheels nearly drowned out his words as well as any sound of fighting. Amaya could almost imagine this a peaceful ride into the country, though one in which no pedestrians thronged the streets. The people of Madrid had either hunkered down to withstand the battle or rushed to join the fight. Amaya leaned out to watch the buildings pass, tall and stony and impassive as if they knew they would be here long after their inhabitants were dead. It was an unsettling idea, but she did not withdraw, preferring to see her enemies approach.

They followed the curve of the street into a place where it widened into a plaza. A fountain several *rikras* tall stood at its center, water splashing placidly into the wide basin. The fountain resembled a miniature tower, complete with dome, atop which stood a robed female figure. Amaya still did not understand what meaning such constructions had for Europeans, whether they meant to memorialize someone or simply liked to celebrate the human form.

She watched the fountain as they passed it and continued watching as it fell to the rear. Now she would never have the opportunity to explore Madrid. The idea made her unexpectedly melancholy. It was not as if this were her home, and she was no longer certain she wished to be Spanish. Her heart ached nonetheless.

Elinor gasped. Amaya turned to look at her only to be shoved away from the window. From outside, Lord Enderleigh shouted, "Elinor!" And Amaya saw, arching toward their line of carriages, a ball of fire bigger across than her outstretched arms hurtling toward them out of the sky.

In the next moment, the fire was gone, extinguished as if it had never been. Elinor awkwardly leaned out of the window and said, "We must find cover! He knows I am here!"

Amaya did not understand what it meant that Valencia knew about Elinor. She could not comprehend how he had discovered them at all. But the carriage jerked, tilted in a sharp turn, and came to a halt. Elinor was outside before Amaya could react, her face turned to the sky. Amaya quickly joined her. Two more fireballs sailed toward them, casting the plaza into hellish relief. Without a gesture, Elinor extinguished those as well, though they came far closer than Amaya was comfortable with.

"You must help the others seek shelter," Elinor said without turning her attention from the sky. "El Encendedor approaches. I am pretending to be less capable than I am, to trick him into complacency, but that ruse will not work for long."

"Why does he come? Because I do not see why he wish to fight you." Amaya found she could not stop staring at the sky, either, straining to see the next fiery missile.

Elinor shook her head. "A line of carriages sneaking away to the west—he no doubt believes it is King Ferdinand, trying to make his escape. I have no idea what he makes of the fact that the king has an Extraordinary Scorcher in his train; did you tell him of my existence?"

Amaya managed not to wince at this reminder of her captivity and her blithe confiding in Valencia. "He knows I was attendant upon you. But he should not believe you support the king."

"Even if he realizes his mistake, he cannot permit me to go free." Elinor gestured at another pair of fireballs, though they did not immediately vanish. "I am more likely to be an ally of Spain than someone interested in simply being free of this conflict, as far as he is concerned. Now, go." The air in front of Elinor shimmered, glowing hot, and a fiery missile burst into existence and shot away from her, sailing into the sky before being extinguished at the height of its arc.

Amaya turned to see the carriages pulled up in an untidy group around hers and men emerging from them in disarray. Lord Enderleigh hovered above the group, surveying the plaza. "Free the horses, and come this way," he commanded, Flying toward the northern side where a building with an ornamental façade faced the fountain. Stone curlicues ornamented its eaves and the sides of its broad double doors, and a latticed window positioned over the door caught the last light of the setting sun. A stone cross ornamented with smaller curlicues surmounted the peak of the roof.

Lord Enderleigh dropped to land lightly on the doorstep and pushed on the door. It didn't open. Grimacing, Lord Enderleigh hammered on the door with his fist, shouting, "Open this door immediately!"

Amaya arrived at his side, pushing through the crowd of men, just as he set his shoulder to it. The door failed to shift more than a finger's-breadth. "Barred, I believe," he told Amaya.

Amaya's gaze fell on the frightened Peter Grimly, whose Shaped beauty seemed so out of place now. "You will help," she told him. Grimly's face paled to ash. Amaya grabbed him by the arm and towed him to stand in front of the door. "Build your Strength—your muscle and bone," she said.

"I have never—" Grimly began in a weak voice.

"You will do it now because you have the talent." There was no time for her to alter a non-Shaper without causing that person tremendous pain. She spoke to Grimly's Strength *sunqu* and sent a command coursing through him. Grimly gasped as his muscles enlarged slightly. Then his eyes narrowed and his jaw tightened in determination. Amaya watched long enough to know that he was building muscle before doing the same herself. Her body strained against her slightly too large shirt, but the power coursing through her felt like nothing else in the world.

"We push on three," she told Grimly, who had become even more muscular than she—well, it was typical of the young to think more was better, and so long as it gave him the strength to help her break the door down, she did not care about his absurdity. She set her shoulder against one half of the door, waited for Grimly to do the same, and counted off numbers.

On *three*, they slammed into the door in unison. There was a still, breathless moment in which she feared they would need to strike again, and then the inner bar cracked and the door flew open. Amaya took a few stumbling steps before catching herself. Then the others pressed forward, pushing past her in their eagerness to reach safety. Amaya stood back and waited.

"No, do not—we will all die!" said a tremulous voice that rose high above the clamor. "This is a house of God!"

"My lord," Amaya said, grabbing Lord Enderleigh by the sleeve as he neared her, "we have attacked a church. Surely that is wrong."

"Miss Salazar," Lord Enderleigh said, "a church is a sanctuary, and should open its doors to all in need. Tell the priest he is in no danger. I must fetch Lady Enderleigh." He pushed through the crowd and was gone.

"Excuse me, ah…" Amaya could not immediately recall how

Valencia had addressed her uncle Leocadio. "Excuse me, Father, but we need shelter. We will not hurt you."

"This is a house of God," the elderly priest repeated. "You bring violence here."

"No, but..." Amaya did not know what else to say. He was correct that even though the ambassadorial party intended him no harm, the fighting would reach this far, and she was not certain everyone who fought in Madrid that night cared about sparing holy men. "We will defend you," she said. "But you must permit us entrance. I promise you will not be hurt." A rash promise, but the man was so terrified Amaya felt responsible for watching over him.

The priest's gaze shifted, and Amaya discovered he was looking at her clawed hands. "You should not fear me," she said. "I do not turn my claws on the innocent."

The priest swallowed once, convulsively. Then he gestured. "We must bar the door again, as you have broken through. But we have no weapons."

"We do," Amaya said. It was a brash statement; aside from the abilities of those with offensive talents and Edmund's fists, they had only a handful of pistols that had originally been intended to defend the party against bandits while they traveled. It would have to be enough.

Lord Enderleigh returned, hustling Elinor along with his arm around her shoulder. Elinor turned to look back once, then hurried through the door Amaya shut behind her. The shattered bar made Amaya feel slightly guilty, but if Lord Enderleigh was correct, the priest should have let them in to grant them sanctuary, and she and Grimly should not have had to break it down.

"I need a window," Elinor told the priest, who looked at her in mute incomprehension. Amaya repeated the request in Spanish, and the old man nodded and gestured to them to follow him.

The narrow front hall opened almost immediately into a much larger room full of wooden benches. At the far end stood an ornate table beneath a tall arch, beyond which the wall was carved with images Amaya at first took for abstract designs. Another glance told her they were human figures engaged in activities she did not understand, their hands clasped together and their heads tilted to stare at the ceiling. The room smelled of an unfamiliar incense, and she commanded her nose to stop itching so she would not sneeze.

More arches lined the walls of the room, and the old priest led them through the second on the left to a staircase. It was unlit, and dark enough that Amaya needed to adjust her eyes to keep from falling. Elinor walked slowly, holding her gown high so as not to trip. The staircase let out on an equally dark hallway, but the priest moved as if he had a Shaper's eyes, and shortly opened a door through which dim light streamed.

This was the room wherein lay the window Amaya had seen, the latticed one over the door. An enormous ball of fire streaked toward them, and Elinor dismissed it before it could strike the damaged front door. "This will be enough," she said. "You must make this place defensible against conventional attack, because I am certain El Encendedor will not be alone when he comes."

"El Encendedor?" the priest said, grasping the one part of Elinor's speech he could understand. "You are also an Extraordinary Scorcher?"

"She is," Amaya said. "She will defend this place." In English, she added, "I will remain with you in case something goes wrong."

Elinor nodded absently. She squeezed her husband's hand and said, "I suppose we will learn to fight a land battle."

The earl chuckled. "How typical of you to see the best in a situation. Mr. Hanley, if you would translate for me, I will explain to this priest what we need."

Edmund looked at Amaya as if he wished he might speak with her privately. She smiled, and his features softened as if she had kissed him instead.

When the men were gone, Elinor said, "I need you to smash this window. I can fight behind glass, but it is easier not to have any barriers between myself and the fire. And I did not like to do it where the priest could see. He has enough worries without seeing his church destroyed by those who would protect it."

Amaya nodded. With her elbow, she gave a sharp blow to the lattice, which splintered and shattered. She used her hands to snap off the remaining pieces and fling them into the street, then Shaped her bloody hands free of the few cuts the glass had given her and wiped them on her trousers. Elinor watched in silence.

"This is like no battle I have ever fought in," she said when Amaya finished.

Amaya said, "I do not know what it is to fight like a rat in a cage. We are trapped here if Señor Valencia comes."

"I know," Elinor replied. Another fireball vanished, and then she flung one of her own that was also extinguished. "For now, we must protect ourselves. I predict—" She pressed a hand to her lower back and grimaced. "I predict this will be a very long night."

CHAPTER 25
IN WHICH THE POWER AND LIMITS OF EXTRAORDINARY SCORCHERS ARE REVEALED

For a time, it did not feel like a battle at all. The occasional ball of fire came sailing out of the darkness, temporarily illuminating the empty plaza. The carriages huddled in front of the church in a random way that suggested their drivers had all been drunk when they stopped. Amaya wondered in passing where the horses had gone. She hoped they were somewhere safe.

Elinor leaned on the window sill, watching the skies. After two or three of Valencia's fiery missiles, she would fling one of her own. Hers were always extinguished more rapidly than she dismissed Valencia's. "He is brash," Elinor said abruptly. "You see how he shows off his distance? I am certain he believes me less capable than he, which will work to our advantage when the fighting is fiercest."

"What is distance? Can you tell how far away he is?"

Another fireball shot toward them, and Elinor extinguished it when it reached the fountain. "There are four aspects to a Scorcher's talent," she said absently. "Distance is how far away a

Scorcher can ignite a fire—or in an Extraordinary Scorcher's case, extinguish one. There is range, which is how far one can make a fire such as these missiles travel before it goes out. Power is how large and hot a fire a Scorcher can ignite. And stamina is how long one may wield fire before becoming exhausted. Señor Valencia's range is exceptional; I have been watching the place where the fireballs come from, and he is quite far away. But his distance is not as good. My missiles travel farther than his before they are extinguished."

"Then he does not approach."

Elinor shook her head. "He draws nearer every moment. I believe he intends to frighten us, or possibly me. He knows I will realize his stamina is great to permit him such an extravagant use of his talent. And he believes me much less powerful." She laughed, a low chuckle that sent a chill down Amaya's spine. "There are men who believe a female Scorcher is necessarily less powerful than a male. I intend to trade upon that misunderstanding in my dealings with Señor Valencia."

Amaya looked out at the now darkened plaza. "If I cared about him, I would fear for his fate."

Elinor laughed again. "I always feel exhilarated when I use my talent. It is like nothing else in the world, like pure life running through my veins. But perhaps you, as an Extraordinary, understand."

"I do." Amaya ran her hands up and down her arms, though the night was warm. "When my body responds to my Shaping, it is like I can do anything."

"You have it exactly." Elinor pressed a hand lightly to the base of her spine. "No, I am well," she said when Amaya exclaimed. "It is how I feel my reserves are low, but I believe this is merely the usual ache of the child affecting my body."

"I will fetch a chair," Amaya said.

Finding a chair was harder than she anticipated. Most of the seating appeared to be the long benches in the central space of the church. Eventually Amaya found an armchair in a small salon off the central space and hauled it up the stairs, bumping against corners and wedging it through the door. Elinor laughed when she saw it.

"I feel as if I am fighting from a throne," she said, but she seated herself with alacrity. "Do you know, I am grateful not to have given birth yet? This would be dreadful if I had to fear for the safety of my child as well as everyone else."

"I suppose that is a way to see it," Amaya said.

She turned at the sound of footsteps to see Edmund entering the room. "We are prepared for a siege," he said. "Though it is possible Señor Valencia's people will be disinclined to attack a church."

"Then what is it we do?" Amaya asked. "It is not a battle if we face each other and cannot attack."

Edmund shrugged. His hair was disordered, giving him a rakish appearance Amaya found appealing. "That will depend on Señor Valencia. I assume your strategy, Lady Enderleigh, is to exhaust him to make him defenseless?"

"You do me honor to assume I have a strategy," Elinor said with a wry smile. Another fireball soared over the plaza and was extinguished. "At the moment, I intend only to prevent him doing damage to this building, and to keep our people safe. I dislike fighting a defensive battle, but as we do not know his intentions, a defensive battle is all we can manage at the moment."

"We are watching the plaza for any sign of conventional attack. Thus far, we have seen nothing." Edmund looked out the window at the fountain. "Have you any idea how far away Señor Valencia is?"

"A few streets, I believe." Elinor cast a ball of fire into the sky; it was extinguished almost immediately. "He is very close."

"Then I will warn the others." Edmund gripped Amaya's shoulder briefly and left the room.

Elinor settled back in her chair. "You and Mr. Hanley," she said. "I confess to being surprised. He has many stellar qualities, but I did not believe one such as him to appeal to a warrior such as you."

Amaya could not reveal Edmund's secret profession. "He likes to see—to show himself as lighthearted and not sensible, but that is not so. I see him fight, and he is strong. And I see him struggle, and he is strong."

Elinor nodded slowly. "I respect Mr. Hanley's understanding of the political situation. He cannot be entirely frivolous if he is so wise. But—no, I will not insult you."

"Insult me?"

Elinor paused to aim another fireball out into the night. "I believed him to be uninterested in any sort of romantic commitment. But I know you are not the sort to wish for only temporary pleasure. Forgive me if that is crass."

Amaya did not understand what about Elinor's words could be considered inappropriate. "He did not meet the right woman until now."

That made Elinor laugh. "Then I am happy for you both. And—" She stood, her words cutting off. "He is here."

Amaya moved past Elinor to stand by the side of the window where she could not easily be seen from outside. At first, the plaza looked as empty as before. The carriages formed an impromptu barrier in front of the damaged church door, their bodies black hulks in the moonless night. The water in the fountain flowed in an endless stream, making a rippling sound Amaya heard clearly despite the nearby shouts and the reports of gunfire. Nothing moved but the water, emerging from half a dozen spouts carved to look like swan's mouths.

Then the noise surged, and the shadows between the buildings shifted and vanished as torches rushed toward the plaza. Men wielding those torches ran toward the church and came up short as if some invisible barrier had stopped them. Their shouts were indecipherable as voices tangled with voices to make a sound that was nearly tangible. A few guns fired into the air, sending the scent of gunpowder wafting toward the broken window.

Amaya realized Elinor had taken a position opposite her and was looking out the window. "I wonder," Elinor said. "Do you believe these have been Coerced?"

"I cannot say," Amaya said. "Does it matter?"

"It may, if the Coercion impels them to attack a house of the Lord regardless of their own feelings." Elinor surveyed the crowd. "I understand the Spanish people are quite devout."

Heat battered at Amaya an instant before fire filled the window. She did not have time to shout before it was extinguished. Then every torch in the plaza died and vanished. "You must find him, Amaya," Elinor said. "I—"

The torches came to life again. The sound of the crowd, which had grown fearful, rose to an exultant roar, and they pressed forward, thrusting their torches at the battered door.

Elinor sat shakily in her chair. "He is quite powerful," she said. "That is a trick I am not sure even I could manage."

Amaya crouched beside her. "More powerful than you?"

Elinor shook her head. "But I am hampered by the need to protect the child, or I would—*duck!*"

Fire bloomed again in the window, hotter than before. "I must know where he is," Elinor continued, "so I may attack him directly."

The sound of blows striking the door filtered up to where they sat. "The others will guard the door," Amaya said. "Sit here."

She again took her position at the side of the window and surveyed the plaza. The fire had not been launched at them as before; it had simply ignited the air at the window. Amaya recalled what Elinor had said about range and distance and guessed Valencia was close enough to ignite a fire wherever he chose rather than lighting one near at hand and casting it out into the sky. That would make it harder to find him.

Heat gathered at the window, and she ducked away from Valencia's fire. A moment later, it went out, and she peered around the window's edge again, scanning the crowd. Valencia would not be with the torch-wielding attackers; he would be somewhere—there. A shadowy figure stood between two buildings to the right and across the plaza. No, two figures, one shorter than the other.

"I see him. I believe it is him," she said, beckoning to Elinor.

Elinor looked where she pointed. "I fear I can see very little despite the torches," she said. "Let us hope you are right."

Fire exploded, hot and bright like a second sun, in the alley across the plaza. A shrill scream rang out before the fire disappeared. The two figures moved deeper into the alley, out of sight. "Ah, that is he," Elinor said in tones of deep satisfaction. "Now, sir, we shall see what you are capable of."

A rumble filled the air, deep and thunderous like the earth shaking, though nothing moved. Then fire filled the alley from one end to the other, blazing as high as the rooftops. It did not go out immediately as the other fires had. Amaya looked at Elinor, who wore an expression of profound concentration. "Yes, I am not so weak a foe as you believed," she murmured. "I refuse to be defeated by the likes of you."

Two figures staggered out of the alley and ran for the western end of the plaza. "They moved," Amaya said.

Elinor let the fire die and lit another in the direction Valencia and Jennet ran. The two changed direction and hurtled into another alley. "Another trap," Elinor said, and set that alley on fire as well. They waited. No one emerged. Elinor extinguished all her fires and, after a moment's hesitation, the torches as well. "They escaped out the rear. And now I do not know where they have gone."

Suddenly, the room filled with fire. Amaya dropped to the floor, waiting, but the fire did not go out immediately. Scorching hot air filled her lungs, and she crawled to the window, desperate for air not on fire. Then the fire was gone, and Amaya faced Elinor, whose expression was wide-eyed and terrified. "The child," she whispered.

Amaya grabbed Elinor's hand and towed her out of the room, slamming the door shut on another blaze. She fell into her awareness of Elinor's body and focused on the place where the babe rested in the womb. "I cannot touch," she said, hearing her voice coming from very far away, "but it moves yet, and your body is cool to the touch. It is well."

Elinor breathed a long sigh of relief. "I was too confident, and I nearly paid a very dear price." Smoke curled from beneath the closed door, and Elinor glanced that way and the sound of the fire licking at the wood ceased. "I dare not put myself in harm's way again."

"And yet he has no such restriction," Amaya said.

Elinor nodded. "I can keep him from burning this place, but that is all. Amaya, I do not know what else to do."

"I do," Amaya said.

She and Elinor hurried down the dark stairs to where the noise was loudest. The mob beat on the doors, which were held fast not by a barricade but, Amaya suspected, a Mover's talent. Lord Enderleigh left the defenders to take his wife's hand. "You are well?" he asked.

"I am, but there is nothing I can do save prevent El Encendedor's fire from engulfing this place." Elinor gripped his hand tightly.

"I will go," Amaya said.

"Go? Go where?" Elinor asked, her expression confused.

"Out. I will find Señor Valencia and stop him." Saying the words filled her with fierce joy.

"You cannot. He will kill you, or that Coercer will enthrall you—"

"I do not burn as others do. And Jennet will not see me." It was not true that Jennet would not see her, but Amaya did not wish to explain her certainty that Jennet would not turn her Coercion upon Amaya.

"This is insanity. Miles, we cannot permit this." Elinor turned an imploring look on Lord Enderleigh.

"Lady Enderleigh is correct," Lord Enderleigh said. "We have only to wait El Encendedor out. He will exhaust himself soon, and then we can attack."

Amaya glanced at Elinor to see what she thought of this statement and saw uncertainty there. "You do not know this," she said. "It is that Señor Valencia has much endurance, and he may burn this place before he is exhausted. I must go."

"Go where?" Edmund said from behind her, startling her.

"Amaya wishes to kill herself fighting El Encendedor," Elinor said.

Edmund came forward to stand beside Amaya. "I have been thinking it is time to take the fight to him," he said. "And as we cannot open the doors to face the mob without being overwhelmed, that means someone must approach stealthily. Amaya and I are experts at doing so."

Elinor flung up her hands in exasperation. "And now you both have gone mad."

"Elinor, it is what I am made to do," Amaya said. "I will—"

"We will," Edmund interrupted her.

She glanced at him. He looked as determined as he ever had fighting for Valencia, and it comforted her to know this time his skills would be put to the right cause. "Very well. We will leave by the back door and make our way around to where Señor Valencia is. And then we will see how well he starts fires with my claws in his belly."

Lord Enderleigh smiled. "A vivid image. Elinor—"

"I know," Elinor said irritably. "But I do not wish to lose either of you. So you must swear to return."

"I swear it," Amaya said. Edmund nodded.

"Speak to the priest," Lord Enderleigh said. "We will hold fast here. And—good luck to you both."

Amaya clasped Elinor's hand. "I will return because I wish to see who the child will become."

"I will hold you to that promise," Elinor said.

The priest, and a handful of men and women dressed in long black robes, huddled together near the table by the strange carvings, muttering in a language Amaya did not understand. When she laid her hand on the priest's shoulder, he startled, but did not react in fear. "What manner of men are these that attack a house of God?" he said.

"They are not in control of their faculties, Father," Edmund said. "They have been Coerced. We intend to put a stop to it, if you will show us the back way out."

The priest nodded and rose to his feet.

Amaya wondered why, if there was a back door, no one had

tried to assault it. When she saw it, her question was answered. The back door was a narrow, black slab of age-hardened oak, barely large enough for one person to enter. The priest unlocked it and opened it cautiously, but no one waited outside to attack them. The door opened on an equally narrow alley that ran the length of the church. It smelled of rotting waste and animal feces, and Amaya had to turn sideways and sidle along it to make her way out. No attacking force could make use of it.

She stopped outside the alley, breathing deeply and wishing the air did not stink. Edmund, for whom the alley was an even tighter fit, joined her after a moment in which she feared he might be stuck. The noise from the mob was duller, but torchlight flickered off the walls and Amaya knew Valencia must be nearby.

"He was in that alley before," she said in Spanish, pointing, "but I believe he has moved on. We must search quickly."

"This way, then," Edmund said.

They made their way around the plaza, staying out of the light and using the alleys between the buildings as much as possible. There were few of those; the buildings were two or three stories tall and many *rikras* long, though Amaya guessed, if they were like English buildings, they were divided internally into several houses. The streets stretched out at random, making odd, sharp turns or curving in places, and without the guidance of the stars to keep her oriented, Amaya would have become hopelessly lost.

Slowly, they worked their way west and south, around the plaza in a drunken path that nevertheless brought them ever closer to their goal. The sounds of battle rose up in all directions now, not just the mob in the plaza but more distant shouts and screams and gunfire. Amaya could hear at least one group centered on the Palacio Real, and despite her anger with King Ferdinand's stupidity, she hoped no one there would be killed.

They crossed a street, temporarily empty, the packed earth of which showed signs of many people having passed that way recently. Amaya circled around the west side of the nearest building, a tall structure with walls darker than its neighbors, and ducked into the alley that ran behind it. The alley's scorched walls caught Amaya's attention. This was the second alley Elinor had burned, the one from which Valencia and Jennet had not emerged.

She held up a hand to signal Edmund to stop and pressed herself against the wall to peer down the alley's length to where it ended at the plaza.

"They were here?" Edmund whispered. He took a position opposite her, his back to the wall.

Amaya nodded. "But they would have exited at this end, where we stand, and we have not seen them. They might be anywhere by now."

"Except they are not, because the church is still under fire." Edmund peered down the alley as if hoping to see Valencia trotting toward them. "We must search this area."

The roar of shouting rose like a windstorm, and torchlight flickered from the west. Edmund swore under his breath. "They should not be this far west yet," he told Amaya. "We must move quickly or be caught up in the mob."

Amaya took a few steps to look down the western street. The mob was a dark, moving mass gilded by the light of a dozen torches. She swiftly assessed their weaponry. "Some guns," she said. "Knives, mostly. They are no threat to us."

"No, but we are on a different mission, remember?" Edmund took Amaya's arm and drew her away from the street. "This street runs between the houses parallel to the plaza. If Mr.

Valencia is not at its end, he is surely in one of the alleys that run like wheel-spokes between here and there. Hurry."

They ran eastward now, slowing every time they came to an alley cutting across theirs. The shouting and clamor rose up on all sides, and the glow of firelight was stronger than before. Amaya refused to let herself dwell on what Valencia might have done, whether the church was on fire and it was already too late. She would not permit him to defeat her by giving up before she knew her cause was hopeless.

Creeping up on the second alley to her left, she pressed against the wall and peeked around the corner. Two figures, one smaller than the other, waited at the far end, backlit by an enormous blaze. Amaya's fear that this was the church door burning passed as the mass of flame sped away to splash against the church's shattered window. Then the end of the alley lay in darkness once more, the two figures darker shadows in the gloom.

Amaya glanced at Edmund, who crouched against the opposite wall. "I go, and you follow," she whispered.

Edmund scowled and shook his head. "As if I would permit you to take the first blow."

"This is no time for you to become chivalrous, Edmund. If Mr. Valencia sees us coming, he will try to burn us, and I can survive that more readily than you. I will draw his attention, and you will attack."

Edmund did not look happy at this proposal, but he nodded. Amaya took a deep breath, assessed her *sunqu* as she let the air out of her lungs, and sprang for the taller figure.

She was as quiet as possible, given the speed of her attack, but she was not quiet enough. The sound of her feet hitting the ground made Valencia and Jennet turn around. In the timeless drawn-out period between launching herself into action and reaching her target, Amaya had time to observe that Valencia looked tense, as if things were not going his way, and Jennet was as impassive as if she had Coerced her own emotions away. But Valencia had not reacted with fire, and Amaya pushed herself harder, not looking to see if Edmund had followed, hoping only to reach the Extraordinary Scorcher before he could attack.

Then the world erupted into flame.

CHAPTER 26
IN WHICH THERE IS FIRE AND BLOOD

For the briefest moment, Amaya's accelerated senses perceived nothing out of the ordinary. Then pain greater than any she had ever experienced enveloped her. Her skin and hair curled in from the heat, all the moisture in her mouth and the insides of her nose evaporated, and her eyes threatened to boil from the fire's proximity. Amaya shot a command to Sense that tempered her nerves' reactions, and the pain dulled but did not vanish. She needed some pain to stay aware of the fire's progress.

She was running nearly blind now, her eyes unable to focus past the fire. Valencia and Jennet were blurry shapes, Edmund was not within sight. She flung herself, not at Valencia, but at the shorter figure, bowling Jennet over and taking them both to the ground. Jennet screamed as the fire engulfing Amaya seared her flesh.

Then the fire died as abruptly as it had started. Jennet's eyes were squeezed shut, and she breathed rapidly, her heart pounding. Amaya rolled off her and sprang to her feet. She lunged at Valencia, her claws extended, snarling.

Valencia was locked in combat with Edmund, the two men grappling for dominance. Fists gripped fists, and they shoved one another back and forth like wrestlers with deadly intent. Amaya, searching for an opening, shouted, "Give up, Mr. Valencia! You cannot win!"

Valencia ignored her. Fire blossomed over his fists and spread over Edmund's hands and up his arms. Edmund cried out and released his enemy, swatting at the fires to extinguish them, but they spread until his whole upper body was consumed by them.

Valencia stepped back and regarded Edmund's struggles dispassionately. Amaya again lunged at him, and he held up a hand and said, "Kill me, and he will burn until he dies."

Amaya instead flung herself at Edmund, tearing the shirt from his body so he could stomp out the fire. Red streaky burns covered his torso, and he was breathing as heavily as Jennet, but he turned on Valencia with a furious, fearless expression. "Coward," he spat. "You know you cannot defeat me in a fair fight."

"Why should I not use all the weapons I have? Is that not a fair fight?" Valencia shrugged. He turned his gaze on Amaya, and smiled. "I did not believe in a Shaper's power over fire until now," he said. "You should be burned to death, and yet you stand here as lovely as ever. My admiration for you grows stronger with every moment."

"I believed I admired you, but that was a lie," Amaya said. "You forced us to follow you, you made us believe—"

"I did nothing of the sort," Valencia said. He gestured at Jennet. "Ned chooses to serve me, and his talent is remarkable, yes. But let us not lay blame where it is not deserved."

Amaya had turned to look at Jennet when Valencia gestured. Jennet had stood and moved some distance from both Amaya and Valencia, almost to the plaza. Her clothes were scorched and her hair was in disarray, but she no longer looked terrified. At Valencia's words, though, the swiftest expression of anger swept across her face, her brows drawing down in the center, her lips thinning to a pale line. Then it was gone almost before Amaya could register it.

Impulsively, Amaya said, "We know she is Jennet, not Ned. And you are wicked to claim no culpability in the things she does. She acts on your behalf."

Valencia raised an eyebrow. He, unlike the rest of them, was untouched by fire and looked as fresh as if he had just stepped from his dressing chamber. "She told you the truth? That astonishes me. Jennet's secret has been her protection for years, is that not so, my dear?"

Jennet nodded once, sharply. Her eyes were fixed on Amaya. Almost Amaya felt Jennet was waiting for her to do something, but she had no idea what.

"But that is irrelevant," Valencia continued. "I do ask Jennet's assistance, but it is her choice whether to obey. It has always been her choice, and the consequences are hers alone. True, she owes me her life, but even so—"

"Then it is you who have manipulated her," Amaya said. "She believes she must help you because of what she owes you, but it is not true. No one should give over what they know to be right simply because they feel a duty to serve someone evil."

"Evil?" Valencia sounded utterly astonished. "I, evil? When I do nothing that is not in the service of Spain?" He stepped closer to Amaya. "You saw the rightness of my cause once, before Jennet made it more appealing than even my rhetoric could manage. Can you not feel so again? This is the new world, Miss Salazar. A world swept free of nobles and kings, where ordinary people have the charge of their own fates. You cannot tell me you do not believe this is the best choice for Spain?"

"Do not attempt manipulation again, Mr. Valencia," Edmund snarled. "We are not fools."

Valencia ignored him. He took another step, then another, until he was within touching distance of Amaya. "You are a magnificent woman," he whispered, "beautiful and terrifying. What might not the two of us accomplish together? Please, Miss Salazar. Join me. Take up your rightful place in history."

For a moment, Amaya wondered if she had once more been Coerced, his words felt so right. But... "You would kill the king, and his brother, and all the nobles?" she asked.

"Amaya!" Edmund exclaimed.

"I would kill all those who stand opposed to freedom," Valencia said in a low, almost seductive tone.

Amaya shook her head. "Your way means death for more than just your enemies. I will not help you."

Valencia's smile fell away from his face. "Jennet?" he said.

"No," Jennet said.

Valencia finally looked in her direction, his brows rising in surprise as if his pet dog had risen up and spoken Spanish. "No?"

Jennet drew in a breath. "It's past time I chose my own damnation and not yours. Let your own words sway them, or not, but I will no longer serve you."

Once more, astonishment touched his features. Then fire engulfed Jennet, who screamed. And Amaya closed the distance between herself and Valencia, claws raised.

She was distantly aware of Edmund rushing past her toward Jennet, and then she slashed her claws across Valencia's face. Valencia stepped back just in time to avoid the razor tips gouging his flesh. He swung his fist and caught Amaya across the chin, rattling her skull.

Amaya felt her every *sunqu* responding to her body's demands, Need and Release tightening their grip on nonessential organs, Heart and Sense tuning themselves to peak performance, Strength building the muscles of her arms and chest and legs until they made the fabric of her shirt and trousers taut. She absorbed the blow to her face and slammed her fist into Valencia's stomach, making him bend double over her hand.

She shifted her weight to drive her knee into his face, but Valencia converted his reaction into driving his head into Amaya's chest, shoving her back a few steps until she hit the alley wall. With her nerves muted, she felt no pain, just the thump of the impact and the scratchiness of the plaster surface, but she lost her breath for a moment, long enough for Valencia to disengage and back away.

"You should burn me," she taunted him, once more raising her claws. "This will not end well for you if you do not."

Valencia's hair was a mess and his cheeks were flushed, but he still breathed normally. "You know you do not burn as others do," he said. "I would expend myself needlessly." He reached behind his back and drew out a pistol Amaya had not seen. "I wonder," he added, as casually as if commenting on the weather, "whether you will survive being shot in the head."

Amaya rushed him. The gun fired with an explosion that filled the alley. Quick as a snake, Amaya dodged the pistol ball and bore Valencia to the ground. Valencia flung the pistol away and grappled Amaya as he had done with Edmund. Amaya dug her claws deep into the flesh of his hands, but Valencia held on, grimacing with pain.

More gunshots, from farther away, and a growing brightness told Amaya the mob was headed their way. "You see what you have done?" she ground out. "How many of the people you claim to care about will die tonight?"

"Better a clean death in battle than the slow death of oppression," Valencia hissed. "You are a warrior. You should know the truth of that."

Amaya slammed her forehead into the bridge of his nose, making him scream and let go her hands to cover his face. "A warrior knows no death at all is best," she snarled. With a single blow, she tore out his throat.

Valencia convulsed once. His hands moved to clutch at his throat as blood poured between his fingers. "Your...failure..." he whispered, and the light in his eyes died.

Amaya leaned over Valencia's body, propping herself on her bloody hands, and commanded Need to expand her lungs just enough to keep her vision from tunneling. She felt empty as she always did after a fight, empty and aching inside. Closing her eyes, she drew in a deep, blood-scented breath. Then she pushed herself up and stepped away from the body, toward Edmund and Jennet and the sound of gunfire.

Two people huddled together at the mouth of the alley. One lay sprawled on the hard, blood-soaked ground, and the other supported the first's head. For a moment, the scene made no sense. Then Heart jolted Amaya with a painful thump that had nothing to do with fighting.

She raced toward Edmund and Jennet and fell to her knees by their side. Edmund's bare chest was covered in blood from half a dozen wounds, and it rose and fell erratically. Jennet knelt with Edmund's head in her lap. One sleeve was saturated with blood, but she seemed not to notice. "They saw us," she whispered. "The men with guns. I couldn't—they were too fast, and I couldn't stop them, Coercion takes too long. He stepped in front of me. He hates me! Why did he do that?"

"...stupid chivalrous notions..." Edmund said, his voice breathy and distant.

"Do not speak," Amaya told him. She gripped his hand and let herself drop into her sense of his body the way she had for Elinor so many times.

Immediately, despair seized her. His *sunqu* were so damaged she could not imagine how he was still alive. Nothing had penetrated his heart, for which she was grateful, but one of his lungs had collapsed and his Need was in a panic trying to compensate. A rib shattered, his upper arm bone cracked, and half a dozen lesser wounds. More despair swept over her as she realized he had taken a ball to the stomach. Gut wounds were almost always fatal.

She sent a command to his heart to slow, to stop spurting blood Edmund could not afford to lose. The flow of blood stemmed. To her horror, his skin began to chill and his lungs labored even harder. She tried to help his Need draw in more air, but that accelerated the blood loss. Terrified, she stopped Shaping him and sat back. She didn't know enough. And Edmund would die for her ignorance.

Edmund's head shifted, and he opened his eyes to look at Amaya. "...not sure...this is...how I wanted...my life...to end," he said. His breathing made a horrible whistling noise, and he sounded very far away, but his smile was as warm and familiar as ever.

Amaya clutched his hand harder. "It is not over," she insisted. "You and I are not over."

"What did he say?" Jennet asked. "I can't hear—his voice is so quiet—he is dying!"

Amaya switched to English. "He say he is done with life, and I say it is not so." Closing her eyes, she dropped into that meditative state once more, searching for a connection she had never thought to need.

Swiftly, one *sunqu* at a time, she gathered her awareness of

Edmund's body to herself. And one *sunqu* at a time, she made links between him and herself, joining his body to work in tandem with hers. She breathed, and Edmund breathed; her heart beat, and his beat with hers. It could not heal him, but it would keep him alive until she could find a solution.

When she opened her eyes, Edmund was staring up at her in astonishment. "I feel different," he said, his voice a little stronger. "What did you do?"

"It is nothing," Amaya lied. "You will be well." To Jennet, she said, "You must find help."

Jennet jerked away from Edmund, and Amaya caught his head before it could strike the ground. Jennet's strange light-colored eyes were wide and horrified in the torchlight. "I? But—you are an Extraordinary Shaper—"

"He is wounded for you," Amaya said. "You owe him. You were willing to work for Señor Valencia because you owe him, so how much more should you do for he who saves your life?"

Jennet glanced out at the mob filling the plaza. Their violence had not ceased with Valencia's death, though they had spread out from attacking the church to wreak destruction on the buildings surrounding it. "But I do not know what to do."

"You must do *something*," Amaya insisted. "And if you start here, that is a good place." She could feel her reserves dwindling like water through a sieve as they poured into keeping Edmund from dying. Arguing with Jennet frustrated her, but if Amaya left to find a doctor or an Extraordinary Shaper, Edmund would certainly die. Jennet was now their only hope.

Jennet looked at the mob again. Her face hardened. "Stay here," she said.

She stood and walked out of the alley into the plaza, into the midst of the mob. The men she passed, some dressed in blue and red uniforms, others wearing the same kind of worn shirts and trousers Amaya did, ignored her as if she were invisible, but made way for her regardless. Amaya watched her go, her heart in her throat. Surrounded by heavily built, armed, shouting men, despite her height Jennet looked almost childlike. Amaya could not believe she had ever mistaken Jennet for a man.

Jennet stopped some ten *rikras* away with her back to Amaya. One hand curled into a fist. Then Jennet tilted her head back—and silence flowed outward from her, spreading like a wave over the mob until the only sounds were the roar of the torches and the more distant sounds of fighting. With a rush of sound like a room full of whispering children, every man in the courtyard fell to his knees facing Jennet. Amaya could see some of their faces, and the looks they bore were of exultant adoration, the way a man comes before his God. She herself felt nothing but numbness, the result of the linkage she shared with Edmund.

Jennet lowered her head. "Go home," she called out in a voice that carried to every part of the plaza. Without a word, without a murmur, the men stood and dispersed into the surrounding streets.

A few of them approached the alley where Edmund lay. Amaya tensed, prepared to fight even though doing so might cost Edmund his life. But the men, three soldiers and a pair of ordinary folk who might have been farmers, walked past as if Edmund and Amaya did not exist. Their faces still had that strange, rapt expression of exultation, as if they were in the throes of the purest passion imaginable. Amaya watched them go, her hand still holding tight to Edmund's. She had believed her own talent unsurpassed in its destructive power. Now, seeing the results of Jennet's Extraordinary Coercion, she felt as small and insignificant as a helpless infant.

She turned her attention back to the plaza. It was almost completely empty now, with a few men moving away into the darkness—and Jennet, standing where she had stopped, now facing Amaya. The look on her face, unlike those of her victims, was unreadable, her eyes cast into shadow by what few lights were left. She stared at Amaya, who stared back silently at her.

Then Jennet turned and ran.

"*Jennet!*" Amaya screamed, rising to her feet. She took two steps and was brought up short by Edmund, whose hand she still held. Her heart beat too fast, and she felt strangely twinned, one heart in her chest, the other in her hand. She looked down at Edmund; his face was grey and pinched, and his other hand closed over his chest as if it pained him. When she looked up again, Jennet had disappeared.

"Jennet," Amaya said, almost in a whisper. She sank down to sit beside Edmund and bade both their hearts quiet. Once more, she attempted to Shape his injuries, and once more had to stop when he let out a thin, keening whimper of pain.

She slashed the bottom half of her shirt with her claws and tore away a large piece of fabric. Wadding it up, she pressed it to his wounds, but realized almost immediately they were too numerous for her to stanch the flow of blood from all of them. She resorted to pressing it against the bloody hole in his stomach, then guiding Edmund's hand to hold it there. His grip was weak, but it gave her the feeling she had accomplished something.

She rested her hand over his on his stomach and closed her eyes. Once more. She perceived the ball embedded in his flesh, a misshapen lump of void her talent could not touch. A Mover could remove it, and she knew from something Dr. Macrae had said that a proper Healing would push a foreign object up and out of a wound as the injury Healed. She drew in a calming breath and let it out slowly, picturing the air tinged red with heat from her body and curling to mingle with the cooler, blue night air.

She compared their twinned *sunqu*, her stomach intact, his torn and bleeding inside as well as out. Carefully, she spoke to one of the many damaged blood vessels, showing it what it should look like. It shifted, then knit itself back together. Rejoicing, Amaya turned her attention to the next. Another success, and another. And Edmund had made no noise of pain.

She examined his body again, and her joy faded. Edmund was still dying. Her vitality could only support them both for so long. And what Healing she was capable of was not fast enough to save him.

She felt hollow and aching inside, not just from having killed Valencia, but from the knowledge that Jennet was gone, and there would be no help for them. Even the church was too far, and there was no help there in any case. Amaya could do nothing but sit beside Edmund with his hand clasped in hers and watch both their lives spin out to their ends.

"Amaya," Edmund said, his voice again surprisingly strong—well, he was strengthened by borrowed life now, so perhaps it was not so surprising. "Amaya, what have you done?"

She smoothed his hair back from his forehead. "I have joined our *sunqu* as one. It will keep you alive for a time."

Edmund's dark eyes were fixed on hers. "And when that time runs out?"

She stroked his hair again. "Do you not find this whole situation strange?" she said. "It is not at all how I expected this day to end."

"Amaya—"

"I told you, if I did not love you now, I would love you soon," Amaya said. Hot tears burned the corners of her eyes. "You are strong, and intelligent, and you always know what to say to me. And I cannot imagine loving anyone else."

"Amaya," Edmund said, more forcefully, "what happens to you if our *sunqu* are linked when I die?"

She smiled through her tears. "You should not worry about that."

Edmund tried to jerk his hand away from hers, but her body was still powerfully Shaped from fighting Valencia, and she held him fast, then caught his other hand as he let go of the cloth and swung a fist at her face. "If you fight, you will injure yourself more," she warned.

"You'll die," Edmund said. "Damn you, let go of me!"

"You cannot force me."

"No, but—" He wrenched at her restraining grasp. "I will not permit you to do this. What good will it do anyone if we both die here?"

Amaya shrugged, a difficult thing given that she was fighting Edmund for control. "If I let go," she said, "I will always have the memory of watching my love die when I could not save him."

"You're a damned fool."

"Then I am a fool." A sob shuddered out of her, and the tears fell in earnest. "I am a fool, because I should never have refused Dr. Macrae's demands. I should have learned the ways of Shaping others, and then I—" She sucked in a breath and tried to control her weeping. "I am a fool, and it will cost me everything."

Edmund stopped struggling. "Amaya, this is not your fault. If you had done as Dr. Macrae asked, you would never have come to Spain, and I would not have put myself in Mr. Valencia's way, and I would not be here now for you to weep over. My love, please, let me go. I cannot bear the thought of you dying needlessly. *Please.*"

A wave of dizziness swept over her as he spoke, and she found she needed her grip on his hands to keep from falling across his body. "It's too late," she said with a watery smile. "Too late. Shaping myself free of Mr. Valencia's fire, and then fighting him...I have extended myself beyond what this body can bear."

With a twist of his wrists, Edmund jerked his hands free of hers. Immediately he sagged, and his wounds began bleeding more heavily. Amaya reached for him. Her arms felt so heavy, like iron rather than muscular flesh. She blinked, and found her eyelids unresponsive. Everything was so quiet she could hear the rush of blood through her veins, sluggish like an icy stream. She rested her hand on Edmund's forehead and tried to make sense of his *sunqu*, but everything was muddled, mixed together as if his body and hers were made of air and earth and water rather than bone and blood. She could not even perceive where her own *sunqu* began and ended.

She realized she had fallen face first across Edmund's body, which was a warm, wet mass beneath her. "Edmund," she cried out, or thought she did; she again heard nothing but the flow of blood, saw only a dark redness that she knew must be the insides of her eyelids. "Edmund, I love you—forgive me!"

The last thing she knew was Edmund's hand coming to rest atop hers, and then nothing more.

CHAPTER 27
IN WHICH A NEW THREAT ARISES

T*hrum-thrum. Thrum-thrum.*
   The distant rhythm of a heart pulsed through her like a drum, making her bones vibrate.
Thrum-thrum. Thrum-thrum.
She became aware of having bones to vibrate, bones that ran through her body like a tree with many branches.
Thrum-thrum. Thrum-thrum.
A body. She had a body. Muscles clung to the bones, skin clad the muscles. One by one, her awareness spread to encompass her heart and lungs and stomach and kidneys and a dozen other organs. *Sunqu*. Heart, Sense, Strength, Need, and Release.

As if giving those *sunqu* names had been some kind of signal, her sense of them as separate entities vanished, and her body gave a *twang* like a plucked string, and she was Amaya again.

She drew in a deep breath. It hurt enough that she knew she had been breathing very shallowly for a long time. Aside from that, she felt no pain anywhere. She blinked her eyes open and saw darkness. That did not worry her; she could tell she was in a darkened room, or it was nighttime, as opposed to having gone blind.

She lay still and let her senses tell her where she was. Dark shapes swam into view, distinguishable only as shadows of themselves: a table, a clothespress, the posts of the bed on which she lay. The bed was a soft European one with a mattress and not an Incan pallet, and a quilted blanket covered her from the waist down. The room smelled of fresh lavender and furniture polish. She did not recognize the room, so she was in no house she was familiar with, but she was certain this was not the Palacio Real, which was a relief.

At the limits of her audial range, she heard conversation, murmuring male and female voices. That was the most she could make out. She strained briefly to try to understand the words, but gave up after only a moment or two. She would have to leave the room to join the conversation.

Memory drifted in like scraps of cloth blowing in a gentle breeze, gradually coming together to reveal the picture painted on them. She had killed Valencia. Jennet had Coerced the mob and sent them away. Edmund had—

Amaya squeezed her eyes shut as sharp pain lanced through her chest. Edmund had been shot defending Jennet. For the first time, Amaya wished she had killed the woman when she had the chance. Edmund, putting himself in harm's way for someone he hated, because he could do no less and still remain himself. She cringed at a particularly vivid memory of Edmund lying in that stinking alley, his bloody chest marked by a dozen small wounds. So small to do so much damage. And she could not Shape him whole. Her lack of knowledge had killed the man she loved.

She remembered, now, that she had pushed herself past her limit, and her body had shut down to Shape itself back to health. She must have…yes, she had let go of Edmund's hand when that happened, which explained why she had not died with him. Linking her body with a dying man's ought to have been fatal. She felt a pang of guilt, not just for being still alive, but for her selfish gratitude that she had not died, after all.

She tried to lift her hand to wipe away the tears trickling down the sides of her face. It trembled, but did not move. Another memory, a more distant one, drifted in. The last time this had happened, she had been weak for a time as her *sunqu* reoriented themselves. She still felt no pain, and no numbness, just a heaviness when she exerted herself, as if her limbs weighed too much for her to raise. She tried once more, and this time her arm below the elbow lifted, not much, but enough to hearten her.

She spent some time moving the muscles of her right arm until she had it under her control, then worked on the left one. That was easier, as her *sunqu* had begun to reassert their dominance, and her muscles began to remember what they were for. The effort allowed her to push her grief to somewhere distant where it could not touch her. Arms lifting, elbows bending, knees flexing and extending her legs and feet. She suppressed Release's urge to sweat from exertion.

Finally, she sat up, feeling like a weary old woman with sticks for bones, and propped herself on her palms. Her breathing was too rapid as Heart made demands on the rest of her, but that would pass. Her legs quivered when she swung them around off the edge of the bed, and her bare feet tingled when they brushed the floor boards (sanded smooth and lacquered, Sense told her). When she tried to stand, her body rebelled, so she sat quietly on the edge of the bed with her hands folded in her lap and waited for Strength and Sense to work together again.

She wore a soft cotton nightgown she thought might be her own, because it smelled like her, but if she had been bereft of consciousness for many days—and based on her previous experience, it likely had been many days—it would naturally have gained her scent. It was too dark for her to make out the room's details, and her eyes refused to sharpen with Shaping. It didn't matter. She was in the hands of friends, or they would not have bothered removing her ruined clothes to make her comfortable. Though she had not been in a position to care, their thoughtfulness cheered her.

The weight of the *wallqa* was a comforting pressure on her breastbone. She fingered it through the cloth of the nightgown and once more relaxed at the touch of the smooth surface stippled with hammer marks. If that had been gone, she truly would have felt naked regardless of what she wore.

She tried again to stand, and this time her body obeyed, though she tottered and swayed with every halting step. A line of light showed where the door was, and she aimed for that, her hands held out in front of her to guide her and prevent her running into a wall or tripping over a chair.

The door opened when Amaya was still some distance away, and Elinor entered. She let out a shriek that made Amaya jerk in surprise. "Oh, you are well," Elinor exclaimed, and hurried forward to put her arms around Amaya. "I apologize, I was simply so startled. In your nightgown and with your hair disordered, you seemed at first glance to be a spirit."

"I understand," Amaya said. She returned Elinor's embrace awkwardly, as she was not accustomed to showing affection by hugging. Reflexively she assessed Elinor's condition and found her well. The child moved within her, little shifts of arms and legs Elinor likely could not perceive, but that told Amaya it, too, was unharmed.

"You must sit—or perhaps not; I do not know what you need," Elinor said. "Doctor Quintana said it happens when a

Shaper exhausts herself, but he said you were likely to die of it." She scowled in irritation. "He was not very optimistic, and I am not sure I approve of him."

"I do not die," Amaya protested. "But—" She fell silent, not wanting to speak of Edmund's death or of how she very nearly had died with him. Her heart ached with memory, and she told herself fiercely not to weep. "Who is Dr. Quintana?" she asked, and hoped Elinor would not hear the hoarse misery in her voice.

Footsteps sounded in the hall. "I heard voices," Lord Enderleigh said from the doorway. He looked at Elinor, and his eyes narrowed. Elinor returned his gaze coolly. "I should not impose," Lord Enderleigh said. "I must tell the others you are awake, Miss Salazar." He backed away from the doorway, and the door gradually swung shut without a hand touching it.

"We are staying at an inn here in Burgos," Elinor said, gently ushering Amaya to a chair visible in the diminishing light from the doorway. With a sizzle, the lamp beside the bed flared into life. Amaya blinked. In the lamplight, Elinor looked tired, with pronounced shadows beneath her eyes and the corners of her mouth dragged down. Amaya considered protesting that Elinor looked more in need of a chair than she was, but Elinor did not appear in the mood for argument.

"Why are we in Burgos?" she asked instead.

Elinor took a seat on the edge of Amaya's bed. "That is a rather long story, and I am not certain you are well enough—"

"I am not ill, Elinor. My body has recovered. It is not that I am an invalid. Please do not protect me." Amaya clasped her hands in her lap to still their trembling from her exertions so they would not give her the lie. She hoped Elinor would not bring up Edmund's death, either, but she steadied herself against the possibility. Elinor knew of Amaya's love for him, and perhaps that would prevent her wounding Amaya further. Eventually, Amaya would have to face her loss, and she was distantly aware that she was being a coward, but she did not care. Pretending would not bring Edmund back, but it eased the terrible ache in her heart for the moment.

Elinor looked skeptical, but said, "Very well, if you are sure. Amaya, so much has happened, and some of it we do not know the truth of. Tell me, did you attack King Ferdinand?"

"I did not!" Outraged, Amaya tried to rise, found her legs once more unresponsive, and pretended she had merely intended to sit forward. "I have said what happened. He says we, Edmund —" Pain gripped her heart, but she forged onward. "Edmund and I, he says we lie to him about Mr. Valencia's intentions and he says we are Coerced to kill him. I stop him threatening us and we…" Again she remembered that Edmund was dead, and swallowed tears. "We run—ran to you, and that is when we all escaped the palace. I did not hurt him."

Elinor's gaze on Amaya was placid, but the set of her jaw told Amaya Elinor was upset about something. "You attacked him," she said, "with your talent."

All at once Amaya saw the truth. Her heart gave a painful lurch. "It is not what you believe."

"I don't know what I believe." Elinor's hands were folded in her lap. "It is why I am here and not another. Though from what I have heard, I might not be able to burn you to death before you killed me."

"I would not—Elinor, you do not know—"

"Then tell me." Elinor gestured with a hand, and the lamp burned more brightly. "Tell me why you kept this horrid secret. Tell me why I should trust you when I know you can kill with a touch."

Amaya gripped her hands together so tightly they felt numb.

"You can kill with a thought," she said. "Why should I not fear you?"

Elinor opened her mouth, then closed it again. "My ability is no secret. You must have a sinister motive not to reveal yours."

"It is not sinister! Edmund—" She swallowed again around the hard lump in her throat. "I believed everyone knew. It is not a secret—that is, it is a known thing, that if one can Shape the heart whole, one can also Shape it to destruction. It is obvious, and that is why I do not say what I can do, because my character speaks for itself. I do not kill except to protect. As you do. Elinor, you must understand!"

Elinor's head bowed. "I do," she said. "Forgive my cruelty, but I needed to know what you would say. You must understand how the situation appears. The king of Spain did *not* know what an Extraordinary Shaper is capable of, and he or someone near to him drew the conclusion that your ability is not unique to Amaya Salazar, but is possessed by all Extraordinary Shapers." She smiled bitterly. "And because he is, of course, a benign and wise ruler, he immediately spread the news abroad that Extraordinary Shapers are to be feared. Since he is a Speaker, that was likely very far abroad."

"He—I see, it is a manner of speech to call King Ferdinand wise and then to tell of a not-wise thing he has done." Amaya shuddered. "Is this why we are in Burgos? We leave Spain?"

"Yes, we are on the way to Santander to take ship for London."

Amaya looked more closely at Elinor. "You still do not sound happy."

"Because none of us know how far that news will spread. We might return to London to discover a warrant has been issued for your arrest, or that Extraordinary Shapers have been banned, or even that many of them have fallen to the mob." Elinor sighed. "If we had a Bounder—but no. Sir William's reticulum in England has heard nothing of any such news, but I believe it is only a matter of time."

"Then what will you do with me?"

"With you? Nothing. You are no more dangerous than you were six days ago when we knew nothing of this secret. And if the members of our party do not fear me, I see no reason why they should fear you." Elinor rose. "What do you need? Food? It is after ten o'clock, but I am sure we can find something for you to eat. You were in that unconscious state for nearly a week, not eating or moving, barely breathing. I was so afraid for you."

"I will be hungry soon," Amaya said, "but well before morning, so it is good I eat now."

"I will have something sent." Elinor hesitated, then extended her hand. "I did not fear you, not ever," she said.

Amaya clasped Elinor's cool, small hand. "You know what it is like to be feared for what you might do," she said. "I do not fear you either."

"Then we can endure the worst," Elinor said.

When Elinor was gone, Amaya sat staring at the flame, watching it flicker like a tiny living thing. It still angered her that every European she encountered believed this one aspect of an Extraordinary Shaper's talent outweighed all the other marvelous things such a person could do. It angered her more that the European Extraordinary Shapers had apparently kept it a secret, likely out of fear rather than from a desire to assassinate others. If they had not been so determined to shroud it in mystery, they would not now be facing another Frenzy.

She considered her bed. Resting was likely a good idea, given that her body was still not fully recovered, but she did not like to eat in bed, and she wanted food more than she wanted rest.

She looked around for her trunk, then remembered it had

been left behind in the Palacio Real along with most of her wardrobe. No wonder she had needed to borrow a nightgown. She checked the clothespress anyway; empty. She hoped someone was in a position to loan her day clothes, as she could hardly travel clad only in a nightgown.

The door opened when she was halfway to the chair. "Amaya?" the visitor said.

It was Edmund.

CHAPTER 28

IN WHICH CULTURES AND
CUSTOMS ARE COMPARED, AND AN
AGREEMENT REACHED

<hr />

Shock like an icicle through the heart and then complete numbness swept over her. She realized she was kneeling on the floor with one hand thrust out before her, preventing her from hitting the wood planks face first. Hands gripped her shoulders, and Edmund's voice came to her ears, speaking words she could not understand. They sounded exactly as if they were coming from some distant realm of the dead, where Edmund surely was.

She squeezed her eyes tight shut and made herself breathe, forced Need to draw sustenance from the air and Heart to work less erratically. Now she understood why Elinor had reacted to the sight of her as she had, that gasp and retreat not of fear, but of total surprise.

Edmund's mumbling, alien speech became intelligible between one syllable and the next: "—not well, you must return to your bed. Can you walk?"

She shook her head, not in response to his question, but in lingering surprise. "Edmund," she managed, "Edmund, how is it you are alive? I felt—" She could not now remember what she had felt, but he had been dying, she was certain of that.

"Back to bed," Edmund said, and he lifted her as easily as if she had been a kitten and deposited her on the bed neatly and without fuss. Reflexively she pulled the blanket over herself, but did not lie back. She gazed at him, searching for signs of hidden injury. He was dressed well, if informally, with no coat or neckcloth and the neck of his shirt open, and did not move as if he hurt anywhere, though lines of worry touched his forehead and the corners of his eyes.

Confronted with his presence, with the solid reality of him, she could say only, "You died."

Edmund shook his head. "I made a very near thing of it, though. Dr. Quintana's Healing was the greatest pain I have ever felt. And I was conscious for all of it, though not in any coherent way. He said afterward if he had permitted me to sleep, I would likely never have woken. It is as well we left him in Madrid, for my sense of gratitude was at war with my dislike of him."

Amaya clenched the blanket in both hands. "Edmund," she said, frustrated and confused and angry all at once, "*who is Dr. Quintana?*"

Edmund dragged the chair to where he could sit beside her bed. "He is a disreputable, drunken physician with the bedside manner of a dyspeptic bear. He also happens to be an Extraordinary Shaper. And I recant every terrible thing I ever said about Jennet, because had she not known of the man, I likely would be dead."

"Jennet? She ran away."

"Ran to fetch Dr. Quintana, or so I gather. I was not exactly lucid at the time. I believed *you* dead because you had collapsed atop me and I could not feel your heartbeat nor breath." He pried her hand free of the fabric and held it tightly in his. "It felt like an eternity, lying there with your dead body over me and feeling the life ebb from mine with every passing moment. And then Dr. Quintana was there, and it was a different kind of eternity. So much pain—though I welcomed it at the time, as sign that I might survive."

"But how could Jennet have known of him?"

"That, I did not ask. There was no time. I believe Jennet watched Dr. Quintana's work, and stayed long enough to tell me she had repaid her debt to me. Then she left, this time for good. I doubt we will see her again." Edmund sighed. "I don't understand her. She did not, as far as I can tell, Coerce Dr. Quintana into following her, as his temperament would have been far more pleasant. The doctor would not say anything about her—became downright surly if I pressed him. So it is a mystery whose depths we shall never plumb."

The humor in his final words eased Amaya's heart. "It is a miracle, as Bess sometimes says about things. And she tells me miracles should not be questioned, for fear God will think one ungrateful."

Edmund's smile faded. "We have indeed been blessed with a surfeit of them. When Dr. Quintana told me you were merely comatose from too much Shaping, I felt light enough to Fly like Lord Enderleigh. Amaya, you should not have exerted yourself so on my behalf. I could not have borne the weight of your death."

Amaya leaned forward. "Come closer," she whispered, making Edmund lean in to hear her more clearly. She put her free hand around the back of his neck and kissed him. His lips tasted of mutton and wine from supper, and they moved softly against hers. "It is what we do for each other," she said, "we who love each other, because I could not have let you die without doing everything in my power to stop it."

Edmund's dark eyes were intent on hers. Then he kissed her again, fiercely, taking her in his arms and holding her so tightly she squeaked. She had believed she knew how kissing felt, but this marvelous passion, this knowledge that they had both come so close to death, made her feel as if she were endlessly falling, held up only by his embrace.

She shifted back, making room for him on the narrow bed, and he joined her there, half-kneeling awkwardly beside her. She had never been this aware of her body, had never realized how blissfully aware her Sense could be, every nerve alight with the need to touch and be touched. Tugging at the hem of his shirt, she slipped her hand beneath the fabric to touch the smooth skin of his body, not to assess his condition but to feel his muscular strength contrasting with the satiny texture of his skin.

He had his hands on her hips, drawing her closer, his fingers straying lower, and she moaned, a tiny sound that seemed to echo in the dimly lit room. "Lie with me," she murmured. "We need this."

Edmund moved from kissing her lips to kissing her cheek. "We should not," he said. "In fact, I should leave. No one knows I am here save perhaps Lady Enderleigh, but your reputation—"

"My reputation can go to the devil."

Edmund laughed. "That is not at all appropriate language for a young lady, as I'm sure you know."

"I do not care about that or anything else. You are my love, Edmund, and I want you the way a woman desires a man. You cannot deny you feel the same."

"Of course not, but..." He retreated to the chair, sliding off the bed but retaining her hands in his. "What are the marriage customs of the Incas?"

Amaya raised both eyebrows. "You would marry me?"

"You sound surprised. I assure you, it is the deepest desire of my heart to have you wed to me, and not only because you are a desirable and beautiful heiress whose fortune will keep me in the manner to which I wish to become accustomed."

That made her laugh. "The Incas marry within *ayllus*, family groups, but that is to maintain their strength. You are not related to me, and I find my own relations not compelling possibilities as husbands." She thought of Mateo and suppressed a shudder. "And a man and woman may marry for a short time, as a trial. Perhaps we might marry for a month or two only."

Edmund's grip tightened. "That would not satisfy me," he said, his eyes twinkling, "but of course if you insist, I would do everything in my power to prove to you during that time that I am the most devoted, most capable, most loving husband you are likely to marry now or at any other time."

Amaya smiled. Now she felt like she was floating, not falling. "Edmund," she said, "I cannot imagine anyone I would rather marry than you, and if I believed it was only to last a month or two, my heart would break. Now, how is it done? I know Bess took a month in her preparations, but perhaps that is because her husband is a viscount. I would prefer not to wait a month. Tonight would be better."

He laughed again. "Not tonight, darling. There are preparations to make, and a license to acquire that we cannot get until we return to England. And Bess would make both our lives a misery were we to marry before she returns."

Amaya scowled. "I like the Inca way better."

"No doubt, but I promise you—" Edmund leaned over and kissed her, a long, slow kiss that roused all her *sunqu* to a fever pitch— "I promise the English way is worth waiting for."

Five days later, Amaya stood at the rail and watched the banks of the Thames slip past. She had forgotten how noisome the river was, that sweetish-sour odor the brisk breezes could not fully dissipate. Elinor had said something about the smell being worse in full summer. Amaya had already begun plotting ways to keep herself and Edmund out of London at that time.

The idea that she was no longer just Amaya, but one of a partnership, had not grown stale in the past several days. Before falling in love, she had been aware of being answerable only to herself, of being a friend to Bess and her family, but still being solely Amaya. Even the discovery of two sets of relations had not made her feel more connected to the Nevilles and the Salazars. But this relationship to Edmund, seeing in him her other half, thrilled her in a way she had never before imagined.

Now she let her eyes go unfocused and air-dreamed a future. London was hot and smelly, yes, but Edmund's employment was there, and perhaps staying away permanently was not possible. But they might travel. Perhaps they could take a house in the country during the summer. Bess would return soon; Amaya wished to spend as much time with her friend as possible. Friend, and soon-to-be sister. That, too, thrilled her.

This time, she heard Edmund's step half a breath before he said, "River travel is not a passion of mine. I much prefer the open sea, if I must spend time aboard ship. I confess to being a creature of the city. I hope that does not disturb you."

"The smell disturbs me, but there is much to do in a city." Amaya glanced at him; he had taken a position next to her, leaning casually on the rail, and was looking off across the city. "It is not so daunting an idea as it once was, that I might live in a European city."

"I am glad to hear it. Though naturally we will live wherever you prefer." Edmund's hand covered hers briefly, a swift gesture only she noticed. "The nature of my employment will have to change, though it would not be so unlikely for me to travel in the company of my wife. You might be surprised at how many gentlemen of leisure are in reality employed as confidential agents of the government."

"I suppose it is not so unlikely, given the English penchant for foreign travel and how so many English men seem connected with men of other nationalities. It is almost a Speaker's reticulum." Amaya surveyed the riverbanks and the many buildings that grew up like weeds along the shore. "How odd that none of the city's turmoil is visible on the surface."

"It is not as if there is rioting in the streets, Amaya. Whatever has happened in the wake of the revelation of Extraordinary Shapers' secret ability, the English are too civilized to permit it to turn into civil unrest."

"The Spanish are civilized, too, and *they* had riots." Amaya found she had unwittingly extended a claw and carved a shallow groove in the rail approximately a handspan long. She clasped her hands in front of her. "It unnerves me to know that others will look at me differently now. I never imagined I would be feared for my talent."

"It will pass. People are afraid now, but their need for Extraordinary Shapers has not disappeared. In time, it will all be a commonplace." Edmund stepped closer so his elbow pressed lightly against hers. His proximity warmed her heart and made her wish they were married already.

She heard footsteps behind her, and Sir William called out, "Miss Salazar, might I have a word?"

"Sir William, yes," she said, turning. "It is that you have need?"

"Not for myself, no," Sir William said. His usually pleasant expression was somber, his ubiquitous smile vanished. He nodded briefly at Edmund, then said, "Lord Sacheverell Spoke to me not five minutes ago. He asked that I relay a message to you."

"I do not know who is this lord."

"He is a member of the House of Lords—of Parliament—with connections to the War Office. He requests that you meet with him this afternoon, after we dock."

"Meet with him?" Amaya glanced at Edmund, but he looked as confused as she felt. "Meet with him for why?"

"He gave me to understand it was a private government matter, and that you are to come alone." Sir William's usual smile had vanished. "Miss Salazar, it is a most unusual request."

"Unusual is putting the matter lightly," Edmund said. "I suspect this has something to do with the revelation of the secret Extraordinary Shaper ability."

"But I do not understand," Amaya said. "You said, Sir William, that England is not in turmoil due to it."

"I said there were no riots," Sir William said, "and that is true. But I have learned from my reticulum that some Extraordinary Shapers have been accused of committing murder with their talent, and distrust of them runs high. The government has almost certainly taken matters in hand, and Lord Sacheverell's request likely has something to do with it."

Amaya looked at Edmund again, but addressed her words to Sir William. "Then you believe I should not go."

"I can hardly tell you to disregard a government request, particularly one that comes close to being a demand." Sir William shook his head slowly. "I don't believe you are in any danger, if that helps. I simply cannot say what demand they will make of you."

"I should go with you," Edmund said.

"But they say, go alone," Amaya said.

"As if you have ever cared for the dictates of persons in authority." Edmund clasped her hand briefly. "If this Lord Sacheverell intends to command you, you may need someone whose grasp of English is better than your own."

"I see your point, but..." Amaya paused, trying to make sense of something she understood only instinctually. "It is possible Lord Sacheverell is afraid of me, or of Extraordinary Shapers, and I do not wish to make him more afraid by coming to him with more than just me. I promise I will not agree to anything until I have spoken about it with you."

"That is very wise, Miss Salazar," Sir William said, regaining some of his usual cheer. "I will arrange for a hackney to convey you to the meeting place."

"Yes, very wise, Miss Salazar," Edmund repeated as Sir William bowed and walked away. "Is that because you are preparing for the time when you will promise to obey me?"

"Is that a thing I must promise?" Amaya said, dropping back into Spanish. "It seems unlikely. And no, it is because you have a devious, twisty mind and will see dangers I do not."

"I choose to see that as a compliment," Edmund said.

CHAPTER 29
IN WHICH AMAYA IS ONCE MORE THREATENED, WITH PREDICTABLE RESULTS

Amaya had seen the Palace of Westminster many times and been impressed by its size. Now, having stayed at the Palacio Real, her perspective changed. This building housing the English Parliament had a few towers taller than the palace in Madrid, but mostly its walls were shorter and unadorned, with strange jagged tops that looked like rows of gap teeth. She did like the enormous window facing out over the river; it was the biggest she had ever seen, and she wondered how it was kept clean.

Now, however, that window was invisible as Amaya's hackney approached the palace from the west. From this side, the Palace of Westminster was mostly sheer windowed walls rising some three or four stories high. Other carriages moved in and out of the pillared entrance to the south, all of them black and anonymous as if visiting the palace were somehow unsavory business. She suppressed her nervousness and concentrated on her hands, folded neatly in her lap. These men were no danger to her. She had no need to be nervous.

LIBERATING FIGHT

The hackney driver brought the carriage to a stop and opened the door to help her down. He showed no sign that he felt this journey was anything out of the ordinary. Of course, he did not know she was an Extraordinary Shaper, since she did not wear the black cap English Extraordinary Shapers did. He would likely not have been keen to offer her his hand if he knew.

As per Sir William's instructions, Amaya climbed three short flights of steps to enter the palace. The steps opened on a gallery filled with portraits of unsmiling men in somber clothes who all looked at Amaya as if she were an interloper. She ignored them. The portraits of the Salazar family had been far more welcoming, and not just because she was herself a Salazar. Here, she knew she did not belong. A tiny spark of resentment at being ordered about by Englishmen flared into life, and she suppressed that as well. She had chosen to obey the summons, and there was no point in resenting her own decision.

Men dressed in formal clothes stared at her as she crossed the gallery. She ignored them as well, or at least pretended to; with her enhanced hearing, she listened to their conversations in case some of them were about her and she might need to do something about them. Most of them did whisper about her, but it was all idle speculation about her identity and her reasons for venturing into this bastion of male privilege. None of them came close to guessing the truth.

She turned left at the end of the gallery and, remembering her instructions, looked for the second door on the left. That door stood ajar, and lamplight burnished a small triangle on the carpet before it, faint but still brighter than the dimly-lit hall. Amaya pushed the door open further and entered.

The room, warm and close and stuffy, was a library, far bigger than either the Hanleys' or Fernándo's, with shelves reaching half a dozen *rikras* to the ceiling. All the shelves were filled with books that looked mostly unread, their spines shiny and untouched. Three tables surrounded by small chairs filled half the room, while the other half was dominated by a set of four sofas upholstered in brown leather, two of them flanking a cold fireplace. A ladder leaned against the far wall, tall enough to reach the highest shelves; *it* looked well-used, though not to the point that it was falling apart. Had it not been for the unused books, Amaya would have called it a working library, one which saw much use in the course of a day. Instead, the smell of dust and old paper told her everything she saw was for show.

Two men sat at the farthest table and rose when she entered. One of them she knew; it was Mr. Fenton of the War Office, he who had attempted to bully and trick her into working for him. His round, rosy cheeks rounded more as he smiled at her, but Amaya was on her guard, and she saw his smile reached no further than his lips.

The second man was taller than Mr. Fenton by a few inches, which made him almost Amaya's height. He was large of stature, with a round stomach and heavy shoulders and fingers like thick sausages. He, unlike Mr. Fenton, did not smile, merely nodded to her in acknowledgement of her presence.

Amaya stopped just inside the room and waited for the men to speak. She did not intend to give up any advantage. For a moment, the room was silent. Mr. Fenton glanced at his companion, then at Amaya, then back at his companion again. His silent companion, for his part, stared at Amaya. Amaya held still so she would not appear nervous.

Finally, the large man said, "Miss Salazar. Thank you for coming. Please, have a seat." He indicated one of the sofas near the fireplace.

"Thank you," Amaya said. She took a seat and immediately wished she had not, because the sofa was too soft, its padding

LIBERATING FIGHT

thick and yielding, and she sank into it so deeply it would take some effort to rise.

Both men sat on the sofa opposite her. "My name is Lord Sacheverell," the large man said. "You are acquainted with Mr. Fenton, I believe."

Amaya nodded. She still did not intend to speak until she had to.

"Mr. Fenton is here as your liaison with the War Office, as I understand you are one of its agents." Lord Sacheverell rested his hands loosely on his knees. Amaya kept her gaze fixed on him as the more dangerous of the two.

"I am not of the War Office," she said politely. "I assist Lady Enderleigh as a sign of my respect for this country, but I am not an English citizen yet."

Lord Sacheverell's dark, well-shaped eyebrow arched in inquiry. "'Yet', Miss Salazar?"

"I intend to marry an Englishman. He says this will make me English, though not by birth."

"And yet you have English family. The Nevilles."

Amaya nodded again.

"In any case," Lord Sacheverell continued, "Mr. Fenton is here as a courtesy to you. You have been out of the country, and therefore are not aware of the new regulations regarding Extraordinary Shapers."

The hair on the back of Amaya's neck prickled a warning. "Regulations?"

Lord Sacheverell's hands closed slightly. "Given the revelation that Extraordinary Shapers have a dangerous, even fatal aspect to their talent, we have decided it is best to allay the people's fears by implementing certain changes. All Extraordinary Shapers are required to wear identifying clothing, not just the traditional hat or cap, but a coat unique to them.

We also have begun a registry of Extraordinary Shapers, consultable by any interested citizen, so that no one need fear accidentally encountering one."

"That is foolishness," Amaya said without thinking. "Extraordinary Shapers are no more likely to kill than anyone else."

"Miss Salazar," Mr. Fenton began, his tone of voice a warning.

"Miss Salazar," Lord Sacheverell said, overriding the little man, "you are in no position to speak to me in such a way. This government must deal with thousands of men and women capable of killing with a touch. That is not an ability that engenders trust in anyone. The populace is on the brink of terror, and all it will take is one death at the hands of an Extraordinary Shaper to push them over that brink."

"And yet they do not fear the thousands of Scorchers who live in London alone," Amaya retorted. "Nor the Movers who might throw someone off a roof with their talent. And no one says that Bounders must be hampered so they do not enter houses secretly and kill their owners. This is a new thing, and the fear will pass." She leaned forward slightly, inviting confidences. "You should not fear me."

"I am not afraid of you, Miss Salazar," Lord Sacheverell said, scorn filling his voice enough that Amaya believed him. "I am afraid of another Frenzy. Can you guarantee it will not happen? I believe not."

"Miss Salazar, please see sense," Mr. Fenton said, casting a wary glance at Lord Sacheverell. "These are temporary measures only. You need not fear, oh, reprisals, or attacks."

As Amaya had not been thinking of those possibilities, his words did not reassure her. "Change happens quickly and it is hard to turn around," she said. "I say it is foolishness. And I will not do it."

"I am not offering you a choice," Lord Sacheverell said, his eyes growing hard and cold. "You will obey, or you will leave England."

Amaya blinked. "I do not understand."

"We cannot tolerate rogue Extraordinary Shapers who might do anything with their talent," Lord Sacheverell said. "If you will not comply, you will be required to leave this country. Immediately."

"You cannot force me."

"We can. And unless you wish to give the lie to your assertions that you mean us no harm, you will go quietly." Lord Sacheverell's hands were fists now, as if he meant to start a fight regardless.

Amaya looked at Mr. Fenton, whose rosy complexion had paled with fright. "You cannot permit this," she said. Then something occurred to her. "It has been only ten days, and you do not—did not learn of this immediately. And yet you have a plan already." She rose, her hands shaking with anger. "You knew before," she said, feeling truth unfold inside her, blossoming into awareness. "You know what Extraordinary Shapers can do and you keep it hidden, and now you pretend you are surprised but you have a plan ready anyway. How dare you!"

"Be seated, Miss Salazar, and do not make rash accusations." Lord Sacheverell did not sound as angry as Amaya believed he should be.

"It is not rash. It is true. Why do you do this thing? Why lie to everyone?"

"Because this country depends on Extraordinary Shapers," Lord Sacheverell said, coming to his feet in one explosive movement. "A quarter of our doctors have talent. They are capable of working miracles. We *cannot* have the people questioning whether their doctor's touch will kill instead of heal!"

"They will not question if they know and trust," Amaya said. "*You* have made it a fear, not them, because you make it a secret and then it looks like truth. If you do not fear, no one else will."

"You know nothing of politics and nothing of ruling a country," Lord Sacheverell shouted. "Your blind, irrational faith will do nothing but kill thousands, possibly tens of thousands."

"My people know what is true," Amaya said, her voice rising to match his. "The Incas do not fear me even though I can kill with my talent. That is because *I do not murder*. Having an ability does not mean one must always and only use that ability."

Lord Sacheverell looked to be ready to erupt again, but when he spoke, his voice was quiet, if intense. "Get out," he said. "You have one day to remove yourself from England, and then you will be removed. And do not think to subvert the law by marrying. You will find no special license available, nor will anyone, anywhere, post your banns."

Amaya understood very little of his statement, but the central point was clear. "It is your foolishness that does this," she said.

Mr. Fenton cleared his throat. "I do not believe Miss Salazar should be banished," he said.

Lord Sacheverell looked down at him as if he'd forgotten the War Office liaison was there. "I beg your pardon?" he said, sounding puzzled.

"We don't yet know what will happen," Mr. Fenton said, coming to his feet. "But Miss Salazar is correct that we do not put restrictions on Scorchers or Movers or Bounders or any other potentially deadly talent."

"This is none of your concern, Fenton," Lord Sacheverell boomed.

"I am Miss Salazar's liaison, and as such, it is my concern." Mr. Fenton nodded at Amaya. "I say it is premature to treat all

Extraordinary Shapers as criminals, and I will make this opinion known to the War Office."

"The War Office does not set policy."

"It is, however, responsible for the actions of the Extraordinaries under its command, and the government's policy will affect the War Office first and most dramatically." Mr. Fenton's color was returning, and he stood his ground without a hint of fear. "And I know this policy has yet to be ratified—is that not so?"

Lord Sacheverell said nothing.

Amaya said, "Did you try to make me obey something that is not actually a law?"

"It is good policy," Lord Sacheverell said.

Amaya had to clench her fists to keep from extending her claws. She settled for saying, "This is bad manners, Lord Sacheverell, and you disappoint me. There is no policy yet, and I will not obey it even if there is. I am going now, and you will not stop me and you will not make me leave England. I know this because you are afraid, not of me, but of these people you talk so easily of. They are more intelligent than you know, and they will not be fools." She nodded politely to Mr. Fenton, who bowed in return, and let herself out.

All the way back to the street, she shook with rage. Tried to fool her—tried to force her to obey a stupid policy—tried to make her leave the country—Lord Sacheverell was a fool, but was he a powerful fool? If the English government knew what Extraordinary Shapers were capable of and had kept it a secret, their plan had been formed years ago, and they would have another plan for implementing the first one. Which meant Amaya might be in trouble no matter what she did.

She hailed a hackney and did not realize until the driver spoke to her that a lone woman requesting a carriage was unusual and likely improper. This irritated her further, and she spoke too sharply to the driver; her retort silenced him completely. Her bad mood stopped her feeling guilty about her words, and she sat staring out the window coming up with worse things she might have said to Lord Sacheverell and wishing she were still in a position to say them.

She had directed the carriage not to the Hanleys' home, but to the Grosvenor Square mansion where Elinor and Lord Enderleigh would live until after Elinor's child was born. Amaya had arranged with Elinor that she would remain with them, since Elinor's confinement was near. Today, the house's dour façade matched her mood, and made her feel, contrariwise, almost cheerful, as if she were not the only one in the world feeling irritated.

She knocked, and waited for the footman to admit her, then crossed the entry to the stairs. Voices coming from down the hall stopped her ascending to her bedroom as had been her plan. Elinor, and Edmund, and—

With a cry of excitement, she plunged down the hall to Elinor's sitting room and flung herself on Bess, saying, "It is so good—why are you here, I know you and Elinor do not know each other?"

Bess, laughing, caught her spectacles as they flew off her nose from the force of Amaya's embrace. "It is all Edmund's doing. He insisted I be introduced to Lady Enderleigh, as she is such a good friend of yours."

"Bess was with Mother when I returned home this afternoon," Edmund explained, "and as I knew you would be returning from Westminster to this house, I took the liberty of bringing her along."

"I am so glad you did," Elinor said from her seat near the fire. "You spoke so highly of Lady Ravenscourt, I have longed to make her acquaintance. Sit, Amaya, and I will ring for refreshments, and we will hear what you learned from Lord Sacheverell."

"Lord Sacheverell?" Bess said, sounding puzzled. "What have you to do with him? You are not a member of the War Office, surely?"

"Then you know him," Amaya said. She sat next to Elinor and untied the strings of her bonnet.

"Know of him, at least. We have never been introduced. He does not have the pleasantest of dispositions, I am told, and my —I understand he is not fond of Extraordinary privilege despite his work with the War Office. Or perhaps because of it." Bess sat opposite Amaya and settled her spectacles more securely. "He is sympathetic to a group within the government that would like Extraordinaries to have somewhat fewer rights than they currently do."

"I see. Now things about my speaking to him make sense."

"Tell us, or I will run mad," Edmund said.

Amaya found her bad mood had vanished. "There is little to tell. Lord Sacheverell says that the government wishes to make Extraordinary Shapers conspicuous so they cannot hurt with a touch. But it is not law yet. I believe he tried to trick me." She frowned. "And threatened to make me leave England if I do not obey."

Edmund rose to his feet. "Leave England? Impossible!"

"Maybe, or maybe not, I do not know. But I tell him I do not obey and I do not leave. Edmund, they knew! You were right that they were afraid of my talent, Sir Maxwell and Mr. Fenton and the other lord. They knew what Extraordinary Shapers can do and they keep—kept it a secret because they fear a riot if people learn of it."

"I beg your pardon," Bess said, "but what is it you speak of?"

Amaya glanced her way. "You have not heard?"

"Lord Ravenscourt and I arrived from the continent only this afternoon. I have heard nothing unusual about Extraordinary Shapers."

A chill gripped Amaya's heart. She took her fears in hand and said, "It is that an Extraordinary Shaper can hurt as well as heal."

"Yes, I know," Bess said, "or rather, I guessed after Mr. Rutledge told me months ago that the government knew something sinister related to your Extraordinary Shaping. I did not realize it was a secret, though as I say this, I recognize that no one ever speaks of it. You mean to say this knowledge was actively concealed?"

Amaya stared at her friend. "How did you guess?"

Bess shrugged. "I did not make the connection immediately, though it is obvious—though perhaps it is only obvious to someone like me, who has been under the care of dozens of Extraordinary Shapers in her life. Anyone capable of enhancing my eyes must be capable of damaging them as well." She tapped a finger beside her left eye. "Such knowledge is only frightening if one does not realize that most people are not evil, and they do not in general use their abilities, talent or otherwise, to harm others."

"That is what I say!" Amaya exclaimed. "You see it. I do not understand why Lord Sacheverell does not."

"Very likely it does not suit him to see it," Edmund said, "if Bess is right that he would like to see Extraordinaries disenfranchised. I am more concerned that he threatened to deport you. How did he intend to enforce that?"

Amaya shrugged. "I told him I will not go. So it does not matter to me what he tries."

Elinor shifted her weight and made an uncomfortable noise. "I am well, just weary," she said when Amaya gave her a concerned look. "If this policy is not law, I doubt Lord Sacheverell has the power to enforce it. But perhaps Lord Enderleigh and I should look into this further. If it is on the verge of becoming law, we should be aware of that."

Absently, Amaya took Elinor's hand to assess her condition as she had become accustomed to do. She stilled, listening to Elinor's *sunqu*, hearing Bess and Edmund's voices without paying any attention to them. "It will have to be Lord Enderleigh who does the looking," she said, interrupting the conversation. "You will be busy elsewhere."

"I, busy? What do you mean?" Elinor asked. A peculiar expression, an inward-turned, questioning look, crinkled her eyes, and she splayed one hand across her enormous belly. "Oh," she added.

"Do not fear, all is well," Amaya said. "But we will go upstairs. Bess and Edmund, I will see you later."

Edmund looked confused. Bess rose and brought him with her. "I understand," she said with a smile. "Lady Enderleigh, it was a pleasure meeting you, and I hope to visit you again. Edmund, I promised Mother we would dine with her tonight, if you would accompany me?"

Edmund caught Amaya's eye. His expression showed clearly his disappointment at being deprived of her company. "Of course," he said with a bow. "Good afternoon, ladies."

When Edmund and Bess were gone, Amaya helped Elinor stand. "Do not be afraid," she said. "It will still be many hours, and I promise it will not hurt."

"Oh," Elinor said again. "I believed childbirth to be quite painful. Is pain not necessary?"

"Not for one such as I." Amaya tugged on her friend's arm. "Come, and let us see who this child will be."

CHAPTER 30
IN WHICH THERE IS ONE FINAL REVELATION

maya twitched aside the curtain, then drew it back fully. Pale morning light lit the bedchamber, not enough to warrant turning off the lamp, but enough that she felt heartened after the long night. "It is almost time," she told Elinor.

Elinor struggled to rise from where she reclined on the bed, but subsided. "I am so tired," she said. "I cannot imagine what this would be like if my exertions were painful."

Amaya took her hand and swiftly assessed her condition, then got her arm beneath Elinor's shoulders and helped her stand. "There is some pain, because the pain and the need are too close together. But you are bringing a baby from inside to outside, so that is not so strange."

Elinor laughed breathlessly as her muscles contracted yet again. "Is this how childbirth happens among the Incas? You said only a female Extraordinary Shaper can attend upon the Sapa Inca's wives."

"Upon any birth." Amaya helped Elinor perch on the end of a

delicate chair with slim wooden armrests. "It is a woman's thing, though a male Extraordinary Shaper can examine the babe once it is born."

"Among the English—" Another contraction took Elinor, and she paused, holding her breath until it passed. "Among the English, we have male physicians as well. There is much argument over whether a midwife or a man-midwife is better."

Amaya chose not to comment on what seemed to her the unnatural practice of having a man in attendance on a birth. She hurried to spread thick cloths beneath the chair, counting under her breath. A second chair nearby held more cloths for cleaning and receiving the child, and a basin of steaming water sat beneath it. "There should be more of us," she said, "more attendants, but it is not needed. That is, it is for holy purposes, to welcome the child."

"I did not feel comfortable inviting any of these servants to help, when you said they were unnecessary," Elinor admitted. "I am a private person, and they are all strangers, and my sister is in the country—oh, that feels so odd." Her face contorted briefly, and she gripped the armrests. "Please, tell me it is time."

Amaya rested her hand on Elinor's forehead. A laboring woman was a strange creature, all her *sunqu* tense and inward-focused, Heart and Need expanding as if under a Shaper's command, Sense keyed to its fullest, Strength and Release in abeyance. She let herself fall deeper into her sense of Elinor's body. "It is time," she said. "You will count with me, and when I say to push, you push down, and I will pull. It will be a few times we do this. Be patient."

Elinor nodded, speechless.

Amaya moved her hand from Elinor's forehead to her bare knee and knelt before her. "Push now." She kept her voice calm, though excitement made her wish to shout.

Elinor bore down with all her might, her face going red. Amaya sent her own commands through Elinor's body, adding her strength to her friend's physical exertion. The child moved, propelled down by the powerful forces of muscle and gravity. Flesh shifted, spread, and held. "Again," Amaya commanded after a pause for breath.

This time, the child's head crowned against her hand, and what had been a void in her senses blossomed into awareness of a third individual, new and perfectly formed. "Oh, she is beautiful," she breathed, and gave Elinor's muscles added power.

"She is?" Elinor gasped. "This is—I feel I am like to tear myself apart!"

"Again," Amaya said, and with a slip and a shift, the head came free, followed by the shoulders, and soon Amaya held the infant in her hands.

She swiftly cleaned its mouth and nose and sent commands to its *sunqu* to make it draw breath. The babe sucked in air, turned pink, and let out a thin wail that made Elinor burst out in laughter and tears. "Oh, Amaya," she said. "It is miraculous."

Amaya smiled. The infant wriggled, testing the limits of this new, cold world. Dropping into her deep awareness of the child's body, she examined her thoroughly. It *was* miraculous, the way in which a newborn's *sunqu* came to life after nine months of dormancy. How they all linked together so perfectly, revealing truths that would fade over time. "She is perfect," she declared. "Let us finish this, and introduce her to her father."

Half an hour later, it was all over, the afterbirth passed, the cord cut, the mess cleaned up, the infant washed and wrapped in soft cloths and laid safely in her mother's arms. Lord Enderleigh sat beside Elinor's bed, touching the child's downy head in wonder. "So very small," he said. "I wish my mother could have seen her namesake. She loved children, and so few of hers survived infancy."

"We are calling her Anne," Elinor told Amaya, "so that a little of her grandmother may live on in her."

"That is a strong tradition," Amaya said. She lifted the impromptu birthing chair and returned it to its place.

"And with luck, she will resemble her mother and not her father," Lord Enderleigh said with a laugh.

Elinor clasped his hand. "You are the most handsome man of my acquaintance."

Amaya did not consider Lord Enderleigh precisely handsome, even without the burn scars, but love did strange things to the perceptions. "She will be very much like her mother," she said. "Though whether she will be an Extraordinary, I cannot tell. That is never evident in the *sunqu*."

"That would be something indeed, to predict her future," Elinor said.

Amaya paused in the act of straightening the drapes. "No, she will be a Scorcher," she said, puzzled at Elinor's response. "That I am certain of."

The baby Anne chose that moment to let out a sharp wail. Elinor absently tucked her child closer to her breast. "You cannot know that," she said. "Talent cannot accurately be predicted. That is all fortune-telling at best and charlatanry at worst."

"It is not prediction as you mean it, and not a guess." Amaya crossed the room to stand at the foot of the bed. "Was that not why you wanted an Extraordinary Shaper to attend upon you, to know the child's future talent?"

"I wanted an Extraordinary Shaper so the birth would be safe and the child well cared for." Elinor's heavy brows furrowed nearly to meet in the middle. "Amaya, what are you saying?"

Amaya raised a hand in a noncommittal gesture. "I cannot say how it is done. The *sunqu* of an infant are unformed and all connected for the first several days. That is, a baby may cry, and suckle, and eliminate waste all in the same movement. It is a kind of confusion. And in that confusion, if there is talent—if talent will manifest later—it shows now. Then, when the baby grows, that confusion passes."

Elinor and Lord Enderleigh looked at each other. Anne gripped her father's finger tightly, but he seemed unaware of it. "Miss Salazar," Lord Enderleigh said, too calmly, "what you speak of is unknown to Europeans. We have no way of predicting accurately if or what talent may arise. Such an ability is beyond desirable."

Amaya shrugged, uncomfortable at being the focus of his intent gaze. "I suppose it is not an obvious thing."

"Is it a thing you could teach others?" Elinor asked.

"Yes. It was taught to me by another Extraordinary Shaper amongst the Incas, when I was new in talent." Her discomfort increased. Elinor and Lord Enderleigh were clearly excited about something, and not sharing that enthusiasm made her feel awkward.

"Then I believe we have a solution to the government's problem," Elinor said.

"But you did not reveal this when you attended Mary's confinement," Edmund said. He helped Amaya down from the carriage and tucked her hand around his arm when she had safely alit.

"If it is no talent, we just—we among my people—say nothing," Amaya explained in English. "There are few born with talent, so it is most common that there is nothing. There is no point in saying this."

"Even so, when I consider that you carried this secret all this time, I am astonished."

They ascended the stairs of the Palace of Westminster and passed down the gallery of disapproving faces. The portraits did not seem to care for Edmund any more than they did for her. Perhaps it was not her sex or national origin that offended them, but something more subtle. Amaya observed them more closely, but still saw nothing appealing about them.

"It was not a secret," she protested loudly, drawing the gazes of the well-dressed men standing nearby. "You English are always saying things are secret when really it is that you resent having not been informed of something perfectly normal."

"All right, not secret," Edmund said, amused. "Lesser-known, perhaps? I imagine 'concealed' has the same connotations."

"Yes. Just because Europeans do not see Shaping as the Incas do does not mean we have concealed from you."

"Very true." Edmund squeezed Amaya's hand gently. "But the men we are here to see will not understand that distinction. You will have to be direct with them."

"I do not believe I am ever less than direct with anyone."

"This is also true, and I am fond of you nonetheless."

Amaya shot him a sharp glance he returned with his blandest expression before smiling so affectionately it made her heart speed up.

They passed the library where Amaya had spoken to Lord Sacheverell and kept going, deeper and deeper into the palace until Amaya was not certain she could find her way back. There were no windows, just dark-paneled, narrow corridors, some hung with more glowering portraits. The further they went, the fewer men they saw, until they were completely alone—and yet

Amaya could hear the murmured voices of a large number of people quite near. She closed her hand more tightly on Edmund's sleeve. She was not afraid, but she never enjoyed being at a disadvantage, and the place she was about to enter would put her at the greatest disadvantage she had ever experienced.

They approached a door flanked by two guards, both dressed in a uniform Amaya had never seen before, who brought their weapons to the ready. Edmund stopped a short distance away, enough to make them feel less threatened, Amaya hoped. "Miss Imelda Salazar to address the House of Lords," he said.

The guards relaxed fractionally, but did not stand aside. Presently, a man dressed in formal knee breeches opened the door and bowed. "Please remain standing out of respect," he said. "Speak when you are addressed. This is a most unusual situation, and one for which there is little precedent. No one not of this august body is normally permitted on the floor." He spoke quietly but with force, as if he were communicating the most urgent message imaginable.

Edmund nodded. Amaya regarded the man steadily and was reassured to see him blush. It made her feel as if she had some control over the situation. The man stood aside, and Edmund and Amaya entered the room.

Amaya's eyes automatically adjusted to the brightness that was a stark contrast to the narrow halls. Arched windows let in the summer sunlight, high enough above that no direct light fell on anyone in the vast chamber and bright enough that the several golden chandeliers did not need to be lit. Rows of benches lined three sides of the room, centered on a couple of large tables. The benches seemed surprisingly informal for the room, which for all its emptiness had ornate paintings covering its walls. An unoccupied chair beneath a canopy faced Amaya, and despite its relative simplicity, Amaya could not help seeing it as anything but a throne.

Dozens of men clothed in red robes with wide white collars occupied the benches. Most of them were speaking quietly to one another, the source of the murmur, but a few noticed Amaya and Edmund and prodded their neighbors, discreetly pointing. Amaya's discomfort increased. "What is it we do now?" she whispered.

The man who had let them in had crossed to the first table and was whispering to someone who sat there. Amaya realized it was Lord Sacheverell. Her heart sank. The antagonistic lord was not likely to care about her proposition, and might make things difficult. She held her head high and surveyed the rest of the room. She had no control over Lord Sacheverell; she only had control of herself.

"Miss Salazar, approach," Lord Sacheverell said in a voice that cut across the other conversations and silenced them. Amaya walked forward between the benches until she stood beside Lord Sacheverell. "The War Office has asked that you be permitted to address us. I would like it stated for the record, Lord Mouldron, that I was opposed to granting audience to someone so patently inappropriate—a foreigner, a commoner, and a woman."

Another man seated at the table stood. "Your objection is noted. Miss Salazar, I hope you are not wasting our time. We have paused in other important deliberations to hear you today."

Amaya wished she had not agreed to this. The men's smug, self-righteous, dismissive comments set her teeth on edge. She wondered if they would dare be this rude to Elinor, in the middle of this highly flammable room. She reminded herself that she was there for the sake of others and not just herself and refrained from shouting.

"I thank you, my lords, for hearing me," she said, as politely as she could manage. "I am here because you wish to make Extraordinary Shapers guilty of crimes they do not yet commit, and this is wrong."

"That accusation—" Lord Sacheverell shouted.

"You do not have the floor, Lord Sacheverell," the other man, Lord Mouldron, said. "Please do not make unfounded criticisms, Miss Salazar."

"I apologize, I do not mean a criticism." That was a lie, but irrelevant. "What I mean to say is that you have decided Extraordinary Shapers are dangerous and you wish to protect people from their fears. I say this is wrong. You are English. You do not punish people before they are criminals. Extraordinary Shapers should be no different."

She paused, but no one else tried to interrupt with objections. Lord Sacheverell looked to be biding his time, though. "But it is as I say, that you are worried about fears and what ordinary people will do out of fear. I do not believe these fears will last. And there is a thing you can tell those people that will make them forget their fear."

She paused again. This had been Edmund's suggestion. Finally, Lord Mouldron, who seemed to be in charge of deciding who should speak, said, "And what thing is that, Miss Salazar?"

She smiled sweetly at him. "I know how to tell what talent a child will manifest."

She had not believed Edmund's assertion that this would be dramatic, so she was startled when the room erupted into shouting and people standing and barraging her with questions. She said nothing, merely waited for the furor to die down and Lord Mouldron to say, "Miss Salazar, if this is a ruse to convince us not to act in the best interests of the country—"

"No, it is a truth to convince you to see sense." Amaya met

his gaze fearlessly. "It is not perfect, because it must be done in the days immediately after birth, but it is completely accurate and easily taught to others. Other Extraordinary Shapers." She leaned on this last phrase and saw the lord flinch.

"Please, all of you, my lords, this is not a trade," she continued. "You have forgot what it is that Extraordinary Shapers do. We save lives. We do not wish to kill unless we are evil, and an evil person will find a way to kill even if it is not with a touch. Please do not fear us. And do not teach others to fear."

The room was silent. Finally, Lord Mouldron said, "Miss Salazar, you are excused. Thank you for your cooperation."

That did not seem very promising. Amaya did not move. "My lord, what is your decision?"

Lord Mouldron did not flinch this time. "You are not entitled to be present for our deliberations. But we will consider your words carefully. You may now withdraw."

Amaya felt Edmund at her elbow and realized this was likely the best she could expect. She curtseyed, and she and Edmund left the room.

They walked back through the halls to the exit in silence. Outside, birds sang, and the passing of hundreds of carriages made the streets hum, and the breeze carried with it the myriad smells of London. It made the over-warm chamber of the House of Lords seem like a room in a dream.

Edmund hailed a hackney, and they rode in silence for a few moments, until finally Edmund said in Spanish, "It was well said. I believe they will change their minds."

"I hope so. It is terrible to live in fear." Amaya played with her bonnet strings and sighed. "But what comes next is worse, for me, anyway."

"Dr. Macrae is a good woman, and will not eat you."

"No, but I dislike admitting to having been wrong as much as anyone, and if she gloats—but she will not gloat, I know." She sighed again. "Thank you for coming with me."

"I believe I have said that I prefer your company to that of anyone else, regardless of the activity." Edmund took her hand and squeezed it gently. "And soon enough, I will have your company all the days of my life."

The hackney let them off at a tall brick building Amaya found distasteful, and not just out of guilt at what it represented. She did not care for its flat façade, its unadorned roof and its many small windows. It looked angry, like an elderly woman whose feet pain her and who has let that pain sour her disposition. It was all an illusion, of course, and the building was no more terrible than any other institution of learning, but Amaya wondered now if some of her resistance to Dr. Macrae had been a reaction to knowing she would have to frequent this horrid building.

Dr. Macrae waited for them in a small, neat office off the front door. It smelled of varnish, and rather strongly so, but Dr. Macrae gave no sign that it disturbed her. She was a tall woman, beautiful and well-formed as only a Shaper could be, with ruddy hair in smooth bands over her temples and a dark gown. She sat with her hands resting atop her desk, a vast ebony structure carved with fanciful leaves and flowers, and regarded Amaya calmly.

Beside her sat a young woman—by English standards, little more than a girl, but she would be a woman amongst the Incas—who would not look at Amaya with more than shy glances. She was dressed in the same kind of dark gown Dr. Macrae wore, with a white long-sleeved apron over it. Curious, Amaya regarded her closely. She could imagine no reason for Dr. Macrae to bring someone with her for this interview.

Dr. Macrae stood as they entered and offered her hand to

Amaya. "Miss Salazar, it is good to see you," she said. "Please introduce your companion."

"This is Mr. Edmund Hanley," Amaya said. "He is to be my husband."

Dr. Macrae's eyes widened. "Congratulations, then! I did not realize. Please, be seated. It is good to see you."

Amaya took a seat. "You know why I am here," she said. "I have changed my mind. I wish to study medicine."

She closed one hand hard on the armrest, waiting for Dr. Macrae to say something exultant. But the doctor only raised an eyebrow and said, "May I ask what accounts for this change?"

Amaya ignored her embarrassment and said, "I was foolish, and my lack of knowledge nearly killed someone I love. I still do not wish to be a doctor—I mean that it is not the job I desire. But I wish to have the knowledge of a doctor. I wish not to be afraid that I will hurt with my talent from my ignorance. I apologize for having been wrong."

"I understand," Dr. Macrae said. "We will be proud to teach you, Miss Salazar. And—" She indicated the young woman sitting beside her. "I wish to introduce to you Miss Maria Neville. She is also an Extraordinary Shaper, and your cousin. She, too, is new to Norwood College, and I felt you might wish to have her companionship as you both learn."

Amaya gaped. "My cousin," she said. "Mrs. Neville, she says I have cousins."

"There are several of us," Miss Neville said quietly, still not looking at Amaya. "You will be welcome."

A family. Amaya looked at Edmund, who was smiling. "You will teach me," she said to Dr. Macrae. "And there is an important thing I will need to teach you."

CHAPTER 31

IN WHICH AMAYA'S HAPPY ENDING IS WHAT SHE MAKES OF IT

The small chapel was stuffy, and too-warm from the many candles lighting its interior, but Amaya found it beautiful. It reminded her of her lost home, how its ancient stone fitted closely together, its narrow windows giving only glimpses of the outside world. High above, shadows clustered, not dispelled by the candlelight. She could almost imagine herself watched over by lost friends, and that comforted her, even though those friends would be as confused by this ceremony as she was.

She did her best to pay attention, but the priest's monotonous voice put strange emphases on certain words, and the subject matter was still alien to her despite her recent instruction in the Christian faith. There had been a day when she despaired of ever understanding this new religion, and had considered whether she dared swear oath to Edmund in his faith when she was not certain what it meant to her. Despondent, she had gone to Bess for counsel. "God is generous with our inadequacies," Bess had said, "and He understands our hearts. That is what matters, in the end."

"I will," she heard Edmund say, his clear voice ringing out over the priest's sonorous drone. She looked at him, and was caught breathless at the way he looked back at her, his eyes alight, his voice more certain even than when he had been in the grip of Jennet's Coercion. Her heart thumped painfully with excitement and joy, and she smiled, only half-hearing the rest of the priest's words.

"...in the holy estate of Matrimony? Wilt thou obey him, and serve him, love, honor, and keep him in sickness and in health; and, forsaking all other, keep thee only unto him, so long as ye both shall live?"

The unexpected silence as the priest stopped speaking startled Amaya out of her reverie. She ran back over his words in memory. Yes, Edmund had said she was expected to promise to obey him, though he did not have to swear to obey her in return. She met his eyes, raising an eyebrow, and was amused to see his smile falter. He did not know her as well as all that if he believed she would cavil at such a small promise. "I will," she said, and Edmund's look of utter relief made her wish to laugh. She trusted him, and that made obedience irrelevant.

No, it was the next part that made Amaya uncomfortable, this giving her away as if she were a trophy or a possession. No one, not even the sagacious Bess, had been able to explain it in a way that satisfied Amaya, and in the end, Amaya had told the elderly priest there would be no one giving her away, and he was to omit that phrase. She had expected him to put up a fight at her objection, but he had merely smiled in a way that said he understood.

She clasped Edmund's hand as he spoke his vows, then took it a second time to repeat her own as the priest instructed. With his hand in hers, she could not help but be aware of his condition, of how his heart beat smoothly and in rhythm with hers, how his every *sunqu* was tuned to a perfect alertness. At home, had they been married the Inca way, their marriage would have been solemnized along with hundreds of others all married in the same year, in a glorious sharing of that ritual. This was beautiful in a different way, and every bit as glorious.

She accepted the wedding ring as Edmund slipped it over her finger, then knelt as the priest droned out more words of which she heard only a few scattered phrases: "…may ever remain in perfect love and peace together…let no man put asunder…in holy wedlock…man and wife together, in the name of the Father, and of the Son, and of the Holy Ghost. Amen."

This part was something she did understand, though it was nothing she had ever learned among her own people, this joining together of two as one, and although her understanding of the Christian God was still imperfect, she felt it spoke well of Him that He honored that joining in one of His most holy rituals.

She listened more or less patiently to the remainder of the priest's words, telling herself he was a good man even if his speech was boring, and rose at his dismissal, anxious to have Edmund all to herself finally.

"Thank you," she heard Edmund say to the priest, and she smiled absently at the man. To her surprise, the priest took her hand and made her look at him.

"My dear," he said, returning her smile, "your path has been an unusual one, and I would like to assure you that God knows the desires of your heart and honors them."

"He does?" Amaya felt unexpectedly irritated, as if the priest had said something presumptuous. Probably she should not feel so, as he did, after all, have the right to speak for his God, but Amaya did not as yet feel at home in this new faith, and the idea of God speaking to her, even indirectly, made her uncomfortable. The Sapa Inca would never have addressed her so informally.

The priest nodded, as placidly as if he did not perceive her irritation. "I am a Seer as well as a priest," he said, "and it is part of my calling to See what I may on behalf of those I marry. God does not bless us with Sight of the distant future, so I cannot tell you what your life holds past the next few days. But I have Seen you in a far land, surrounded by those to whom you owe loyalty of blood, and it is my judgment that you will not be happy until that Dream comes to pass."

Amaya's face was hot with confusion and anger. She controlled a hasty response and said, "Thank you, Father, I will remember."

The priest's smile deepened. "You do not like my interference. Very well. Your choices are your own, regardless of what I See. Go with God, my dear." He released her and turned away.

"He Saw you in Spain," Edmund murmured.

"I do not know why I resent his interference, but I do. Oh, Edmund, let us not speak of this now. This day is a happy one, and I would rather not dwell on unpleasant possibilities."

Edmund squeezed her hand, but said nothing more, and they turned to receive their friends' happy wishes on their marriage.

But Amaya could not forget the priest's words, however she tried to lose herself in gaiety and celebration. She had left Spain behind, and England was now her home, but memories of Fernándo and Graciela and Leocadio and even the defiant Mateo persisted in intruding on her day. Guilt became resentment, resentment became anger, and by the end of the celebratory gathering hosted by the Hanleys, she was caught up in such turmoil it was all she could do to speak pleasantly to those she loved.

She accepted Edmund's arm and found herself in a hired carriage before realizing she had no idea where they were going. "Edmund, what is this?" she asked, falling back into Spanish in her turmoil and weariness.

"We are setting off on our wedding trip," Edmund said. He put his arm around her shoulders and drew her close, though he did not attempt to kiss her.

"We did not plan a wedding trip."

"*You* did not. I, on the other hand, have exercised my multitudinous powers of secrecy and intrigue to make preparations you are not aware of. Feel free to thank me at any time."

Irritation flared again. "Suppose I do not desire a wedding trip?"

Edmund smiled and brought her hand to his lips, grazing her knuckles with a kiss. "You promised to obey me, so in this case, your desires are irrelevant."

"Edmund!"

He laughed. "I apologize, darling. You are in quite a temper, and I should not tease you. In truth, this is not a pleasure trip, or not entirely; I do anticipate with great pleasure seeing the sights of Toledo and its many artistic treasures."

A chill passed over Amaya. "Edmund," she said again, less vehemently. "I do not wish to return to Spain."

"Amaya, you have every right to decide for yourself what family you will embrace." Edmund's expression was as serious as she had ever seen him. "But you will not be happy if you simply pretend you have no family at all."

"I am not Don Fernándo's heir, no matter what he says. It should be another."

"Don Fernándo's wishes are not what matters now. This is about who you are, and who you choose to be. Our stay was cut unnaturally short, and I would not have Mr. Valencia's cause prevent you from making that choice on your own terms."

Amaya sighed and closed her eyes. "I wish you were not so wise."

"I know. It is the most tremendous burden." Edmund's sigh was more dramatic than hers. "But you cannot tell me your mood has not improved now that I have made this decision for both of us."

She did feel better, though she did not like to admit this. "Perhaps it is just the knowledge that we no longer need fear censure at being alone in one another's company," she said with a demure smile.

"That is a much better answer," Edmund said, and kissed her.

···

THE ROAD TO THE SALAZAR ESTATE WAS HOT AND DRY, AS unlike their first journey as possible. The air smelled of dust and sunshine, baking the earth as thoroughly as an oven. Amaya considered the possibility of her running beside the carriage, feeling the hard, dry dirt against her bare feet, but not in any serious manner. She wore a fine muslin gown that would be ruined by such exertions.

Edmund had his head tipped back as if he were asleep, but she could tell by the regularity of his breathing that he was simply resting. She paused in her surveying of the landscape to watch him, her heart warming with pleasure at how handsome he was, how firm the line of his jaw, how his eyes were softened by thick black lashes that were the only feminine thing about him. A moment's desire washed over her, and she smiled at the knowledge that she might indulge in her desire for him whenever she chose.

"You are staring at me again," Edmund said without opening his eyes. "Dare I hope it is a mark of your deep and abiding love for me?"

"You may," Amaya said. "Oh, Edmund, suppose this is a mistake?"

"You know it is not," Edmund said, sitting up and looking at her. "At worst, you bid a true farewell to your relations, and we return to Toledo."

"Don Fernándo will hate me if he learns I killed Mr. Valencia. He loved him like a son."

"Then we will not tell him. I confess I am curious to see how much of Don Fernándo's affection for El Encendedor was the result of Coercion. He may be grateful rather than angry."

"You are hopelessly optimistic, Edmund."

"Not hopelessly. Hopefully." Edmund took Amaya's hand. "Darling, you have nothing to fear."

The carriage bumped over the small stone bridge crossing the Tagus River, and in no time it jounced and jolted its passengers up the short road to the Salazar estate. Edmund handed Amaya out of the carriage, and the two made their way to the house. The door's upper half stood open, and Graciela waited there as if she and not Leocadio was a Seer, to know of Amaya's coming.

At sight of her aunt's somber expression, a jolt of fear shot through Amaya. It was a thing out of a novel for her to have arrived just as Fernándo died, and she knew it was unlikely, but her imagination persisted in playing out a host of dramatic scenarios.

"Miss Salazar," Graciela said. "I feel I owe you an apology."

Startled at the unexpected salutation, Amaya blurted out, "An apology, to me?"

"To you and to Mr. Hanley," Graciela said. She did not look

ashamed despite her words, merely regarded Amaya with a directness that increased Amaya's discomfort. "You were Coerced, and I did not inform you of the truth of your emotional state."

"Because you are a Discerner, and immune to Coercion as well as aware of its presence in others," Amaya said, remembering Don Balthasar's words. "But it would have done no good."

"Even so, I regret so much that I permitted such a thing to happen." Graciela still did not look away. "I hope you both can forgive me."

"Amaya is right. We would not have believed you," Edmund said. "Pray, do not hold yourself accountable for what is another's evil."

Amaya impulsively laid a hand on her aunt's arm. "We all of us have regrets," she said, "and it is better to make the future right than to live in the middle of those regrets. If you wish, I will forgive you, but I would rather you forgave yourself."

As she spoke, her words echoed strangely in her mind, and she found herself wishing she could repeat them to Jennet. If anyone had regrets, it was the strange young Coercer, and Amaya wondered briefly where Jennet had gone—and hoped with an unreserved sense of peace that wherever in the world Jennet was, she might find absolution.

Graciela nodded once, as soberly as a queen. "Thank you," she said. "My father is happy to make you welcome. Please, enter, both of you."

"Thank you," Amaya said, deciding not to reveal that she was now Mrs. Edmund Hanley, or Mrs. Salazar Hanley, or Mrs. Hanley y Salazar. So many possible names, so many possible meanings.

Graciela led them through the house, which felt darker and less welcoming than before. That was certainly Amaya's imagination. Fernándo's drawing room was hot from the blazing fire he sat next to, the air even warmer than outdoors. Fernándo himself, however, sat bundled in a heavy shawl as close to the fire as he could manage without catching on fire. His eyes gleamed in the firelight.

Amaya curtseyed politely. "Thank you for welcoming me," she said, though he had done nothing welcoming. "I am glad to return."

Fernándo jerked his chin at Graciela. "Bring refreshments," he said. Graciela departed without a word. "Take a seat," he told Amaya. "You and your companion."

Amaya sat next to Edmund on the sofa opposite Fernándo. No one spoke until Graciela returned with a tray and glasses of water. She set them within easy reach of Amaya, then handed a glass to Fernándo and retreated to stand by the door, watchful and obedient.

Fernándo's hand shook as he grasped his glass, and a few drops of water spilled over his chin as he drank. Amaya chose not to draw attention to this, even with an exclamation of sympathy. It surprised her to realize she shared Fernándo's fierce independence and hatred of being thought weak. She did not know how she felt about having anything in common with her cantankerous grandfather.

Finally, Fernándo said, "What do you know of Spanish politics these last few weeks?"

"I know Mr. Valencia is dead," Amaya said without a trace of self-consciousness. "I know there have been riots over the revelation that an Extraordinary Shaper's talent may be used to kill, and I have heard that King Ferdinand has taken the opportunity arising from these unrelated events to take a hard line against any who would challenge his regime."

Fernándo shifted in his chair and drew his shawl closer about his body. "And thus the dream dies," he mused, almost to himself. "Is that why you have returned?"

That did not make any sense. "I have returned because I am a Salazar, and I did not like the abrupt manner of my leaving before," Amaya said. "If you mean, do I intend to take up Mr. Valencia's mantle, I fear not. Revolution is not to my taste."

"However much you might have fought in its name." Fernándo fixed her with his sharp gaze. "I should chastise you for breaking your vows, but Alejandro is dead, and I find myself not so eager for blood as I once was." To Amaya's surprise, tears rolled down Fernándo's cheeks that he did not wipe away. "I had hopes—ah, but it does not matter now, the death of this old man's dreams as well as Alejandro's."

"I regret—" Amaya began, not sure why she was apologizing, but Fernándo cut her off with a wave of his shaking hand.

"You will stay," he said, sounding tired rather than obstinate. "You are a Salazar. Ernesto's child. You will stay."

Amaya glanced at Edmund, who looked impassive. "I am a Salazar. And not. Mr. Hanley and I are married."

Again, Fernándo surprised her; she had expected her announcement to cause him to fly into a rage, but he merely smiled. "I see. You know that ladies of Spain do not take their husband's names? You are correct, you are still a Salazar."

"And..." Amaya swallowed an unexpected nervous lump in her throat. "I have made promises to England. To teach their Extraordinary Shapers, and to be taught in turn. I cannot stay."

Fernándo's smile disappeared. "Take my hand," he said, thrusting it at her.

"You do not fear my touch?" Amaya said.

"I am old, but I am not a fool," Fernándo replied. "Talent is what one chooses to make of it. It is not destiny. Come, take my hand."

Amaya clasped his hand and reflexively assessed his health. Her jaw fell slack in astonishment. "Don Fernándo," she said, then could not think of anything else to say.

"You see I am dying," Fernándo said as matter-of-factly as if he were commenting on her gown. "Of course we are all dying, all of us, every day, but for me the time draws rapidly near. I must see my inheritance settled soon. You will not return to England. I command it. Your duty lies here."

For a moment, Amaya considered lying to the old man. He was correct, his death was only days away, and she might stay here until then and leave immediately after. She did not like him, she did not know if she respected him, and she owed him no consideration simply because they were related. But looking into Fernándo's eyes, she felt a twinge of sympathy for his pain at having loved and lost her father. She understood now what drove him, and in the face of that knowledge, she could not lie to him.

"I am not Ernesto," she said, as kindly as she could. "I know you regret the harsh words that came between you. But you cannot make up for past sins by giving me his patrimony. And I am not your salvation."

Fernándo licked his cracked, dry lips. "And what would you have me do?" he exclaimed. "Give everything to that wastrel Mateo? You are a warrior, Imelda Salazar. You will fight to keep this place whole. I will not go to my grave knowing my entire life meant nothing in the end."

"Aunt Graciela is a warrior," Amaya said impulsively. Out of the corner of her eye, she saw Graciela twitch at mention of her name. "She loves this place. She has given her life to serve it—you know that, you cannot be ignorant of what that means."

Fernándo waved a dismissive hand. "Graciela knows her duty."

"It is more than that. She might have left at any time—she is of the endowed, just like you, and as entitled to status and wealth as any of those. Why do you think she stayed? She loves this place as you do, and she will not see it destroyed." Amaya could not tell where her words came from, but she felt deep within herself that she was right.

Fernándo said nothing, but he turned to look at Graciela, who returned his gaze impassively. Finally, Fernándo said, "You resent me, do you not, daughter? Because of the Ocampo matter. I did it for your sake. Juan Ocampo was a layabout and a drifter who would have made you miserable."

Graciela shrugged. "You were right," she said.

Fernándo jerked in surprise. Amaya had never seen him so nonplussed.

"I was angry, yes, because I thought I loved Juan," Graciela continued in her soft voice. "But he married Magdalena Sobrano instead, and I have seen him make her life a misery. You were right. And I do not resent you. You are what you are, and there is no point wishing otherwise."

Fernándo licked his lips again. "You are more like your mother than I realized," he said. He turned back to Amaya. "And you say she should be my heir?"

"I say she *is* your heir, and you did not know it," Amaya countered. "But I am still a Salazar. My children will bear the Salazar name. I believe Papi and Mama would be proud to know I returned."

"Ah, Ernesto," Fernándo said. He blinked back more tears. "You will stay until I pass?" he asked, and for the first time he did not sound argumentative or demanding, just lonely.

"We will remain here until that day," Amaya said.

"Thank you." Fernándo made as if to rise, and Edmund helped him stand. "You are a worthy husband for a Salazar?" he demanded of Edmund, his voice strong again.

Edmund smiled wryly. "I hope so, as Amaya insisted on choosing me."

"Well said. We will eat soon, if that is acceptable?" Fernándo said to Graciela.

"You know it is," Graciela replied. "Miss—Imelda. Amaya?"

"Imelda was my grandmother's name, and I am proud to own it," Amaya said.

"Then, Imelda, I will show you to your rooms, and we will dine shortly." Graciela's back straightened, and although her voice was as soft as ever, she spoke with a confidence that pleased Amaya deeply.

※

Supper was over. Such a different affair from that first terrible, awkward meal with Fernándo; the mood was cheerful, and Edmund made everyone laugh with his droll jokes and ready wit. Amaya spoke less frequently, preferring to observe as was her habit. She watched Graciela speak respectfully but firmly to her father; watched Leocadio's smile blossom as he realized what a change had passed between them; watched Fernándo's eyes as he saw his daughter anew for the first time in years. It was not so bad a thing, she decided, to be a Salazar, and regretted only that Papi and Mama could not be here as well.

Though, how would her life have been different had Ernesto de Salazar y Ortiz not sailed for the Americas? If he had stayed in Spain, reconciled with his father? Or made a life in England with the Nevilles? She tried to picture herself a society miss, or an Extraordinary Shaper in service to King Ferdinand, and failed utterly. Whatever the differences, she could not have said her life would be better, and in her heart, she felt it would have been much worse.

After supper, Edmund proposed a walk in the garden. Remembering how dismal the place was, Amaya almost refused, but she could tell he wished to be alone with her for a time. So they walked through the overgrown maze to the neglected heart of the garden. Someone had disposed of the weeds Amaya had shredded, but the gazebo still lay bare to the skies, a pitiful sight.

"I am certain Aunt Graciela will have this place restored once Don Fernándo is gone," she said. "It eats at her, I know."

"I agree. And I believe it will be a better tribute to both her parents once it is beautiful again." Edmund swept dust off a bench and sat, tugging at Amaya's hand to make her join him. "Are you glad, darling?"

"That I returned?" Amaya traced the line of the wood grain where she sat. "I am. And yes, you were very wise, and I thank you."

"You are welcome." Edmund gripped her hand more tightly. "I have spoken with my superior, who was remarkably understanding about my indiscretions while Coerced. He rejected my offer to resign, claiming that those to whom I revealed my identity are either dead or in no position to compromise me."

"That is what I suggested. Your superior is very wise."

"He is, indeed. He assures me my clandestine role within the government need not change now that I am married. We will travel as directed, and pretend to be nothing more than two ordinary people in love. And you will study medicine, and teach other Extraordinary Shapers your trick—"

"It is considerably more complex than a trick, Edmund. I assure you it is quite difficult to learn the knack, especially for Europeans who are unaccustomed to seeing the body in terms of *sunqu*."

"I apologize for my casual dismissal of your skill," Edmund said with a smile. "But will that be enough?"

"Enough?" Amaya asked, puzzled at his sudden seriousness.

"I know this is not the life you anticipated for yourself a year ago when you were still an Inca jaguar warrior. I worry that it will be too tame by comparison." He turned to face her, taking her hand in both of his. "Should I tell Mr. Rutledge we should be sent to the farthest reaches of the British Empire, to fight in bloody conflicts against England's enemies? We are still at war in India and Nepal, after all. And no one knows where Napoleon is; perhaps we might hunt him down and bring him to justice, preventing another war?"

His tone was light, but his dark eyes were serious, so Amaya did not laugh. "I have had my fill of death," she said, remembering with another flash of shame the final moments of Don Balthasar. "It is true, I do not wish to pretend I am something other than I am. But I am finding there is more to me than killing, and it would be just as wrong to pretend those things are not true simply because I have set the jaguar warrior aside. And there is so much to this world that I have not yet discovered. So if you fear I will become bored, Edmund, you need not worry for me."

"That is a relief," Edmund said, his smile growing more genuine. "I understand the Indian climate to be quite enervating."

"So Bess says." Amaya leaned her head on Edmund's shoulder and was drawn into his embrace. "But if Napoleon returns? Having endured Coercion, I cannot bear the idea of it being inflicted on anyone. If he returns, and I have the opportunity to fight, I will take it."

"I would expect nothing less from you," Edmund said.

She put her arms around his waist and closed her eyes. The sounds of the garden increased in volume, the whisper of the breezes over the weeds, the songs of birds settling into the trees for the night. Distantly, horses whickered in their stalls, reminding Amaya that Fernándo would likely entreat her to ride over the estate with him as he had said at supper. She did not like to deny him the pleasure despite her fear that the exertion would be too much for him. Perhaps that made her a true Salazar, after all.

The wind shifted, and for a moment, Amaya imagined she heard the cry of the jaguar echoing through the forests of her lost home. The coughing roar came again, and she recognized it now as the sound of distant thunder. A summer storm was rolling in over the hills, pushing the sweet smell of rain before it. How she had mistaken it for a jaguar, she could not understand —but that part of her life was over, and a new life beginning.

When next the thunder roared, she heard nothing but the storm.

THE TALENTS

The Corporeal Talents: Mover, Shaper, Scorcher, Bounder

MOVER (Greek τελεκινεσις): Capable of moving things without physically touching them. While originally this talent was believed to be connected to one's bodily strength, female Movers able to lift far more than their male counterparts have disproven this theory in recent years. Depending on skill, training, and practice, Movers may be able to lift and manipulate multiple objects at once, pick locks, and manipulate anything the human hand can manage. Movers can Move other people so long as they don't resist, and some are capable of Moving an unwilling target if the Mover is strong enough.

An EXTRAORDINARY MOVER, in addition to all these things, is capable of flight. Aside from this, an Extraordinary Mover is not guaranteed to be better skilled or stronger than an ordinary Mover; Helen Garrity, England's highest-rated Mover (at upwards of 12,000 pounds lifting capacity), was an ordinary Mover.

THE TALENTS

SHAPER (Greek μπιοκινεσις): Capable of manipulating their own bodies. Shapers can alter their own flesh, including healing wounds. Most European Shapers use their ability only to make themselves more attractive, though that sort of beauty is always obvious as Shaped. More subtle uses include disguising oneself, and many Shapers have also been spies. It usually takes time for a Shaper to alter herself because Shaping is painful, and the faster one does it, the more painful it is. Under extreme duress, Shapers can alter their bodies rapidly, but this results in great pain and longer-term muscle and joint pain.

Shapers can mend bone, heal cuts or abrasions, repair physical damage to organs as from a knife wound, etc., make hair and nails grow, improve their physical condition (for example, enhance lung efficiency), and change their skin color. They cannot restore lost limbs or organs, cure diseases (though they can repair the physical damage done by disease), change hair or eye color, or regenerate nerves.

An EXTRAORDINARY SHAPER is capable of turning a Shaper's talent on another person with skin-to-skin contact. Extraordinary Shapers are sometimes called Healers as a result. While most Extraordinary Shapers use their talent to help others, there is nothing to stop them from causing injury or even death.

SCORCHER (Greek πιροκινεσις): Capable of igniting fire by the power of thought. The fire is natural and will cause ordinary flammable objects to catch on fire. If there aren't any such objects handy, the fire will burn briefly and then go out. A Scorcher must be able to see the place he or she is starting the fire. Scorcher talent has four dimensions: power, range, distance, and stamina. Power refers to how large and hot a fire the Scorcher can create; range is how far the Scorcher can fling a fire before it goes out; distance is how far away a Scorcher can ignite a fire; and stamina refers to how often the Scorcher can use his or her power before becoming exhausted. The hottest ordinary fire any Scorcher has ever created could melt brass (approximately 1700 degrees F). When she gave herself over to the fire, Elinor Pembroke was able to melt iron (over 2200 degrees F).

Scorchers are rare because they manifest by igniting fire unconsciously, in their sleep. About 10-20% of Scorchers survive manifestation.

EXTRAORDINARY SCORCHERS are capable of controlling and mentally extinguishing fires. As their talent develops, Extraordinary Scorchers become immune to fire, and their control over it increases.

BOUNDER (Greek τελεταχύς): Capable of moving from one point to another without passing through the intervening space. Bounders can move themselves anywhere they can see clearly within a certain range that varies according to the Bounder; this is called Skipping. They can also Bound to any location marked with a Bounder symbol, known as a signature. The room must be closed to the outdoors and empty of people and objects. Bounders refer to the "simplicity" of a space, meaning how free of "clutter" (objects, people, etc.) it is. Spaces that are too cluttered are impossible to Bound to, as are outdoor locations, which are full of constant movement. It is possible to keep a Bounder out of somewhere if you alter the place by defacing the Bounding chamber or putting some object or person into it.

An EXTRAORDINARY BOUNDER lacks most of the limitations an ordinary Bounder operates under. An Extraordinary Bounder's range is line of sight, which can allow them to Skip many miles' distance. Extraordinary Bounders do not require Bounding signatures, instead using what they refer to as "essence" to identify a space they Bound to. Essence comprises the essential nature of a space and is impossible to explain to non-Bounders; human beings have an essence which differs from that of a place and allows an Extraordinary Bounder to identify people without seeing them. While Extraordinary Bounders are still incapable of Bounding to an outdoor location, they can Bound to places too cluttered for an ordinary Bounder, as well as ones that contain people.

The Ethereal Talents: Seer, Speaker, Discerner, Coercer

SEER (Greek προφητεία): Capable of seeing a short distance into the future through Dreams. Seers experience lucid Dreams in which they see future events as if they were present as an invisible observer. They may or may not be able to recognize the people or places involved, so Seers tend to be very well informed about people and events and are socially active. Their Dreams are not inevitable and there is no problem with altering the timeline; they see things that are the natural consequence of the current situation/circumstances, and altering those things alters the foreseen event. Just their knowledge of the event is not sufficient to alter it.

No one knows how a Seer's brain produces Dream, only that Dreams come in response to what the Seer meditates on. Seers therefore study current events in depth and read up on things they might be asked to Dream about. Seers have high social status and are very popular, with many of them making a living from Dream commissions.

An EXTRAORDINARY SEER, in addition to Dreaming, is capable of touching an object and perceiving events and people associated with it. These Visions allow them not only to see the past of the person most closely connected to the object, but occasionally to have glimpses of the future. They can also find a

Vision linked to what the object's owner is seeing at the moment and "see" through their eyes. Most recently, the Extraordinary Seer Sophia Westlake discovered how to use Visions attached to one object to perceive related objects, leading to the defeat of the Caribbean pirates led by Rhys Evans.

SPEAKER (Greek τελεπάθεια): Capable of communicating by thought with any other Speaker. Speakers can mentally communicate with any Speaker within range of sight. They can also communicate with any Speaker they know well. The definition of "know well" has meaning only to a Speaker, but in general it means someone they have spoken verbally or mentally with on several occasions. A Speaker's circle of Speaker friends is called a reticulum, and a reticulum might contain several hundred members depending on the Speaker. Speakers easily distinguish between the different "voices" of their Speaker friends, though Speaking is not auditory. A Speaker can send images as well as words if she is proficient enough. Speakers cannot Speak to non-Speakers, and they are incapable of reading minds.

An EXTRAORDINARY SPEAKER has all the abilities of an ordinary Speaker, but is also capable of sending thoughts and images into the minds of anyone, Speaker or not. Additionally, an Extraordinary Speaker can Speak to multiple people at a time, though all will receive the same message. Extraordinary Speakers can send a "burst" of noise that startles or wakes the recipient. Rumors that Extraordinary Speakers can read minds are universally denied by Speakers, but the rumors persist.

DISCERNER (Greek ενσυναίσθηση): Able to experience other people's feelings as if they were their own. Discerners require touch to be able to do this (though not skin-to-skin contact), and much of learning to control the skill involves learning to distinguish one's own emotions from those of the other person. Discerners can detect lies, sense motives, read other people's emotional states, and identify Coercers. Discerners are immune to the talent of a Coercer, though they can be overwhelmed by anyone capable of projecting strong emotions.

An EXTRAORDINARY DISCERNER can do all these things without the need for touch. Extraordinary Discerners are always aware of the emotions of those near them, though the range at which they are aware varies according to the Extraordinary Discerner. Nearly three-quarters of all Extraordinary Discerners go mad because of their talent.

COERCER (Greek τελενσυναίσθηση): Capable of influencing the emotions of others with a touch. Coercers are viewed with great suspicion, since their ability is a kind of mind control. Those altered are not aware that their mood has been artificially changed and are extremely suggestible while the Coercer is in direct contact with them. By altering someone's emotions, a Coercer can influence their behavior or change his or her attitude toward the Coercer.

Coercers do not feel others' emotions the way Discerners do, but can tell what they are and how they're changing. Many Coercers have sociopathic tendencies as a result. Unlike Discerners, Coercers have to work hard at being able to use their talent, which in its untrained state is erratic. However, Coercers always know when they've altered someone's mood. Coercers do not "broadcast" their emotions, appearing as a blank to Discerners. Because Coercion is viewed with suspicion (for good reason), Coercers keep their ability secret even if they don't use it maliciously.

An EXTRAORDINARY COERCER does not need a physical connection to influence someone's emotions. Extraordinary Coercers are capable of turning their talent on several people at a time, and the most powerful Extraordinary Coercers can control mobs. The most powerful Extraordinary Coercer known to date is Napoleon Bonaparte.

HISTORICAL NOTE

As with all my Extraordinaries books, I did a lot of reading that did not make it into this novel. The history of Spain's interactions with Napoleon is tangled up with its own desire for government reformation, and I was fascinated by the struggle to create a constitution that would give more rights to the downtrodden—a struggle that was interrupted by forced abdications and the installation of a puppet government controlled by Napoleon's brother Joseph. It provided an excellent backdrop for what came before Amaya's return to Spain, as well as giving me an excellent justification for creating a guerrilla leader whose cause was both just and abhorrent.

Another thing I wish I had been able to include more fully is the important role the Catholic Church played in 19th century Spain. I had not read about the fight for Spanish independence in the Peninsular War when I wrote *Wondering Sight,* where Sophia refers to the reverence in which the Spanish held Seers, and in writing *Liberating Fight* I realized I had set myself up well for a culture in which Sight is considered a holy thing, and Seers

HISTORICAL NOTE

are destined for a religious life. But, as with much else, this became a background note evident only in Amaya's few interactions with her Uncle Leocadio.

In real history, Napoleon was driven to defeat in 1814 and was banished to the island of Elba. Clearly, that was impossible in my history; no Extraordinary Coercer could lose control of his Coerced followers so completely. But I wanted that same cessation of hostilities as actually existed, so in my world, Napoleon goes into hiding for a time. The discovery of where he went and what happens when he returns is the subject of another story.

ACKNOWLEDGMENTS

As always, I am indebted to the careful reading and commentary provided by first readers Jacob Proffitt, Jana Brown, and Sherwood Smith.

ABOUT THE AUTHOR

In addition to the Extraordinaries series, Melissa McShane is the author of many other fantasy novels, including the novels of Tremontane, the first of which is *Servant of the Crown;* the Company of Strangers series, beginning with *Company of Strangers;* and *The Book of Secrets,* first book in The Last Oracle series.

She lives in the shelter of the mountains out West with her husband, four children and a niece, and four very needy cats. She wrote reviews and critical essays for many years before turning to fiction, which is much more fun than anyone ought to be allowed to have. You can visit her at her website **www.melissamcshanewrites.com** for more information on other books and upcoming releases.

For news on upcoming releases, bonus material, and other fun stuff, sign up for Melissa's newsletter **here**.

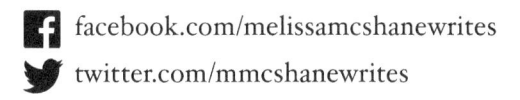

facebook.com/melissamcshanewrites
twitter.com/mmcshanewrites

ALSO BY MELISSA MCSHANE

THE CROWN OF TREMONTANE

Servant of the Crown

Exile of the Crown

Rider of the Crown

Agent of the Crown

Voyager of the Crown

Tales of the Crown

THE SAGA OF WILLOW NORTH

Pretender to the Crown

Guardian of the Crown

Champion of the Crown

THE HEIRS OF WILLOW NORTH

Ally of the Crown

Stranger to the Crown

Scholar of the Crown

THE EXTRAORDINARIES

Burning Bright

Wondering Sight

Abounding Might

Whispering Twilight

Liberating Fight

Beguiling Birthright (forthcoming)

THE LAST ORACLE

The Book of Secrets

The Book of Peril

The Book of Mayhem

The Book of Lies

The Book of Betrayal

The Book of Havoc

The Book of Harmony

The Book of War

The Book of Destiny

COMPANY OF STRANGERS

Company of Strangers

Stone of Inheritance

Mortal Rites

Shifting Loyalties

Sands of Memory

Call of Wizardry

THE CONVERGENCE TRILOGY

The Summoned Mage

The Wandering Mage

The Unconquered Mage

THE BOOKS OF DALANINE

The Smoke-Scented Girl

The God-Touched Man

Emissary

Warts and All: A Fairy Tale Collection

The View from Castle Always